国家出版基金项目
NATIONAL PUBLICATION FOUNDATION

Planned by Zhuang Zhixiang   Edited by Pan Wenguo

READINGS OF
CHINESE CULTURE SERIES
── ESSAY III ──

Translated by Xu Yingcai

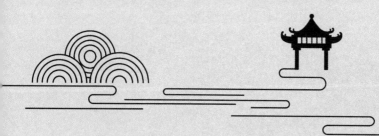

中国经典文化走向世界丛书

散文卷 三

庄智象◎总策划   潘文国◎总主编

徐英才◎译

上海外语教育出版社
外教社 SHANGHAI FOREIGN LANGUAGE EDUCATION PRESS
www.sflep.com

图书在版编目(CIP)数据

中国经典文化走向世界丛书. 散文卷. 三/潘文国总主编；徐英才译.
—上海：上海外语教育出版社，2018
ISBN 978-7-5446-5158-5

I.①中… II.①潘… ②徐… III.①中国文学—综合作品集—英文
②散文集—中国—英文 IV.①I211

中国版本图书馆CIP数据核字(2018)第078888号

出版发行：**上海外语教育出版社**
　　　　　（上海外国语大学内）　邮编：200083
电　　话：021-65425300（总机）
电子邮箱：bookinfo@sflep.com.cn
网　　址：http://www.sflep.com
责任编辑：杨莹雪

印　　刷：上海华业装璜印刷厂有限公司
开　　本：700×1000　1/16　印张 18.5　字数 409千字
版　　次：2018年7月第1版　2018年7月第1次印刷
印　　数：2 100 册

书　　号：ISBN 978-7-5446-5158-5 / I
定　　价：58.00 元

本版图书如有印装质量问题，可向本社调换
质量服务热线：4008-213-263　电子邮箱：editorial@sflep.com

PREFACE

"Cherish one's own beauty, respect other's beauty, and when both beauties are respected and cherished, the world will become one", said Fei Xiaotong, a famous Chinese sociologist at a cerebration party in honor of his eightieth birthday about thirty years ago. In a time of growing interest in intercultural communication today, these words sound especially wise and far-sighted. Translation, as one of the most important means for cultural communication, is usually done into one's mother tongue from other languages by native translators. This largely guarantees the quality of translated text, so far as the linguistic readability is concerned. However, this method implies a one-sidedness in correspondence, as only the translator's "respect for other's beauty" is concerned, regardless, though not completely, of how the local people look upon and cherish their own beauty. It should be compensated by translations on the other way, that is, works selected, interpreted, and translated by the local people themselves into languages other than their own. This approach may go directly against the prevalent views in modern translation theories but, in my opinion, is worthy of practicing. It is perhaps an even more effective way to bring about successful communication in cultures, and the beauties of the world can really be shared by the world's people. It is with such understanding that the Shanghai Foreign Languages Education Press is organizing a new series of books, entitled *Readings of Chinese Culture*, to introduce Chinese culture, past and present, to the world, with works selected and translated by the Chinese scholars and translators.

The series will cover a wide range of writings including but not restricted to works of different literary genres. For the first batch, we are glad to provide three books of essays and one book of short stories, all written by authors of the 20th century. They will be continued by a batch of serious academic writings on premodern Chinese classics in philosophy, literature, and historiography, written by influential scholars of our time.

Later, we will offer more books on classical Chinese drama, classical Chinese poetry, etc.

Some of the books in the series have been published before, but they have been revised and rearranged for the new purpose to meet the current needs of broader readers. We are looking forward to hearing comments and suggestions on the series for future improvement.

Pan Wenguo

CONTENTS

Snow

◎ *Lu Xun*[1]

Tropical rain has never had a chance to turn into ice-cold, solid, and sparkling snowflakes. Erudite people consider this fact boring, and the rain itself takes this as a misfortune. In contrast, southern snow is the pinnacle of sleekness and beauty. It is simply a herald of emerging adolescence and the skin of the most vigorous and healthy virgin. In the snowy fields, there are scarlet Treasure Pearl camellias, white-colored and blue-green-tinged single-lobe plum flowers, and deep yellow Alms Bowl winter sweets. Underneath the snow are pale green weeds. There are indeed no butterflies, nor do I remember if bees have come to gather honey from the camellias or plum flowers, but I seem to have seen winter flowers blooming in the snow-covered fields, on which many bees are busy flying around, and I seem to have heard their buzzing clamor.

A group of children, seven or eight in total, have gathered to make a snow Arhat. Occasionally, they puff warm breaths on their little, frozen hands, red and purple like ginger sprouts. Because they have failed to make the Arhat right, someone's dad has come to help. As a result, the snow Arhat now looks much taller than the figure the kids have made previously. Although it is nothing but a tapering pile of snow — and looks as much like a gourd as it does an Arhat — it appears, on the other hand, very white and eye-catching as a big shiny mess, bound together with the power of its own gluey moistness. The kids use longans for its eyeballs and put on its lips some rouge snitched from a make-up case of someone's mother. Now

---

[1] Lu Xun (Zhou Shuren, 1881-1936), the most famous and influential of modern Chinese writers. He was best known for his short stories and topical essays.

it does look like a big Arhat, and it sits there on the snowy ground with its eyes glittering and its lips glowing.

Although a few children have come to visit it the following day and give it a round of applause, a few nods, and a chorus of laughter, in the end, it has to sit there alone. A sunny day has scraped off its skin, and a chilly night has covered it in a layer of ice, thus turning it into an opaque crystal, and several sunny days in a row have taken the rouge off its lips and made it completely unrecognizable.

On the contrary, like permanent powder or sand, northern snowflakes, after they fall, remain non-sticky solids. When they are spread onto the roofs, onto the ground, or onto the withered grass, they remain the same shape as before. Of course, the snow on the roof has long since melted in the warmth of the fires lit by the residents of the houses, but in other places, the snow flies vigorously in the sudden whirling wind and shines brilliantly in the sunlight. It whirls up and fills the sky like a heavy fog with flame wrapped in it. Thus, it makes the sky flash in a spinning and soaring manner.

In the endless open fields and under the piercingly cold firmament, what is spinning and soaring is the spirit and soul of the rain...

Yes, that is the solitary snow, or the rain in an afterlife — the spirit and soul of the rain.

An Autumn Night

◎ *Lu Xun*

From my backyard, I can see two trees beyond the wall — one is a date tree, and the other, also a date tree.

The night sky above the yard looks alien and high — so alien and so high that I have never seen anything like it. It looks as if it were pulling away from this world so that nobody can see the sky anymore when looking up. But it is very blue at the moment, and flashing in it are dozens of stars that look like eyes — cold eyes. At the corner of its mouth, it wears a smile, which seems to reveal a self-flattering inwardness, as it spreads its heavy frost over the plants and weeds in my yard.

I do not know the official names of the plants in the yard, nor do I know their common names, but I still remember that tiny pink flower, now still in bloom, but tinier. She huddles in the chilly night air, and dreams. She dreams of the arrival of spring, of the arrival of autumn, and of a skinny poet who sheds his tears on the last of her petals, telling her that after autumn and winter, it will be spring again, when the butterflies will dance here and there and the honeybees will sing vernal lyrics. That makes her smile. Although huddling in the freezing cold, she turns pitifully red.

As for the date trees, they have lost all their leaves. Earlier, they saw one or two children come to knock from them the dates left behind by others, but now, none of the dates is left, and none of the leaves is even left. They know about the dream of the tiny pink flower — after autumn, it will be spring; they also know about the dream of the fallen leaves — after spring, it will be autumn. They have simply lost all their leaves, so only their bare branches remain. After recovering from the bending position earlier, when they were laden with dates and leaves, they now enjoy a comfortable stretch. But a few of the branches remain curved downward, to protect the bruises inflicted by the date-knocking rods, while the straightest and longest of the branches, like silent iron, have already pointed themselves directly toward the high and alien sky, making it flash like a ghost, and directly toward the full-orbed moon, making it look embarrassingly pale.

The sky with the ghostly flashing eyes is now far bluer. It looks uneasy and as if it wants to pull away from this world, escaping from the pointing of the date trees, only to leave the moon behind. But the moon has also snuck to the east corner. Only the branches of the date trees that have nothing left on them are still pointing, like silent iron, directly toward the high and alien sky, as if they are determined to prod it to death, ignoring its various wicked, flashing eyes.

"Caw —!" With a screech, an evil nocturnal raven flies past.

Suddenly, in the dead of night, a laugh tickles my ears, in such a tittering voice that it seems reluctant to wake the sleeping people, but the air all around seems to laugh in response. I immediately recognize that the laughter comes from my own mouth, because nobody else is around at such a late hour, and driven by it, I immediately return to my room. Once I am in, I immediately turn up the kerosene burner.

There are tinkling noises on the glass of the rear window, as many tiny flying insects strike against it. Before long, a few of them get in, perhaps through the holes in the window's paper panel. Once they are in, they begin to go for the chimney of the glass lamp, making more tinkling noises. One of them has gotten into the chimney, and has therefore come into contact with the flame — I believe that it is a real flame. About two or three of them recline on the paper lampshade to catch their breath. That lampshade is a replacement made last night, with snow-white paper folded into a wave-like pattern and a spray of scarlet-colored gardenia painted on one of its corners.

When the scarlet gardenia blooms, the date trees will dream the dream of the tiny pink flower, and will bend down like green onions … I begin to hear the midnight laughter again, but immediately interrupt my thoughts so that I can watch the little green insects, each the size of half a grain of wheat, with big heads and small tails shaped like sunflower seeds, scuffling on the white paper lampshade. Their entire bodies are adorably and pitifully green.

I yawn, light a cigarette, and puff out the smoke. Looking at the burner silently, I begin to pay my respect to these verdant and exquisite heroes and heroines.

The Cicada

◎ *Xu Dishan*[1]

The sudden shower has drenched the cicada's wings. So the poor thing cannot fly but crawls along on the ground. It has taken him a great effort to climb onto the prop roots of an evergreen pine, where the raindrops come sliding down upon his wings from the slack needle clusters thousands of feet above. With a short buzz, the poor thing slithers off the roots and back onto the ground.

Raindrops, are you playing a prank on him? Look, ants are coming! And wild birds will soon spot him!

---

[1] Xu Dishan (Xu Zankun, 1893-1941), trained at Columbia and Oxford University, was a scholar-novelist whose academic interests covered history of religion, Indian philosophy, and Sanskrit literature.

The Wild Wood in Spring

◎ *Xu Dishan*

Because the radiance of spring nestled in the mountains takes more time to fade away, the peach blossoms here are still in bloom. Thin, wandering clouds fly from one mountain peak to another and sometimes pause to shade the flora under them from the glare of the sun. The shady spots under the rocks and the area next to the valleys teem with osmund, pteris, and other kinds of ferns, with small red, yellow, blue, and purple flowers dotting the tips of their green leaves. The larks in the sky and the orioles in the woods sing to their hearts' content while the breeze carries the chorus of birdsong to everything in the mountains, whether it has an ear for the singing or not. The peach blossoms are so absorbed in the music that they cannot help shedding a few drops of pink tears that then lie still on the ground; the little grasses are so intoxicated that they cannot remain still, but swing to the rhythm, bending for a moment and then straightening for another. A group of children picks the peach petals in a wood, when suddenly one among them, Qing'er, bursts out, "Look, Yongyong is coming!" The children all stop to look up into the clearing in the peach wood, where the girl Yongyong is picking flowers.

Qing'er says, "Let's try Ah Tong out. If he can make it, we will then honor him as our big brother, and we will make him a necklace with all the flower petals we have picked and deck him out, yes?" The children all agree to the idea.

So Ah Tong goes up to Yongyong and says, "We are waiting for you."

Ah Tong wraps his left arm around Yongyong's shoulder and walks with her, saying, "They are preparing trousseaus for you today, so that you can be my wife. Will you be my wife?"

Yongyong turns around, shoots Ah Tong a stare, and pushes him away, not letting him put his hand on her shoulder. This makes everyone double up with laughter.

The children all shout out, "We have now seen Yongyong push people away with her hands! So Ah Tong has won."

Yongyong never turns anyone down. How does Ah Tong know what to say to upset her and make her push him away? Has this spring radiance inspired his wit? Or is it just the way of nature?

Look: thin, wandering clouds still fly from one mountain peak to another.

And listen: the larks and the orioles still fill the sky and the wood with their singing. And in the peach wood, surrounded by the massive mountains, everything is dazzled by the radiance of spring, except those naughty children.

Pear Blossoms

◎ *Xu Dishan*

They continue playing in the garden, ignoring the drips of rain that fall onto their silk garments. The pear blossoms next to the pool have been washed whiter and cleaner in the rain, but each of their heads droops slackly.

The elder sister says, "Look at those flowers! They are tired and dozing off!"

"Let me shake them awake."

Before the elder sister can open her mouth, the younger sister has grasped a pear tree and given it a few shakes. Flower petals and water drops start to fall, spreading all over the ground, looking like a large expanse of silver shards. Indeed, it is great fun to look at them.

The younger sister says, "Cool. Once they leave the twigs, the petals come alive."

"Nonsense! Look, the flowers' tears have fallen on me," says the elder sister somewhat angrily. Giving the younger sister a push, she continues, "I don't want to play with you anymore. You stay here by yourself."

Watching her elder sister leave, the younger one stands dazed under the tree. After a long while, their nanny comes over. Taking one of her hands, she says to the younger sister while walking with her, "See, you are wet to the skin. Where can I find any sun to dry your clothes on such a rainy day, if you keep changing them?"

Some of the fallen petals are trodden into the mud; some get stuck on the younger sister's clothes and are carried away by her; some fall onto the pool and are dragged into the water by the fish. And a swallow — a spontaneous volunteer — continuously picks, with its beak, at the petals and the mud left in the footprints and carries them onto the beams of the house, to build its cozy nest.

Claver on Sojourning in the Hills of Florence

◎ *Xu Zhimo*[①]

Here, if you go out for a hike in the mellow dusk of May, whether going uphill or downhill, it is exactly like going to see a beauty pageant. For instance, if you walk into an orchard, you will see that each tree is laden with the most poetically luscious fruits; if standing there watching the fruits does not bring you enough contentment, simply hold out your hand and pick some, as those fruits are within easy reach, and then indulge yourself in their taste. This experience alone will be enough to intoxicate your heart and soul. The sunlight is balmy, but not in the least overly warm. And the breeze is pleasantly gentle. As it often comes through the flower-abundant woods in the hills, traveling with it is a whiff of the remotely delicate fragrance mixed with a thin scent of humidly pleasant mist, which caresses your face and winds around your shoulders and waist. Therefore, the act of breathing the air here itself gives endless pleasure. The air is always clear and clean — without any smoke produced by humans in the nearby valley or haze above the distant hills. This enchanting panorama, like a painting, unfolds right in front of you — for you to savor leisurely.

The beauty of being a sojourner in the hills lies in your freedom to choose your clothing and appearance. You can leave your hair unkempt and your chin bristly and unshaven; you can indulge yourself in any clothing you like — you can dress up like a shepherd, a fisherman, a farmer, a Gypsy wanderer, a hunter; you no longer have to worry about whether your tie needs rearranging — you don't even have to wear one, so you can

---

① Xu Zhimo (Xu Zhangxu, 1896-1931), famous modern poet, essayist. He was also a founder of Crescent School, the most influential poetry school in the 1930s.

free your neck and chest for half a day or a full day; and you can wrap your head in a long shawl, in the local colors, imitating a leader of the Taiping rebels or Byron in his Egyptian garb. But the most important of all is to wear a pair of your oldest shoes! Although they may not look nice, they will be your best friends, as they will carry your weight but won't make you aware of your feet under you.

For this type of fun, you are better off without a fellow tourist to accompany you. I strongly urge you to dispense with companions, so you can be alone. That is because a companion would more or less distract you, especially when the companion is a young female — the most dangerous and dictatorial of the kind. You should stay away from her as you would from a prettily-patterned snake in the grass!

It is like nothing more than switching from one prison cell to another within the same jail when we walk, as we usually do, from our homes to our friends' homes or to our working places, because when we do this, inhibitions always follow us and freedom never finds us. But if you can ramble all by yourself in these beautiful hills or in the country, during this transition of spring and summer, it is a time when the Lucky Star shines on you, it is a time when you actually experience and can personally savor freedom and liberty, and it is a time when your body aligns with your soul.

My friends, don't you know that each year that we advance in age is often just one more unit of weight we add to the yokes around our necks and one more link in the chain we tighten to the fetters around our legs? Don't we feel jealous when we see children rolling about for fun in the grass, on a sandy beach, or in the shallow water, or see a cat chasing its own tail? But our yokes or fetters always dominate our actions. Hence, only when you throw yourself into the arms of nature, without anyone else to accompany you, like a naked child running into the embrace of his mother, can you then understand the happiness of the soul, the happiness of living itself, and the happiness of breathing, of walking, of opening your eyes to look, or of pricking up your ears to listen! Therefore, you have to exercise complete egoism and be extremely selfish, allowing only yourself — your body and soul — to merge into nature: to beat to its pulse, to dance to its musical rhythm, and to be content with itself in this miraculous universe.

Our ingenuous innocence is as delicate as a sensitive plant. Once challenged by our companions, its leaves will fold, but under the clear sunlight and in the mild wind, its character will be natural and its life will be smooth.

When you travel alone, you will lie down on your back in the green grass, or sometimes even wallow in it because its soft, warm color will spontaneously arouse your childishness; you will feel an irresistible impulse to dance passionately on a secluded street so that you can see in your shadow the various amusing silhouettes of your own body, because the gentle swinging of the shadows of the roadside trees will awaken your urge to frolic; you will burst out in a song, or a random melody you happen to remember, or a ditty of your own creation, because the orioles or swallows in the woods will remind you that spring should be eulogized; moreover, your mind will naturally broaden as you ramble along the long hilly path, your heart will be calmed as you look at the pure blue sky, and your stream of thought, as it flows to the tune of the spring babbling in the ravine between the hills or to the rhythm of the water gurgling in the gorge, will sometimes stay still to reveal a limpid quality and will sometimes splash into literary waves that roll forward into the cool olive tree woods, into the charming Arno River....

During such a tour, you not only dispense with companions, but also do away with books. Books are ideal company on trains or in your living room, but not when you take a hike alone. What great, erudite, inspiring, lucid, or beautiful sources of thought cannot be found in the singing of the winds, in the hues of the clouds, in the rising and falling of the hills and terrains, or in the colors and fragrances of the plants and flowers? Nature is the greatest book. As Goethe once put it, "Nature is, after all, the only book that offers important content on every page." Besides, this book is so explicitly written that everybody can understand it. And what's more, such information is ubiquitous — from the Alps to the Five Elders' Peaks, from Sicily to Mount Putuo, from the Rhine River to the Yangtze River, from Lake Leman to Hangzhou's West Lake, from the sword-leafed cymbidium to the wild Chinese viburnum, from the snow on the reeds in Hangzhou's West Marsh to the red tides of Venice in the glow of the setting sun, from larks to nightingales, not to mention the fact that all the universally yellow wheat, universally purple wisteria, and universally green grass grow on the same earth and ripple in the same breeze. The symbols they embody always remain the same and the significance they reveal is always apparent. Unless you suffer from a heart ulcer, blindness, or deafness, you are always entitled to this unconventional but supreme education; you can always take this free and most treasured remedy at will. Once you become acquainted with this book, in this world you will not feel lonely when loneliness strikes you; you will not feel poor when you are in poverty; you will be comforted when you are distressed; you will be inspired when you experience setbacks; you will be encouraged when you encounter obstacles; and you will be given a compass when you are lost.

Rain

◎ *Yu Dafu*[1]

Mr. Zhou Zuoren named his study "Bitter Rain", which is opposite in meaning to the "Pavilion of Happy Rain", the title of an essay written by Su Shi, but because of its rarity , any rain that falls in the north can be considered a happy blessing. Take, for example, the big flood we had this year. It was not necessarily caused by excessive rain, and blame should be placed on the river controllers who failed to take necessary precautions, but were only good at finding excuses to muddle through and were only interested in wasting the government's money. If anything happens, they try to shift their responsibilities to others and save themselves from blame. Wouldn't it be boring if things in one's life remained static? For instance, doesn't death draw attention to birth and tragedy highlight fortune? If this inference is true, isn't the same true of climate? Without the rain, what would reveal the loveliness of a sunny day? Without the night, what would underscore the brightness of daytime?

Because I was born in the south, it would be natural if I disliked the rain, but what a lovely blessing it is to get a few drops of rain on a hazy spring day when the flowers are drying! Our ancient poets clearly described the benefits of rain: "The vernal rain pattering outside my attic fascinated me the whole night;" "Apricot blossoms, vernal rain, and the south;" "The mist and drizzle over the capital look dewy and gentle." Summer rain has the effect of mitigating the heat and watering the crops — there is no need to elaborate on its benefits here. The misty and chilly autumn rain,

---

[1] Yu Dafu (1896-1945), a founder of the Creation Society and a representative of melancholy romantic individualism at his early times, became a newspaper editor in Malaysia and Singapore when Anti-Japanese War broke out in 1937 and was finally assassinated by the Japanese soldiers.

on the other hand, conjures up a different picture. The ancient poetic line "Late autumn often has spells of rain; drizzle after drizzle makes my mood dejected" is composed, in particular, to describe the thought-provoking effect of the autumnal rain. As for "Autumn rain and autumn wind — autumn, a season that dispirits," the prosodic sigh made by Miss Autumn (Qiu Jin) is nothing but a lament uttered by someone in a special mood — her feelings are ones of sadness, but they have nothing to do with the rain. Not many people, I am afraid, like the chilly rain of winter, but without having actually experienced it, who can see the true beauty pregnant in the poetic line, "The indistinct quacking of the wild geese from the distant south; the deep rustling of the hourglass in the faintly lit palace"? I remember that Zeng Bingu once used some famous lines from *Poetry Taste* to name a poetry book *Poetry Collection from a Thatched Hut for Rain Appreciation*. I have no idea how good he is at creating poetic imagery, but what a thought-provoking expression those words are: "*a Thatched Hut for Rain Appreciation.*" These words are especially evocative when it comes to the shift between late autumn and early winter, when "The chill of the green mountain is deep; the frost in the tall woods is thin."

Winter Scenes of the South

◎ *Yu Dafu*

Anyone who has spent wintertime in the north will speak highly of the joys of sitting around a stove making tea or of eating stewed mutton while cracking peanuts and drinking white liquor. For the families that have installed pit furnaces, heated earthen beds or the like, those two to three months of indoor life — when outside their houses, the snow is several feet deep and the wind roars as loud as thunder — are the most enjoyable season of the year for living a secluded life. Along with the aged, even the most active children cherish those days, for during that season, there are fruit snacks like radishes, pears, etc. to enjoy and there are exciting festivals like New Year's Eve, New Year's Day, Lantern Festival, etc. to celebrate.

Things are different in the south. Beyond the south side of the Great Yangtze River, even after the winter solstice, the leaves have not yet completely fallen, and the sporadic cold wind — a northwesterly wind — only brings chilly weather for one or two days at most. On early mornings when the grey clouds have cleared up in the sky, the fallen leaves are all over the streets, and the morning frost appears as white as cosmetic powder applied to the face of a dark-complexioned woman, as soon as the sun rises above the eaves, the birds start twittering again, the warm air, as usual, begins to squeeze vapor out of the earth, and the old and the young resume their outdoor lives — going to the open spaces in front of their doors to chat with each other as they expose their bare backs to the sun. Such are the winter scenes of the south! Isn't that delightful?

I grew up in the south, and my childhood impression of the southern winter is deeply rooted in me. Although I am now entering middle age and

17

have fallen in love with late autumn, which I believe is the prime season for scholars to be engaged in reading and writing, I always think the scenes of winter in the south have a special appeal, more than that of a summer night in the north — a kind of lucid appeal, to put it in a modern way.

I have spent wintertime in the Fujian and Guangdong provinces. It is so balmy there that one might have to wear his cotton sweater even as the Spring Festival turns around the corner and one can still see various kinds of autumnal flowers as he passes by the farmers' hedged courtyards. A shower accompanied by rumbling thunders will chill the weather a little bit, but one may just need to put on a jacket to adjust to the change in climate — there is absolutely no need for a fur-lined robe or a padded cotton jacket. However, those extreme southern climatic anomalies are not the winter scenes of the south I want to discuss, for they can only be referred to as a southern evergreen spring — an extension of spring or autumn.

Due to its fertility and moist, the southern land is apt to retain warmth and, hence, better sustains crops. This is why the reed catkins along the Yangtze River remain in bloom until the winter solstice, and sometimes remain red for more than three months. Take as another example the Chinese tallow trees growing on both banks of the Qiantang River. Even when the red leaves fall off, the snow-white seedpods remain, drooping in dots and clusters on the tips of the twigs. Photographs of them can be passed off as those of plum flowers. While the worst scenario for the grass is that it turns ochre, it still keeps some of its gentle green color close to the roots. A wild fire cannot wipe out the grass, and the chilly wind cannot beat it down. If you do not mind traveling to the suburbs on a breezy and balmy afternoon, under the azure sky, you will not feel the bleakness of the season, but instead get in touch with some kind of vitality with which the place is inexplicably pregnant. Percy Bysshe Shelley's well-known line of poetry "If winter comes, can spring be far behind?" can be easily appreciated in the hilly area of the south.

An outdoor stroll in the wintry suburbs is indeed a special favor the southern winter bestows on the inhabitants of the south. Those who live in the frozen and snowy north will not, in their entire lives, ever have an opportunity for such leisurely and carefree enjoyment. I have no idea what would happen if one compared the winter in Germany with the one in our Jiangsu and Zhejiang provinces, but judging from the fondness of many writers for the use of the word "Spaziergang" in the titles of their works, it may be about right to assume that the climate of the four seasons in southern Germany is approximately the same as that in our south. Take the 19th-century bucolic poet Peter Rosegger (1843–1918), for example. He made liberal use of the word "stroll" in the titles of his writings, and what he wrote about is also applicable to the mountainous area in Jiangsu and Zhejiang provinces, China.

Southern China is crisscrossed by rivers and tributaries, abundant in lakes and marshes, and adjacent to the sea. These geographical facts help keep its air moist and create a sporadic drizzle, even in the winter. What an ethereal, peaceful image the scene of a hamlet during a winter drizzle creates! Imagine, after an autumn harvest, a hamlet perching by a riverside and composed of three to five families, with their doors facing a long bridge and windows looking to the distant hills. In between the huts and the hills are heavily wooded areas with various kinds of forked or bifurcating trees. Then, apply to this painting of a rustic winter scene a thin layer of white-colored drizzle — as thin as powder, plus a thin layer of background — so thin that the ink is barely discernible. Isn't this already a scene of leisurely peace? To embellish the painting a little bit more, moor a small black-roofed boat in front of a door and add a few vociferous drinking friends in one of the huts. To suggest the time of twilight, use a reddish-yellow color to paint a halo on the window of the thatched hut to hint at the light of a lamp inside. In such a scene, a person would feel broadminded and carefree, and eventually grow unconcerned about the ideas of gain or loss and nonchalant about the matter of life and death. We must still remember the poetic line composed by the Tang Dynasty poet, "The riverside hamlet in the drizzle of dusk." Sojourning here, even a poet would tolerate outlaws and bandits. What else but the mesmerizing charm of a southern winter scene would cause people to feel this way?

Speaking of rain, it is natural to think of snow. While the poetic line "The nightfall is to usher in a snowfall; 'Tis the time to tipple a little alcohol" is a description of a southern snow scene at dusk, "A chilly, sandy path in the shade of a plum tree; a hamlet with a thin wine aroma in a flurry" draws a picture of the three winter regulars: snow, moon, and plums, meeting together to flirt with barmaids. And if "The barking at the wooden door signals the return of the owner on a windy and snowy night" is a sketch of a southern snow scene on a deep, serene night, then "From within the deep snow in front of the hamlet burst a spray of plum-blossom last night" shows the scene of the next morning, with the kids of the hamlet, who are as fond of snow as dogs are, coming to report the snow scene. Perhaps not all of these lines of poetry were written in the south, and perhaps, not all of the poets who wrote these poems were southerners, but isn't it striking to use these poetic lines to depict the southern snow scenes? They are much more captivating than the prose under my clumsy pen!

For a few years in the south — yes, in the south — there may be winters without rain or snow, but there might be a little spring flurry following a cold wave late in the first month or early in the second, by the Chinese lunar calendar. Last year (1934) was like this, and this winter looks about the same, I am afraid. Judging from this, the coldest days may fall toward the end of February in 1936, in the Gregorian calendar, but may not last for more than seven or eight days. Seasons like this are referred to by farmers as dry winters, which are beneficial to wheat growth but harmful to humans because if the dryness lingers too long, humans will become vulnerable to diseases like diphtheria, flu, etc. But for those who take delight in the winter scenes of the south, this is the kind of winter they enjoy more, because there are more clear days and, hence, naturally more opportunities to stroll in the suburbs. This is also the kind of winter mostly favored by Japanese hikers and German Spaziergangers.

Outside, it is as sunny as it is in late autumn. The sky is so pleasantly high and the sunlight is so pervasive that I can no longer sit in the room. Action speaks louder than words. I am fed up with writing such a humdrum essay. Let me put down my pen, pick up my walking-stick, and go to the lake for a stroll!

I Have Run Head-on into Autumn

◎ *Yu Dafu*

Because early morning is the most pleasant time of the day in this long, hot summer, I have developed a habit of getting up or going to bed at daybreak, which is around four thirty, for sure.

That is the pattern of my life.

But last night, I went to bed earlier, at about eleven o'clock. When I wake up, it is still dark outside. I am about to go back to sleep when I suddenly become aware of the unusualness in the buzz of mosquitoes and the flow of the air. They don't seem to be happening during the thick darkness of midnight! Looking at my watch, I find it already five o'clock, as I have expected.

After rolling out of bed and rushing through my morning routine, I walk out of my room, which is as hot and smoky as a kitchen. No sooner have I stepped out of the hallway than I run head-on into autumn, almost to be knocked back!

First comes the wind, slowly, like a huge fluttering skirt, caressing me from head to toe. Like toothpaste being squeezed, I feel an immediate, thorough relief in my heart. I am not as energetic in the summer as I am in the winter, mainly due to the lucidness of my mind. Now, an earlier autumn has come to resolve my problem. Why not go with it?

The sky that has borne me down throughout the whole summer has suddenly lifted. Looking up, I see numerous small-sized clouds, as white as sterling silver, neatly lined up in the limpidly blue sky. The more I gaze at them, the more they look naughty and resemble my innate inspirations. How I wish I could bring them down and take a few bites at them! I now remember a song I wrote quite a while ago, *I See a Face in the Sky*, but now my mood is quite different from what it was then, and I am also much older — am I? So I stand there looking at those clouds. I want to continue looking at them — until they slowly disappear and are firmly implanted in my mind.

There are more and more passers-by. Some of them look up into the sky, like me — those are romantic types and I bless them; some of them give me a weird look and then hurry away — those are people whom I bless too, because they have a purpose to be busy. This is what life should be like: you have to do something or feel something. Each of these two choices is respectable and cannot be taken lightly. This is just like me at the moment: I now stand my ground. Like an old antelope, I have to be cool-headed in holding myself in my own territory, next to the earthen wares and the wire fences. Everything will be alright by six o'clock, when by the park gate, there will be vendors selling delicious and succulent minced pork dumplings, to go with jellied tofu soup thickly dressed with fresh green parsley over brightly red chili oil and loosely dotted with chopped, smoked turnips. And there will also be deep-fried dough sticks as hot-tempered as felines, soybean milk as demure as a lovely girlfriend, and crispy-crusted, tender-hearted, green-onion-flavored pancakes as intimate as a bosom friend.

Of all the houses tightly lined up here, every window has behind it a story that I have also experienced or that I am interested in hearing; every sleepwalking man cannot help fidgeting like me and every woman in pajamas has been loved or is now in love; every old man is rich with experiences and every child fresh; every dog is animated and every pigeon keen. Every morning I do the same thing, although I am now different from before, always dreaming of unusual encounters and always wishing to inspire fervent passions, yet always being fooled by peevish reality and awakened from fanatical visions by such unusual weather, like today. I am now no longer lonely. Right?

This loneliness is like a padded cotton quilt, spread out high in the sky. It can be depressing, descending, entwining, or uplifting, depending on the change in the number of people who share my room. Beautiful, isn't it? Yes, but a little cruel, I know.

Wow, my Beijing, the one that just had a traffic control yesterday, the one that has had the highest temperature in the country this summer, the one that has revitalized my nerves with a fresh autumn, and the one that has thoroughly disordered my life, completely unfolded my story, and carefully turned me into a new paper to write the story on!

Greenness

◎ *Zhu Ziqing*[1]

Upon my second visit to Xianyan, I was greatly taken by the color of the Plum-Rain Pool — the greenness.

The Plum-Rain Pool is a cataract pool, consisting of three cascades, and the Plum-Rain Cascade is the lowest. You can hear the gurgling sound as you approach the hill, and, raising your head, you can see that inlaid between the two damp, dark hillsides is a long, bright white screen of water.

The first sight we went to see was the Plum-Rain Pavilion, which was right across from the cascade. Sitting by the pavilion, you didn't have to raise your eyes to see the entirety of the cascade, and lying deep down below the pavilion was the Plum-Rain Pool itself. The pavilion sat at a projecting corner of a rock, and it was suspended there with nothing above and nothing below, looking like an open-winged goshawk floating in the sky. It was surrounded by hills on three sides, like in the center of half a ring. Thus, the tourists below seemed to be walking at the bottom of a well.

It was a semi-clear autumn day. Above our heads, thin clouds flew, and down here, the moisture gave the rock surfaces and the grass clusters a light touch of oily greenness. All this seemed to have made the cascade sing louder. Rushing from above, the water seemed like a smooth, neat piece of cloth that had been torn into several differently sized bundles of thread. Because of the many bulges and lumps, when the water struck the

---

[1] Zhu Ziqing (1896-1948), educated at Peking University, he was professor of Chinese literature at Tsinghua University and National Southwest Associated University, as well as a renowned essayist.

rocks as it fell, it sent out random splashes like flying flowers or broken shards of jade. Seen from afar, the crystal-clear, sparkling splashes flew up like myriad tiny white plum blossoms and then fell in a drizzle — hence, the name "Plum-Rain Pool". In my opinion, however, "Poplar Blossoms" might be a better name for the place, because the sprays of water drifted in the breeze just like poplar blossoms. Right at this moment, a few of those poplar blossoms came flying our way, jumping in our warm arms — nowhere to be found.

Enticed by the flashy greenness of the Plum-Rain Pool, we began to trace the magical flickering of its source. After clutching at weeds, grabbing at randomly scattered stones, and carefully leaning forward and bending over to squeeze through a rock passage, we reached the edge of the pool, brimming with green water.

Although the cascade was so close to me as to be within my reach now, my heart was no longer with it, but instead was mesmerized by the rippling greenness of the pool. That intoxicating greenness! It was like a huge lotus leaf spread over the pool — oh, that abundance of extraordinary greenness!

I wanted to open my arms to pull her into my chest, but what a vain attempt that would have been! Standing by the water and looking across it, I thought she looked very wide! This greenness of spread-out flatness and solid deposition was indeed attractive. Loosely pleated, she was like the train of a skirt a young lady would pull behind her; softly ruffling, she was like the palpitating heart of a virginal girl in love for the first time; smoothly bright, it was as though she had been anointed with "nourishing oil", which was as soft and tender as egg white, inspiring tourists to associate her with the most tender skin they had ever touched; unblemished in any way, she was like a piece of soft, smooth jasper stone, dressed in only one clear color — but you can never see her through. I had once seen the green willows in Beijing's Shichahai Temple, but that greenness was a little too light since there always remained an undercoat of pastel yellow. I had also once seen the high, thick "green wall" by the Tiger Spring Temple in Hangzhou, but that greenness was a little too exuberant, as it was comprised of lush clusters of green weeds and leaves. As for other places, the greenness of the waves in West Lake was too bright, while that of the Qinhuai River was too dark.

You are so worthy of adoration, but with what should I compare you? How could I compare you with anything? Is it because you are so deep that you are able to maintain such exquisite greenness? Is it because a piece of the sky has melted into you that you appear so fresh and smooth?

That intoxicating greenness! If I could turn you into a ribbon, I would present you to a graceful dancing girl, who could surely wave you in the wind. If I could shape you into a pair of eyes, I would present you to a talented blind singing girl, who, with you, would surely be able to see. However, I have gotten too attached to you to give you up! How can I give you up without regret? I pat you and caress you as if you were a little girl of twelve or thirteen years. I cup you into my mouth, which is like kissing the girl on the cheek. Let me give you a name — from today on, I will call you "Maiden Green". Do you agree?

Upon my second visit to Xianyan, I couldn't help being struck by the color the Plum-Rain Pool — the greenness.

A Lotus Pool in the Moonlight

◎ *Zhu Ziqing*

I feel very restless these days. Tonight, while I sit in our yard and enjoy the cool air, it strikes me that the lotus pool that I pass by every day must look different under this full moon. The moon sails slowly up into the sky, and the laughter of the children playing in the street behind the wall is all gone. In the house, my wife pats our son Run'er to the beat of the lullaby she drowsily croons. I quietly slip on a gown and walk out, leaving the door closed behind me.

Winding along the side of the lotus pool is a cinder-paved path. This is a secluded road with very few pedestrians, even during the daytime, and therefore, it is quieter at night. Encircling the pool are dense clusters of trees, and growing by the path are willows and some trees unknown to me. On a moonless night, this path appears eerily somber, but it is fine tonight, although the moonlight is pale.

I am the only one on the path, strolling with my hands behind me. This gives me a sense of possessing the entire vicinity, and also a sense of sublimating myself into another world. I enjoy the hustle and bustle of life but am also fond of peacefulness. I like socializing, but don't mind being all by myself. Like tonight, under this filmy moon, all by myself, I can think about anything I want to or nothing at all. I therefore feel I am a free man. I can completely ignore what I have to do or say during the daytime. This is the beauty of being alone. So let me just enjoy this boundless view of the lotus in the moonlight.

Gazing at the meandering pool, I see an abundance of lotus leaves. Standing high above the water, they look like the flared skirts of ballerinas; interspersed among the layers upon layers of leaves are white flowers, some of them blossoming gracefully and others budding shyly. They look very much like bright pearls, or stars in the azure sky. When a gentle breeze wafts over them, a whiff of lingering fragrance follows, which is as ethereal as the music flowing from a high tower in the distance. Right at this moment, there is a slight shiver from among the leaves and flowers. Like lightning, it flashes to the other side of the pool in the blink of an eye and zips open the densely clustered leaves in a jade-green streak. Underneath the leaves are innumerable ripples, which may be invisible, yet this invisibility is what accentuates the charm of the leaves.

Like water, the moonlight quietly streams onto the wide expanse of leaves and flowers. Over the pool, a thin greenish mist floats up. Thus, the leaves and flowers appear to be washed in milk or cloaked in a piece of fine gauze, as misty as a dream. Although a full-orbed moon sails in the sky tonight, it cannot shine brightly, because of the clouds, flimsy though they may be. In my opinion, however, this is where the beauty lies — although one cannot dispense with sound sleep, sometimes a little nap has its own appeal. As the moon shines through the trees, it casts across the pool irregular and mottled shadows from the bosky shrubs standing high above. The sparse silhouettes of the winsome, sinuous willows seem to be painted onto the lotus leaves. The moonlight does not shine evenly onto the pool, but the lights and the shadows thus formed are rendered so harmoniously that they are like a famous melody being played on the violin.

Surrounding the pool, far and near, high and low, are trees, and most of them are willows. They encircle the pool tightly, except for a few spaces at the side where the path winds along. These spaces look as though they have been designed particularly to receive the moonshine. All of these trees appear dim, and look, at a quick glance, like a cloud of smog. But through the smog, the graceful stance of the willows is still discernible. At the tips of the trees are vague outlines of the distant hills — faintly recognizable at the most. And dripping through the sporadic gaps among the trees are the lights of street lamps, dimly torpid like drowsy eyes. At the moment, the most animated sounds in this scene are the singing of the cicadas in the trees and the crowing of the frogs in the water, but these joys are theirs, not mine. I have nothing!

My thoughts suddenly drift to the lotus-gathering event. The lotus-gathering event is an old southern tradition, which can arguably be traced far back in time but was the most popular in the Six Dynasties (the 3rd century to the 6th century). Details about the lotus-gathering events are revealed, to a certain extent, in the ancient poetry. The lotus gatherers were usually maidens, who traveled on dinghies while singing love songs. There were not only a lot of lotus gatherers, but also many spectators. It must have been a joyful and romantic event. In his verse, *Ode to Lotus Gathering*, Emperor Yuan of Liang gave a vivid description of this scene.

Therefore,
Fine young men and fair ladies,
In a courting mood, ride dinghies.
Here they wind back the egret-shaped boats,
To pass their goblets for amorous toasts.
With the oars tangled in water leaves,
They row their dinghies through the duckweeds.
In plain skirts dangling from their waspish waists,
The girls, glancing back, move in slow gaits.
While summer proceeds, spring lingers,
With tender leaves and fresh flowers.
They giggle and hope to keep off the splash and spray,
And lift their attire in case the boats tilt and sway.

This verse clearly reveals the merry spectacle of such an event. It must have been an interesting event, but we now do not have the fortune to enjoy it.

This reminds me of a few lines from *The Song of Xizhou*.

I went to gather lotus in South Pool,
Where the autumn lotus flowers outgrow me;
The seedpods I stoop to toy with and pull,
Are as fresh as the green water can be.

The lotus flowers in this pool tonight can also be considered high enough to "outgrow gatherers", if there is any gatherer, yet unfortunately the water ripples are hidden from sight. This makes me nostalgic for the south. Right at this point of my thought, I suddenly raise my head and find myself already back in front of my door. I gently push the door open and walk in. Inside the house, there is not a single sound to be heard. My wife has already been sound asleep for quite some time.

A Red Leaf

◎ *Shi Pingmei*[①]

It is late night with dreary wind and rain.

Everything has quieted down — only the rain falls on the plantain leaves, producing a heartbreaking patter. Perhaps this sound is the heartbeat of the universe, wailing on this quiet, late night.

Quickening for a moment and then slowing down for another, the rain outside the window sounds as majestic and mighty as battle drums and as rhythmic and swift as jazz swings, and its fall is as thin as the willow twigs tousled by the wind, wetting only a few budding chamomiles. With a broken dip-pen in one hand and my face toward the light of a lamp, I am lost in deep thought, as the images of past events glide through my mind. Abruptly, I put down the pen, slide open a drawer, pull out a red-covered diary, and flip through it until a red leaf appears. As brightly colored as a rose, the red leaf has already been kept in my diary for two months. Because of a propensity towards avoidance, I have not dared to look at it until now, for it is the embodiment of a soul and the symbol of a tragedy. Who would have expected that a thin leaf would be veined with the insolvable mystery of life and death? Looking at the leaf, I am now a captive to my tears, but I cannot complain. Of the tens of thousands of maple leaves that have fallen, this is the one that carries with it such an unfortunate fate. Let me tell you the story behind it.

The story took place on the night of October 26, 1923, when I was

---

① Shi Pingmei (Shi Rubi, 1902-1928), woman essayist and social activist. She was considered as one of the four talented women writers in the second quarter of the 20th century in China.

reading a book entitled *Annals of Sorrow-Free Lake*. Because I was a little tired, I lay down on a couch to take a catnap. The feverfew on the desk was in bloom, and the breeze coming through the window screen puffed whiffs after whiffs of its fragrance onto my face. The sweet scent lulled me into a state of deep slumber — or rather a gentle intoxication. Seizing the moment of my body's relaxation, many petrels of reminiscence begin to dart over the undulating waves of thoughts in my mind. I was lost in the recollection about my childhood, when friendship — as firm as gold and as pure as jade — was formed, and unshakable determination — as strong as iron — was forged. I could not help smiling when my thoughts had reached the prospect of my future which aimed as high as a soaring bird in the cloud-embellished sky. When I opened my eyes, I saw, however, that the feverfew blooms were all drooping. I began to worry about their fate. It looked as if they were heading toward their tombs, where the angel of death, with his black wings open, awaited them. My heart was filled with an inexplicable sadness.

At about ten o'clock at night, the servant girl came in and handed me a letter. I opened it and saw a blank piece of paper. When I pulled it out, a red leaf slipped out. "Oh, it's a red leaf!" I cried out involuntarily. Confused for a while, I picked it up with my trembling hand, and saw written on it two lines:

As uncontainable as the enticing autumnal mountain scene,
I resort to this red leaf to send to you my tender feelings.

— Picked up by Tian Xin from the Azure Cloud Temple
in the West Mountain on the Twenty-Fourth of October

Thus, quietly, the night wind stirred up the peaceful lake in my heart, in which waves upon waves surged as if it had turned into a sea dominated by a fierce wind. Leaning forward on the desk, I tried to think it over, and immediately a heavy burden of sorrow began to pile up on my brows. I had never expected that such an uncontainable emotion would have erupted in me after an ordinary meeting, but still, I felt sorry to him for I couldn't accept his leaf. Because of the goal I had long cherished, I couldn't accept the leaf; even if I did accept it, I wouldn't be able to fulfill the duty behind it. Because I could not give him my heart, I couldn't accept the leaf; even if I did, I would not be able to bear the pain of deceiving him. Even though I didn't have to think about myself, how could I not think about him? This filled me with heart-rending agony.

Bats slid by the window. The noises they produced under the dark, somber mantle of night made me shudder! I lifted the drapes off the window and saw lying on the moonlit ground mottled tree shadows as motionless as if they were dead, deepening the sense of chilliness and silence of the universe. I slid on a jacket, pushed the yard door open, and walked out. The chilly wind starting up dispelled all the annoyances in my heart. Wandering the yard for a few aimless rounds, I sat down in a thatched pavilion to watch the moon. The silvery moonlight, chilly, clear and bright, made me feel the emptiness and the solitude of the world. So, before long, I returned to the room, dipped my pen fully in the ink, and wrote a few words on the back of the leaf:

The withered basket is too shabby for a fresh red leaf.

Wrapping it in the same white paper and enclosing it in an envelope, I mailed the leaf back to him. Thus, I crumpled with my own hands the bud that had begun to bloom. Although he was extremely sad about my rejection, he never stopped seeking a relationship with me. After he died, I went to Lan Xin's apartment to sort out his mail. That was when the letter suddenly appeared again. I opened the envelope, and there I saw the leaf with the handwriting of both of us still on it — only the leaf had dried up; it had a narrow crack down the middle. Seeing it, I felt as if I had been stabbed in the heart with a dagger. Although I had turned him down when he was alive, now after his death, I felt that this leaf was a symbol of his life. Dear God, allow me to pray for him. I will now accept what I refused when he was alive. However, a leaf can come back, but what about him? He will never be able to return, and only this everlasting leaf, the bearer of my regret, will accompany me. As I pick up the leaf with my trembling hand, I wish that the feeling with which he sent me the leaf would remain in it forever.

Evening and Morning Views from a Ferry

◎ *Zhu Xiang*[1]

Beauty is everywhere — even over a ferry berth outside the old town.

It is nine o'clock on a late autumn night, and there is a light, chilly wind. I wait for and then board a ferry rowboat. Both the sky and the river are dim, but, upon a closer look, the water is still suffused with an amber glow. The pitch-black strip that stretches in between is the southern bank.

With the evening stars strewn around it, Hesperus twinkles like an electronic light in the relatively far distance. Swaying on the river is a silver beam of light, which, as it can be seen, comes from a red fishing lamp.

The houses on the bank are outlined in black.

There is a pontoon about forty to fifty feet away. Usually unattractive, the dim electronic light on the pontoon now is not only pleasing to the eye, but it is simply beautiful. It casts some human figures in outlines, but you don't hear anything from them, just as you don't hear anything from us on this rowboat.

Suddenly, in the center of the river ahead, several dark sailboats rush downstream, soundless, like birds released by giants.

Now, it is early morning near a commercial port.

The sun has climbed up to a twenty-degree angle or so from the horizon, while the moon looking like an upside-down bowl has dipped to a forty-degree angle. A few huge clouds, like mackerel scales, are glued to the light-azure sky. They look as though they are far behind the sun.

The mountains are clad in an antique bronze-colored garment, with pleats like pictures.

---

[1] Zhu Xiang (Zhu Ziyuan, 1904-1933), important modern poet and essayist.

Over the river, the mist rises more than two feet. A few corpulent gulls now flash brightly in the sunshine.

The moon hangs over to the portside of the boat.

And this is where the mist is over a foot high. It is sometimes visible and sometimes invisible on this side, but it is completely invisible in the shadow of the boat. —

The only things that are brightly and wildly colored are the lines of trees on the distant land and the sails on the horizon.

The water is rendered from yellow by the boat, to grayish-blue in the center of the river, to silver-gray next to the bank. A few small steamers are puffing out soot, which is black around the openings of the chimneys, light-green, ecru, and pale in the shadow of the boat, and pale-brown in the slanting sunshine.

A ferry trip in the early morning is colorful.

Lamplights

◎ *Ba Jin*[①]

I'm startled awake from a midnight nightmare. Feeling smothered, I get up and walk into the cloister to breathe the chilly night air.

It is pitch dark all around. My feet seem to walk upon a slumbering sea, but soon, like waves rolling one upon another, the off-white streets emerge. Then, as the darkness of the night gradually recedes, I can finally discern where the hills are, where the houses are, where the vegetable gardens are.

To my right, lamplights gleam from inside a few bungalows that stand against the hills. The lights dilute the darkness of the night.

I look at the lights. The gleam they cast is pale yellow, and the lights seem to flicker slightly in the cold air. Once or twice, I almost think they are going off, but in the blink of an eye, they come back on again. These lights that burn so late at night are probably the only ones to quietly spread a little bit of illumination and warmth — not only for me, but for those who cannot fall asleep on such a chilly night, and also for the walkers who still grope their way in the darkness. Yes, over there — isn't that a burst of hurried footsteps? Who is this person walking back from the city to the country? Soon, a dark figure walks past me, so fast that he might be running or fleeing. I understand very well why he is rushing home. And therefore, I believe, to his eyes and heart, the gleam in front of him must seem brighter and warmer than usual.

I had the same experience as this man is having. A faint light — a

---

① Ba Jin (Li Yaotang, Li Feigan, 1904-2005), one of the most important novelists, essay writers, and translators, who had been elected chairman of the China Writers Association.

light, it seemed, that could be swallowed by the darkness at any minute — once encouraged me to walk a great distance. Large snowflakes brushed against my face; my leather shoes kept sinking in the muddy dirt road; and several times, the wind tried to knock me into the mud and mire. I felt like I was trapped in a labyrinth, and it seemed like I would never find an escape or see any way out, but, holding up my head and throwing out my chest, I continued to stride ahead. I kept walking because I saw a little light at the time, although it was only about the size of a bean. Light, no matter whose house it comes from, can always reveal direction to walkers — even to a non-native like me.

That incident occurred many years ago, and since then, many great changes have taken place in my life. Now, I stand in this cloister, watching the gleam of the lights coming from the foot of the hill. Aren't these lights like those from many years ago? I can hardly see a difference between them! But why do I fail to see the difference? Am I not standing peacefully in the open corridor at the front of my house? I am not fumbling for direction on a rainy night, but looking at the glow of light, why do I suddenly feel reassured and inspired? Is it because my heart, after being misled into a labyrinth by a nightmare and wandering in the dark night, has finally found its way out?

I do not have an exact answer to my own question, but I know for sure that my heart is growing peaceful and my breath, much smoother. I should be grateful to those people who have shared their lights, although their names are beyond my knowledge.

While I am not the one for whom they have lit the lights, nor will my image appear in their dreams, I have still benefited from the lights that have comforted my heart. I love lights like these. One light — or even several of them — may not be powerful enough to clear up the entire darkness, but it can lend a little courage and a little warmth to those who cannot fall asleep on a chilly night.

A lighthouse beacon on a solitary sea can save many boats from sinking — in fact, any boat sailing on that sea will benefit from its guidance. In an obscure European legend, a lonely maiden living on an island set up a light at her window all night long in hopes of calling back her little brother at sea, but to no avail; however, her light helped many nearby fishermen on their return journeys.

Let's trace further into ancient times. The torch that the Greek priestess Hero set ablaze on her tower lit up the eyes of Leander in his nightly swim to her across the Hellespont. One night, a storm blew out the torchlight. Unguided, the brave lover was drowned. Yet that blazing torchlight seems to continue illuminating us even to this day, as if it had never sunk to the bottom of the sea along with the ancient beauty.

Although none of these lights is lit for me in particular, I receive a share of their benefits, too — a little illumination and a little warmth. Light disperses the darkness from my soul, and warmth allows my soul to grow. A friend of mine once said, "Food is not the only thing that makes us live," and this, of course, is also true for me. My heart often drifts over the dark sea. If it were not for the guidance of the light, my heart would someday sink for good into the bottom of this dark sea, too.

I remember a story about a friend of mine. Filled with incurable pain and a strong determination to die, he threw himself into a river in the south. The last thing he remembered, as he sank into the water, was hearing someone cry for help, along with various other noises; he also saw a tiny light before he lost consciousness. When he woke up, he found himself lying in bed in the home of a stranger. There was a kerosene lamp on the table, and he was surrounded by several hearty, friendly faces. "There is warmth in this world," he thought in gratitude. And after that, he changed his attitude toward life: his sense of hopelessness was gone, his pessimism disappeared; he became an enthusiastic person and began to love life. This incident occurred twenty or thirty years ago, and I recently met this friend again. That little light had encouraged a person with a suicidal propensity to lead a long and healthy life. Although I have not broached the topic of the light with him, I believe that the dim light still burns in his heart.

In this world, light will never die out! As I think this, I cannot help but smile at the other side of the hill.

Myriad Stars

◎ *Ba Jin*

I love moonlit nights and am also fond of the star-strewn sky. Back in the old days, in my home town, when I was in our courtyard enjoying the cool nights of July and August, what I enjoyed most was watching the stars fill the sky. As I watched them, I forgot everything, as though I had returned to my mother's arms.

Three years ago, in Nanjing, the house I lived in had a back door. Whenever I opened that door at night, I saw a tranquil nighttime view, with a large vegetable garden below, and above, the blue sky densely studded with clusters of stars. Though stars seem small and weak to the naked eye, the brightness of the starlight seemed ubiquitous. I had been reading about astronomy then and knew about some of the stars, so they were like my friends and would often talk to me.

Now, I am on the sea. Because I gaze at the stars every night, I have come to know them well. Lying on my back on the deck and looking into the sky, I see myriad stars, half-bright and half-dim, hanging in the deep blue sky. The ship moves and they do, too. They look so close to me, as though they are falling! Gradually, my vision blurs. I seem to see innumerable fireflies dancing around me. Night at sea is mellow, tranquil, and dreamy. Looking at the many familiar stars, I seem to see them twinkling at me and seem to hear them whispering. Now, I am completely lost in them. Nestled in their embrace, I smile and fall asleep. I feel like a child, sleeping in my mother's arms.

The Hen

◎ *Lao She*[1]

I have always disliked the hen. Once it gets a little startled — in whatever ways possible — look, it clucks and clucks and clucks, from the courtyard to the backyard and then from the backyard back to the courtyard, endlessly, and for no reason at all. Simply obnoxious! Sometimes, it may stop its random clucking, but then, tiptoeing, in a gingerly manner, along the foot of a wall or along the ridge of a field, in a thin and sissified voice, as if it has something to worry about, it strains its throat and drags out some kind of a noise like a grievance or a complaint. The sound immediately gives me the creeps!

The hen never resists the rooster, but it sometimes bullies the most benign ducks. And what's more scandalous about it is that it will viciously attack another hen — biting fiercely and yanking a handful of feathers from the unprepared victim.

When the time comes for the hen to lay eggs, it reaches its most conceited point, itching to let the whole world know the little achievement it has made — by then, even a deaf person would not be able to stand the noise it makes.

But I have changed my opinion about it, for what I see now, instead, is a mother that has hatched out a group of chicks.

No matter where it goes now, in the yard or outside of it, it always stretches out its neck, showing that there is nothing in this world to be afraid of. Even when a bird flies over or something makes a noise, it

---

[1] Lao She (Shu Qingchun, 1899-1966), with his novels and dramas, was regarded as one of the best writers in modern China, and "master of the Chinese language".

immediately becomes vigilant, tilting its head to listen and tightening its back in preparation for a fight, looking forward and then behind, and cawing to alert its children to gather around their mother!

Whenever it finds something edible, it cheeps and makes a few pecks before immediately releasing the precious find to its children. As a result, each baby chick has a round and bulging belly, as if it were stuffed with one or two glutinous rice balls, while the hen itself becomes skinny. If an adult rooster or hen dares to swoop in on their food, this mother will most certainly launch a counterattack to drive the challenger far away. Hence, even a big rooster is somewhat afraid of it during this period.

The hen teaches its chicks how to peck at food, how to dig in the dirt, and how to take a dirt bath. It teaches them many times a day. It also semi-squats — I think this posture is very tiring — to let its children squeeze under its wings and bosom to keep warm. When it crouches on the ground, some babies climb onto its back and peck at its head or at other places, but it remains silent.

If anything stirs in the night, it will squawk. Its voice is so sharp and sounds so sad that even the heaviest sleeper will get up to check whether a weasel has sneaked in.

It is responsible, motherly, courageous, and hard-working, because it has a group of chicks to take care of now. It is noble-minded, because it is a mother now. And a mother must be a heroine!

So I dare not dislike the hen anymore.

The Pavilion of Cherished Dusk

◎ *Xie Bingying*[1]

The rustling breeze fans the murmuring leaves, and the babbling stream hums with the birds' sweet singing — what an enchanting symphony of nature!

Are the chirping cicadas on the tree branches somewhat exhausted, perhaps? If not, why is their singing so disjointed and so melancholy?

The water in the stream gently gurgles along, through the sand, over the stones, and across the little blades of grass — day and night, always in the same way. Perhaps the stream never stops. Does it?

The gracefully dancing butterflies have ceased their activity and now perch in the clusters of weeds, while countless mosquitoes continue to glide back and forth around the tree branches in a disorderly manner.

The crescent moon that has just popped out from behind the eastern horizon sails against the light blue clouds. She looks as if she is gazing at me closely, fixing her wide-open eyes on me and my wild antics under a green tree by the Pavilion of Cherished Dusk, in front of a stream.

Encouraged by the rising wind, I begin to shout, and now and then, I jump up and down, my hair disheveled. Oh, oh, what fun! Then, with my left hand holding out my silk skirt and my right hand raised over my head, I begin to dance slowly. My childish, artless and ridiculous gestures are perfectly reflected in the clear water. I laugh at the dancing image reflected in the stream. And the image in the stream laughs back — which, in turn, intensifies my laughter, only to further intensify the laughter of the girl

---

① Xie Bingying (Xie Minggang, 1906-2000), first woman writer who had served in the army, her prolific writing of novels, short stories, essays, letters, etc. covered 20 million Chinese characters. Her best known novel was Autobiography of a Woman Soldier.

in the stream. And so I begin to cry to her. And so she frowns, opens her mouth, and starts to cry back, which makes me shed real tears, only to make her shed hers. She has shed as many tears as I have, and our tears fall into the stream at the same speed.

Sometimes, I follow a toad and imitate it. When it jumps into the weeds, I jump there, too; when it leaps onto a rock and squats upon it, I leap onto a rock and squat there, too; but when it suddenly flops into the stream, all I can do is to disconsolately watch it swimming freely.

Sometimes, when a bird sings, I sing, too. But when my throat goes dry and my voice turns hoarse, the bird keeps singing in joyful complacency.

And finally, lying down on my left side, with my left hand supporting my head, I gaze at the filmy moon that seems to smile at me, and I gaze sideways at the few white, cottony-soft clouds which stand out against the remaining azure ones.

After a long vigil, my eyes are so sore that they feel as though they have been numbed by many needles. Exhausted, I slide down onto the thick, tender, green grass and fall asleep. The balmy springtime breeze, with its various scents, and the sweet birdsong, with its various melodies, send me into a dreamland.

In the dream, I see my grandma, who passed away two years ago, and my two cousins, who died last winter. My friendly, smiling grandma hugs and kisses me, and my two cousins tug at my clothes, asking me to tell "The Story of the Red-Haired Savages". In a semi-awake and semi-asleep state, I find myself grieving and sighing long and mournfully.

Waking, waking, and finally completely awakened from my dream, I open my eyes, and my view is filled with a full spring scene. This scene has driven away the dream I have just had.

Yet, when I lean on the stone balustrades and listen attentively to the murmuring maple leaves and glance at the water of the stream, recalling my honey-sweet and happy life in the past, "my tears start to fall onto my shirt" involuntarily again.

Then, when my tears dry up in the light wind and my hair covers my face in uncombed tresses, I perk my head again, to look at the scene of floating clouds, running water, green hills, and flying birds, at which I can only smile bitterly.

Alas!

I want to trade this listless, dark, dull and boring life of mine for a flourishing and vibrant one; I want to exchange this depressed and impetuous soul of mine for that of my tranquil and leisurely elder sister; I want all my past and future tears to be forever gone with the running water.

I want to release all my sorrow and indignation to the spring breeze!

I want to pass along my melancholic elegies to the twittering birds in the woods!

I want to commit my ties of love and affection to the branches of the trees!

I want to hang my pure and eager heart in outer space!

I want to have all my possessions melt into non-existence! Non existence!

The thin sunlight sweeps through the dense forest, glides across the heavenly vault, and gradually recedes into the western corner of the world. "Caw-caw-caw," the ravens crow as they return home and skitter over my head; the cicadas chirp and clamor; the sound of the running water seems louder than before; and the evening breeze begins its course through the woods. An abrupt shudder makes me aware of the chilliness in the air. Standing up, I tug at my shirt and skirt to straighten them out, and then I lower my head to look at the grasses on which I have sat. I have ravaged them so much that they now look squashy and limp.

"When the spring breeze comes and the dewdrops take shape, the grasses should be able to recover, shouldn't they?" Sadly, I sigh to myself.

I hold up my skirt and step down from the pavilion. A farmer abruptly stops hoeing his fields. He stretches his back and then turns around and fixes his eyes on me — until I turn around a corner.

Before the Rain Arrives

◎ *He Qifang*[1]

After circling and whistling softly in the breeze, the last flock of pigeons is also gone. They have flown back to their warm, wooden cote earlier than usual, perhaps because they have mistaken the bleak, grey sky for the color of nightfall, or have sensed the imminence of the storm.

Clad in dust and dirt, the tender green shoots, having sprouted in the sunshine of the last few days, look somewhat haggard on the willow twigs, and hence need a wash-up. And the chapped earth and the dried tree roots have also long been expecting this rain. But the rain withholds itself.

I miss the thunder of my hometown and its patter of rain. Those powerful rumbles and rolls of thunder resound in the valleys, and they shake, wake, and burst open the buds of spring, dormant in the frozen soil. Then the patter of rain, as soft as fine grass, begins to caress the buds with its gentle hands, pulling out from the buds the oily green leaves, opening up from among the leaves the red flowers. These reminiscences, like nostalgic sensations, frequently ring in my heart and depress me. The climate in my heart is like the one of this northern land — lacking rainfall. Just as the raindrops hang in the gloomy sky, a tender teardrop lingers in one of my dry eyes, persistently refusing to come down.

The white ducks also seem restless. From the turbid creeks in the city come their anxious quacks. While some of the ducks are happy with their own slow, boat-like gliding, others are doing headstands, plunging their long necks into the water and stretching their red webbed feet out behind their tails, continuously thrashing the water so as to balance themselves.

---

[1] He Qifang (1912-1977), modern poet, essayist, and literary critic.

45

No one knows if they do that for the purpose of looking for crumbs of food at the bottom of the creeks or just to indulge themselves in the cool water deep down there.

A couple of the ducks have already climbed onto the bank. After waddling back and forth like gentlemen under a willow tree, to dispel the weariness that results from their swimming, they then stand there, each in its own pose. Using their beaks as combs, they begin to meticulously preen their white feathers, sporadically shaking their bodies or flapping their wide wings to get rid of the drops of water hidden between their feathers. Done with its grooming, one of the ducks twists its neck to the back of its shoulder and tucks its long, red beak into one of its wings. It quietly closes its small dark eyes, set in downy, white eye sockets, and looks as if it is going to have a nap. Oh, poor little duck, is it in this way that you have your dreams?

This scene reminds me of the duckling-herder in my hometown, where a large flock of light-yellow ducklings swims in the streams. The clear, shallow water, the green grass flanking both banks, and a long bamboo pole in the herder's hand — how tamely his little team waddles over the ridges and slopes of the hill and how exultantly the ducklings chirp! When night falls, the herder makes a home by setting up a tent-like bamboo hut. But what a distant image that is! In this dusty and muddy land, all I hope for is to hear a little patter of rain on the leaves. If a cool rain could break its hesitancy and drip into my wrecked dream, it can perhaps grow into a green bower to shade me.

I raise my head. From the drooping sky, as grey as a pall of mist, some cold drops fall onto my face. As if in a rage — a rage over the heavy grey color of the sky, an eagle coming from afar, with its wings stretched out motionlessly, slants down from the sky, almost touching the earthen hill on the other bank of the creek, before it flaps its two wings with a roaring noise and soars back into the sky. I am astonished by the size of its broad wings, under which I can see the mottled white feathers on the underside of its chest. Then I hear from it a powerful cawing, like a shout from its tremendous heart or, perhaps, a call in the darkness for a companion.

Yet, still no rain.

Ode to Camellias

◎ *Yang Shuo*[1]

After a long stay in a foreign country, I sometimes find it very hard not to miss my motherland. To alleviate these feelings of nostalgia, I once came up with the idea of painting a picture that fully embodied the essence of my motherland, so that I could hang it up and look at it from time to time. I suggested my idea to an artist and asked her to paint such a picture for me. But, to my disappointment, she replied, "You have given me a hard nut to crack. What subject could one paint that would embody a theme like that? A few hills or rivers? A particular person or object? None of those subjects would work, I'm afraid. Besides, what colors would one use? Even if you put all the existing colors together, you still would not be able to portray the full view of your motherland." I thought it over and felt the same way. So I changed my mind and gave up the idea.

In February, I returned to my native country. Ever since I set foot in Kunming, I have been intoxicated by what I see. I used to be a northerner, and in the north at the moment, it may well be the season when the wind and snow lash the earth, and the mountains and rivers freeze. Yet in Yunnan Province, spring has already arrived, as though it were fleet of foot. Like a catalyst for flowers, it has brought out the blossoms everywhere.

The best place for a view of flowers is the Huating Temple in the Western Hills. Approaching its gate from afar, I already catch a whiff of sweet scent, which helps to soothe my mind. This scent comes from the plum blossoms. There are red, white, green, and vermilion plum trees, each of which is laden with blossoms that could inspire poetry. While the

---

① Yang Shuo (Yang Yujin, 1913-1968), famous journalist, lyricist and essayist.

white Yulan magnolia has slightly faded now, the bright yellow jasmine is in its prime. This springtime scene is much more lively than that at the Dianchi Lake.

Yet this is not the most lively springtime scene. Look up at that tree! Set off by the oily, smooth, dark green leaves are hundreds and thousands of bright crimson, large, multi-petalled blossoms, each like a blazing flame, blooming high up there next to the eaves of the temple portico. These are the famed camellias. Without having actually seen them, one would be unable to fully comprehend the intricacy in this line of poetry: "Spring is as deep as the sea."

This is a good season to see camellia blossoms. So after visiting the Huating Temple, I brave a scattered drizzle and visit the Black Dragon Pool, which is also a good spot for a view of camellia blossoms. I had the impression that camellias were rare, but to my amazement, I see many blossoms here, appearing now and then by a bamboo fence or near a thatched cottage. My friend tells me, "This isn't much of a surprise. In Dali, almost every family grows camellias. During the blooming season, all kinds of camellia blossoms seem to compete for rarity and beauty. That area is really stunning!"

This makes me think: "Yes, camellias are beautiful, and beauty comes from work. Who has cared for the camellias as though they were their own children, nurtured them day and night, year after year, and finally, with their own sweat, cultivated such rare flowers? We should be grateful to those who have beautified our lives!"

Pu Zhiren is one such skilled nurseryman. I have met him by the Jade-Green Lake, where there are many camellias in full bloom. There is an abundance of red, as though a colorful cloud has descended onto the lakeshore. As he leads me through the flowers, Pu Zhiren points to each camellia and tells me its name. This one is called Colossal Carnelian and that, Snow Lion; this is named Butterfly Wing and that, Large Purple Gown... So many names and so many colors! Then, he tugs at a twig of a camellia tree and says, "This one is called Kid's Face. It is late to bloom, and that's why it is only now just beginning to produce buds. But once it blooms, it is a deep red. This kind of camellia is the most pleasing to the eye."

"An old saying goes, 'It is easier to appreciate flowers than to grow them.' " I ask, "It must be quite a job to grow and cultivate camellias, right?"

He replies, "Yes and no. The camellia has its own habits, and one must be very meticulous in handling its water, soil, and climate. It grows best in cloudy weather, but it is quite delicate and suffers in the wind and the sun. Insects are its worst enemies. There is a kind of insect called a borer. Once a borer gets into it, the flower is bound to die. Camellia cultivators face lots of worries all year round."

"Their life span isn't very long, is it?" I blurt out another question.

He replies, "Yes, it is very long. The Huating Temple has a camellia tree called 'Scales like Pinecones'. It dates back to the Ming Dynasty. So it has been alive for more than five hundred years. Once it blooms, it produces over a thousand flowers."

I utter an involuntary exclamation, for I had not expected that the camellia tree I saw earlier in the temple had such an extraordinary origin.

He misunderstands my surprise and adds, "You don't believe me? Dali has an even older camellia. Elders say that it has already lived more than a thousand years. When it blooms, it is full of flowers — too many to count. It has, thus, earned the popular name 'Ten Thousand Camellia Blooms'. And the trunk is so thick that even several people with their arms extended and their hands joined wouldn't be able to reach all the way around it." He makes a hugging gesture as he says this.

I look at his hands, deeply touched. They are full of calluses and covered with fresh soil. Then, I look at his face. There are deep wrinkles around his eyes. You don't need to ask him about his life — you can learn about his life just by looking at him. This middle-aged man must have experienced much hardship. He is such an ordinary workman that if he takes leave and walks into a crowd, he will be immediately engulfed in it and can hardly be identified again. But these are the very people who have devoted all their time and energy, their mental and physical work, year after year, to the cultivation of trees and flowers and to the beautification of our lives. This is exactly how beauty is created!

Right at this moment, a group of children come to look at the flowers. With their little red faces tilted up, they giggle and titter.

"Kid's Face camellias are now in bloom," I cry out.

Looking bewildered for a second, Pu Zhiren understands me instantly. With a smile, he replies, "Yes, indeed. There is nothing more attractive than these kids' faces."

This inspires me to imagine the composition of a painting. An idea suddenly occurs to me: could a picture of a large, dewy Kid's Face camellia in full blossom, painted in the heaviest and brightest red, represent the essence of our country? I make a simple sketch of the idea and mail it to the artist, who lives far away, in a foreign country. Perhaps this time, she will be able to conceive of a painting for me.

The Beach on a Midsummer Night

◎ *Jun Qing*[1]

Shortly after the setting sun dips behind the mountain, the western sky still burns, a vast stretch of tangerine-red evening glow. The sea, dyed red by the glowing rays, looks more spectacular than the sky. Because the sea is in motion, each time the rolling waves surge forward, one wave after another, the glowing rays that shine along the crests of the waves appear not only red but also bright, like billowing and blazing flames, now flashing and then vanishing — only to shift to the next flashing, rolling, and surging movement of the sea.

Gradually, the glowing rays in the sky begin to fade from crimson to bright red, and then, to light red. And finally, when all the red rays are gone, the sky, which suddenly seems higher and wider, begins to take on a sense of deep solemnity. The Evening Star, the earliest star to come into view, begins to twinkle against the dark blue vault of the sky. This star, so big and so bright, is the only star that glitters at the moment, with a light that catches the eye, against the vast stretch of the dark blue firmament, looking exactly like a bright lamp hanging from a great height.

The night is thickening, but in the vast firmament, more and more "bright lamps" are emerging. Meanwhile, everywhere in the city, electric lights are also lit up one after another. Among them, the most visible are those that hang high on the hillsides that encircle the harbor. Mirrored on the dark blue water from their mid-air sources, the lights create reflections that flash and rock with the rolling waves, so they look like layered strands of flowing pearls. Setting off one another in the rays that they cast, both the pearls flowing upon the sea and the stars densely spread out in the sky

---

[1] Jun Qing (Sun Junqing, 1922-), famous military writer, essayist and painter.

look especially enchanting.

In this serene and charming night scene, I ramble along the seashore, treading on the cottony-soft, sandy beach. The water tenderly strokes the fine, soft sand of the beach, making a gentle rustling noise. The sea breeze, late to arrive at the scene, is fresh, clear, and cool. All this gives me a sense of indescribable excitement and joy.

The evening breeze gently rustles, a mixed scent of the sea and the crops of the field wafts in the air, and the warmth left by the sun lingers on the soft, sandy beach. Small knots of people who have worked various posts during the day now come over to this cottony-soft, sandy beach to bask in the cool sea breeze, to watch the star-embellished night sky, to engage in conversation and light banter, or simply to relax. Just like the rolling waves that surge here and there, now and then on the tranquil sea, cheerful and merry laughter breaks out here and there, now and then on the beach.

I ramble along the beach, among my fellow townspeople and friends.

Over there, next to a wooden boat keeled over on the beach, I see a group of people who have just finished harvesting wheat in the fields and are now discussing this year's harvest. Because the ample rain in this spring gave the wheat a good growth spurt, productivity is better this year than last. And now, as we have just had a thorough rain, a bumper harvest in autumn is almost guaranteed. Highly encouraged by these great auspices, the harvesters' talk is filled with cheerful and merry laughter.

The moon is up.

It is a splendid, full-orbed moon. Like a silver disc, it springs out of the tranquil sea, shining in all directions; a vast expanse of waves, the silver of fish scales, flashes in the sea. This flashing instantly brightens the beach, where many groups of dimly visible visitors — sitting, lying down, or walking — now emerge more clearly in my sight. Ah, it really surprises me that there can be so many visitors here, enjoying the cool night air. The entire beach is filled with the sound of chatter, laughter, singing, and frolicking.

The moon sails very high now. It is so clear and so bright.

And it is also very late at night now.

On the beach, some visitors have fallen asleep as they lie on the cottony-soft sand, and others continue to chat and laugh. The pleasant, cool breeze continues to rustle, and the clear moon continues to shine. Let these fine people thoroughly enjoy their varied conversations and their time of utter relaxation, on this clean beach under the limitless sky.

A Humorous Analogy for Prose

◎ *Feng Jicai*[①]

A young friend asked me what prose was and how to distinguish it from fiction or poetry. In reply, I offered him a humorous analogy:

A person walks along a road as he normally does — that is like a piece of prose.

A person is suddenly pushed into the water — that becomes a novel.

The earth catapults him onto the moon — that is a poem.

To create prose is to write down the happenings of everyday life most worthy of being written down. There should be no special effort-making, no calculated seeking, no artful feigning, no purposeful fabricating, and absolutely no "wracking" of the brain. The ultimate purpose of prose is to convey, in writing, a little feeling, a little sentimentality, and a little flavor. That's all there is to it. Of course, this "littleness" very often engenders heartfelt and unforgettable depth.

In art, no depth is manufactured.

The initial inspiration for a piece of prose is also distinct from that of a novel or a poem. A novel is thought out; a poem jumps out. A novel is the result of intense mental labor; a poem, in contrast, seems to involve no brain work at all. Immortal verses are all like visitors from outer space that serendipitously descend into the hearts of poets.

But what about prose? Prose-writing is like the clouds in the sky. You don't know where they will come from and when they will appear. Your life and your heart should be as pure as the blue sky. You raise your head, aha!

---

① Feng Jicai (1942-), famous novelist and painter. He is also an ardent advocator to protect folk arts.

Like bits of a white cloud, some fragments of the prose will begin to emerge.

This is what I like to say about prose-writing: prose is felt in your heart.

Buddhist Pilgrims — Travelogues of Mount Tai in the Old Days: Story One

◎ *Feng Jicai*

The piety of religious believers is sometimes so amazing that it goes beyond the comprehension of non-believers. While shrewdness and slickness often go hand in hand with vacillation, single-minded and persistent piety can often work miracles. However, what may seem miraculous to non-believers is merely ordinary to religious believers, such as the religious old women who have ascended a high mountain to burn incense and worship Buddha.

I

A considerable number of travelers on Mount Tai are Buddhist pilgrims. That has been the case since ancient times, and has remained so even during the "Ten Years of Turmoil," when all the temples on the mountain were locked up and all the religious idols were removed from their divine pedestals and stored in the main hall of the Azure Cloud Temple on the very top of the mountain. Among those idols were Sakyamuni (the spiritual founder of Buddhism), Rulai (the divine form of Sakyamuni, or Buddha), Lord Guan (a protector of fortune), Guanyin (Bodhisattva of mercy), God of the Land (Buddha of earth), Lohan (Arhat), Weituo (a protector of Buddhism), and Dai (the local god). For centuries upon centuries, each of these deities had been sitting alone in his or her own sacred shrine, minding his or her own business with no opportunity to get to know the others. Once they were packed into the same room here without the necessary introductions, all they could do was to stare blankly at each other with wide-open eyes. Even so, those pious old women could still name each of them. Unable to get into the locked hall, one would stealthily poke a hole through the papered window with her fingertips and then squint through the open lattice-pane to locate her desired god. Seizing a moment of occasional absence of the strict temple-guard, she would pull out a few homemade straw sticks, insert one end of each between the stone tiles on the ground, light them up as incense, and then kneel down to kowtow to her god behind the door guarded with a big brown copper lock.

That was an odd but popular practice on Mount Tai during those ten years. How funny it was to worship gods by burning incense and kneeling down before a locked door, rather than directly facing them according to the century-old tradition! However, although the lock on the door could not be opened, the spirit of their piety could not be locked up or impeded in any way, but was all the same expressed to those senseless idols. While what they did was ignorant and ludicrous, it clearly revealed their deeply ingrained sincerity. This tells us that the most intractable thing in this world is the human heart. A song can be banned, but it can still be sung in the heart. You cannot hear anything, but the singer is listening to it in his heart.

This is called — the existence of the intangible.

II

It is said that women are kind-hearted, and therefore, most Buddhists are women, especially those old women living in remote, isolated mountain areas. People come to Mount Tai to worship Buddha from different places, with the closest being the nearby villages, within dozens of *li*, and the farthest around Dezhou area, hundreds of *li* away. Whether from nearby or distant areas, one has to trudge more than a dozen *li* on a mountain trail to get from the foot of Mount Tai to the top, not to mention that a large part of the trail is a winding and steep route made of rock steps. Because most temples are built halfway up the mountain, it is indeed a very daunting and laborious task for those old women with doddery small feet, already in their seventies or eighties, to accomplish. I wonder why the original selection of temple sites couldn't have been done in consideration of those old, kind-hearted women, but I am told that they were purposefully selected so as to test their sincerity. Without such taxing and grueling labor, how could the gods possibly see their piety? Besides, gods are not at all understanding of humans. Whether this explanation is a joke or not, those pious old women went ahead with what they believed they were supposed to do. Their piety and persistence would not only touch the gods, but would often move non-believing young tourists, who would go into a temple and perform a few kowtows themselves.

After completing the divine service, each of those pious old woman would pull out a copper coin from the chest of her blouse to grind it against the imperial stele in the garden of the Azure Cloud Temple. It is believed that if one grinds the coin edgeless on the stele, takes it home, pierces a hole in the middle, threads a red string through the hole, and then hangs the coin around the neck of her grandson, it can ensure her grandson an "endless long life." As nothing in this world is endless, the gesture with the coin is, in fact, intended only as a good wish, as is suggested in the implication of the word "edgeless."

Satisfied with the completion of her service and grinding, she would pick a wild flower and then saunter down the mountain. If you, on your way up to Mount Tai, run into an aged woman heading down with a flower in her hand and a contented look on her face, she must be a Buddhist pilgrim. There is no doubt about that.

Upon the arrival of spring, when the breeze is gentle and the view clear in the tranquil mountain, you can often see aged women, in small knots, edging their way up or down the rock steps of the mountain trail, which, as perilous as Jacob's ladder, is ten thousand *zhang* high. The women wear clean clothes, have sleek hair and solemn countenances, and are accompanied by a few young girls who walk ahead of or behind them and carry in their arms some clothes and food in a homespun blue-cloth wrapper with a white-flowered pattern. The clear and melodious clatter of the old women's bamboo or wooden sticks on the rock steps coordinates well with the soughing of the pines, the humming of the spring water, and the chirping of the birds all around, thus creating a harmonious and mellifluous music. The pretty faces of the young girls, the white hair of the old women, as well as the freshly yellow winter jasmine in the hands of every one of them, constitute an eye-catching view against the secluded, verdant ancient valley.

The pious old women stop from time to time. They sometimes have to sit down on the rock steps to rub their sore and stiff small feet, or to take a breath as they wait for their fellow travelers who lag behind, or to untie their cloth wrappers to take out a pancake, the size of a wok cover toasted yellow in color, some emerald-colored Chinese onions, and a jar of savory jam — all authentic Shandong roughage — to fill their stomachs already strained from exhaustion. If you approach them at this moment, they are likely to be in a happy mood to answer your questions. Smoothing their sweaty hair away from their head temples, enlivening the deep wrinkles all over their faces, and showing their few remaining crooked, yellow teeth, they would tell you with a broad smile that they came last year to pray to the gods for a grandson for each of them and promised to redeem their vows in return for the fulfillment of their wishes. Not long after they returned home, their daughters-in-law all got pregnant, and each of them now has a chunky grandson to cuddle in her arms. They have traveled over hills and dales today in particular to redeem their vows to the gods.

Hearing this, you will be touched by their simplicity and piety! And therefore, you will not laugh at their ignorance, but instead will respect their purity and faithfulness. What adorable older ladies they are! As long as gods keep their word, they do too, no matter how hard it might mean to them. Because piety originates from a pure and fair mind, you will sincerely congratulate them and send them on their happy way home.

III

This story took place during "the Cultural Revolution," when the society was plunged into a gloomy and stifling atmosphere. I was on my way to Mount Tai to do some sketching. After going past the Pavilion of the Fifth Marquis Pine, I caught sight of a rock cave shrouded by pine and cypress trees. Inscribed on the wall by the entrance was the name of the cave: "Morning Sun." Out of the dark cave wafted faint wisps of bluish smoke. I crouched down and groped my way into the cave. Immediately wafting into my nose was a thick aroma, suggesting the burning of incense and redolent of a temple. Through the smoke permeating the cave, I gradually found myself standing in front of a stele with the image of Guanyin (Bodhisattva of mercy) engraved on it. The lines were bold, vigorous, and fluid, producing a godly image of solemnity, peacefulness, and benevolence. The top of the cave was black, an obvious indication that incense had burned there for hundreds of years. It really surprised me to see a Buddhist idol so well-preserved during a time when the cultural heritage of the country was almost thoroughly purged. I was about to step forward to take a closer look at the idol, when, abruptly, several figures sprang up near me. Looking closely, I saw that they were country women above middle age, all in blue padded coats and black pants, and all with strands of hair like crow wings hanging by their temples. I couldn't associate their dressing style with any particular area. They all looked fidgety and tense, as though I would flare up at some kind of mistake they had made. One of the women was stepping on something. It was a few incense sticks resting on a small mound of earth, with the top ends still burning bright and the smoke swirling up. She was trying to knock them over with her toes and cover them up with earth. It suddenly dawned on me that they were here to worship Guanyin, but mistook me for a "rebel" cadre from the Mountain Brigade, because it was a policy back then that anyone who came to the mountain to burn incense would be detained.

I faced a dilemma: If I chose to stay, they would be afraid to continue their worship; if I opted to leave, they would suspect that I was going to report them to the "rebels" and have them detained, and I would thus scare them away. They had plodded all the way here just to burn a few incense sticks before Guanyin, make a few kowtows, pray for some comfort, and reinforce their wishes. How could I drive them away and ruin their wishes because of a bad decision? I would never be able to make up for the mistake, no matter how repentant I was. I was at a real impasse... So those women and I stood there in confusion.

Suddenly, a bright idea struck me. As if blessed with a literary inspiration, I immediately proceeded with it: I took a step forward and cupped up the small mound of earth to set up the incense sticks again. Although I did not believe in the non-existent Buddhist deities at all, I dropped to my knees and started kowtowing to the idol. Stunned for a moment, the women all followed me; they fell to their knees and started to concentrate on their kowtows. When we stood up, each of our knees was marked with a large spot of yellow earth. Standing there face to face, we all burst into elated grins.

They were happy, because they had fulfilled their wishes; I was happy, too, because I felt I had been quick-witted. And what a good deed this wit of mine had brought about!

Nuorilang Falls in the Morning and at Dusk

◎ *Zhao Lihong*[1]

The fading glow of the setting sun peeks out of the thin clouds and spreads onto the rippling mountain ridges. Basking in the golden rays, the pine trees standing on the ridges are rimmed with translucent and glittering hues, thus bearing a resemblance to jewel-and-coral sculptures. This view, distant and serene, looks like an oil painting — still, but spectacular.

The bus races on a highway where not a single soul is in sight. My destination is Nuorilang Falls.

Abruptly, from a wood next to the highway, the sound of running water wafts into my ears. It is faint at first, like a long sigh from an extreme distance, then grows louder and louder, as though swift raindrops were beating tree leaves, tumultuous, yet clear and tinkling; finally, it sounds like a gusty wind whistling through forests and soon develops into air-rending and earth-shaking rumblings, creating the illusion that a mighty force of numerous soldiers and horses is running and galloping in the woods. The neighing-and-roaring sound rises from the wood, resounds over the valley, then expands in the air until filling it up, and in the end, dominates the dusk-bathed sky, mountains, woods …

From among the shady green clusters, a burst of white light flashes into my view, then another one, and then — the great waterfall!

I get off the bus and stand by the roadside. From far below, massively unfolding into my view is the Nuorilang Falls, no more than a hundred meters away from the highway. The waterfall comes out from a huge

---

① Zhao Lihong (1951-), poet and essayist, who has won several essay prizes and is the chief editor of Shanghai Literature.

expanse of green bushes and then abruptly tumbles into the deep valley, forming stream after stream of snow-white water screens that hang in myriad shapes and poses on the wide precipice of the cliff. Hovering over the deep valley is a huge cloud of drifting mist.

The waterfall in front of me appears a little underwhelming in comparison with what I have in mind for the majestic Nuorilang: though wide enough, the downward-flying water screens seem somewhat thin, somewhat delicate, and somewhat lacking in magnificence. Only the rumblings of the water live up to my expectations. That air-rending and earth-shaking sound is a kind of percussive music produced when falling water strikes the precipice and the rocks. Unconstrained, the music reverberates with untamed force and in unruly wildness amidst the mountains and forests.

"Nuorilang" means "masculinity" in the Tibetan language. Perhaps the local Tibetans want to use the name as a symbol for man's robust potency and burning passion. If that is the case, then, is there an endless downpour of passion in this terrestrial world?

I want to walk to the waterfall along the trail in the wood, but dusk is already thickening and the air is dimming all around. The waterfall in the distance becomes obscured. Amid the unceasing rumblings and in the mist-permeated darkness, those streams upon streams of white, moving water screens appear nebulous and mysterious, as if unapproachable to any mortal man ...

Lying in bed in Nuorilang Hotel that night, I cannot fall asleep. Floating into the windows are mingled sounds — the rustles of the leaves in the breeze, the gurgles of the streams in the mountains, the enchanting whistles of the autumnal insects... From within the chorus of nature, I try to discern the roaring sound of the waterfall, but cannot. Why does that air-rending and earth-shaking sound fail to reach me? Perhaps, the wind is not in the right direction?

Early the following morning, when dawn just begins to break and the mountains and the forests are still cloaked in the morning mist, I hasten out of bed and start a hike towards Nuorilang alone. All around, it is unusually quiet. Only the gauze-like mist, as flimsy as if it were nonexistent, drifts in the air now and then.

I suddenly hear a clip-clop from behind me. Turning back, I see two horses, one snow-white and the other jet-black. They walk toward me in a leisurely, content manner. They must belong to the local Tibetans, but the horse herdsman is nowhere to be seen.

The two horses also head in the direction of Nuorilang. Though I walk shoulder to shoulder with them — only about a meter away at most, traveling with a stranger like this does not send them into a fluster at all. Instead, they stroll along quietly and steadily with their eyes fixed on the front. They have such a graceful walking carriage that they look like a white cloud and a black cloud floating along in the morning mist. When they reach Nuorilang, they continue on their journey without stopping or looking aside. Amid the rumblings of the water, I gaze after them until they disappear in the distance, like an uncanny dream lingering in my vision.

Once again, Nuorilang unfolds itself in front of me. Compared with the one seen in the glow of dusk yesterday, this waterfall, cloaked in the morning mist, looks bigger, wider, mightier, and more magical. Hidden in the drifting clouds and fog, the mountains behind the waterfall are still indistinct at the moment. Myriad water screens seem to gush out of the clouds and fog and look like countless white dragons soaring from the bottom of the valley, with their heads plunging into the mistiness and their bodies and tails still dangling in the air, perpetually lashing at the cliff ...

Step by step along the damp trail in the wood, I approach Nuorilang. As the distance between me and the waterfall shortens, the rumbling sound becomes louder and louder, and the mist brushing against my face becomes thicker and thicker. By the time I get to the waterfall, my hair, face and clothes are all soaked with water. However, it is right at this moment, as I tilt my head up to admire the great waterfall, that I begin to have some idea of the waterfall's raw power and sheer grandeur.

The sky, hazy from clouds and fog, seems to have been ripped open in a gigantic crack, from which the heavenly water, abundant, incessant and precipitate, gushes out and pours down. Each tumble from the crack goes down a great distance into the deep valley, sending out flying sprays and creating deafening echoes. Now, both visually and acoustically, Nuorilang is a manifestation of the topmost magnitude. Facing such a great waterfall, I feel I am a mere particle of dust in a sky full of drifting mist.

This reminds me of the waterfall I saw on Mount Yandang many years ago. As I stood in front of the famous waterfall, the Colossal Dragon Pool, my mind conjured up an image of a huge dragon being nailed to the precipice of a cliff, struggling. But what I see now is a vision of many dragons hovering and dancing, and many carefree "water nymphs" singing a most reverberant chorus in the otherwise serene valley. This awes me and stirs my soul. Confronted with such a magical natural phenomenon in such an energetic show of magnificence, I feel how small and tame human beings are!

Yet the front of the waterfall is not a place to stay long. The dense mist in the air makes it difficult to breathe. So I rush back up to the trail. After a while, I turn back to look. To my amazement, Nuorilang has taken on a brand new look: shining from the rushing water are thousands upon thousands of golden-red beams of ray, reflected from the rosy morning clouds above the mountains across from the waterfall. Blended by the drifting mist, these light beams rise and fly in dazzling colorfulness, creating a fairytale-like atmosphere …

Right at this moment, the sound of people cheering comes from the mountain trails in the far distance. These early birds are heading this way for a visit to the waterfall.

In the morning, when the bus takes us on a trip around the mountain slope behind Nuorilang Falls, I see a vast, dark green lake hugged by a group of green mountains on three sides. Like an incomparable gigantic emerald, the tranquil lake water is so green that it looks transparent and mysterious, and I begin to doubt if it is real water. Local Tibetans call this mountain lake "The Son of the Sea". Pointing to the lake brimming with green water, the friend who accompanies me on this visit tells me, in a detached tone, "This is the Nuorilang."

Is it? I can hardly associate this abundance of still water with a great surging and roaring waterfall. But what my friend has told me is true. This lake, the Son of the Sea, in the U-shaped encirclement of mountains, has a long opening on one side. That is the very diving platform from which the deluge of water plunges into the deep valley, and the very gigantic crack in the hazy sky of clouds and mist I saw earlier this morning, when I looked up from the bottom of the valley.

Walking closer to the Son of the Sea, I notice that the water is so limpid that one can actually see the bottom of it, and I realize that the seemingly still water is actually moving slowly — toward, of course, that gigantic opening. This body of high-mountain water — the gathering of all the meltwater from the myriad mountain peaks and valleys — can be contained for some time, but its surging and roaring nature can hardly be changed. Nuorilang Falls is exactly the break-out and gush-out from that containment. So long as this seemingly tranquil containment exists, its throbbing passion will never abate.

The Backs of the Best Musical Conductors

◎ *Zhao Lihong*

The best musical conductor is not self-styled, but acknowledged after he passes the tests of countless performances and the analyses of myriad eyes and ears. Once he stands in front of the orchestra and starts to move his baton, we will see his extraordinariness. Everything that emanates from him — such as his hand movements, facial expressions, the look in his eye, and his stance — manifests a mellifluous rhythm, an impeccable musical note, a marvelous empyrean chant, or a heavenly revelation. The movements of his body are music; his image is an embodiment of music. Through the tips of his fingers, he transmits the composer's soul, perching in his heart, to every player in the orchestra, to every musical instrument, to every listener, and to every bit of the air in the concert hall.

When he abandons himself to the music he is conducting, we can only see his back, because he stands facing his orchestra with only his back to the audience. He turns around to us only when the last bit of music fades away from the orchestra, letting us see his face, with a smile lighting up his face with subsiding excitement, and sweats sparkling on his face and forehead. This is the moment when we, the audience who have just woken up from the enthrallment of the melody, realize what labor and energy it has taken the maestro to conduct the music that has danced in the air a moment before.

How many such conductors have been imprinted in my memory?

Herbert von Karajan is one of them. I saw his picture on the covers of phonograph records and cassettes. A portrait of a silver-haired man facing the camera, with his downcast eyes slightly closed, he seemed to be in a state of sleep, intoxicated in his intricate and solemn dream. He was perhaps the most popular conductor in China during the 1980s. In the early 1980s, I bought from the Shanghai Music Bookstore a set of tape recordings of the Beethoven symphonies he had conducted, and I listened to it many times on a mono-channel cassette player. Now I know that the sound quality of that cassette player could never convey the true aura and spirit of the stately symphonies. It only gave a rough approximation, in terms of sound quality. Still, it enchanted me and aroused my feelings. I pictured not only Beethoven's thoughts and feelings but also Karajan's stances and facial expressions. In my imagination, Karajan, a serious man, was a thinker, because when he conducted, he often closed his eyes and indulged himself in a musical reverie. The strokes of his hands and his body movements were only part of his thinking. Although I would never be able to know what was on his mind, I knew that in his contemplation, his hair turned white, like a pile of snow covering his forehead...

Karajan finally came to China to conduct the great Berlin Philharmonic Orchestra as it played a Beethoven symphony in Beijing, and I finally saw his live performance, during which I learned that while conducting, he not only closed his eyes to indulge himself in musical reveries, but also sometimes opened his eyes. In Beethoven's *Pastoral* symphony, when he reached the point of the thunderbolt blasting in the sky over the open country, he abruptly struck his baton from high in the air, as if he had struck sparks and lit a lightning flash powerful enough to illuminate the world. Right at that moment, his eyes shone, as if the lightning flash and the sparks in his heart had clashed and burst out from his pupils. When the storm subsided, the balmy sunbeams seeped out in between the clouds, the world returned to peace, birds started to sing in the shade of the woods, and fish to swim in the limpid water. This was when he sank back into his thoughtful reveries and reveled in his heavenly melody. With his head lowered and eyes slightly closed, he looked like a thinking statue. Only the baton in his hand still moved lightly to usher his orchestra, and his audience as well, into various exhilerating scenes after the storm between the terrestrial and celestial worlds.

Like a child dwarfed before an ocean, Seiji Ozawa, short in stature with swaying and bouncing black hair, stood in front of the Boston Symphony

Orchestra comprising over one hundred musicians. But as soon as he lifted his baton, he turned into a decisive giant and as soon as the music started, he became the master and the soul of the ocean. Under his guidance, the ocean surged and billowed, splashing in a stunning variety of formations. The looks in his eye were imposing, and his hands, along with his eyes, continuously swung to different instruments, as if he wanted to grab each player and put him or her on the tip of a wave, to be tested by a storm.

It is a rarity in the world's history of music for an Asian to convincingly conduct a large, famous Western symphony orchestra to play the works by Western composers. When he was conducting, Seiji Ozawa's black hair swayed and bounced in front of the orchestra while the music drifted and swirled over his black hair. What a marvelous integration it was of the golden Western melody and the Eastern black hair, with the black hair leading the golden melody! Music swept away national boundaries as well as the barriers of races and languages.

The most unforgettable image of Seiji Ozawa in my memory was how he conducted *The Moon Reflected in the Second Spring* by the blind composer A Bing. The famous Chinese Erhu solo — a heartfelt lament from an abject vagrant musician in the old time facing a stream of crystal clear spring water — merged into a Western orchestral ensemble, a brilliantly illuminated chorus, and a series of rolling and surging waves of music. It seemed that Seiji Ozawa must have known A Bing and could picture how the lonely blind man was playing by the spring water, for all musicians are empathetic. The moment the music arose, all was communicated without any need of speech or explanation. This was exactly like spring water spilling over a rocky beach. It soon filled up all clefts and gaps, whether tangible or intangible. I saw his eyes filled with sparkling tears. What a touching scene it was when his tears sparkled in the melancholic grace of this music!

Among all the contemporary conductors, Carlos Kleiber is perhaps the most charming. One can never forget his unique way of conducting Strauss's Waltz for the New Year Concert, held in the Golden Hall of Vienna that year. That little baton in his hand seemed to have been ordered to give a magical dance, and every joint in his body seemed to have been charged to dance to the beat, but there was no exaggeration, no ostentation, and no frivolity. Thus enlivened, both the orchestra and the audience were enticed to dance with the music. Every year, the Golden Hall witnesses the performance of Strauss's Waltz, but none of these performances can match the one given by Kleiber in heightening the atmosphere of the hall to a state of gracefulness and fervor.

Kleiber, perhaps one of the very few spiritual aristocrats in contemporary society, is said to make little of money. He is reluctant to join worldwide tours, and he never accommodates himself to engagements with undesirable orchestras or works. Of course, he has never been to China. His sparing acceptance may be because he only wants to interpret the pieces he wants, from the apex of musical performance, and he has often reached that summit of glory. I have owned quite a few of his records. One of them is Brahms's *Symphony No. 4* by the Vienna Symphony Orchestra, which he conducted and which, in my opinion, has the best sound quality of all recordings of the same work. Through Brahms's somewhat grievous melody, I can picture Kleiber's woeful and stern look.

Zubin Mehta is an Indian. He was the chief conductor of the Israel Philharmonic Orchestra at the time I saw him. In that old municipal auditorium in Shanghai, he conducted the Israel Philharmonic Orchestra in a violin concerto by Itzhak Perlman, the Israeli-American violinist. In the eyes of the Chinese, Mehta did not look oriental, but white. Neither did he look any different from European or American conductors. He was said to be heavily censured by the Israelis because of the Wagner works he had conducted. This is an injustice to Mehta, because rejecting Wagner is unthinkable for any conductor. It is also an injustice to Wagner if people simple-mindedly associate him with Nazi because Hitler liked him. Would Wagner be in favor of killing Jews, like Hitler? Fortunately Mehta was still with the Israel Philharmonic Orchestra. The bold and epic characteristics of Wagner and the virile style of Mehta got along quite well, but Mehta might never have another chance to conduct Wagner in Israel.

The other day, I went to enjoy Felix Mendelssohn's *Violin Concerto in E Minor*, performed by Itzhak Perlman. The joint performance by the stocky Mehta and the wheel-chaired Perlman could perhaps be acclaimed as a heavenly collaboration. Mehta was noted for his flamboyant style and vigorous and powerful movements, which harmonized well with his stout appearance, but this violin concerto of Mendelssohn's was not something that could be conveyed through vigor and strength alone. It was the sound of spring that rang with the finest vernal breath, the rustle of a breeze in the woods, the raindrops under the sunshine, the dew on blades of grass, the crystal-clear streams winding amid clusters of flowers... Controlling his force, Mehta jiggled his baton, carefully led his orchestra, and appropriately moderated the background sound for the violin theme. This was a moment when both his performance and his expression were like a lion dancing on a high wire and a tigress licking her newborn cubs. The eye contact between Mehta and Perlman struck a chord in my heart. Such an exchange melted in the enchanting music and unveiled a myriad of spring charms to me.

Speaking of Mehta, it's natural to think of Wilhelm Furtwangler, a German conductor. Some people consider this German conductor a spirit, and some simply regard him as a surrogate — or a reincarnation — of Beethoven, because no one else understands Beethoven as profoundly as he does and no one interprets Beethoven's symphonies as exquisitely and hearteningly as he does. Conductors since him all feel they cannot match him in that respect. He dominated the first half of the 20th century. The musicians who played in the orchestras under his conduction would recall: Once he stood on the podium, the divinity of the music descended from heaven. Either the players or the audience would feel involuntarily "magnetized" by his baton. Claudio Abbado, the world-famous Italian conductor, put it this way, "The moment Furtwangler steps onto his podium, time and space freeze; the audience and the orchestra are under a tremendous impact as if struck by thunderbolts." However, the angel was possessed by devils, as this great maestro was a member of the Nazi party and a most favored musician of Hitler himself. After the Second World War, he was brought to trial and found guilty for what he had done. He was often compared to Faust, the protagonist in the eponymous drama in verse by Johann Wolfgang von Goethe. Faust sold his soul to the Devil in exchange for unlimited knowledge and worldly pleasure. I have seen *Mephisto*, a film based on the true story of Furtwangler, which exposes the twisted soul of this musician during the Nazi reign in a breathtaking fashion. The glory that his talent brought him and the ingratiating way he secured that glory stigmatized his purity and integrity as a musician.

Of course, there is no way for me to hear Wilhelm Furtwangler conducting Beethoven's symphonies, no way to see how he waved his baton in front of his orchestra, and no way to imagine how Beethoven's soul once perched on his baton. I do not believe the claim that he is unprecedented and will never be surpassed in conducting Beethoven's symphonies, for Beethoven's soul will never disappear. So long as Beethoven's music continues to touch our feelings, new conductors will appear to interpret his music in more exquisite and expressive ways. However, what Wilhelm Furtwangler has left in me is but a blurred image of his back.

In China, no one outside the music circle is familiar with Valery Gergiev, I'm afraid? Actually he is a true maestro, who, with his courage and audacity, his talent and charisma, revitalized a declining orchestra. I have been to two of the concerts under his conduction: One was the Mariinsky Theatre Orchestra performing Tchaikovsky's *Symphony No. VI* and Mahler's *Symphony No. 3,* and the other, the Tchaikovsky opera, *Eugene Onegin.*

He is a conductor of passion. Tall, with a thin face and bright, deep-set eyes, he looks handsome and young, although he has a short beard. Standing in front of the orchestra, he radiates vitality and masculinity with his every movement. His curly hair and beard, his deep-set eyes, his gestures — all remind me of the Russian poet Pushkin. In the historical site of Pushkin's home in St. Petersburg, I saw an oil painting of the poet. The poet resembles this Russian conductor in shape and facial expression. While listening to the opera *Eugene Onegin*, as Valery Gergiev conducted in the orchestra pit, I had a hallucination of the Russian poet, standing there with his back to me, reading aloud his poems in a measured cadence. His passionate voice reverberated in the terrestrial world.

These conductors have made our terrestrial dreams come true and have eliminated the distance and space between us and remote history.

The Lily in My Heart

◎ *Lin Qingxuan*[1]

In a remote valley, there was a cliff a few thousand feet high. Since nobody-knows-when, on the edge of the cliff there grew a tiny lily. From the time it appeared, it hardly looked different from a weed, but the lily itself knew that it was not a weed by nature. In the innermost recesses of its heart, it had a singular belief: "I am a lily, not a weed, and the only way I can prove this is to produce beautiful flowers." With this belief at heart, the lily made a great effort to absorb moisture and sunlight, to root itself into the earth deeply as it grew upright, and finally, on an early spring morning, it produced its first bud at the top of its stem.

The lily was happy, but the nearby weeds were scornful. They laughed at the lily behind its back. "It is a weed, and there is no doubt about that, but it insists it is a lily and is so deluded that it actually believes as much! I don't think that thing on its head is a bud. It must be a tumor growing out of its brain." They scoffed openly at the lily as well. "Stop dreaming. Even if you are able to bloom in this wild and desolate area, you aren't any more worthy than we are."

The lily responded, "I want to bloom because I know I can produce beautiful flowers; I want to bloom because I wish to fulfill my solemn life as a flowering plant; I want to bloom because I prefer to validate my existence with flowers. Whether or not there is anyone to appreciate me, and no matter how you look at me, I will bloom all the same!"

Therefore, under the scornful looks of the weeds, the wild lily strove

---

[1] Lin Qingxuan (Qin Qing, Lin Li, Lin Dabei, 1953-), famous essayist, who has been awarded numerous essay prizes in Taiwan.

to exert its inner will. One day, it finally began to produce flowers. Its dainty and erect stance in an inspiring pure white made it the most striking beauty on the cliff. At this point, no weed dared to laugh at it anymore.

So flowers began to burst from the lily one after another, and crystal-clear drops of liquid appeared on the flowers every day. The weeds thought the drops were just dewdrops from the night before, but the lily itself knew that they were the tears it had shed because of the utmost happiness it felt. So every spring, the wild lily worked hard to bloom and seed. And with the help of the winds, its seeds spread to the valley, to the grasslands, and to places near the cliff. Thus, pure-white wild lilies began to grow and bloom everywhere.

A few decades later, people came from towns and villages as far as several hundreds of miles away, to watch the lilies bloom. Children knelt by the lilies to enjoy their fragrance; lovers shared hugs before the lilies and made lifelong vows of love; and numerous people, witnessing a scene more beautiful than any they had ever witnessed, were moved to tears, for the lilies had tapped into their untainted sense of tender affection.

No matter how others admired them, the lilies all over the mountain remembered the aphorism that the first lily had passed down to them: "We shall not boast but will bloom wholeheartedly, because blooming is how we prove our existence."

Perception of Spring

◎ *Zhu Guoliang*[1]

In the south, spring always descends quietly amid the pitter-patter of the vernal rain. The line of poetry that describes this natural phenomenon — "Apricot blossoms, vernal rain, and the south" — has even made its way into the literary hall of fame. As I recall the dozens of springs I have lived through, all have been like this: only after hovering between the initial warmth and the lingering cold, and repeatedly breaking through the piercing west winds and the recurring cold waves has each spring then begun to reign over the terrestrial world. This makes the vernal season as valuable as gold. Spring is often seen through rain and then, in the blink of an eye, it slips into early summer, making people lament over the brevity of the season.

Cherishing spring is a natural outgrowth of a persistent love of life. It is also an actual judgment made after comparing and weighing the season against winter. The frigid cold of winter is not only a purifying and testing process for the world, a precondition for the rebirth of life, and a requirement for the revival of life, but also serves as contrast and reflection: Without the solid ice, who could appreciate the brilliance of the plum flowers? Without the white snow, who could recognize the nobility of the green pines? Without the bitter cold, who would praise the towering height of the trees? However, these seem to be the ideas of philosophers or the imaginings of poets. Only the season of spring belongs to all ranks of people. It is recognized and acclaimed by both the great and the ordinary and by the poet and the farmer.

---

[1] Zhu Guoliang (1954-), essayist and journalist.

Who wouldn't say that spring is wonderful? "'Tis the season when everything thrives; I am not alone in relishing it," exclaimed the poet Bai Juyi. Flip through a book of Tang poetry, and your eyes will be filled with sentimental verses about spring, composed by Li Bai, Du Mu, Han Yu, and Li He. Don't moralistic figures also sing of spring? The poem *Spring Outing Improvisation* written by Cheng Hao, an idealist philosopher of the Northern Song Dynasty, was chosen as the very opening poem for *The Selected Poems of a Thousand Poets*. Touched by the vivid spring scenery and the radiant spring mood, Zhu Xi, a sage in Confucianism, sang in his poem, *Spring Day*, "Spring is easy to perceive, for it glamorizes everything in a riot of colors." Buddhist monks believe in the creed that everything in the physical world is illusory, yet as "mundane beings" they are not immune to the effects of spring. Zhi Nan, a monk of the Tang Dynasty, wrote the well-known poetic line, "What bedews but does not soak me is the apricot-seasoned rain; what fans but does not chill me is the willow-twig-swung wind." From classic Chinese poetry, one can see that spring is eulogized in all its aspects, from singing of spring breezes, spring water, spring rain, spring grass, spring willows, spring birds, spring hills, spring outings, spring nights, spring slumbers, etc., through the admiration of spring to the description of treasuring it.

Through an appreciation for spring — contemplating its scenery, gazing at its flying birds, basking in its breeze — anyone, whether Chinese or not, can elevate his nature, examine his life, lament worldly concerns, and be thankful for living.

"From her boudoir on a spring day in full attire,
The blithe lady sauntered up to her green tower;
The sight of the roadside willow evoked from her,
A regret for her husband as an official pursuer."

If this lady in the feudal times could not sustain her spring-evoked solitude, then George Santayana, a modern American philosopher, went even further, as to be a willing captive of spring. This gentleman had been teaching at Harvard for a long time. One spring day at the age of fifty, while giving a lecture, he caught sight of a robin perched on a window lattice. This reminded him of the arrival of a new spring. He turned to his students and said, "I have an appointment with spring!" That being said, he dashed out of the classroom and began an European tour.

Life and the four seasons are bestowed without exception upon all of us, but of the four, the vernal season is the one that can best open the doors to our feelings and souls. No wonder that the first excavated pictographic-phonetic character of the ancient Chinese oracle bone script was the word "spring". No wonder that an ancient person, when bidding farewell to his friend, fervently advised him, "Once in the south, make sure to fully enjoy spring." And Xiangyun, a lady residing in the Grand View Garden, even exclaimed, "Cease, cease, and don't let the spring elapse!" To the contrary, however, spring is in fact impossible to retain forever. Where there is birth, there is death. "Blossom falls, water flows, and spring goes" is an inevitability that nobody can deny. Whether blossoms fall intentionally in the direction they aim, or water flows uninterruptedly in the same course, they both illustrate the axiom — the natural phenomenon that time runs its course. Time may run as it desires; however, people of determination and aspiration should always keep the spirit of spring in their commitments, their motivations and their endeavors to forge ahead.

The Eagle in My Heart

◎ *Tang Min*[1]

No more eagles hover in the sky.

And now, children no longer play the game "An Eagle Preys on Chicks".

When I was a child, I lived in a small wooden cottage under a long row of tall eucalyptus trees, with a wild meadow in the front and a lot filled with weeds at the back. The blue sky seemed especially wide. One day, we were racing in the meadow when someone burst out: "An eagle! Here comes an eagle!"

Lifting our little hands to shade our eyes from the sun, we gazed at the eagle for a long time. Stretching out its wings like a taut bow, the eagle looked as if it were frozen right at the heart of the blue sky. After a good while, the eagle tilted its wings, gave itself up to the force of the air current and began to glide around.

In our hearts, eagles are the music of the sky.

The most unforgettable memory I have of eagles is watching older ones teach a younger one to fly. With the tiny little eagle in the middle and its father and mother on either side, they flew and flew, either with the wind or against it. At times, they closed their wings to let themselves drop, and then, flapping their wings, they lifted themselves up again.

And then, with the eagle father and mother flying side by side and the child behind them, they soared, they dived, and they glided across the blue sky — all in this triangular formation.

No matter how hopeless and heartbroken one is, when one sees

---

① Tang Min (Qi Hong, 1954-), woman essayist and novelist.

eagles flying across the sky, his or her heart will be filled with hope.

In arranging a schedule for birth and death, nature allows eagles to maintain their dignity forever: eagles are one of the very few species that can foresee the arrival of their own death.

When an eagle foresees its imminent death, it leaves its nest quietly and flies to a remote, uninhabited mountain, where it soars again and again into the high, blue sky until it is utterly exhausted. Then, with its huge wings closed, like an arrow, it shoots itself into a deep pool, lashed by waterfalls.

The pool it chooses is so deep that even its feathers are submerged.

Every time I see a waterfall with splashing deluges of water miles high, I seem to hear the singing of eagles, a singing so powerful that it pierces the blue sky, from the netherworld at the bottom of the pool below.

Eagles have low survival rates. It takes a couple of eagles two years to lay one egg, and on average they can hatch only one young eagle from every two eggs. And whether the young eagle will survive depends entirely upon the food they can find.

So far, there is only one eagle that I have laid my hands on.

On its lifeless body.

That was when I lived in that little wooden cottage. One day, my little playmates and I saw four or five soldiers, armed with rifles, walk quietly under the eucalyptus trees. They looked surreptitiously into the sky. We followed them here and there and finally asked, "Soldier Uncles, are you trying to shoot airplanes?"

"Keep your voice down! We are shooting birds."

"Who is the best shot among you?"

They pointed to a dark-skinned soldier. He was very young. "Him! His family has hunted for generations."

We were immediately fascinated by this short, serious-looking soldier.

But they were not shooting sparrows, for they were patient and waited four or five days. I suddenly understood and asked the young soldier, "Aren't you here to shoot eagles?"

He clapped his hand over my mouth and said to me in a low voice,

"Don't say that. It will hear! If it knows we are shooting it, it will not show up. Eagle is the most extraordinary bird of all!"

I was stunned! When they were absent for a while, my playmates and I shouted into the sky, hoping to ruin their plans: "Eagle, don't come here!"

But finally, the soldiers opened fire! I heard the rhythmic, clear, continuous reports of a semi-automatic rifle. I dashed out of the little cottage and saw an eagle dropping slowly toward the earth, along a waving, slanted line.

"Ah, eagle! Ah, eagle!"

I ran across the broad meadow.

Ah, eagle! The eagle lay in the meadow, without making a sound.

The hunter, that young soldier, ran over from a distance, looking agonized. He ran so lightly — as nimble as a deer — that he did not make a sound either, but his eyes were bewildered and his mouth, open.

I crawled over to the eagle. It was so young, like a sixteen-year-old person. One of its wings was open, still in a flying position. One of its eyes, still looking toward the blue sky, opened to full roundness, like a mauve-colored agate, bestrewn with tiny little honeycomb-shaped facets, in which the sun was reflected in a myriad of shiny spots, very clear and very bright.

The concierge Mr. He ran over, waving his big palm fan and bawling loudly. Drawing on his experience as a veteran hunter, the old man yelled at the soldiers: "You fools! How dare you shoot eagles? From today on, you will be cursed and will never be able to hit your targets again. Whoever kills an eagle will go blind."

The young soldier fell to his knee next to the eagle and began to stroke its feathers. He looked dejected and sad. "I did this for our squad leader. He is the best person in the world! Let me go blind! Take away my hunting skills!"

The rest of the soldiers stood a little farther off, with their heads down, voiceless. From that incident, I learned that some people went eagle-hunting because of their belief that eagle's brain was a cure for the severe headaches resulting from brain injury.

The soldiers took the eagle with them.

Before they left, I sprinted up to them and said, "Can I touch it, Uncle Soldiers? Let me touch it!"

My hand made contact with the smooth, cold feathers. Thus, with a sound from within my heart, the little sparkling bottle in my heart was broken.

Since then, all the eagles in my heart have been shot and have fallen one after another into the splashing waterfall — gone forever!

A sky without eagles has no solemnity and no music.

Now, only when the wind howls continuously or the blue sky is clear can I seem to hear the flapping of wings. Is it a gigantic, transparent eagle stretching out its wings? And does it have feathers, bones, talons, a beak, and a pair of sharp and penetrating eyes?

And since then, I have never again seen a flying eagle.

The Sea in My Eyes

◎ *Jiang Nan*[1]

A summer beach.

The sound of the blue sea waves wafts in the air rhythmically — brightly for a moment and dimly for another. With a few strokes, the sea wind has caught my hair, and I pluck a strand and poke it between my lips — oh, the seawater has even salted my hair! Geologists argue that it is the salinity of streams and rivers that has salted the sea, while some poets lament that it is the sweat of fishermen and the tears of the poor that have done so. But I shall say — how shall I put it when oceanographers are engaged in a heated discussion about whether seawater is becoming saltier or less salty? I shall say — oh, well, a sea is a sea after all, isn't it?

A tidal wave comes crashing down upon me.

The entire world begins to sink and sink and sink... and the ice-cold water, shrink-wrapping me up, begins to draw heat from every pore of my body. The more I release the heat, the more the water absorbs it — maybe complying with the law of equivalent exchange is a human instinct! But, anyway, the battle between humans and Mother Nature is a major theme in the earth's symphony, while the fights among humans themselves are but an accompaniment.

The sea looks me in the eye with a supercilious expression...

The Sea: "What are you here for?"

Me: "To seek..."

The Sea: "Another one, huh? Humans marvel at my depth, but only

---

[1] Jiang Nan (Yang Zhi, 1977—), contemporary bestselling writer, was regarded as a representative of Chinese fantasy literature.

in my shallowness do they seek refuge. Ha-ha!"

Me: "I'm here to look for chemical elements in your veins — uranium, deuterium, and tritium — to free them from the spell of solitude."

The Sea: "What for?"

Me: "For it is inevitable! For it is unavoidable! And for I am a HUMAN."

The Sea: "What if I flare up? You can be..."

Me: "Then, that will fulfill me."

A long, deep drowning kiss! I can hardly breathe! Then, the sea frantically tugs me into his arms and starts a jive dance with me: One sweep after another, one sweep after another — endlessly... but suddenly, he releases his grab, and I am thrown, along a parabola onto the crest of a wave. Opening my eyes, I see, through countless triple prisms of broken waves smashed by sunlight, a reflection of life in a riot of colors...

The view spirals up —

The setting sun, a hypertension sufferer!

Dark clouds, like grievances, hanging under the firmament!

Seagulls, musical notes, expressing a sense of nostalgia!

The firmament, a combination of myriad sine curves!

...

A succession of blurred visions floats up from the bottom of the sea, to be quickly devoured by foam as each vision pops out of the water surface — one after another, one after another... until none is left!

I stride onto the beach. Barefoot, step by step, I tramp on the sand, in an attempt to leave larger and deeper footprints... But the sea, unrolling his watery tongue which is bubbling with foam, licks them all up. — Error marks? — Typewriter white-outs?

"Click." A camera has captured the scene: a wry grin, wet hair, water drops hanging halfway down, splashes flying in the air, reflections rippling on the sand... and the large pile of transparent ash Vesuvius has dumped here. Time tried to creep away from the scene, but I thrust out my leg and tripped him into the exposure of sunlight. Thus, quietly, I have frozen the "eternity" permeating the universe into the unrepeatable but elusively familiar moment.

The sea is vast, very vast... and this is the sea seen in my eyes.

In the Hometown of the Daffodils

◎ *Zong Pu*[①]

"What impresses you most?" That is a question people often ask me, in recent years, on my homecomings from abroad. So this time, when I am back from London, before anyone flings the question at me, I tell him or her that the most impressive thing is the daffodils — those flamboyant flowers that gently sway over the green grass.

The first time I saw a daffodil was at a friend's home in Britain. It was planted in a pot. "This is the very daffodil William Wordsworth wrote about." She pointed at it. The plant had a cluster of yellow flowers, the petals somewhat resembling those of our Chinese water-grown univalve narcissus, but the heads were much larger, the size of a Chinese wine cup. Nothing seemed special about this plant, as its flower heads drooped over the window sill.

In my memory, the poem describes the plant like this:

Ten thousand saw I at a glance,

Tossing their heads in sprightly dance.

A pot on a window sill is certainly not the right place to reveal its true nature.

London is no longer shrouded by man-made haze, but because of its whimsical climate and frequent drizzle, a distant scene always looks blurred, as if it were a Chinese ink-wash painting, permeated with a southern Chinese flavor. Driving by any of London's several city parks, one can see, through thin mist, on a large green lawn always appearing

---

① Zong Pu (Feng Zhongpu, Feng Hua, Ren Xiaozhe, 1928-), modern woman writer, daughter of famous philosopher Feng Youlan.

rain-washed, a bright yellow spot. "Those must be daffodils!" We would talk about and point to them, but never stopped to observe the plants.

Unlike the unusually short spring in Beijing, spring in England is exceptionally long, lingering from initial warmth to recurring coldness, alternating between sunny days and rainy days, and hesitating over whether to stay or not. One day, we went to the county of Buckinghamshire to visit the Waddesdon Manor, formerly a privately owned residence and now a government property. After feasting our eyes on the multiple towering steeples on its exterior and the luxurious and opulent furniture pieces in its interior, we started to head for its outdoor grounds. Rambling through an aviary, a rose greenhouse, and a place with some kind of soft-barked trees, we reached a slope rich with green grass, which filled our view with abundant and fully saturated verdancy, and looked as if it were newly rain-washed. As we sauntered along, something abruptly brightened our view.

There, right on the lawn, a large stretch of daffodils sprang into view! They gently swung in the breeze, making it hard for us to see any individual flower — what we saw was a great stretch of gamboling tender yellowness. They brightened our view and lightened our hearts. They looked so bright and so light that they seemed to have abruptly lifted the blurry mist in the air, heralding, despite the recurring chilliness over the initial warmth, the presence of a radiant and enchanting spring.

I gazed — and gazed — but little thought
What wealth the show to me had brought.

Again, this is a stanza from William Wordsworth's poem *Daffodils*. To a writer, what he or she has once seen or heard may in due course shine in his or her writing better than any other treasure can, but to an observer of flowers, the joy that Mother Nature has brought to him or her preponderates over the joy that a work of art can bring. You may not agree with the latter assertion, but it could at least serve the artists as a kind of encouragement.

Later, in Greenwich Park and Park Royal, I also saw large stretches of daffodils dancing vivaciously, and every time, the great stretch of them took my fancy. Because each stretch was always accentuated by a background of still-larger green lawn, the abundance also gave me a sense of wideness and reassurance. Alone in London, after all my friends had returned to China, I walked for about twenty minutes every day, to take a subway train to the British Library for some reading. The twenty-minute walk went past some houses lining the roadsides from end to end. Although the front yard of each house was limited in size, it was well taken care of and adorned with all kinds of plants. Among them, the daffodil was, of course, a must-have. Standing in clusters in the green grass, they naughtily swung their heads.

And so, as the poem suggests, there is no doubt that Englishmen have a special affection for daffodils, which, judging by their ubiquity, must be easy to grow. Daffodils are a common species, unostentatious and modest by every single plant or flower, but once placed in large groups, they look so vivacious, so joyful, and so eye-catching, but simple. Their beauty is revealed only when they are bundled together. They rely on each other and cling to the bosom of the grass.

Ten thousand saw I at a glance,

Tossing their heads in sprightly dance.

Beautiful daffodils, you must have withered by now, I am afraid.

The Many-Hued
(Two Supplementary Chapters)

◎ *Guo Feng*[1]

As our train enters the remote, densely forested mountainous area of Shunchang, I notice that all the pine-and-fir woods stand atop of the mountains, while azaleas, cluster after cluster, bloom in the crevices of the rocks by the streams. This is the continuous, slowly backsliding, window-framed view outside of our train — a view composed of various distinct hues: At the highest point of this view is the hue of the dark green pine-and-fir woods mixed with the emerald-green camphor trees; down below is the hue of the flaming red azaleas. But these are not the only two hues! There is yet another one: That is the reflection of the azure sky, the mountain rocks and trees, and the azalea clusters in the streams. This reflected, rippling, and shimmering blended hue is extremely enticing.

April is the season of flowers. I remember taking my children on a mountain tour during the early '70s, when I was sojourning in a high-mountain hamlet in northern Fujian. This memory tells me that in the grass under the pine-and-fir woods and between the azalea clusters also bloom various kinds of wildflowers in a riot of colors. However, the moving train obscures the details of yet another subtle, scattered, but equally appealing color composite in Mother Nature. To see such a splendid, rich hue, one has to delve into the innermost recesses of the Great Mother.

---

[1] Guo Feng (Guo Jiagui, 1917-2010), famous essayist, poet, and children's book writer, who has published more than 50 books.

Moonlit Night

From the train that slowly departs from the border of Shaowu County, I can see that the mountain ranges flanking both banks of the Futun Stream assume myriad positions. The moon has already emerged in the east. Viewed from the train in motion, the moon sometimes looks as if it were a rose crowning a forest, and sometimes it is blocked by the mountains and trees and slides out of sight. Its thin light appears as if it were an opalescent mist, shrouding and toning the mountains and forests. I notice that, bathed in the moonshine and accentuated by the shadows of the mountains and forests, the reeds on the slopes or by the streams and the azaleas in the rock crevices look more brilliant and splendid than they do during the daytime.

This mountainous area must have been washed by a few heavy rains, for now and then I can see from the moving train that a bright cascade falls along a joint in the dim mountain façades. I believe that falling in the clefts must be other bright cascades formed by the convergence of many hidden, thin streams running in the rock crevices or even among the grasses on the slopes. I can see that the moonlight has invigorated and enlivened the Futun Stream, which, besides rainwater, I believe, also has to take on a great number of water currents and cascades, and then carries them all with it to forge forward.

Mountain Village

What is this place now that has a few mountain hamlet-style wooden houses vaguely visible through the encirclement of a verdant fir-wood that has filled up my view? What is the name of this mountain village bathed in April's bright moonshine? Through a window of the train, I see that clusters upon clusters of red azaleas are in full bloom all over the slopes in front of and behind the village, looking like blazes flaring up here and there.

The Futun Stream, when gathered at the rock base of the village, looks wider, and seems to have formed a deep, irregular oval-shaped pool through the encirclement of the lushly jumbled reeds. Exposed in the water are a few reefs that continuously send out snow-white splashes. No sooner have I begun to gasp in admiration at its beauty than from amidst the green grass by the water comes flapping an egret. It glides along close to the flowing water, circles around in a leisurely manner, and then disappears in the reeds.

It strikes me that beauty sometimes flashes in and out of our view in the blink of an eye — or in other words, it sparkles on and off in our hearts for a split second, but through hard work, we can retain its effect forever with literary and artistic re-creation.

The Parable of the Hillock

◎ *Le Weihua*[1]

This hillock looks like a handful of earth.

It is said that they come here to climb it in order to pursue life's truth.

They are both young. The guy has just bought his first razor, and the girl has just started writing in her diaries. Thus, the girl is still immersed in "How sweet love can be." The guy, to be honest, is also keen on diary-writing. After some eyebrow-knitting thought every night, he writes down such sentiments as "What a hardship life is."

When the guy and the girl meet, they look at each other without saying anything, and they just hold hands.

The hand-holding is, however, no longer a bashful experience.

They then fling behind them the small town at the foot of the hillock, where walking-tractors are puffing black smoke against a dazzling sunshine-bathed background composed of a noisy snack bar, a pie room, and a fly-haunted fish stall.

They come here to climb the hillock, trying to find a little peace in the woods of poplars and metasequoias, of bamboo as densely planted as window railings, and of verdant towering pines and ancient cypresses all over the hillock.

Thus, one bend after another, a sunlight-flecked path crawls from out of the secluded, verdant woods to where their feet are.

This is the route up the hillock.

The girl twines her arm around the guy's. The guy drags her along,

---

[1] Le Weihua (?-2017), contemporary writer.

breathlessly. Small as the hillock may be, there are hundreds of nose-touching rock steps to climb and tangles of old tree trunks and withered vines to cross in the way. Here comes the sunshine, which, diffused by the pine and cypress needles as it cascades onto the ground, turns into streams upon streams of fog-like rays. Through the gaps between the mossy tree trunks, the two see the wandering sunlight casting strips and spots of shadows on the protruding rocks on the ridge.

Suddenly, the girl slips on a loose rock step, which rolls all the way down with some earth, creating a faint echo of a thud. This tranquilizes the quiet hillock even more. A dumpy toad with bulging eyes hops next to her feet and then slowly flops into the wet weeds.

With their sturdy boughs and branches fully extended, the pines and cypresses shroud the hillock with their dense twigs, which, despite the small size of the hill, are numerous enough to ripple and sough in wind. The two have now disappeared into the wood, but their disorderly footsteps can still be heard when the rippling and soughing of the wood subside.

Sunlight brushes the leaves in a circle, mantling them with a fascinating touch of light. While these leaves are so verdant that they seem restless, the slope underneath them is shady and damp. A limpid stream zigzags around a mossy boulder and gambols down the hillock.

"What are you doing with a knife?" From the wood comes the girl's confused voice!

"Peeling an apple for you," replies the guy after a moment of disturbing silence. With a smile, he unburdens himself of the heavy duffel bag. The shirt over his muscular right shoulder is already wet with sweat.

Not another sound! Following their footsteps, we see the two sitting on a rock, the guy peeling an apple with a fruit knife. The peel falls onto the ground like a necklace. The sun shines through the foliage and casts the boy's shadow on the ground, and next to his is hers. A wisp of a smile creeps into the corners of her closed lips. It is a relaxed and contented smile.

A horde of insects swarms over, fluttering around their legs complacently. It flutters as if it were drifting.

The young man waves his hand to drive them away.

"Don't," says the girl. "They are butterflies."

"How come they are so small?"

"They are the little ones."

Therefore, one of them goes on with his apple-peeling and the other waits to eat the apple.

Their ankles start to itch. They slap and get their hands full of blood.

"Oh, mountain mosquitoes!" He shows her his palm.

"Yes... mountain mosquitoes!" She lowers her head and wipes her blood-smeared palm against the grass, trying not to be seen.

Finally, they have reached the hilltop.

There is a half-wall there, with dark-green ivy sprawling all over it. The ivy leaves shift constantly between the light and the shadow, like many blinking eyes. Over there, a path rimmed with green grass and bush winds to the back of the hillock, and by the side of the path stands a small tea stall — a mere piece of wooden board supported by four sticks. Placed on the board are a few cups of tea, and sitting in front of the tea stall is an old man, with silver-white hair, silver-white eyebrows, and silver-white clothes in the sunshine, looking as if he were semi-transparent. He is watching the two youngsters.

The two also sit down.

"What a pity! Such an aged man has to carry water up the hillock." The girl is fondling a little weed swinging in the wind with her feet.

"Let's get a few cups to drink. This old man is indeed pitiful." The guy turns to look at the girl's face as he reaches for his money.

"Didn't we just have two cups of orange juice before we set off? I am full." The girl pats herself on the stomach, and then whispers to him, "Besides, the teacups may not be clean."

The guy nods thoughtfully.

The hilltop is a flat, palm-sized piece of land. They circle it three times and shout into the air a few times: "Oh, blue mountains and green waters!"

And then, they head down.

Turning back to look at the old man, they see that, in the radiant sunshine, the old man remains the same — as white as if he were solid and semi-transparent.

Postscript:

Back in the small town, a faint chill squeezes into their necks. Letting out an "ouch," the girl rushes to hide under the eaves. Then, with a few drops here and a few there, the rain begins to pitter-patter. Thus, a poetic scene of mist, fog, and wetness begins to emerge.

Despite the rain, walking-tractors continue shuttling back and forth, shipping pork or manure while puffing black diesel smoke into the air. The snack bar and the pie room are crowded with farmers in mud-smeared clothes. The fish stall, now dragged to a spot under the eaves, remains noisy and swarmed with flies.

Displeased by what she sees, the girl grumbles, "You see, what an annoyance! No wonder it's peaceful up there. Wish I could stay there for the rest of my life..."

Eyebrows knitted, the guy is perhaps thinking again of the line in his diary: "What a hardship life is."

"Let's go back, OK?" mutters the girl, tugging at the hem of his jacket.

"It is raining."

"I have an umbrella."

"Alright."

The girl produces an auto-open umbrella from her bag and pops it out. It looks like a flaming red mushroom.

With nothing else to do, they begin to retrace their steps back to the hillock.

Sheltered under the umbrella, the two are on their way, tottering back up. Whispering in their ears are the pitter-pattering of the rain on top of the umbrella and the rustling of the wind by their side.

Walking closely abreast under the red mushroom, they are sometimes discernible and sometimes indiscernible in the lushly verdant woods.

The rain-rinsed sky begins to darken; the rain-washed woods appear even more serene. Lushly verdant as the leaves still are, that verdancy now creates a sense of watery blur, reflecting an amber hue. The rain-caressed tree trunks look as dark and rigid as black iron rods.

They accidentally step in a puddle and wet their shoes.

Then, they accidentally tread on a mossy spot and fall on their backs.

Up again, they continue their trip, so the red mushroom keeps floating in the lushly verdant woods.

Here they are again, at the apple-peeling place. To tease her, he pulls out his knife again.

But she is no longer in the mood as before. Pouting her lips a little, she responds, "You want to feed those mosquitoes again?" Lowering her black, velvety eyelashes, she fixes her eyes on the apple peel that has been left on the ground earlier. It is already withered, looking as if it were a bloodless human limb, with mountain ants crawling on it.

The red mushroom quietly changes its course uphill in another route, leaving the squelching footprints of the two on the muddy path, as the rock steps are not paved here.

The hilltop is a rainy world, where ivy creeps on the half-wall. In the lingering rain, the ivy branches and stems intertwine with each other, and from the tip of each leaf, water-beads slowly dribble.

Looking back, the path that winds to the back of the hillock remains the same, but the old tea-seller is gone, with only four eyelets poked by the sticks in the muddy ground, now filled up with water.

Looming at the end of the path is a sea of clouds and mist. The sky takes on a distinct hue; so does the water. Where they merge is an ethereal void.

Under the red mushroom, the two look at each other, wordless. They hold hands but then fall into silence again.

Looking back at the footprints they have left behind, they decide to go downhill.

They know what it is like in the small town down there, but still, they head down.

Over the hillock, a bank of saturated clouds crawls heavily, shrouding the tip of the hillock into a hazy silhouette.

By nature, the cloud has its own disposition, and so does water.

If so, what about humans?

Besides, this hillock is only a handful of earth.

Haloes

◎ *Mu Xin*[1]

Both in the East and the West, all the deities depicted in the fine arts — whether gods, saints, or accomplished monks or nuns — have haloes around their heads. However, oriental paintings or sculptures favor a frontal approach in portrayal, which allows an easier rendering of haloes, and has, as a result, boosted the incessant creation of gaudy divine images of the so-called Dharma Wheel. Western paintings or sculptures prefer unadorned single-line circles or solid disks. Although, viewed from the perspective of the entire work, a frontally rendered Western halo is simple and pleasing to the eye, the problem comes from a profile approach or a semi-profile approach, which Western painters and sculptors often seek, after they are satiated with the frontal approach. This profile approach or semi-profile approach, however, forces the halo to turn with the image of the head, producing an oval-shaped iron hoop or bronze disk suspended over the head. It creates a sense of uneasiness — how can this be considered a divine halo? It looks odd — so odd that it actually offends the eye.

Although medieval artists already knew how to apply the sciences of anatomy and perspective into works of art, when the West was still, at the time, likely ignorant of how many dimensions there were in space or how many directions there were to light, Western haloes do not comply with the laws of common physics. Juxtaposed against the precise principles of anatomy and perspective, some renderings of Western haloes appear

---

[1] Mu Xin (Sun Pu, 1927-2011), famous painter and literary writer, whose literary work covers essays, short stories, classical and modern poetry.

incongruous, odd, and hard on the eye. They are, at least, faulty strokes in the final touch of a painting or flaws in otherwise satisfying images — or rather, obvious sarcastic indications that all haloes around the heads of gods, saints, or accomplished monks or nuns are fake and awkwardly forced on. Isn't this a serious warning from natural truth that artists should not run wild? But are they the ones to blame?

I have not become a Christian, perhaps because I have discovered this ridiculous flaw. Oh, omnipotent God, this is indeed a shameful flaw. It lays Western religion open to the criticism of atheists.

I have not become a Buddhist, either, probably because I have found the divine images of the Dharma Wheel overly splendid. How could you compose yourself in front of such an exquisite, extravagant, and ostentatious display? It dazzles you even when you lower your head and close your eyes.

If this is "drollery", then there is something more, which is almost "heartbreak".

Any relatively old Chinese intellectual knows the story of Buddhist Master Hong Yi, who also went by the secular name Li Shutong. Mr. Li extensively studied literature, music, painting, and especially calligraphy. He also played the female protagonist in *Lady of the Camellias* when he was young. And as an elegant and talented young man studying in Japan, he could well be considered a paradigm in the mortal world of our time. As he must have married before he went to Japan, his first wife stirred the whole family into a tempest when he brought home a Japanese girl. Having lost his wits in settling the complications, as the story goes, he abandoned himself to despair and abruptly saw through the emptiness of the secular world. Alone, he went to Lingyin Temple in Hangzhou to be tonsured and initiated into monkhood. By the time his two wives rushed to the Fly-by Peak, their husband had already locked himself up in Buddhist Seclusion. Buddhist Seclusion is a self-imposed confinement, when the head monk in the temple seals off the tiny seclusion room with his own hands and won't remove the seal until the scheduled time is over. Food and water are served only through a small window. The two wives knelt down in front of the room and started to wail. They cried for a day and a night, imploring Li Shutong to change his mind, but for the whole day and night, he didn't even give them a word of reply from inside the seclusion room. Once determined, nothing could pull him back — his persistence is indeed something to be admired and respected.

Mr. Zhao, a friend of my father's, is also a friend of Master Hong Yi. Once, at a birthday party for Mr. Zhao's mother, I went to pay my respect; I saw *The Vajracchedika Prajnaparamita Sutra*, handwritten by the Master, specifically for Mr. Zhao's mother. I was indeed taken by the Master's assiduous effort in attaining both detail and preciseness, in rendering neither ostentatious nor restrained artistic appearances, and in providing neither saturated nor dry ink effects. Buddhist scriptures have many repeated characters, but those repeated characters in his handwritten Sutra all look exactly the same as though they come from the same Chinese typewriter — not only his calligraphy skill, but his inner tranquility is indeed transcendental. Such an inner purity as he had achieved awed me. Looking at the Sutra, I was too overwhelmed by admiration to let my eyes linger on it.

Quite a number of times, on the walls of wealthy families, I have seen couplets written by Master Hong Yi. These couplets are, of course, well-written, all revealing a sense of tranquility, but I take umbrage in this matter: Why would a religious adherent become an artistic associate of such people? Even though I can take it as the Great Vehicle — Buddhist altruism — trying to save mankind from the sea of miserable life, I have still sensed in it the fawning of the almsgivers. It doesn't seem pure or equanimous to collect alms this way, does it? I find myself in a quandary: It is harder to sympathize with the predicament of a religious adherent than with that of the common people.

Mr. Zhao is a renowned scholar, noble, eminent, and erudite. He claims to be a Lay-Buddhist, so he is a combination of Buddhist and scholar, with a high spiritual pursuance. One day, while chatting over tea during an outing, we broached the topic of Master Hong Yi. Shortly before his decease, Master Hong Yi took a tour to Mount Yandang with Mr. Zhao. Silently, they stood on top of a boulder, shoulder to shoulder, feeling the vast wind coming from all sides. Such a scene would naturally calm one's heart and purify his mind. A person's face would easily reveal his thoughts. Catching a slight change in Master Hong Yi's eye expression, Mr. Zhao couldn't help asking:

"Thinking about something?"

"Yes," Master Hong Yi replied.

"What is it?"

"Mundane matters. Family affairs."

Upon recalling, Mr. Zhao lamented, "You see, a Buddhist of such a high attainment as Master Hong Yi could not even desist from missing the world of man; how can we ordinary people or mundane beings, then?"

Back then, I was not over twenty years old yet, but I was so deeply touched by the story that I can still remember it freshly, even to this day. As a respectable and cautious person, Mr. Zhao never judges people. He mentioned this to me only because of his extremely close relationship with my father. The fact that he is not likely to mention this again to anyone makes it especially valuable to write this down. I take this as a Buddha's relic.

While Mr. Zhao was intuitive and inquisitive, Master Hong Yi was ingenuous and sincere. How terrible it would be if Master Hong Yi had answered the question that day with the word "nothing" or using Sanskrit transcripts or Buddhist sutras to evade it! Hypocrisy is despicable. But Master Hong Yi expressed his thought with candor. This is indeed something. It is a lasting light of enlightenment, making me remember it better than those haloes, be them gaudy ornaments or circular or disk-like unadorned highlights. Thus, I can forget any good or bad impressions about him, but remember this true, hearty expression of his, given shortly before his decease. How many tightly closed inner recesses open without outside force? All living hearts throb with blood.

I remember I didn't ask Mr. Zhao if any halo of light emerged over Master Hong Yi's head when the Master so replied. I didn't ask, because I knew that it must have emerged. Well, this is not because Mr. Zhao and I differ in reflections — we differ completely, and such a "generation gap" is better than none.

Yet, this is nothing but just heartbreak — heartbroken to the point of being bright. There is yet another kind of halo that is almost cruel — cruel to the point of being dark.

Night fell. A few friends were chatting in the corner of a bistro.

George, in biophysics, commented: "A human body emits some kind of light, and anyone with an innate special power emits more intense light. This light is so strong that one can sometimes see its blue-purple glow with the naked eye, and the glow around the head is more noticeable."

Matsuda, who had the keenest interest in Unidentified Flying Objects, took over the topic, "Those divine haloes over the heads of gods on ancient carvings and frescoes are the helmets of outer-space creatures. Those haloes can be seen in Egypt, Mexico, and Russia. They are images abstracted from recollections and legends by ancient people."

Ouyang, a painter and sculptor, said, "That circle can help observers better focus on the face in the portrait." He continued with a smile, as if talking to himself, "My head used to have one, too."

Seeing everybody bewildered, the smile still on his face, he related the following event.

"In a certain country, during a certain decade toward the end of the twentieth century, some kind of political persecution in the style of the Inquisition took place. Although I was not a political heretic, because of an accusation regarding some details of a relief sculpture I had created, I was soon put in jail. The prison cell, about twenty square meters in size with walls on three sides and iron bars on one, contained over fifty people. When the inmates sat or stood in the cell during the daytime, there was a little space between them, but at night, when we lay down to sleep, no one could lie face-up. We had to sleep on our sides, one's belly against another's back with our legs straight. We really suffered on steaming hot summer nights, when everybody was sweating like wet mud... Well, let's leave this to focus on the halo part!

"During the long day, among the crowd of the old, middle-aged, and young prisoners, only the 'veterans' had the privilege to sit against the walls. Newcomers had to stay in the middle area, where there was nothing at all to support their bodies. This would exhaust the back and weaken the waist, and make each day feel a year long. According to the prison rules, no one could reveal his name or talk about his case to anyone else; no one could inquire about the cases or the names of others, either. I bore those rules firmly in mind and told nobody anything about my case and had no interest in chitchatting with anyone. Two months later, luck befell me, and I was allowed to sit against a wall, and that was indeed a great boon — or rather, a luxury — to my back. 'What is this gentleman's involvement?' When that old man with long and white hair next to me tried to ask me this question in a low voice for the third time, encouraged by what I saw about other inmates who tried to kill time by whispering to each other, I replied in a low voice, 'My sculpture got me into trouble.' He brightened at my answer, as he believed he had met a like-minded soul; it turned out that he doubled as quite a renowned art connoisseur and painter. He lowered his head to my shoulder and gently whispered, 'Don't give up! Don't!' I retorted, 'How do you know I have given up?' 'From the look in your eyes,' he murmured. 'You are exhausted, walking on the road of art, and because you have no intention of taking the evil road, you simply wash your hands of it.' I thought he was insightful, because I was at that time, indeed, thinking about breaking with the clay and plaster once I saw outside daylight again. He continued, 'Look at me — this pile of dry bones. I will continue painting till my dry bones turn to ashes. And even then, my ashes can be used to make pigments. You are so young, only half my age. You shouldn't give up!' I retorted again, 'Till death? What is the point of clinging to this painting and carving?' 'Yes, exactly, but nothing else is more interesting.' This struck home with me. I had been engaged in carving for so long. Nothing else would be interesting enough to be worth the change. I couldn't help turning to glance at him. His white hair was silvery! He gave me a sly smile and asked me, 'Done any Buddhist sculpture in relief?'

'Yes.' 'Do you know the one with a round thing over — around the back of the head?' 'A Buddha halo.' Taking a breath, he said, 'Do you know how it is formed?' 'Bestowed by Heaven.' 'Not necessarily... Look at the wall across from us!' I took a look but didn't notice anything. 'Look at the heads of those people sitting there!' Once he had pointed it out, I came to know what he meant: I noticed that each man's head did have a halo behind it. They were the many hair-dirt-smeared spots left by the inmates on the white lime-washed wall — the collaborative result of many people of different body heights. In terms of size, as they related to those inmates, they resembled the solemn haloes on paintings or carvings. The inmates, when relegated to such a condition, all had their heads shaven clean according to the rules. During the summertime like that, sitting there against the wall, legs crossed, barebacked and barefooted, with those haloes and their bald heads, they looked exactly like the eighteen Buddhist Arhats, disciples of Sakyamuni Buddha, if not more — I couldn't help laughing out loud. The revelation in this is beyond my ken. I couldn't help admiring the old man for using a sense of humor to balance the suffering — especially with an implication that was far beyond the humor itself.

"Knowing that I saw the point, he felt a sense of relief and heightened spirit. After that, despite our age difference, we became friends united by hardship."

Hearing our laughter and seeing our expressions, Ouyang, the narrator, was content.

We all lifted our cups. Although we didn't know what we were drinking to, we went ahead and drained our cups anyway.

Family, Night, and the Sun

◎ *Ke Dou*[1]

You have never figured out whether you are a pair of eyes or a hand.

You always have the urge to touch something, and that something you have the urge to touch is nothing but that face. You run your hand on him lightly — your fingertips stroke him in such a way that it is as if you are in awe of the blood running under his skin.

He looks at you, passionless, eyes blank. But unfortunately, he is the person you cherish. When you are near him, you want to melt into him. And that is what you have been longing for since you were young.

You are thirsty for a pair of big hands to squeeze your back.

He is supposed to come home tonight for dinner. You took the time to cook a few dishes for him. Now you are waiting.

You have been waiting for many years, and these years seem longer than your life. You have always been waiting. You have gone to every possible corner of the world and taken a lot of time — to find this pair of big and warm hands.

He finally arrives, but doesn't stay for long; he tells you that his affection is an illusion. You have to face the world alone.

The thick velvet drapes are swaying slightly. The window has a big crack, and the wind keeps coming in through it. Seeing the drapes moving, you always think that the pair of hands is right behind it. To keep that feeling, you purposefully leave the crack unrepaired.

You know he is in love with another woman, but you do not want to

---

[1] Ke Dou (Chen Pan, 1954-1987), woman poet, a member of the New Poem Tide movement in the 1970s.

figure out what type of relationship that is. You are tolerant of him because you believe this is a big world and the human heart is boundless. It does not matter whether he loves you or not. All you care about is whether you love him. When you close your mind to what he has done to you and only consider him as a human being standing in front of you, you know that all you need is to love him. How he treats you is irrelevant. All you are concerned about is your own heart. All you need is a form of love. You take the form as the content, believing that happiness is only a matter of subjective feeling.

You stand up and pull open the drapes, but that hand behind the drapes has disappeared immediately. You look out of the window into the yard and see that the boughs and branches of the old tree are swaying, and its leaves are drifting away one after another, slowly. Against the deep grey sky, the scene looks like a distinct silhouette, as if it were a stage set. The food is getting cold, but he is not home.

He has betrayed you quite a number of times; he takes you for granted; his heart is very distant from yours — and he is on constant alert against you.

You extend one of your hands, slightly trembling. What you want to touch is not his heart, but his face — the face with a beard. You hope your hand will not be flung aside.

Both of your hearts are tightly closed to each other.

He always believes that his heart is his, completely separate from yours. He is a man, and you are a woman. He is a husband, and you are a wife. He now loves a different person, but you still want to stay with him.

You certainly know that a human heart is hard to tie up, but you can give yours away to him, and that, you do every day.

You are calm when doing so, because you understand him. You know he dislikes you — coercion causes hatred. But to you, his detestation is as clear as the blue sky.

He does not feel awkward or guilty. He is so unperturbed, either when he falls in love with you or when he betrays you.

There is nothing at all to be guilty about, to begin with. Neither of us has hurt the other. To think that you are hurt is just a warped idea, because when he hurts you, he hurts himself at the same time. You look after him and care about him, and your kindness is like a dagger stabbing him so that his heart is bleeding and the wound cannot heal.

It is not that you intentionally try to win him back. It is not that you purposefully use tactics to win his affection. It is a need, an intuition, or a natural inclination that drives you to do so. You do so in order to fulfill your urge to love.

The kettle on the stove in the next room is sizzling as if it were whispering endlessly.

Everyone has merits and demerits, but which are the ones that reveal someone's true nature? The saying "He is good in nature, as his merits preponderate" is as stale as a spoiled vegetable soup. What are merits and what are demerits? They are all human biases in the final analysis.

Ignore these biases. Humans can only be categorized into the pure and the impure.

Some people send you anonymous letters while others advise you to leave him.

How come you have never understood?

You two have never been truly together, and you two have never been the same type of person.

Love has always been your single-sided matter. It has nothing to do with others, not even him. You love; that's enough. And even if he wants to leave you, that will not remove the love from inside you and make you a hollow person devoid of affection.

In you, there is an eye that sees nothing but another world — that is your own heart.

An ice-cold nose of a puppy.

The moon, so lightly colored, indistinct from time to time like a dream.

He doesn't come home, and that gives you the chance to face yourself.

You examine yourself. The person in the mirror is pretty. And you give her thorough consideration. She lacks nothing. She succeeds at whatever she does. She is full of confidence and believes she can live very well. As for how her husband behaves, it is totally a matter of his own choice. There is no need to be distressed.

She loves him, but not for any particular reason. Love is spontaneous, a fulfillment of one's own passion. As to how her beloved responds, it has nothing to do with her. There is some kind of intangible thing in it that has grabbed her, attracted her, and she cannot resist it. That is the true nature of life — fate.

Everybody says that he is no match for her — in all respects. She cannot understand that, because love is someone's inner feeling, which has nothing to do with material conditions. Because she knows she cannot quench a feeling that is beyond rational explanation, she just lets it drift in its own way.

Although his feelings have changed, she cannot turn herself into a chain to lock him up anyway.

There is nothing about the other woman that is worth envying. Of course she is okay, but you are fine, too. She has nothing better than you.

That he has fallen in love with that woman must be a mistake, to a large extent. If not, then you must be a mistake; it is a mistake that you have come into this world. If it is indeed a mistake, then will it be found out someday? But is it necessary to find it out?

She was tense when she saw you, so tense that she was at a loss of what to do.

That was the moment when you felt you were not the pathetic one. You wanted to tell her to relax and live as she did, because you were thinking about love-fate at that moment.

Love-fate is not hinged on human qualities.

What can you do if the two of them were fated to bond?

A rotating cloud. The distant sun.

There are many suns in the universe. Give up your own centering gravity, and you will face a brilliantly radiant world.

You hear a broken clock ticking. It is already dark outside.

If you were that shabby, paint-flecked clock, would it tick along all the same, as happily as it does?

That little rabbit on the wall chewing on a carrot has a pair of eyes as sweet as cherries. That is a birthday gift he gave you.

You begin to do your work, for you do not want to waste the limited amount of time you have. You should make your efforts worthwhile for yourself in the years to come.

You open your book, but you begin to think of your father again. You cannot remember his face or smile clearly. As you close your eyes, the first image that appears in your mind is his stiff, white face. That pair of eyes is permanently closed, as if under his eyelids were two ice-cold glass balls.

You didn't often stay with your father when you were young, and you always turned down your father's help when you grew up. This was all because you used to believe that having your man was already enough. But later, you realized that you couldn't do without your man because he was like a father. In his arms, you felt you were as little and cuddly as a child.

Huddled in his arms, you felt as safe as a small cat.

You liked to swing one of his arms while you walked with him, or you sometimes just let your face rest on that arm, listening to him humming a tune. When you looked up at him, he hugged your head into his chest with his big hands, so tight that you found it hard to breathe.

But you had always been aloof with your father.

When you were little, you wanted to grow up, but when you grew up, you wanted to be little.

Don't worry. You will be little again someday. You will feel the littleness again and again, as there must be a bigger life to love you, if that is what you wish for.

Like a human vocal cord, the wind outside keeps mumbling. Humans always worry for nothing.

When you miss him, you involuntarily fondle his clothes, which smell of his body. It is a pleasant smell. You have a very sensitive nose and can smell much more than other people do.

When you stand up to get some water, you have the illusion of seeing his lips in the basin. These two lips are honest-looking.

You are not surprised. Life has been like this — you can always find a way to comfort yourself.

He is not a bad man. He never hurts anyone on purpose. Even though he has committed a great deal of wrongs, he can always get himself pardoned, for he is a genuine man and never fakes anything.

Genuineness has immunity.

Night is a stage curtain. When the curtain falls, the performers can exit the stage, remove their makeup and costumes, and relax. They no longer have to rack their brains and strain their nerves to search in their minds for the right lines. This is the time when they are most adorable. But some of them, unfortunately, cannot or will not remove their makeup or costumes. They have to act, even in bed. But you don't want him to be like that.

For when he feels good, you do, too.

But how can you feel good if he does not treat you well?

Feeling good is merely a matter of sensation.

You are thus suspended in the air, tilted. You are never able to straighten yourself up.

Again, you are absent-minded. Picking up a pen, you write down a few words: Be the sun to illuminate yourself.

The Moon over Mount Orchid

◎ *Yu Qiuyu*[1]

The first day I came here, the place was so dark and so unfamiliar to me that I mistook that light atop the mountain for a star. There were no other stars around that night. It was the only light, high up there, like a lonely beacon hanging from a raging sea, flipped upside-down to loom overhead. It perplexed me a bit, but I was so exhausted by the trip that I didn't give it much thought — I only glanced at it before plunging into sleep.

I was surprised early the next morning, when I pushed open the window: A huge mountain blocked my view of the sky. On top of the mountain, vaguely discernible, was a pavilion, which should have been where the light came from. When night fell, that light still looked like a star to me. I took a long look at it, but again I was bewildered. Because each time during the first several days I looked at it I had the same feeling, I decided to climb up the mountain one night to find out the truth. Therefore, I waited for a moonlit night.

It came one night, when the moonshine suddenly painted everything around translucently silvery — so silvery that the mountain huts, the small trees, and the earthen ground would clang if one knocked on them with a bare hand. The massive mountain had no rugged rocks, no swaying weeds, nor streams — in short, nothing was there to snag or trap a walker. It was just one single boundless stretch of broadness and smoothness — of no other colors but dim, tinfoil silver. Striding on such a mountain path, one would feel his entire body as ethereal as if he were an immortal on a trip

---

[1] Yu Qiuyu (1946-), famous Chinese contemporary cultural scholar, theorist, essayist.

to heaven, mindless of what was by the roadside, but just marching on and on. So far as the road ahead extended, he would keep floating along, never stopping. Although quick enough, he would be careful in treading, so as not to ruin the quiet simplicity of the scene.

I must have climbed quite high by then, for the wind was beginning to intensify and the chilly light to drench the skin. I crossed my arms to hold my shoulders and shuddered. Looking up, the moon seemed smaller than it had been when I was at the foot of the mountain. Just as I was about to wonder why, I realized: How could my walking speed beat the movement of the moon? I would never be able to walk fast enough to get a bigger image of it, but the opposite would happen instead. I patted myself on the back of the head.

The mind can hardly sustain stimulation. Once you provoke it with thoughts, you drive away from your heart a sense of detachment. Now the endless distance started to turn into an endless time stream. So I could not but conform to the ordinariness and started to randomly recall the remote history of the mountain. I seemed to remember that Huo Qubing (a famous general in the 2nd century BC) once fought a ferocious war here — a very exhausting one. *The Book of Han* mentioned the mountain when relating the general. I remembered that in referring to the war, the book applied a simple adjective "fierce", so sparing in its choice of words that it left the reader to his own wild imagination. What an ill-fated mountain it was! It stood here in the strategic spot, so it was inevitable that it be used as a battlefield where there were repeated attacks and killings. A mountain could hardly withstand wars. What could it retain after the frequent felling of its trees and the repeated burning of its flora? The streams were dried, to be filled up with thick blood; the surface of the earth was scraped away, to be strewn with broken arrows and damaged halberds. But what was the use of these remains of war? Filled with dread, the mountain rushed to cover them with layers upon layers of yellow earth, so that it could swallow the sorrow into its stomach. If it could digest these remains in its stomach and turn the place into a salubrious mountain with soothing breezes and a cooling moon, so much the better, but unfortunately, its long-exposed bare back was destined to carry the burden repeatedly. That was why it closed its eyes and its mouth forever, as if it were an old man, who, after going through many afflictions, finally became stoic.

This place could have enticed benign-looking Zhang Qian (an outstanding explorer of West China and Middle Asia in the 2nd century BC) and Xuanzang (an eminent monk traveling to India for Buddhist sutras in the 7th century) to frequent it, but I guess they didn't bother to climb it. There was no easy path, nor any appealing scenery. Besides, each of the two great men needed to save his strength for the long trip ahead. Most likely, they looked up a few times and then passed it by. If Xuanzang did have had those fabled disciples with him, he might have had Sun Wukong, the almighty monkey, make a somersault to get on top of the mountain for a look, but Zhu Bajie, the incarnated pig, was too lazy to bother, and Sha Wujing, the grisly mendicant, had the load of luggage to take care of.

Perhaps Lin Zexu (a high-ranking official who destroyed imported opium shipments in the 19th century) had climbed up the mountain. He had the time and energy. Once up, he could breathe out the sigh suppressed in his heart, while looking over to the southeast, thinking about his home, and pondering the blaze he had set in Humen that had long died out. Zuo Zongtang (an important official in the Westernization Movement in the 19th century) could also have climbed up. He was in command of troops, and therefore it was routine for him to climb up mountains wherever he went to check out the terrain. This man had done some sly stuff, but he did something admirable here. He could keep looking over to the northwest, while, from time to time, ordering his man to get him the map of the remote areas. When he was in a good mood, he could also have had his soldiers plant some willows to keep the barbarous wind from blowing in.

Had the current road been built earlier, the latter two officials could have dropped by a few more times. One would watch over the southeast and the other, over the northwest. But it was not until forty years ago that the groundwork for the road was initiated, and again for the purpose of waging war. It was a quick, rushed job. Among the road builders, there were soldiers and common laborers. They must have dug out countless human skeletons, which bore no signs of dynasties, but were pale to the eye under the moonlight. A few of those skulls must have laughed bitterly and eerily, for many generations ago they were also the builders of this road. The very thought of this must have sunk the hearts of the current road builders, who must have cursed their bad luck for seeing the skulls.

I was scared to continue thinking this way. It gave me the creeps to let my thoughts linger on this subject on such a barren mountain on such a late night. I quickened my footsteps, trying to complete the long journey quickly. Free of luggage, I started to tramp with great intention, as though I were trying to create a cheeriness of a pampered child to comfort a reticent grandma. Did any of those early road construction coolies, provoked by the moon he chanced to look at while shaking off his sweat, had the notion that this road would have been used for tonight's purpose, I wonder?

I tramped along and reached the top of the mountain. The pavilion was built with grey-colored bricks on top of an old military beacon tower. I had not expected to see a crowd of folks already gathered there, none of whom was making any noise. It seemed as if they were all awed by the height at which they were now standing. They were all looking down at the densely strewn lights with contented smiles, searching for their houses. A wife, in a low voice, grumbled to her husband, "What made you turn off the light? You see, we can't locate our home now." "Gee, what's the big deal?" replied her husband. "It won't walk away!" I chuckled to myself — we may have indeed walked out of that long, mountainous road.

As my home was not in this area, I didn't share the same interest as those folks. Besides, those lights below were not that extraordinary. As a wayfarer who had surveyed quite a few seas of lights in foreign metropolises, what was originally called the splendid Silk Road couldn't kindle my interest at all. Therefore, I had to leave those folks tonight to stand on the other side of the pavilion. What I saw, standing alone, was an endless scene of mountain after mountain, taking advantage of this fine moonshine to sprawl up to the very edge of the sky — not the real edge of the sky, though, for when I tried to look farther, I had already raised my head to the utmost and seen the sky overhead. These mountains, for thousands upon thousands of years, had stood here clutching each other, but at the same time billowing and surging forward. Any one of those waves was big enough to dwarf me. I could also hear them roaring, but found no onomatopoeia was good enough to describe the sound — it was so loud that it turned out almost silent, looming in the universe and able to drown one's ears and engulf his heart. As one of our ancient philosophical epigrams puts it, the most appealing sound is silence. Perhaps this was what the historical sound was.

I remember hearing the same sound when I was fumbling through a thread-bound historical book. Each page of the book was the same color as each layer of the mountains. It must have been an intentional design so that readers could use their eyes, already accustomed to the yellow earth, to listen to the historical archives and to decipher the mountain bodies. If that is the case, I have found my home here.

According to the sages, this place used to abound with orchids — it must be the hometown of orchids, otherwise it wouldn't be named as it is. This, on the whole, can be trusted, for the ancients were honest people who didn't quite know how to fake anything. My hometown is also lush with orchid plants, even to this day. Once you set foot on a mountain tract there, even the flying cascades send out a deep, pleasant orchid scent. But who would have expected that this place is the origin of the orchids of my hometown? And where have the orchids here gone now? It is really embarrassing to have a gigantic mountain carry the stigma of an empty name. But, on second thought, it shouldn't matter, for aren't there those quiet, huge waves and the big, silent sounds? Once they wash this away, they will roll that in. Is that the case? Perhaps! Let me think about them again, and let me listen to them again.

The people on the other side of the pavilion had all left, and the lights down at the foot of the mountain were turned off one by one. All were gone except me, standing motionless, like a weathered stone pillar.

I would rather be weathered so that I can avoid the protection of layers upon layers of the high walls of the human world and so that I can have all my warm and rich moisture dried up. Thus, I can be stark naked to face the deserted mountain ranges and search them for a misery-filled soul of an ancient civilization in a perpetual journey. I believe that Lin Zexu and Zuo Zongtang, in such a search, once reached the epiphany of the significance of the armed forces. Tonight, I will continue my listening.

With a fleeting frown, the moon slunk into a mass of clouds, and then slid out of it to sail west. She kept sailing forward, and during the course of her journey, she became bright and unrestrained. With a silent puff of cool breeze, she suggested that I get back on my way. Yes, neither Zhang Qian nor Xuanzang had stayed. They, looking ahead, trailing their cinctures, and dragging their weary feet, had trod the slumberous land into a smooth path.

Go! Only going can produce sound — solid sound ringing in the valley, like those Tang Dynasty camel bells did.

So get going.

Click-clack, click-clack; clink-clank, clink-clank.

(Mount Orchid is located near Lanzhou, Gansu Province.)

Journals from America
(Excerpts)

◎ *Wang Zengqi*[1]

Flowers, Grasses, and Trees

In America, real flowers and artificial ones look alike. Here, when you see a bouquet of flowers, you often need to feel its leaves with your hands before you can tell if it is real or not. Even old-time Chinese-Americans here have to resort to their hands before they can say, "Real! Real!" Most American families grow flowers. Here, houses are not walled in and are not connected to each other; instead, they have walking passages in between them. Outside the house, there is usually some land, often with flowers growing on it. Most of the flowers are yellow daisies.

American daisies look pretty much the same as Chinese ones. There is also a ruby-colored flower, but I do not know its name. The two touch-me-nots I saw in the garden outside the poet Carl Sandburg's historical site looked quite lovely to me. I asked an American lady what those two flowers were, but she didn't know. Americans are casual about planting flowers. They just randomly spread out some seeds without any serious plan. There is one design, but it is not up to my taste. The designer plants some brightly colored flowers in a ring on a lawn, with even space for each kind of flower. This kind of design is quite odd. Most American homes have indoor plants, such as Chinese radix asparagus, spider plants, and the like, each planted in a shiny brass pot in the shape of a half-ball, hanging there. This design is not up to my taste, either. Many an American likes

---

[1] Wang Zengqi (1920-1997), contemporary writer, essayist, dramatist and was regarded as a successor of Beijing School writer. He was famous for his short stories and essays.

flower arranging, and chrysanthemums with short petals, mauve or white, are a common preference, but here I have never seen chrysanthemums with tube-like petals, curly petals, or long petals. Even if they do have them, they for sure do not have "Kylin Horn", "Lion Head", "Unkempt Hair", and the like. In flower arranging, Americans focus on quantity and color only, thrusting a large bunch in a glass vase and that's all there is to it. They are not very much into flower-shape arranging, which the Chinese are enthusiastic about, an arrangement that uses short stems to set off tall ones, curved ones to balance straight ones, and matching vases to accentuate flowers. This is also true with American still-life paintings, in which flowers are set in a vase randomly. They do not understand the composition of Chinese offshoot-flower painting. They do not ink-paint bamboo or cymbidium orchids. All Chinese arts are associated with Chinese calligraphy, but it is hardly feasible for an American to learn to appreciate the Chinese calligraphic handwriting of the *"Note on Yatou Pill"* by Wang Xianzhi. America also has lotus flowers, but I have never seen any paintings of them. Because Americans do not know how to use Chinese Xuan paper or calligraphy brushes or ink, even if they try to paint this type of flower, they will never achieve the effect Shi Tao and Bada Shanren did. Since Americans also have lotus, they have lotus seeds too, but I am skeptical about whether they know how to stew Rock-Candy Lotus Seeds. Instead, they let those seeds wither and dry for flower arranging purposes. This is unique — they do so, maybe because they fancy the unusual shape of the seeds, but some people dye the seeds red before inserting them into vases. This is simply a joke and certainly not up to my taste! Americans also use reed catkins for flower arranging. This is worthwhile. I saw this in Amana, a German community where they sell a bunch of it for fifty American cents.

America is young, and so are its trees. Those trees flanking the highway between Iowa and Springfield look only like shrubs. And that hundred-year-old oak tree in Amana — perhaps planted by the early German immigrants — was already considered rare and was therefore protected with wooden fences around it. Cypresses over five hundred years old, like those in Zhongshan Park or the Temple of Heaven in Beijing, are absolutely nowhere to be found here. Broadleaf trees overwhelmingly outnumber conifers in America, and among the former ones, oak trees are the most common. America does have pine trees, but very few. I have seen a few in front of Abraham Lincoln's grave and in Mark Twain's hometown. Like Americans themselves, American pine trees are sturdy, tall, straight, and very green, but America does not have the Suzhou type of pines characterized by "a fresh look, surprising shapes, remote antiquity, and unique beauty;" it does not have the Yellow Mountain type of pines, or the Mount Tai type of Five Marquis Pines. Chinese pines boast plentiful shapes and postures, which are often the result of natural disasters caused by wind, snow, thunder, or fire. Those unique trees bear scars upon scars of wounds. Chinese pines are shaped by Chinese history, culture, and people's characteristics. Chinese pines grow in the patterns of Chinese paintings.

American grasses resemble Chinese ones, but the dog's tail has smaller grain ears — usually in red. Across the May Flower apartment is a large lawn, which looks like a massive, thin, silvery fog bank when dandelions puff out their flower heads. Among the cotton grass grows a lot of clover. You can fry its tender shoots to make a dish, which the Shanghai people call "grass heads" or "golden flowers". It will be delicious if you fry it on a big fire with a lot of oil and a little bit of kaoliang brew. Americans do not know this clover is edible. Even if they do, it doesn't matter, because they do not know how to make a dish with stir-fried vegetables.

Nostalgia

The short history of America makes Americans very nostalgic.

By the river in Iowa City, there is a restaurant. This restaurant has good food, especially its Sunday buffet dinner, which provides various kinds of salad, fruit, and all kinds of seasoning and flavoring. This place used to be an old factory, but it went out of business, and the current restaurant owner bought it. He did not bother to remodel the building, but kept all its huge, crisscrossing iron pipes, painted the color of wine, and the thick chains on the roof and the walls. But this is exactly the kind of place where customers feel an emotional appeal when they are relaxing by the windows, drinking dry gins, chewing French fries, and eating beef steaks.

Amana used to be a village of German immigrants, where, it is said, villagers preserved the old custom of using carriages instead of vehicles, but now villagers have changed the tradition, and the village even has a large freezer factory and a microwave manufacturer.

However, because it used to be an old village, quite a number of tourists still come to visit it on holidays. What, then, is "old?" I can hardly figure it out. There was a yoke hanging by the door of the restaurant where we dined. For a sign, yes, that is a little old. Lined up on the walls inside the restaurant were various-sized old-fashioned carpenter's tools, indicating that this place might have been a carpenter's shop. Yes, that is also old. The lights they were using were kerosene burners, each with a lamp chimney. When I asked the waitress if the light was a kerosene burner, she burst into a smile, replying, "A fake one." It turned out to be an electric light in the guise of a kerosene burner. She was not a German by birth, but was, instead, a British descendant. Her family name awed me — Shakespeare! She confirmed that she was a descendant of Shakespeare. We chatted a little, but I didn't know what had prompted her to mention that she was not going to get married, as she believed marriage was not beneficial to women. Is this also an old tradition, I wonder? Displayed in Amana's museum were an old cot and a wooden chair. Everything on sale in the museum's antique store was made less than a hundred years ago, but the prices were sky-high. For an ordinary bronze plate, used by someone's grandma, they were asking $50. Such villages are ubiquitous in China and such "cultural relics" fill up our recycling stations. Amana had quite a few local wine stores, where they offered free wine tasting. I tried two or three glasses, but did not buy any, for I am a downright layman about grape wine — don't know what's good in it.

John Deere Ottumwa Works is a large, quite up-to-date modern farm-equipment manufacturer. Made of steel and glass only, its famous administrative building, through the contrasting effect of its natural rustic steel and transparent glass, gives a sense of great stability and firmness as well as luminosity and capaciousness. While a Henry Moore abstract sculpture is set up on a small islet in the middle of a small lake, the workshop handed down by John Deere's great-grandfather is preserved at the other end, which forms the opening page of the history of John Deere Ottumwa Works.

American Insurance is quite a sizable company. In a big office in its Iowa branch, which we visited, on each of the desks, grouped together to form a larger meeting table, stands a computer. This company has a large collection of modern artwork hanging in the reception room, in corridors, and everywhere. Even each of the small personal offices has quite a few abstract paintings and sculptures.

I wondered about the company manager's fondness for modern art. Later, I learned that the American government has a policy that the money a company spends on modern art is tax-deductible. This is like getting free art. It is absolutely a phenomenal policy to encourage companies to cultivate art.

After visiting the large, modern company and seeing its countless works of modern art in the morning, we went to visit a completely different place in the afternoon — "The Farm of Living History," which has retained its century-old lifestyle. We rode an old-tractor-driven tourist-wagon with a few rows of seats installed on it, saw some little Indian teepees, and wove along a rough, undulating path through an oak wood for quite some time. We saw a soft-coal-burning forge shop, still using old-fashioned leather bellows, where a blacksmith was striking iron. It was all for show.

There was a thrift store selling all kinds of used stuff. The store owner, quite eloquent, explained some of the goods in a conventional way, and one of them turned out to be a Chinese *Sheng*. He was accurate, though: "This is a Chinese musical instrument, called a *Sheng*." The store was also selling black bowlers that were popular in America a hundred years ago (but these are newly made) and fruit slush drinks made locally, following a traditional recipe.

By the time we returned to the forge shop after visiting every nook and cranny, the blacksmith had already forged a work of art from some wrought iron: a snake-shaped candle stand, with the snake's head pointing downward, tail upward, and body coiled up.

We also went to visit the town where young Lincoln lived. It was preserved in its original state through a great deal of effort. The earthen paths, the wooden houses, Lincoln's former residence, and the post office where he used to work had all been preserved. We saw an old woman quilting with various pieces of differently colored cloth in a dim wooden house, a worker soaking cotton threads in melted wax and then hanging them up one next to the other on a wooden rack in an open space — this type of candle is called a "foreign candle" in Beijing and is still available there — and a very white-complexioned, stout lady, barefoot and in a white skirt — in the style of women of Lincoln's time — weaving a basket under the eaves of Lincoln's former residence while answering the questions of passers-by. Of course, all of these people — the old woman, the candle maker, and the barefoot, bulky lady — were acting for wages. They were there working during the daytime, and after work, they would drive home, eat their meals, drink their cokes, and watch TV.

An Afternoon's Sporadic Clarinet Chanting

◎ *Su Ye*[1]

It is a spring afternoon, perhaps some time after three o'clock, when I gradually wake from a deep slumber. I do not budge. Slowly, I begin to see sunlight slanting onto the east wall through the lace curtain. Bright yellow. Then, I hear a clarinet chanting, now and then, in a grievous tone.

Still I do not budge, as I am too feeble to; I close my eyes again and remain lounging in the soft, warm bed. For quite a few days and nights, I have not been able to sleep like this — the effect of the medicine, perhaps! No one is at home. This is really good for quietness and idleness. I am an invalid, and I deserve this solitude.

Listening to the low-pitched, deeply meaningful expression of the clarinet, which chants like a gust of wind sweeping over a large stretch of violets, I almost fall asleep again — I seem to sleep in an English village or see a windmill in a Norwegian mill from the last century... Thus, in a state of doze, while listening to the solo of the clarinet, I am immersed in remembrance and cherishment.

Finally, I come fully awake, beginning to remember that the solo comes from the small yard of the Western-style house below us. I used to hear it. It was practice, rather than a performance. I had never tried to picture the player, but I was sure that he was a member of a music troupe, who would usually sit next to an oboe player in a stately concert of symphony.

But what has made him return to his crony again today, playing it fitfully, spontaneously, and heavy-heartedly? Is he sitting in his room? Why

[1] Su Ye (Su Bixian, 1949-), contemorary woman essayist.

123

have I never seen him? Or did I see him without being aware of it?

Look at those two towering white poplars over there. They have been there since yesterday and the day before yesterday, and they are still there today. The sun, with his beaming hands, strokes and caresses those shards of foliage so that the leaves rustle naughtily like book pages, and the silver backsides of the leaves ripple like tidal splashes. I am constantly worried that the two trees will be cut down. I wish the new building sites would be far from us. I wish moonlight would remain, dusk would remain, clouds would remain, and pigeons would continue their circling.

This is the moment when that lonely clarinet often chants, sounding like an old man, clad in black, roaming around. I have no idea from which room the sound comes. On that not-so-small piece of land in the backyard stand a winter-sweet, a hydrangea, and a princess tree. Except in winter, that moist, mossy spot first sees big, purple flowers dropping from the princess tree, then, on top of them, the snow-white petals flurrying down from the hydrangea, and then, the foliage casting a dappled shade, and finally, the yellow leaves falling. Perhaps because it is a bit too far from where I live, in winter, I do not see the winter-sweet withering, but instead see its strong branches and golden flowers when it is in full-blown bloom. Maybe the death of winter-sweet flowers is beyond the ability of the naked eye to see? Because her soul and spirit have gone long before she physically dies, her bodily deterioration becomes unnoticeable. This is, perhaps, how winter-sweet flowers pass away.

That clarinet never sounds vehement or dejected, but just a little grievous, like an unknown piece of violet-colored grassland lying in the recesses of a forest. Although the sound is often fitful, three notes in a row for a moment and then two, it never annoys anyone.

Behind that winter-sweet, there is also a steep-roofed bungalow. Going back in time, it must have been the servant lodge of that Western-style house. Now it looks like a family is living there. On a balmy day, an old man with streaks of white hair, guided by an old woman also with streaks of white hair, would come out to sun in a rattan chair. A few times, I caught him taking a moment when nobody was around to try to stand up by himself, with the help of his walking stick. As I watched him, I would tighten my fists to give him strength, but he couldn't manage it, although he didn't fall, either — but only bent his head further down. Once, a pregnant young woman with a bulging belly appeared from that bungalow, and some days later, a rope appeared between the winter-sweet and the princess tree with beautiful diapers flapping on it in soft wind. Then, I saw that benign old woman bottle-feeding a baby huddled in her arms. And then, I saw that the baby was able to sit in a roller and that the old man who had been unable to stand was teasing the baby with a rattle.

Is the clarinet player the father of the child?

What an ordinary, routine and quiet yard it is!

I remember seeing two boys, each less than two feet tall, stealthy but highly-strung and excited, hanging a cat from the lintel of the small door on the second floor, when I happened to open the balcony entrance to air a quilt in one quiet, late afternoon. I yelled at them, and they slipped away like thieves, but the poor cat couldn't get down. Like a stuffed toy with the stitching pulled off, it went limp first and then rigid...

For every Spring Festival and on some other holidays as well, this little yard sees the lighting of firecrackers. It has also seen the arrival of dowries labeled with red big characters: "Happiness." Behind that grey wall at the back of the building, three chickens are being secretly kept. When that clarinet chants like whistling wind coming from a valley, everything here remains the same — the same as it is this late afternoon when I am sick, lying in bed without budging while listening to the clarinet telling the story of our life.

The chant took my mind back to 1959, when I was ten years old, suffering from a serious disease accompanied by a continuous high fever. Like today, I woke up in a daze late one afternoon and saw sparkling sunlight creeping on the window frame. "Bang, bang." I heard the banging of wood from downstairs, and in my fever, mistook it for bullets flying during an ongoing war. I was scared and started to struggle up, wanting to jump out of the window to escape, when right at that moment my mother came in, carrying a big glass of drinking water in her hand. What crystal-clear water: Limpid! Bright! Sparkling! It must have been sacred! And so was my demure and elegant mother!

That was the first time when I, as a little child, had perceived life!

Maybe because I have been too ill for too long, I have finally had a good sleep and a quiet afternoon wakeup.

As if from another world, I have now come back to this dejected but hard-to-escape reality.

All life has to bear something, as is calmly expressed by this clarinet. You will surely agree with me if you have ever seriously pondered the topic of death.

When Summer Is Here

◎ *Dong Dong*[1]

From that day on, he has been constantly with you. Under the roof, baked by the direct summer sun, with an electric fan buzzing aloud, you two play poker, but never turn the game into a fortune-telling séance. Then you two roam on heat-wave-stricken streets. He always sees you home before parting. Thus, you are fully exposed to an outdoor summer, evening scenes, and all the sweat as well.

In fact, you are afraid of such a harmonious relationship. You no longer gesticulate when you talk, you echo what others say, or you talk to everybody while facing just one person. As you have expected, he has kissed you — you have not been persistent enough in turning him down, and since then, you no longer want to be yourself. When you become aware of what has happened, it is already too late to change anything.

Back in the small, wooden bed placed in a corner, your hair rustles against the wall in the dark, producing a sound as faint as wheat awns scratching on a piece of paper. Now, the star-strewn sky over your head has extended to the riverbed, and you have been complaining that you are tired after your feet have traversed myriads of check-patterned concrete pavers during the daytime. You are not a good girl. So he told you. That is when you wanted to abandon yourself but found it hard to abandon him. You remained calm — your face remained neutral. Whenever he was about to broach that topic again, you started to rub your feet on the ground and felt your shadow dwindling. Maybe he enjoyed seeing you routed, but you didn't say anything.

---

[1] Dong Dong, contemporary writer.

Now you have come to the point of blaming yourself for being selfish and narrow-minded. You are trapped in a net as empty as the darkness of night, and as your fingers run on it, each thread of the net unfolds a story of the past. All is vapid, so vapid that words fail to depict it. They are like hospital CT reports, running out one by one while you are awaiting your result on tenterhooks.

Here you are again. You have been wandering around that dust-filled construction site for hours, hoping to see him appear on the balcony of the high building across the way. You believe that he will eventually see you. You keep humming some kind of nameless, melancholic song, and have lost the sense of time, until the road you have been treading on begins to subside into silence. That fading face is a long-ago image in your mind.

Now he sees you, but you have no idea from how many divergent paths he has run back to you. You bury your face in your arms and want to say something to him, but he does not listen. Instead, his fondling hand has felt in your hair the teardrops that have rolled down from your lower cheeks. Does he know that you no longer cry lately, even when you are mistreated? For quite a while, you become so big-hearted that you refer to all those shocking happenings around you merely as stories.

You are now so badly beaten down in front of him. Since the very first day of the reunion, you feel that something you have long been expecting is missing, and hence you are worried. And so, here recur those fruitless days, like a revolving scenic lamp set in motion. You sigh because you do not want to draw your melancholic plight into your heart. You feel a sense of loss in your heart, and the closer you are to him, the stronger this feeling tortures you.

In a dream, countless bugs attack you. You are horrified, screaming like a big bird that does not want to lose its wings.

Instead of going to a restaurant to cheer yourselves up with wine, shortly after your birthday, he brings you a bottle of wine labeled with the animal symbol of your birth year. You raise your head and take a gulp, pretending your expansiveness, only to follow it with heavy panting. He sees through you — you are a scarecrow at most. If you shed tears again, you will be a chicken forever. But you ignore the idea of hopelessness. Instead, you grieve over your own misfortune: Why can you never accept denial? You have now come to the point of being stoic to others. He has been watching you. It is as if you are back in the depressing dream, in which the wind has smashed the thick wall to pieces, and you drift away silently and aimlessly. Night has sunk, and tears have soaked the backs of your hands. He says that he will never let you be like that again.

But when he tells you he will be on a business trip the following day, you feel a sense of strange relief and walk into a theatre by yourself to watch random movies. How long will you keep deceiving yourself? You can't tell. You can remember this particular lesson only because the wound has existed for too long, but even so, you have never wondered if the earlier intimacy was real or not.

Too many people are keen observers of others but are dense-minded and easily pleased about themselves. That is why half of your brain starts to cry while the other half seeks assuagement.

Lights

◎ *Shi Zhongxing*[1]

The stars have vanished, the moon hides from sight, the lights at the windows are gone, and the fishing-boat lamps over the river are turned off; darkness — the boundless, ubiquitous, and prevailing darkness — has devoured the sky, the earth, the river, and the village. By veiling my eyes, darkness has turned the road under my feet into an unbridgeable abyss.

Where am I? Should I go forward or backward? Should I turn left or right? Am I at the verge of a cliff, or at a trifurcation, or at the end of a darkness-sealed tunnel?

Flop! A scree in front of me rolls into the water. A chill runs up my spine, and my legs go limp. I'd better change direction! But it is pitch-dark all around — I cannot get any sense of direction.

I hope and pray and shout — shout for the reappearance of the stars, of the moon, of the window lights, and of the fishing-boat lamps, but, like a stone thrown into the sea, my effort meets no response at all. Darkness has looted the stars and abducted the moon; as this is a famine-stricken area, the village sees no kitchen smoke and the river produces no fish — what is the use of fishing-boat lamps, anyway? Oh, a firefly, please fly here to tear up the shroud of the vast darkness, but where are you? Oh, a storm, please rip open the curtain of the thick night with your thunder and lightning, but why is there not even the slightest trace of you? Oh, a wildfire, please break out to blaze off the darkness, but why does the land stay so stagnant and indifferent?

I struggle, wrestle, and battle, but my fists hit nothing — all around,

---

[1] Shi Zhongxing (1933-), writer and senior editor.

there seems only a void. I am sweaty all over, breathless, and exhausted. Why didn't I bring a flashlight or a storm-light, or even a match with me? Although the older companions don't blame me for my negligence — they only say I am "just a kid," I have learned my lesson: A light is a must-have for a night walk.

There will be more nights and more night walks.

I am on a desolate beach on a starless night. The sky, the earth, the banks, the reeds, and the rice seedlings and cotton sprouts we have nurtured with our sweat — all have been submerged into the darkness. The sea has changed color. It now looks like an old man splashed all over with black ink when being publicly criticized as a "counterrevolutionary non-human" on a stage. Is that sound of sea waves lapping on the beach a hint of groaning, weeping, or roaring? As the sound comes nearer, water rises over my ankles. Should I go back to our campsite or go ahead into the sea? Should I break through the enemy's heavy siege or sink into the gulf of death? But refusing to be scared or daunted, I continue striding forward. Fortunately, the sound turns out to be the water from an overflowing stream. Now here comes the levee ahead. I see a light, the size of a cup. It is from a storm lantern, the very one I used last night right over there to pick up our people, who are now there to use the same lantern to pick me up. Thanks to this light, for many dark nights, I have never gotten lost on desolate beaches.

Lights can brighten dark kingdoms, airports, wharfs, train stations, workshops, and laboratories, where, thanks to the forever-on lights, darkness fails to prevail.

However, not all people treasure lights. Lights have illuminated people not only while they perform noble deeds, but also while they perform debauched activities. Gluttonous, dissipated, and licentious lives; unscrupulous, criminal, and sinful deals — all are carried out under lights.

Overt, lawless bandits also use lights.

Many years ago, for example, the place where the iron heels of Japanese invaders had tramped was infested with robbers and bandits. To avoid falling victim to robbery, every night, my parents would grab my hand in one of theirs and tuck a quilt under another, and, under the twilight, rush out of our house to hide in a ditch or a wood nearby. A gang of bandits, torches and flashlights in hands, would arrive, snarling and harrying. Curling up in my mother's arms, I, a child who was just beginning to understand the way of the world, held my breath so I would not make a sound. I was shaking. As I remember, had that light from their torches and flashlights, which look like the wide-open mouth of a horrifying beast, angled a bit more, we could very well have been exposed. To avoid falling prey to the ferocious beast, I would rather stay away from light and hide myself in the darkness.

Therefore, in the hands of pillagers, a light can terrify people and scare them away in no time. During the Cultural Revolution, when a "criticizing meeting" on an illuminated sports ground reached its climax, as another example, the participants would rather dodge those beams of lights — as if to avoid poisonous snake tongues — and hide in the corners that no lights could reach. Only those few jesters on the stage needed the lights to embolden them, but their vicious nature was also thus revealed by the lights.

We should take the lights back from the pillagers, and let the lights forever illuminate us, warm us, and kindle our hopes.

I long for lights! I cherish lights!

Lights are a necessity on the journey of life!

I wish lights would always be with us!

A Hometown Visit

◎ *Wu Zheng*[1]

He didn't know until he had arrived in Hong Kong that his was considered quite a wealthy family here. Looking out from one of the units in the luxurious mansion standing erect in Mid-Levels on Hong Kong Island, one had a daytime or nighttime fairytale-like bird's-eye view of Hong Kong and Kowloon. Yet, this tangible asset, something that others would take as a glory, a pride, or a fortune, had brought him nothing but a sense of loss or emptiness. He, who suddenly had to leave the land of Shanghai, had to temporarily depart from Meimei, his girlfriend in Shanghai, and had to be isolated from poetry and music, felt that his red, pulsing heart had suddenly been emptied, to be stuffed with an appetite for fame, money, personal interest, sexual desire, and all those loveless and insincere feelings. What especially annoyed him was the presence of skeptical looks, emotional head-shakings, and sarcastic comments he constantly received from his many relatives and friends. He knew very well that to achieve something in this world, one should rely on nobody — not his parents nor his family — but himself. That was why he turned down all the so-called offers of "help," but surprisingly decided to go to the company that employed him after several interviews, to start training from a low position.

A year later, when he went to Kowloon Hongkan Train Station to welcome his other half, who had been left in Shanghai but now came to join him, he said, extending his arms to hug her, "We can start our career

---

[1] Wu Zheng (1948-), famous writer, novelist, poet and literary translator who has been settled in Hong Kong since 1978.

now, Mei."

"Then, let's start, but we have to carry on our Shanghai 'Pedaling-Tricycle' spirit," — a spirit of diligence with which one starts his career by pedaling tricycles — she replied with a smile.

Thus, a brand-new enterprise model, characterized by the concept of coupling art with business, was set up in the following half a year in the Taiko Terrace Shopping Mall, which was still under construction at that time. This model was a multi-functional commercial organization, which he named "Lodo Music Center", specializing in selling and leasing musical instruments and providing music books and music training. In ten years, this company had developed into an entity with three branches, thirty teachers, and nearly a thousand students, and every year it produced quite a number of rising stars, but that was a different story. He sometimes had an impulse to put aside all those business affairs for some time to open up and take a whiff of that old vintage sealed in his heart all these years, bottled in which were literature and poetry, but he clenched his teeth and quenched his urge. He repeated to himself the old saying, "To tame floods, Sage Dayu didn't stop at his home in the three times he passed it." Time had finally streamed to that golden twilight toward the end of 1983, when he was rambling on the flora-strewn Taiko Terrace with his Meimei, preparing to make a life decision. That was the moment when the "take-off" was finally triggered, a moment that can be described as "Flying over the sheer precipice toward the sky!" He advised himself, "Let go of everything! Follow your urge. No use going against it." Thus, he plunged into the world of literature, letting the frantic poetic whirlpool engulf him and sweep him along a roaring and billowing route, into the boundless ocean of letters...

At the end of 1986, he returned to Shanghai — the headstream of his life. The seas upon seas of people he saw here were no longer clad in that drab blue, but multiple colors rioted among them; masses upon masses of buildings were no longer grey, but the dust-covered granite mansions, he noticed, were being washed one by one to reveal their true, century-old looks; traditional streets and store names, time-honored brands, and even the stock market, he was told, were all being restored. People say that history sometimes plays jokes. If that's the case, that period of his most dramatic and most familiar life experience falls right in one of the jokes. He was walking, as if in a trance, on those familiar streets. He wondered if he should consider himself a native or a visitor. He was not sure if he was here to seek his old dream or to have a new dream. He was wandering, hesitating, admiring, and struggling between joy and sorrow over what he had gained and what he had lost...

He stood right in the center of the street, as bold as a traffic island, letting glide by him taxis puffing black smoke and trucks with blaring, high-pitched horns. That eight-year life in Hong Kong was now as remote and ethereal as a bank of smoke or fog left behind him, a thousand miles away. Suddenly, a sense of vacillation struck him: Had he indeed gone through that life experience? If he had not written those few volumes that were tangible and bearing his name, that luxurious mansion in Mid-Levels, that rich fortune his father had bequeathed him, and that high, ten-million-dollar tower, built at only a cost of three hundred thousand dollars, would all mean nothing. He made this clear to himself, as he roamed in the center of the streets in Shanghai eight years later — nothing more than just to show the people of a money-worshiping nation that an art lover or an admirer of poetry, though not worshiping money, can create wealth, too, if needed. Yes, apart from this, he had done nothing.

He began to cross the street. The will to survive by dodging the moving vehicles shuttling in both directions woke in him again a sense of direction and shrewdness. In the long run, this is a fair world: You get what you have paid for. This is true in a career and also true in love. That is what he had concluded when he reached the other side of the street.

In the following days, he also went to visit that Japanese-style garden house. For fear of disturbing the current occupants, he didn't dare knock on the door and introduce himself. He was told that the government had assigned the building to a few families, and at least one of them was a young couple, because he noticed that diapers, recently hung on a clothesline, were fluttering in the northwest wind over where the pomegranate tree had been uprooted. These diapers were like a declaration of new life and gave him a sense of fullness, satisfaction, reward, and of a worthy trip.

The chilly wind in the high air pinched his ears as he strode down from the top of the arched Sichuan Bridge. He caught sight of a pedaling tricycle among the stream of vehicles that had stopped at a red light at the intersection of Beijing Road and Sichuan Road. The tricycle was right next to the sidewalk, and the rider, a long-haired young man about twenty years old, was waiting for the traffic light to change color, with one of his hands gripping the handlebar and the other pressing the brake handle. On the back of the tricycle, he carried a set of new furniture of different sizes. Driven by some sort of inspiration, he approached the tricycle driver.

"Excuse me," he said to the stranger. "Moving?"

"Hm... no. Getting married."

"That's good! Hey, can you give me a lift? I will pay you ten yuan."

"You will pay?" A surprised look flashed in the driver's eyes. "Are you going far?"

"No. Right on one of the cross streets at Beijing Road ahead."

"But my cart is already full of furniture."

"No problem. I can sit on the side rack. I like that."

The traffic light changed. "OK, get on, if you like." Hurried on by a succession of bicycle rings from behind him, the driver made a quick swing of his hand. "Get on!"

As he resumed pedaling with his two feet alternately, the tricycle wobbled along, tailgating Bus 21. The driver couldn't help asking, "I say, mister, why don't you take a taxi, since you are willing to pay ten yuan?"

"Hmm — how should I put it? I have a special feeling about pedaling tricycles."

The Boeing was accelerating, and then came the sensation of an abrupt take-off. Thus, he departed Shanghai. The large sprawl of the city, towns, and suburbs bathing below in the early sunlight outside the porthole reminded him of Taipei, Singapore, Los Angeles, New York, and all those metropolises he had visited — and Hong Kong, of course. A warm teardrop rolled out of his eye, and a short poetic stanza burst into his heart:

How can I not adore it?
Strange land can be millions more,
Hometown is one, but no more.

The Expected Return Home

◎ *Cheng Limei*[1]

I have long felt grateful to dusk.

It is late autumn, when the fallen leaves are swaying, each tinged with a sense of tranquility and longing born of maturity. Dusk, through shards of random leaves, spreads onto my shoulder its mottled warmth, which is permeated with a sense of long-retained remembrance and reflections. Such a moment, like déjà vu of an expected and unforgettable return home, deeply touches me.

At dusk, I can always remember your radiant smiles, which, just as how your face looked upon your leaving — half-exposed in the glow of the setting sun and half-dimmed in the shadow, were wordlessly saying that life is endless.

Now, I am sitting here alone in the thickening dusk, whereas you are already on your way, far away from me, traveling tirelessly day and night. I wonder if your world also has dusk like this.

Under a bus sign in the distance, a girl in green, with a prune in her mouth bulging her cheek, stands waiting for a bus. An urge to re-experience youth sends my reckless heart onto the bus with her. Then, the quickly vanishing, window-framed young face sparkles up and blossoms into a scene of sly adolescence in the deep autumn.

A middle-aged woman walks by gracefully, her maxi-skirt trailing along, fully exhibiting an air of maturity, which causes the young girl to glance back at her frequently. Such charm will imprint on the girl until her middle age, when she will not be afraid of losing her youth, but will keep

---

① Cheng Limei (1960s-), contemporary woman essayist and publisher.

her head high all the same.

Among withered grasses, there are always green ones that riot for attention; among shriveled leaves, there are always live ones that will the fall. Each of the remaining ones is murmuring that life is endless, while it quietly finishes the last part of its journey...

Everything — even a piece of leaf or a puff of wind — affects our life and feeling.

The gloaming beach and coastline no longer see me in tears, as they did when I first came here at the age of eighteen. Back then, with two boys who had never seen the sea, I probed my way to the seaside. As I approached the sea from afar at dusk, the tides gradually filled my vision; my eyes abruptly went wet with tears. Squatting completely down and thrusting my hands into the golden sand, I let my tears run.

When the lapping waves washed over my feet again, I suddenly woke myself up: I was here for an appointment, a promise I had made in my past life. Now I had finally reached this heart-felt place, which had frequented my dreams. I was here to fulfill my promise. There shouldn't be any sentimentality of searching everywhere in vain or ecstasy to the point of hysteria. There was only the tranquility and comfort of an expected return home.

Nothing romantic, like what those two boys had expected, happened during that seaside visit. The passions had long drifted far away, with that fishing boat.

For a few dusks in a row, I had been roaming alone at the seaside, cherishing what was in the distance and the almost-blank past. On the sandy beach in those few days, I had left many colorful footprints — that was an important page in the life of a young girl.

Even to this day, I feel no regret for that immature age when one tends to arbitrarily believe that life is melancholic. Gone forever is that adolescent period of my life, which flew away along a simple, straight line, with only the young, black hair remaining fluttering in the distance.

When we are young, everyone takes youth for granted. While the once-blossoming flower, extraordinarily beautiful but evanescently short-lived, will drift away, the affection between you and me, deeply engraved in our bones, will remain.

Like this wedding ring on my finger, it doesn't need to make any promises — a love pledge is just a drifting cloud in the sky. But when someone from among a sea of people comes to you from afar, with deep love and an open, sincere heart in exchange for yours, you will feel that your long-held dream has come true as foretold in destiny.

When you stop to face me, that purchasable wedding ring has turned into a priceless feeling. When a beautiful rainbow flashes across my heart, the world has receded in my eyes. I think I know now what real love is.

God is my witness.

A life's course is endless and filled with hustle and bustle. As long as it has displayed flamboyance, it will be rewarded with an equal measure of colorlessness and loneliness to carry with it in return. This solitude after much clamor mirrors the long past and the remote distance. But what is the mentality one should take at the moment to go with the autumnal implications of this dusk?

The arrival of a life, as destined, is a state of grace, a bestowal of joy, and a star of luck. When we travel on our life journey in the terrestrial world under the celestial heaven, we are doing nothing but walking, which itself is accompanied by solitude and loneliness. God is not a dominator, but a responsible door guard. He bestows on us all the same kinds of bodies, the same types of hearts, the same levels of intelligence, and the same journeys with the same destinations. He lets us choose a way of life for ourselves and then waits there for us to return home.

He said: Do not bicker about death, nor haggle for life. Life or death is only a soul bound in time. Eternity lies beyond the boundary of life and death.

He is not a judge of success or failure, but a witness.

That is why I only stood here, quietly waving my hands to you when you were leaving me at dusk to travel afar — all that is a part of life. That which really belongs to us cannot be waved away, and what lies far from you and me is long gone without even a trace, like wind and clouds on the distant horizon.

A human life, whether lived under the illumination of hearth lights or by sitting alone at dusk, is like water in the nature. It comes from where it comes and goes where it goes. As there is no criterion for what solitude or clamor is, we should not have to put too much weight on it. Clouds dwell in the sky, while water accommodates itself in the bottle — the Enlightenment of Zen has already told us how to look at life. With real understanding of life, we will be tolerant and refrain from haggling or bickering over the size of the rivers we face, for all rivers flow to the sea and everything converges into one.

Whether life is a happy one or a miserable one, so far as you accept it as it comes, you are enjoying a real life.

Hence, we should not run away from anything, nor should we refuse anything. Let whatever is to come, come in due time. Do you remember the song we once heard? It's an English song called *The Answer Is Blowing in the Wind*.

When we open our long-stored memories many years later, they are already laden with life voyages. Seeing a head full of gray hair, we will not turn back, for the scene before us is still as beautiful as before.

Returning to our heart is our initial soul, which has completed its visit to the mundane world.

When the present dusk looks like a painting by Vincent Van Gogh — heavily colored life and deep-rooted misery, life has been assigned a different meaning in my eyes.

Unfortunately, I am not able to project the impact of this scene, even though what I am using is not a paintbrush. To me, to depict such a scene is as laborious as a woman having a difficult delivery. But that throbbing, burgeoning life makes my heart pounding. All I can tell you is that what is destined to come or end is what is true.

Aren't the dusk in your place and the relay-stations you now pass one after another the life codes that we couldn't decipher many years ago?

Let me not worry about your dusk, for a true feeling should lie at the bottom of everyone's heart. The strongest urge in life is the most beautiful and agonizing; it is the most solitary as well.

It is too early to wish to have everything. What we expect is the true meaning of life.

To me, the best moment is when my snow-white, floor-length drapes are drawn down, just as a huge stage curtain is closed after a show. What differs, though, is that I have my drapes drawn down only at dusk.

This is the moment when, as expected, a long-familiar dreamy scene descends in front of me: A bright fleck begins to bounce on the wall, as if a solemnly pledged, fervent love has returned on a daily basis as expected. The dusk that filters in through the drapes oozes a sweet, warm affection which wets my eyes with tears. My mundane heart has completely disappeared, to be filled with only gratitude and a sense of transcendence, while my fingers undulate over the black and white piano keys, letting the instrument do the narration.

Then, quietly, I sit alone by the west window, waiting for you to return.

The Old House

◎ *Zhou Haiyan*[1]

I like living in an old house, any of those in an old southern town that have sliding wooden windows, wide protruding eaves, red-painted wooden partitions, and whitewashed grey-brick walls. Often when I pass a slightly open wooden door between the old walls, I feel that the dilapidated door has kept behind it a long history and many stories, as well as desolation and the coziness of leisure. An old house is like an old book — every corner or every tile carries a wordless story. An old house is like a lucid philosopher who has objectively witnessed worldly glories and riches, decaying and declining, despairing partings and heartbreaking separations, and bitter grudges and relentless feuds. And an old house is also like a black stream — it lets you rinse in it and savor the best of it and in the meantime leave your own smell in it...

It was by sheer chance that, through an exchange, we got this old house, which really took my fancy. Because it was a detached house at the east side of a walled-in compound and had a small yard and its own entrance, it was very quiet. When friends came to chat at night, no matter how late into the night we talked and how vociferously we aired our voluble and bombastic views, we wouldn't affect our neighbors. All the friends who had seen the house thought it a desirable, good residence.

For those few years, my lifelong companion Xiao Yu and I were the only two residing in the house. Except for one or two nights each week, when I had to go to teach at an evening school, I could stay at home, reading books or preparing for classes, living the conventional, leisurely

---

[1] Zhou Haiyan, contemporary writer.

life of a member of the old-time literati.

After moving into this old house, I had someone lay a small flowerbed under the southern window and ship in some plants and soil from a distant nursery, and then I planted in it grape trees, asparagus ferns, camellias, azaleas, Chinese roses, valley lilies, scarlet Kaffir lilies, cypresses, strawberries... In over a year, the grape and fern vines had crept up over the wide southern window, and completely green-shaded the study room on the first floor. When the strawberry began to bear fruit, I didn't have a child yet. What a lack of fun it was to go without a pair of small, pudgy hands to pluck those freshly watery red berries! I had been frequently turning over this sorrow in my mind, but all I could do was watch the berries ripen and then rot in the earth. The year when my daughter was able to toddle, those strawberry plants didn't bear fruit, but instead lots of grapes began to hang from the vines. We gathered the grapes and found, to our surprise, that they filled up a small basket. Small as they might have been, they were quite sweet. With the basket in hand, in a merry spirit, my daughter bustled about the entire compound, giving out her grapes.

There was a big jar sitting in a corner of the dooryard, with over a dozen fish in it. As that corner was quite wet, it was fully covered with green moss. In the evening, after a rain, a small tortoise would often come out to peer for food. In the years of our daughter's babyhood, when we held her in front of the jar to train her to pee, we would often sing to the jar:

Tort', tort', up show, show;

Drink, drink, my pee, pee.

When the tortoise happened to come out at that moment, our daughter would burst into laughter. Later, she started to sing the lines herself:

Tort', tort', up show, show;

Drink, drink, my pee, pee.

As this tortoise was timid and docile, our daughter would often tease it. Before we were to relocate south, we were a bit concerned about who would come to take care of the tortoise, but one morning, to our dismay, the little thing was lying right in the middle of the dooryard, its head and four limbs stretched out. When our daughter went merrily to tease it, it didn't budge. The tortoise was dead! When it was alive, it was afraid of everything, but when it was dead, it didn't want to huddle under its shell anymore, as if to remove its lifelong stigma as a coward.

In the east wall of the dooryard, there grew an outlandish tree called "Jue".

It didn't grow on either side of the wall, but right from within the wall. Its thick trunk, acquired over the years, squeezed its way out of the gaps between the bricks — a lump here and a lump there, like modeling clay. As the old people in the compound told us, this tree was likely to have grown from a sapling that happened to be left in the wall during the construction of the house. Nobody had ever expected it to grow up like that, but it did, for sixty to seventy years by now. For fear that it might break the wall, the former house owner tried many ways to kill it, such as soaking the trunk with toxic liquid, scalding the roots with hot water, peeling off the bark, and nailing in the bones of a Fu fish, which were said to be highly poisonous, but none had destroyed it in the past six or seven decades. Instead, it survived and was still thriving, and didn't show the slightest sign of aging. During the typhoon season in autumn every year, we would always pollard the tree at the top of the wall, for fear that its enormous crown would swing off the high wall in the wind and the enormous quantity of fallen leaves would clog the gutters on top of the kitchen sector. But when the spring breezes came, myriad green shoots would sprout from the trunk on the wall, and these shoots would soon grow into a huge crown, canopying the dooryard. For the entire summer, it would keep off the burning sunbeams and dance in the wind, favoring this old house with pleasant cool air, a sense of luxuriant greenness, thriving vitality, and lyrical whispering, completely mindless of its fated beheading in the coming autumn. Before the typhoon came each year, we had to pollard the tree. So its stylish green branches and twigs would disappear within the spell of a morning, to yield to a large, vapid ash-colored sky. Through the chipped bricks and broken tiles, we could see the beaten-up

145

neighboring gable across the lane outside. It was a picture of dilapidation. So for quite a few days, a sense of loss would linger in our hearts, refusing to go away...

Even if you called it a tree, it didn't look like one, for it did not have an erect trunk, but only wood lumps squeezing out from the gaps in the wall. And only from these wood lumps could one roughly figure out what its deformed body might look like, and only from the bucket-sized ugly-looking stump seen through the crack formed by missing bricks at the top of the wall and the repeated knife scars all over the top of the tree could one tell its age. I often had the feeling that this "Jue" was not a tree, but a monument sculpted from the soul of a tree. Since the day it was kept in the dark wall during the construction, it was doomed to endure misery for the rest of its life. Its unyielding determination to survive, its perseverant temperament for sunlight, and its tenacious spirit and soul had prevailed over the brick wall and the repeated decapitations. Every year, its ugly-looking body displayed its extraordinary, bold, and stylish soul to spring and to the sunshine. I think this is the enlightenment as well as the gift this old house has given me.

A Life That Never Matures

◎ *Han Xiaohui*[1]

Nothing today seems different from the way it was before. The clear sky is a lovely blue, and when the sun rises, the great earth shimmers in golden yellow.

But, to me, this is a day with a brand-new meaning.

Today, even without counting it on my fingers, I know that I have to bid farewell to my adolescence upon the third repetition of my birth year in China's twelve-year zodiac cycle.

For the entire day today, I have been muddle-headed, with a question screaming inside me:

Why am I still immature?

1

Driven by some kind of caprice, I dig out my old photos — of the period from elementary school up until yesterday, when my thirty-fifth year ended. Eighteen images altogether! Among them are a photo showing a "red-scarfed" image of me taken at the age of nine when I joined the Young Pioneers League, a photo showing a "working-class" image of me taken at sixteen when I started to work in a factory, a photo showing a "university student" image of me taken when I started to go to university after eight years of working in a factory, and a photo showing a "reporter" image of me taken when I started to work in a newspaper office after graduation. So they look as simple as that — but not really! I paste them on a piece of white paper in chronological order and place them under the

---

① Han Xiaohui (1954-), woman essayist, senior editor and literary critic. She is the first Chinese writer to be invited to make a speech at the Library of Congress in the United State since 1949.

glass on my desk.

Then, taking on a stranger's perspective, I start to closely examine myself over the past three decades.

Those few pictures taken in my teens reveal some naïveté between my eyebrows, showing that I was still trapped in the immaturity of worldly matters. Those few taken in my twenties have my eyes looking up, unreservedly exposing to the world my longing for and trust in life. In my thirties, as the rest photos show, the look in my eyes has gradually changed — to a pensive and perplexed one, to a complicated and embittered one, and to a sunny and gloomy one — betraying a soul that has spent thirty years in pursuit, which has gone through a full tempering in the matters of life. Those three decades of worldly affairs have left on me not only physical wrinkles and a coarse character, but also a lot of obscure things under the surface.

However, in the wilds of an obscure life, there is a soul seeking truth, benevolence, and beauty.

2

"But, have you found them?" I ask those pictures.

They look at me seriously, without saying anything.

Perhaps the way we look at life in childhood makes more sense. We believe, in our little hearts then, that adults know everything about the world. Back then, I had a real admiration for those grown-ups I was familiar with. I particularly admired their carefree way of living and their reassurance in dealing with matters — for them, this world had no unsolvable problems.

Therefore, even when I was still a little kid, I began by instinct to long for maturity. This instinct involves the same amount of investment we humans make in the pursuit of light, truth, progress, advancement, and improvement, required throughout the course of our lives.

Now that the thirty years of struggles, setbacks, laments, and feelings are all gone, I am even more nostalgic about the nursery rhyme, as a result:

Pick, pick, pick plantains,

Let's pick plantains;
Pick, pick, pick plantains,
Here are plantains;

...

To me, the world is always as naïve as when I looked at it as a toddler. I have never learned to hedge, lie, or parrot when talking to people, never learned to fake, deceive, or bluff when socializing with others, and never learned to be suspicious, vigilant, or irresponsible when dealing with the outside world. Although I keep my eyes wide open, still, I believe everyone is a good person to me, kind at heart, and therefore I am always truthful with them...

It does save a lot of hassles to confront complexity with simplicity, but I cannot stay a child forever!

If we switch the positions of the earth and the sky to look at the world upside-down, will we perceive the world in the same way as we did in childhood? When I was a child, I took it for granted that I knew everything, as if I had seen through the world. But now, the opposite proves true, as I have been repeatedly made a spectacle of in this world.

3

Not just once, not just for one period of time in life, and not just in one new environment has someone asked me, "Why are you so serious about everything?"

Once someone drove the point home by saying that I was not only punctilious to myself but also to others. "Not good," he said. "Change your way of life. Pure water does not raise fish, and extreme sincerity hurts your health!"

The problem of being too sincere has existed since ancient times, and those who suffer it have a shorter lifespan.

However, the reason why I cannot change is not that I am not affected by what this person has said, but because I am not mentally powerful enough to change.

I have tried many times to change the way I live. I really envy the smiles that dimple my daughter's face right after she has cried. I am really touched when I see happy couples walking down streets with their hands intertwined, as if this world were theirs alone. From these I have sensed the meaning of life.

But for this life, I don't think I can be like them.

4

Romain Rolland once said, "Life is hard. It is a continuous struggle for all those who cannot come to terms with mediocrity. For the most part it is a painful struggle, lacking sublimity, lacking happiness, fought in solitude and silence."

But I'd say, "Nothing is harder than life, and this is especially true for the immature."

If Qu Yuan had known how to fawn on the King of Chu or his wife, the Southern Queen, would he have been exiled to live a lamentable life? If Mozart had known how to please the First Bishop of the Salzburg Church, would he have died young, of poverty? This is true in any human life — whether it is a happy one or an unhappy one, whether one is alive or about to die, whether in ancient times or now, or whether in China or not in China — the only difference is what you are seeking in life.

"So what were you looking for?" I examine each "myself" in the eighteen photos, trying to figure out what type of a person she has been.

I know them better than anyone else, of course. There is no doubt about that. They have all been scrupulous rather than unscrupulous, good persons who have never stooped to a despicable existence, but I also worry about them, for such persons are bound to live a hardship-ridden and exhausting life, or even a life that beats them down badly.

"Are you all regretful about the past thirty years of your arduous life?"

They still look at me seriously without saying anything.

I look beyond them and see a picture of my daughter. Seeing her adorable little face and the naïve look in her clear eyes, and turning around, seeing our humble but clean home and my fully loaded bookcase, once again, I choose and will forever choose to be a person:

Who seeks integrity,

And who seeks a true self.

5

Therefore, viewing this issue from a different perspective of life, I do not have the slightest feeling of shame.

Being immature, in many cases, is a gift bestowed by heaven.

Immaturity means truthfulness.

I have seen the sagacious sparks of great writers and poets in all of their works, and at the same time the repeated failures in dealing with their social lives. Honoré de Balzac never matured in all his life; Johann Wolfgang von Goethe didn't lose his childhood innocence even when he was old; in the eyes of unenlightened people, Leo Tolstoy was hard to understand when he made the decision to abandon his family...

That is the very reason why they are great people.

None of those who are slick, obsequious, all-pleasing, and sophisticated in their social lives can create great works of art.

We are lucky that this world has not matured to the point of losing its sincerity. If it does reach the point of being sealed off in sophistication, then no one can really live in such a world.

6

Of course, I am not denouncing maturity.

From the perspective of the betterment of the world, life calls for mankind to mature as quickly as possible. But this does not refer to the type of fake "maturity" that comes with hypocrisy, slickness, trickery, and self-degradation; this, on the contrary, refers to a real maturity imbued with intelligence, thought, and power, which promotes social progress. Only on the wings of maturity can mankind fly to the realm of freedom.

Let's forge forward from immaturity to maturity — the maturity that the world needs to benefit mankind.

For this end, I am willing to raise the requirements for myself every day to continuously cultivate and temper myself, so that I can reach an ideal state as soon as possible.

Watching Stars from a Roof

◎ *Jiang Er*[①]

Let me climb onto the roof to watch the stars alone.

It is an early autumn night, a night with riotous wind, when, on a whim, or rather on a sudden surge of sentimentality, I turn off the lights in the house, close the door, and sneak up onto the roof to lie down there. It gives me an odd feeling! At first, the world up there in the sky looks like an immense stretch of dark clouds portending wind and rain — devoid of even the slightest trace of anything sparkling. This gives me a sense of disappointment and timidity. But I remember seeing splashes and splashes of stars on the sky every night when I raised my head while walking on my way through the basketball court, back from my shower down the hill. Maybe my long exposure to glare has fatigued my eyes so that I fail to see the stars now. So I close my eyes and ease my breath to relax a bit. When I open my eyes again, to my surprise, out of the ink-like black heavenly pond overhead emerge four or five stars. As I am more and more tranquilized at heart and settle into a lying-down position, my eyes become sharper. To my further surprise, what I can see tonight is not just stars, but luxuriant and bright overlapping nebulas, like rain-washed, fully blooming lotus, clusters upon clusters of them, in a pond. Watching them melts my heart. I feel an impulse to say something, but for fear that I may only be able to describe a tiny bit of it with mere words, I decide not to say anything; let me just watch them like this for a whole night.

Watching stars for a long time, one will naturally think of the belief that everyone is associated with a constellation. But, unfortunately, not

---

① Jiang Er, contemporary writer.

many people take a real interest in perceiving or cherishing such a beautiful spiritual hope, for if trapped in a financial plight or embroiled in worldly complications, one would lose the "leisurely and carefree mood" to savor its nuances. No doubt, such fate-related retrospection or forethought will not dawn on anyone engaged in a busy life.

While I am lost in my gaze, each of those star-sparkles hanging high up there seems like a human face — like what happens when you walk in a stream of pedestrians; you may not get lost, but after some time, your vision gets blurred and you don't see what you are looking at. As a result, the more people come into the flow, the less chance you'll have to recognize them. Human faces vary greatly, but seldom can a person distinguish their subtleties. They thus all look like those stars.

Looking up at the star-strewn sky, one will also want to probe the secret of the universe. With human knowledge, however, we may never be able to get to the bottom of it, for the answer lies as far as outer space or on the sun for one thing, and the question itself is too big for a possible answer for another, isn't it? If, say, this Milky Way galaxy is not the end of the universe, then how much deeper and broader is the universe? If, say, this galaxy is already the edge of the universe, then what is beyond that edge? Although imagination can travel two or more times faster than light to reach the very end of this bottomless Milky Way galaxy, if it does reach an end, then what is next to the end it reaches? The challenge of a reverse supposition would still remain. If there is no end, then what is this endless place that can prove this opposite supposition? Is it a loop? If it is, a loop itself has a limit in space, and in time, it continues only until it is exhausted... Such inferring, however, can only make me feel impractical, and solitary as well — just like those stars hanging in the abysmal night sky; although they exist, each lies so far away from another, revealing an aura of ice-coldness and distantness. If humans are like them, in that they each seal their hearts, communicate with nobody, and stay aloof from others, then what is the reason to dig into the secret of the universe, the future, and life itself?

The more I watch the stars alone, the lonelier I feel. However, who will be in the mood to join me, even if I invite a person or a group of people on days other than the Mid-Autumn Festival? Our ancients could learn about their past and about their own time by observing celestial phenomena, make travel decisions by looking at the stars, and understand life by visiting secluded and cold places. We could very well follow them to improve our cognition or provoke our enlightenment by gathering under the sky every night. Even if we do not talk about these matters, there are still all kinds of celestial and terrestrial joy and leisure such as:

Lying on a straw mat to enjoy the warmth;
Resting my head on clouds to dream of the stars.

People nowadays can laugh at you for talking about these topics: "Come on! Give me a break! What's there to see on those stars? Stop being so romantic and starry-eyed, OK?" Or "You are just being dumb. Where can you see the stars, to begin with? I'd rather watch TV at home. They have superb programs!"

Yes, this world has turned into something like that, and therefore, make sure you do not make this type of "joke" with anyone. Jeopardized by man-made strong lights, most of the stars nowadays are suffering from the syndromes of depression or dejection and they thus shy away, while the only ones that still stay at their posts are a few direction-functional ones, like the South Star and the North Star. However, even to locate these stars, you have to avoid crowds, urban clamor, and high buildings, and to go to the field ridges in the quiet country, the seaside, or the high mountains, where, to your delight, you will surely discover that stars still exist, but only seem to have found themselves a new home. Or, facing such a miraculous scene as if it were a world of aliens, you may wonder where you come from and where you will go after life ends, but you will get no answer from those twinkling stars.

Lying on the roof, I gradually feel sleepy. The earth remains tranquil, in spite of the sporadic insect chirps and frog croaks. This current vacation in the mountain resort has reminded me of those long-gone old days and nights when I was here accompanying the stars. Back in grade five or six, when dusk fell, I would take a walk along the turbid stream, from where I could always see, as the sky began to dim, a star shining alone in the whimsical, dark, wave-like evening twilight. Who was that one, that crystal-clear, eye-catching but most lonesome thing hanging toward the edge of the sky, I wondered? Every time I looked up and saw it, I felt like I was running into myself. This is still true, even to this day. When I was in Danshui, either from the sheep's fescue plot on the mountain or from the riverbank, I could see, with my young eyes, a view full of stellar beauty. Although I once brought myself to ponder the subtle relationship between literature, religion, and the celestial entities, I was in an escapist mentality and, most of the time, I was reluctant to figure it out. On the snowcapped mountain, the stars looked abruptly closer, as if abundant fruits were drooping from low trees, so close that I seemed to be able to raise my hand and pick them easily. Although the distance to the sky was no different on the mountain from on the plain ground, the sense of excitement and freshness this closeness has brought me is a hundred times more dramatic. After joining the army, through the island woods, seeing a sky full of stars keeping me company, I was touched and thrilled without knowing why. Suddenly, I felt that those heavenly eyes could indeed see through us travelers, soldiers, and wanderers, and that gave me a benign and extremely warm feeling.

Looking up at the starry sky and contemplating it, I almost fall asleep. During the contemplation, the waves of my thought once ran into the disorderly time-stream, sometimes undulating to the period imbued with sweetness and sometimes, with restlessness. The sweet period refers to the days when I was dating her. What makes the story meaningful is that although we were on two small islands far separated by the sea, a year-long separation deepened our love and feeling instead, for I was not the cowherd on Aquila and she not the weaving-maid on Lyra, who were separated by the Heavenly Emperor and allowed to meet only once a year on the seventh day of the seventh month each year by the lunar calendar. However, while the celestial world has remained constant since ancient times, involving no changes in happiness or unhappiness, the terrestrial world has undergone a fundamental change within a short duration of the last twenty years. Right at this point, I come awake and spring up with a dull heartache, but find nobody to assuage it. A mountain breeze puffs over, swaying the broken leaves of the forget-me-not; the earth remains tranquil and lonely. Alas, what is there to disconsolate me? I won't often come to this mountain to watch the stars. I should learn from them instead and accompany this terrestrial world happily and magnanimously, at the same time being forever self-illuminative, spotlessly bright, and completely detached.

A Clipping about Winter

◎ *Liu Yeyuan*[1]

They will never be able to follow him again — never! Behind him, there used to be a ravine, but now it is gone. It has gradually "degenerated" into what is currently a street, where many old acquaintances he now has no time to think about have chosen to stay. People have their own preferences. It is natural that they don't have to follow anyone. He now has no energy to turn back, and that is exactly the gap that used to confuse and disturb him so much. If someday he has to sink, too, he muses, he will sink into the bottom of the sea — that deep, blue bottom, where many deep-sea creatures are swimming and large submarine benthos, glittering. He will rest there, together with the fish and the sea grass and his pre-evolutional ancestors, where there will be no mirth, but no stupid questions either.

In the beginning, he was the one who followed them. That was when he was very young. Then, they walked abreast for quite a while. But one day, while looking at each other, he said something to them, and then realized that he had nothing more to say. Those extremely important words fell into an abyss between him and them, a very deep abyss that slowly but surely split the two wide apart into different generations. He lowered his head, for nothing was obscured any more.

Although he still sees them from time to time, there is only formality left between the two. That is all there is to it.

The one who once told him that he had gone too far became his friend later, the earliest and most lasting friend of his.

---

① Liu Yeyuan (1954-), contemporary essayist.

He left them to walk all by himself, through one winter after another.

But winters were rigid. Do you know how crude and rough a small scales-making factory with just over a hundred workers was twenty years ago? In the middle of a dark, damp shed of a factory house, covered with a leaking roof, bestrewn with ore, metal, and other items randomly thrown on the ground, stood a small, wobbling and primitive furnace which released its exhausts into open air. Standing, in wind and snow, on a decrepit, shaking wooden rack, in the deafening noise of a booster fan, sweating all over his dust-covered body, he had to continuously pour buckets upon buckets of heavy pig-iron lumps into the firewood- and coal-fueled blaze in the furnace. This was what the fellow workers called "material feeding." He worked there for over four years — hammering iron, spraying paint, grinding metal, drilling holes, sand-casting, and repairing and installing platform-balances, platform-scales, and wagon-balances... Whatever he was asked to do, all because he was classified as an "untouchable" of the "denounced class". He had to constantly carry those 25kg balance weights, constantly lift and pour the 50kg-plus ladle filled with flaming-hot molten iron, constantly worry about those repudiation meetings — all as vivid as if they had just happened. However, that physically exhausting and mentally repressive period was exactly when he came to deeply understand what his father once told him — "Look far!" What a plain, philosophical, and artistic advice! Look far — far into the distance where there are height and depth, humans and spirits, Heaven and Earth, future and history, and abstraction and physical existence. This belief toughened up his weak body and made meaningful what he was going through. It really worked, worked better than Qigong or a faith in Buddhism or Taoism. It later became his life-long companion and a totem that no large rivers or oceans could carry away. Like those feelings of "endless winters" that keep welling up nowadays, it has re-created him. Therefore, whenever a winter befalls him now, his body comes to where his heart dwells.

You will be solemn, when winter comes, he said.

Winter is what we deeply and painfully adore, which is a deep feeling purer and sturdier than the first love.

Even in the desert, he said, you don't have to look for water.

For you, yourself, are the source of water;

Of spirit, of knowledge, of wealth;

Of creativity, of strength;

Of humans, and of gods.

By then, for as long as it lasts, it will forever signify the truth that a real feeling is not as worthy as a deep feeling.

"Hello, winter!"

Indeed, no greeting is as touching and significant as this.

In Honor of Moonlight

◎ *Lin Qi*[1]

It was in a fleeing hurry that I got out of that "Blue Moon" club. Of the two possible scenarios: either "go downhill" or lose a job, I chose the latter. Although this choice leaves my balance in the red, it has given me a sense of relief — I have not been drowned by that huge flood of neon lights, and I hug myself over this little feat.

It is now a night in Kyoto. Alone on this rare occasion, I roam along the Kamogawa River, at the complete disposal of the moonlight that rustles between my eyebrows, over the tips of my hair, and around the corners of my lips, while listening to Mother Nature's harmonious melody performed coherently by the moonlight and the glistening ripples.

Long time no see, Moonlight! The effort to survive as a modern person has deprived me of time with you. Although we Chinese students in Japan always encourage each other by chanting, "Far apart as we may dwell, the moon unites us so long as we are well," who has the leisure to appreciate you?

Loitering alone over the moonshine and shadows by the riverside, I suddenly let my thoughts drift to Li Bai, my favorite great poet, in whose poetic images the moon was the most beloved one. According to statistics given by some scholars, out of the 1,059 poems Li Bai composed, 341 involve the moon, and that means one out of three of his poems has a moon image in it. Li Bai was indeed fanatical about the moon — so fanatical that he even died of it when he was trying to capture it in a river. That accident is recorded in *Selected Quotations*, composed by Wang

---

[1] Lin Qi (Mo Ming Qi Miao, 1957-), Chinese woman writer in Japan.

Dingbao of the Tang Dynasty: "In a palace-silk robe, as lordly and content as if nobody was nearby, the drunk Li Bai waded into River Caishi, but was drowned while attempting to capture the moon reflected in it." Although the research by later generations points out the lack of veracity of such a story, I would rather believe it.

The moonlit water laps along. Oh, Li Bai, the poet of moonlight, as I have no wine with me, let me chant a stanza from one of your poems to honor you:

Oh, Lady Moon, what a loner to be in the blue sky;
Oh, Lady Moon, what sorrow to take the herb and fly.

That eternal loneliness echoes in me!

Moonlight in western Fujian was wet, always drenching us, the group of "Educated Youths". Back then, every time when it was my turn to do night-watch at that large warehouse, I would bring with me my two-string fiddle and play *River Water* the whole night... On that spacious ground for sun-drying grains, the moonlight was my only audience, the most intelligent bosom friend as well.

I do not know why, but humble days bring me closer to Mother Nature.

Once in a while, Mr. Y would come to keep me company on the night-watch. He would show me his diary. I can still remember the quotation from Chairman Mao he had copied neatly on the opening page: "Educated Youths must go to the countryside to receive re-education from the poor and lower-middle peasants!" He underlined the word "must." The next page revealed a small piece of his skin peeled off after a sunburn. It looked like a piece of fish scale under the moonlight at that moment.

I knew I was touched, and even to this day, I am not in any doubt of his sincerity.

Here and there in the diary, there was that type of "emotional appeal" which was meant for me to sense under the moonlight. Moonlight may not be as resplendent as the sun, but it reveals a sense of romanticism that comforts and transcends you.

161

At that time, when there was moonlight, I was fond of listening to him sing, "Roaming and roaming, I'm lured into traveling to distant places by fate." That melancholic but romantic tone flows with the stream of moonlight into the far distance...

I was only seventeen back then. I thought I had already "roamed" far enough to be sent from Xiamen, my hometown, to the countryside in western Fujian to work and live. Never had I thought that I would have roamed even farther away as to be in a foreign country now.

Oh moonlight, my loyal friend, only you have followed me here.

When I was little, I was most afraid of being tailgated by the moon, because I was afraid of being followed by ghosts. I always walked in fear at night...

Weijun took my timidity as a precious opportunity. He volunteered to be my "bodyguard," to see me from the classroom to my dormitory, which involved crossing a path on a hill. Back then, the Chang'an campus was quite desolate, which made the tomb-ridden Chang'an Hill even more eerie, but I preferred evening classes, and every night, I had to return to the dormitory after twelve o'clock.

I dared not hold his hand even during pitch-dark nights. On campus, there were "peering eyes" everywhere, for even when there was no moonlight there was starlight.

On a moonlit night, I would always rush to keep an even distance from him, but never even half a footstep closer — I followed him because I was afraid of hearing footsteps behind me. Once, he suddenly disappeared. Right at the moment I was bewildered, a menacing "ghost" dashed out at me from a dark hut by the roadside. "Oh, my sainted aunt!" I was terrified and went limp, but when I took a closer look at it, the ghost, into whose arms I had gone limp, turned out to be him, dipping into the moonlight to stroke it on my ice-cold forehead. His touch was so tender and passionate.

A rugged and valiant man can be tender and affectionate in the moonlight.

But most of the time, men are in the sunny category. If we say that women live for men, then men for society. A sage once said: "Pursuing material desires and yielding to vanity are the two most direct causes of loss of intelligence."

If that is what is going to happen, then call for the moonlight.

Feeling suffocated in a high-rise office building, some young people proposed a moonlit evening party by the West River, and the proposal was well-received.

Unfortunately, of the three in our family, we could only send over a "representative", my husband, for our child was too little to stand an autumn night's chill.

The next day, our "representative" returned in high spirits. Even though he couldn't fall asleep the whole night — a great departure to his strict routine of going to bed early and getting up early, he instead claimed in a jubilant tone: "Good, the moonlight was really beautiful!" It seemed that he was indeed moved this time, but just didn't know how to express it better.

Later I learned that at the party, they had played a game called "Flower Circling on Drum Beating." Whomever the bouquet of circling flower had landed on when the drum stopped had to perform something, or drink vinegar as a penalty. Because the show's host had actually brought some vintage Zhenjiang vinegar with him, it was a real game. With whatever broken voice one had, whoever got the flower had to screech one or two songs, such as *The Moon Moves While I Do, Too*. But our "representative" was the only one who drank the vinegar.

I am sorry for the hard nut he had to crack, but I know him: It is most likely that he didn't want to spoil the brimful of moonlight in the river with his not-so-decent voice. Don't people say that those who like to drink vinegar are usually romantically sentimental? I wish he had also drunk the moonlight.

Now, I am used to night walks.

Of all the things in this foreign country, I like the moonlight most.

I enjoy slowly riding my bicycle along the Kamogawa River after work, when I let the limpid streaming moonlight and the lapping of the water wash away a day's fatigue from me. This is exactly like what is depicted in

Raising my cup I beckon the bright orb;
With my shadow, we three bodies hobnob.

...

How wonderful it is to bathe in moonlight, which can be considered the most intelligent natural light of all! To see its merits, one has to be alone and tranquil. This is just like what is depicted in *The Cambridge I Know*, a piece of famous prose by Xu Zhimo:

"To know 'the true personality' of your friend, you have to be with him alone; to know the true nature of yourself, you have to let yourself be alone; to know a place (which is also considered intelligent), you have to play in it all by yourself. To be serious, in our entire lives, how many people do we truly know and how many places? We are all too busy to be alone... Unfortunately we all happen to be modern people. The more we throw ourselves into society, the farther away we are from nature. "

I am fortunate to have the chance to be alone tonight, loitering in the moonlight, bathing in the moonlight, and talking about the moonlight.

A-Fan has many moon stories. Although I am not sure if they are legends or his own creation, they are all beautiful — so beautiful that I start to think that his eyes can retain the moonlight.

A-Fan told me that each of our shoulders has a light on it called the light of life, and our foreheads have another one called the light of wisdom. Therefore, never pat anyone on his or her shoulder at night...

From that day on, every time I look at him, his forehead glows as if he has been bathing in moonlight. Of course, I cannot see my own forehead, but I can feel that it often reflects moonlight, too. When this light guides me on a night walk, I am not afraid that "the long trip I have completed is just the beginning of a new trip."

The Autumn Rain and the Mountain Forest

◎ *Chen Xinhua*[①]

It has been windy and rainy the whole day, and the temperature has dropped abruptly. Withered leaves fall everywhere, mottling the street with golden yellow blobs, looking like random colors scrawled on an oil-painted canvas. Through the raindrop-strewn window, the framed scene outside appears like a dreamland of an autumn night in the remote past. The gloomy sky is depressing! For a few days in a row, I have not set foot beyond my threshold, but instead pressed my forehead against the window, watching wet pedestrians silently streaming by. Over the hustling and bustling city life, something floating in the sky is dripping down with the rain into people's hearts. Two simple, whistling lyrics that tell an old story about the sadness and happiness of a simple-minded person in the rain keep ringing in my heart. The two lines keep ringing repeatedly and randomly, as if a musical record has gotten stuck on my mind's gramophone. For fear that it might explode in me at any minute, I grab an umbrella, and out I am on the street. I cannot help shuddering when the wind flings the raindrops onto me while I try to lock the door.

Pedestrians coming up under their umbrellas are expressionless — as if their spirits had flown to somewhere very far away. Each of them has a vacuous face.

As the roadside buildings appear lower and lower, the scene around me becomes more and more rustic and closer and closer to nature. Standing at the end of the street is a verdant mountain, quiet and sagacious-looking in the rain. A gentle, short-grass-covered slope unrolls

---

① Chen Xinhua, contemporary writer.

to its foot, looking like a square-shaped carpet spread out in front of a mountain-god temple. Still greenly velvety, the early autumn grass sprawls farther and deeper toward the mountain. Dotted here and there on the slope are a few pines and cypresses, with layers upon layers of upward-growing needle-clusters, straight and towering, highlighting the sturdy and hardy tree shapes. With the clouds hanging low and the fog drifting, it seems it is drizzling again. The mountain feels especially tranquil and reassuring before an imminent rain. Those trees and that grassy slope, in their tranquility, radiate an overwhelming power. Then, this must be the very place I am looking for. Now those vacuous faces in the rain flash back into my memory — their owners must have left them and come here.

Ascending a little more, the flora becomes denser. And the trees snuggle against each other, leaving only a narrow path amidst them. Washed by rain, the tree branches and boughs that twist and cluster together to veil the sky appear even more vibrantly unfolded and sturdily poised, and look even more saturated with greenness and spangled with dripping dew. And from among the tree branches, once in a while, a broken spider-web or a few stems of withered rattan hang down, blocking my way. Plucked by a slanting raindrop, the cobweb, dotted with transparent, crystal-clear, and sparkling raindrops, gives an abrupt quiver, and then slowly stills — only to be abruptly plucked again. Fallen leaves, varied yellow in hue, lie thick on the ground in the forest, with the ones at the bottom already turned black and dog-eared and the ones on top still fresh and flat. With each step I take on them comes their fracturing sound, clear and melodic. While those under my feet sink, those next to them roll up over my feet, dampening my shoes and socks with the water that saturates them.

Unknowingly, the ringing of those two whistling lines has trailed off to a volume just loud enough to serve as background music for this forested mountain; it sounds both sad and happy. On my way up, I have come across a few trees that are sallow green from their bases up to their topmost branches, with their roots soaked in a dark green puddle, unable to absorb the spring of life. One can hardly find any trace of life in them. Wise trees know the necessity of giving up rotted twigs or withered leaves for the burgeoning of new sprouts next spring. But these blighted trees will die from their rot. This prompts me to think that humans also fall into two similar categories, and I have been constantly in an agonizing struggle between the two choices — sometimes treasuring life but sometimes squandering it away.

Although the drizzle slants down silently, when the various-sized raindrops that have accumulated on the tree leaves slide off onto the withered leaves on the ground, they produce melodious music to accompany my footsteps. It fills up my ears, but behind it, I can also vaguely hear something else. Out of curiosity, I stop walking to listen closely to it. It is a thin, rhythmic sound! What can it be, besides the pitter-pattering of the rain? Oh, it must be the sound of the trees breathing — the rustling produced when the wind brushes the twigs. But — but there is yet another short, fitful sound. What can it be? Listen — but it's gone again. Taking a few more footsteps forward, I stop again to listen to it. "Flap-flop, flap-flop;" here it goes again. Suddenly, I understand. The sound comes from a bird that is hidden in the foliage and flapping off raindrops from its wings. Thinking that there is such lovely life in this rainy forest, I cannot help smiling. Right at this moment, I see a golden leaf, with a few crystal-clear raindrops on it, drifts past me.

As I have no tour guide, I do not know where this path leads me in the rain. I just climb up and up...

Resting in a small pavilion, I lean on its balustrade to look down. The wind, coming down from the mountaintop, drowns all the noises. I cannot hear or feel the rain, but only see its drizzling threads sliding down from the pavilion's eaves. The mountain is shrouded in mist, as if the rain has frozen into fog. Over the valley is a huge stretch of thick milk-white; above it is light green-white, icily steadfast. The autumn rain and the mountain forest create a kind of concurrence: that is, the rain takes its time to come down while the mountain forest does not rush to absorb; there is no rapture and no impatience involved. Opening my umbrella, I want to wedge myself into them, but immediately, the slanting drizzle licks my clothes wet, and so I have to back up — I am contaminated with much too heavy worldly dust, and that's why the autumn rain and the mountain forest do not accept me. They belong to such forest deities that their skin is thirsty for the cold rain's caress, and their beautiful hair can still flutter in the rain like green seaweed, while I can only roam on the margin of nature. While the eternity of great nature touches me deeply, the smallness and moribundity of each individual life shows me how ordinary life is.

By the time I turn to head down the mountain, the evening lights are just switched on. Seeing the city down there, filling the sky with illumination, I begin to think again about those vacuous, but somewhat enlightened faces. The minutiae of daily life have blinded their wits. This has reminded me of those dead trees. I will have to bear them in mind. When I feel cramped living in a tiny room like a trapped animal — when raising my head, I can only see the grey sky and skyscrapers, and when lowering my head, I can only see the flying hems of raincoats under umbrellas, without being able to see the eyes or hearts of the people, I wish to mingle with Mother Nature, and wish that this ink-wash painting of "lingering out in the slanting wind and fine drizzle" would creep into my grey-colored city dream to comfort me.

Lifelong Lament

◎ *Wang Kailin*[1]

Because a river runs in my heart, I do not know — and will never want to know — what drying up feels like. Amidst the mulberry leaves of time, mankind, for transient happiness, food and clothing, fame and gain, and this worry-embroiled life and beyond, spins a self-imprisoning cocoon. But I am a pupa that never wants to turn into a silkworm and that is trying to get away from the lure of mulberry leaves.

From an unknown recess of an unknown world immediately emerges an annoying voice: No one in this world can break the bond; how can you expect to detach yourself from it? You really believe you can enjoy the sea while staying on land?

This is the voice of fatalism — I have heard it many times — which sounds so cold, so banal, and so apathetic, as if it is filled with disdain and sarcasm. It feels like countless venomous spines poking into my heart, but I do not know how to get rid of them.

All I can do is sigh. As this hustling and bustling world has kept me on the move, I have long forgotten about chanting — will there be another chance for me to sing?

You and I are on a riverside facing each other far apart. The sky is like an indifferent face and our carefree smiles form a contrast to it. In the distance as far as our eyes can see, the green mountain looks like a freshly painted fresco, with the autumnal brush-touches still vague. The sky is a vast void with no returning sails or flying birds over the horizon. Close

---

[1] Wang Kailin (1965-), contemporary writer.

to us, the waves riot, lapping against the lonely rock embankment and sending white froth and grey foam high into the air.

We have been friends for a very long time, because you believe that it is better to have a friendship-only relationship, which can be food for the hungry, water for the thirsty, and enrichment for a deficient heart. Although the mellow wine of love intoxicates, one would be in a daze right after sobering up, and then find it hard to sustain the sad days of the lost amour. Real love is utopian. Besides, it is transient, and detached from desire and reality. Once it evolves into daily life — meaning once it settles into its final nest — the color of love will crumble immediately. Although it can be glorious in times of difficulty, it will eventually melt under the sun, just as will a snowfall, heavy though it may be. We should thank Death for creating romantic tragedies with lasting appeal. He opens up a sleeping bag to accommodate those lovers who cannot be together in life — such as the Chinese "butterfly lovers" Liang Shanbo and Zhu Yingtai and the Shakespearean couple Romeo and Juliet — but can rest in the same tomb after their death.

You gaze at the water flowing at the horizon without saying a word. So I give up the topic. This, in effect, is a surrender, but you accept it without revealing any inner emotion.

If we can talk about love in a mood as peaceful as stagnant water or in a manner as nonchalant as if we were talking about something that had nothing to do with us, then why do we cross the city to come to this rural area? Here, as we face the rolling river, it is hard to control our surging emotions. Fortunately, my dwindling rationality is still lucid enough to warn me not to take the risk, not to press the sensitive topic too far.

Perhaps it is indeed better to have a friendship-only relationship — who knows? Between tea and honey, don't most people choose the former, because tea has a light and lingering flavor while honey can't maintain its sweetness for long?

On the riverside, there is a vagabond, shabby and smelly — yes, this is exactly a portrait of poverty and sadness in wildness and despair exposed under the sun. When a passer-by covers his nose and walks past the vagabond with a hidden sense of superiority, even though the passer-by is harrowed by great distress, he feels the world-apart difference from the vagabond and hence is content and free of bitterness. Therefore, the passer-by returns home and admonishes his children and grandchildren by saying: "There are the shamed and the shameless, the fortunate and the unfortunate in this world. Go and take a look at that beggar, who wallows in mud and looks for food in trash cans!" But what can we say when the wretched man starts to sing as we do? Are you sure that you are nobler, more fortunate, and more favored by this world? The vagabond is free to make an appointment with Osiris — the King of the Dead, but Osiris has run away from him in fear. In that sense, isn't the vagabond's life tougher than ours? His personality is surely impaired, but not despicable, not filthy. His impaired personality does not contain sin or evil. He does not claim anything through force or through trickery; he is content to be beneath others; he does no harm to anyone. When he sings, the flower in his soul blossoms and inflames all the same.

I don't think we are wealthier or more worry-free than he is. Since we are already trapped in haggling and wrangling about gains and losses, honors and disgraces, what is the difference between degrees thereof anyway?

The fate of love is a deciding factor in a love relationship. A forced relationship, once obstructed, will lead to the suffering of a long-term separation. Friendship, on the other hand, involves only a matter of good faith, so it is unobstructed like mercury falling onto a floor. Since each of us can open the door of the heart to love and can also close it with the excuse that the relationship is friendship only, why should we linger and lament at the threshold then?

If we cannot bathe in the river of love together, we shall then roam the plains or the wilds, so that we can appreciate completely different scenes.

Let's imagine: If, thirty years from now, we could come back to sit at the riverside together on the same afternoon in the same season, would we be in the same mood as we are today? Maybe by then, time would have already faded our interest to look back at the past. As our foreheads would have been covered with wrinkles by then, our hearts must have deposits of the thick dust of time, too. After we whisked off the dust, some long-ago events would emerge into our view: Unafraid of going astray when young, we felt lucky to have walked out of one labyrinth after another. But right at this moment, it is hard to say if our past decisions were well-advised ones. What we had tried to neglect could very well have been a real feeling. Therefore, although diluting it and eventually drowning it may help build a friendship-only relationship between us, it will remain forever unanswerable whether this choice of ours is correct or not.

I shouldn't hesitate, for one should be decisive. Even if this is a mistake, I shouldn't regret it, because no one in this world can have everything. This is like choosing a route: Even if there are two roads available, you can only take one. However, each can provide you with its own scenes or encounters, and that is what leads to different fates.

I remember that pitiful vagabond again. Apart from food, he has no mood to care about anything else. The least bit of desire for mundane love has vanished in him, while Heaven's light has not yet shined upon him. Even though he is living the lowest life in the world, he can laugh and sing all the same. This is indeed not something that can be speculated about with ordinary experience or common reason.

A great river is not in the least concerned about such insignificant joys or sorrows. In the stream of time, our life is not any more substantial than is a tiny drop of water spray in the river; yet we spend half of our lifetime thinking, one fourth of it talking, and so, do we have enough time left to keep quiet, to hesitate, or to linger? It is no surprise that things usually end up a fruitless endeavor.

Going North

◎ *Zhang Liqin*[1]

Again, I will be going north from here.

The long stretching sky is neither cloudy nor clear. The sun, like a piece of round lowland, caves in on the thickly stagnant sky, and its halo looks like a yellow fence. I stand by a grey-colored, square-shaped concrete pillar, waiting for my train. It is still early. Time inches its way in the gently streaming air.

Things around me are no longer familiar.

... What would the new world be like? Who would come to pick me up at the train station? Under what quilt, in what bed and in what room would I sink into dreams? And then, in what factory would I begin to work, as a means of making a living on my own? I seemed to have thought of answers to none of these questions. I was too young back then to concern myself about how tomorrow would be like and too young back then to care about where I would be the day after tomorrow. All I remember is that Mother pushed me onto a black train that day. And then, her expressionless face started to blur. And finally, the world I knew disappeared from the dusky station. That vanished world became a vague outline that sometimes swelled up and sometimes dwindled — there seemed to be a familiar yellowing wall with a grey latticed glass window in its upper part and a little dark brown bookcase under that window. The green silk curtain behind the glass door of the bookcase had once been my beloved skirt. When night fell, I would climb onto the high plank bed, every bit of which would squeak when I tried to shift from my kneeling

---

① Zhang Liqin (1955-), woman writer.

position. The quilt was folded into a high stack. I would tug it down before going to sleep, and Mother would fold it back into a high stack and stand it under the ceiling in the morning. I had not seen my father in quite a while. We got used to life without him. Therefore, every day, Mother had already bolted the door shut when the tangerine-colored sunlight still slanted in through its cracks. Although I had never tried to figure out if Father was already old or still young, I could still recognize him instantly whenever he came into my dreams. But I couldn't remember if his mouth or eyes were good-looking or not. I seemed to understand that fate had determined that Father had to leave us, because so many other people were also gone like him. Supposedly there was a land of punishment for these people in a distant mountain. For that reason, Mother had to get up early, be out in the early morning and return late at night, and she became peevish at me about trivial things. And for quite some time, the rushing of daily life contracted my heart.

That simple-patterned fence in double rows is still there. Although one cannot see the weather-beaten marks on it, like before, it continues to corral streams upon streams of northbound travelers into a spacious waiting place.

What a specific wait — all for that sound of a wind-shaking whistle! First came the vibration of the railway tracks, then the iron gate clanged open, and then the boarding travelers started to rush. Done! Then the train resumed its rattling. Suddenly, while I was still a young girl, I was all on my own. My pale mother, that slender dark figure, burst into gasps. With those ordinary and extraordinary days thus flung behind the tail of the train, I suddenly felt the pain of the lost past, when, despite those setbacks, tears, annoyances, and perplexities, no matter what, there were many cheerful and vivid events. Although I never begrudged my own endurance or even went so far as to pretend not to be aware of it, I tended to sympathize with others. I would feel highly ebullient after dropping my change into the broken bowl of a street vagabond. But I began to feel bewildered now — I was so thoroughly without anyone to rely on for the first time. Floating around me were unfamiliar odors, and the choking smell of tobacco. The night outside glided against the black train windows in a furious torrent; the dull and shrill clashing sound from between the wheels and the railway tracks squeezed in through the gaps in the windows. I pressed my forehead against the ice-cold glass, leaving on it the mark of naïveté of a young girl who now heartily wished to understand what was there in the massive flow outside the window.

History and human life rush past in the same way. It makes sense that one cannot discern what is in the distance on a dark night, but on this dark night, I was spreading a girl's perplexity and panic into the coming and unknown distance.

Panic is the most precious and cruel feeling a girl can have when she first plunges into life, because this is when she begins to extend her wings, and then she takes a deep breath, closes her eyes, and holds up her quivering thoughts and feelings. By the time she lifts her eyelashes again, she is perhaps already a brand-new person.

The moment when the massive force of society smashes open the seal upon a young girl and embraces her, no matter how — whether it comes with a panicked start, with a joyful smile or a sorrowful heart — sooner or later will be inscribed in her memory as an eternal entry, due to, her lack of preparation, both in thought and feeling.

So many years have elapsed, but that iron fence remains fixed there, without moving. It seem that fixed objects are all tough and durable while flowing ones are fragile and transient. When something flows away, it is gone, and even if it returns someday, it is already beaten by time, isn't it?

This is how I had been flung away, to the north — straight to the north!

That was a frigid piece of land, where the wind whistled loudly when it blew; the sky, always yellowish and hazy, dramatically bent over and closely capped the dark grey mountain peaks all around; sunbeams, with their dazzling and tenacious dry radiance, pierced the windows and plunged into the houses; all the poplar leaves outside the windows seemed to turn yellow within a night and then, within another night not long after, they were all gone. As if things there were in chase of each other into a recurring cycle — all of a sudden, the warm days were gone; all of a sudden, all the leaves were gone; and then, what would happen to the people there?

Since I finally settled down there, over a decade has already elapsed — a decade of lost adolescence in exchange for wrinkles, a baby son, and what I am today.

That iron fence seemed to have long disappeared from my memory and never to have appeared in my dreams either, as if it were waiting for this moment, in particular, to present itself to me. That iron-fenced area, which is always crowded and always corrals life, leads to a dark, dank underground channel, which exits to a waiting platform with a few railway tracks stretching in both directions, far into the horizon at both ends. Not far away is the place where my mother's pale face and dark, slender figure had disappeared. These are what have come into my mind at the moment.

What amazes me is how fate has driven me back to this place again, which, as the land of my maidenhood, has long since changed — it has grown older, bigger, and into a densely populated city, although I have long lost my attachment to it. Why have I come so early today to stand by the square-shaped concrete pillar? Is it just to experience this outburst of agitation and surging thought? Gazing at everything around, I wonder why they are so enticing to me. There is a large stretch of flowers over there. How wonderful it would be if I could melt into their permeating fragrance! There is a little lane over there. Is that walled-in grey-tiled bungalow still there? How wonderful it would be if I could go and take a look at it! There are little girls there, still pretty in my memory. How wonderful it would be if I were still like them...

I rushed there, into the far distance, and then came back without finding what I was there for and afraid to lose. Why had I gone there to look in the first place? It might have been better not to have gone there, for it could well have been a disaster or a real loss if I did have found what I was looking for there. OK, let everything there be a big and fuzzy mess that quietly dominates me in the distance. As I think in this way, those broken feelings and senses start to come together and spread out again distinctively and perplexingly.

For a long time, I have lived in my young heart.

When "there" is mixed with "here" — life does involve such changes — and when everything continues into the future like before, I find myself still mediocre and shallow, and my parched soul is still gasping for something.

The crowd between the parallel iron fences begins to flow, and so do I with it.

By the time I look up again, after spilling out of the somber channel with the crowd, the sky remains neither cloudy nor clear, the sun remains caved-in, and the iron fence remains standing.

On the north side of the roof of the waiting hall, across the platform, a bright red word is posted: NORTHBOUND. Seen from my angle, the word is in reverse, though.

Anxiety Pacified

◎ *Si Yu*[①]

1. This Is Not the Type of Life I Want

I do not know how my life has become like this, but it is never the one I want. The one I wish for can have no high mountains or flowing water, nor sunlight or grassland, nor even bread or milk, but it must have deep affection and tender care. Life is cynical. It takes away the most important things and leaves the least important things that we can live with or without, that we can have more or less of, and that we may or may not need.

Often, I tell myself to be realistic. Reality is always gloomy when you look at it, and full of bumpy stones when you walk on it. Being realistic is an inevitable part of reality, just as being idealistic is always a rebirth of idealism. The incontrovertibility and immutability of reality startles the heart and wakes us from our dreams. But even if I understand this logic, why do I still often look back or around when facing reality?

Often, I swear to heaven that I will be tough-hearted, because a tough heart is strong enough to fend off any type of wind coming from any direction, whether from the north or the west, whether it is a typhoon, a storm, a whirlwind, or even a hurricane. A tough heart looks down upon these winds as if they were just dirt under the foot. But still, why does a vivid show or a touching line from a play cause me to cry heartily all night?

Often, with a disdainful sneer, I make secret plans to exile myself: I can give up the advantages of a city life — its hustle and bustle, its flow of traffic, and even applauses from a possibly large audience — to go to the north. Although it is cold in the north, it is the final destination for an

---

① Si Yu (Zhan Shaojuan, 1954-) contemporary woman novelist and essayist.

independent spirit to perch. I can wear a shabby hat and wander, or carry a travel-pack and perform a pilgrimage. But why do so many sentry posts block the pilgrimage route?

Often, finding it hard to go on, I dream of a termination of existence. The moment of termination is certainly a beautiful and peaceful one, when that gradually cooling body brightens and shines. This makes the living blush, the killer shameful, and serves as a mirror for all survivors. But why can a tenuously thin red thread released from that pair of chubby hands easily but firmly bind me to this world?

At least I am aware that I will not live long, though, because people who enjoy long lives do not often shed a lot of tears, nor do they often grieve excessively until their hearts ache. People of longevity are as hard-hearted as unshakable mountains or rock-firm castles. But we, the soft-hearted lonely souls, are sensitive, melancholic, and fragile. All we can do is inflict wounds on ourselves until we die and are buried.

2. Eastern Style

More and more, I am apt to feel a sense of emptiness welling up in me, not knowing what I am, what the world is, and to what degree my meditation or assiduous reading is real. My empty heart stares at my vacuous mind, and then, the two clash and send out a sad sigh and squeeze out a bitter smile.

Then, I begin to think about Li Shutong and Xu Dishan — think about their knowledge and composure, their helplessness and endurance. Eastern poets, of course, have an eastern style, while the western Allen Ginsberg and Jack Kerouac howl to get on the road. They do drugs, indulge in liquor, and incline toward homosexuality. They use all kinds of extreme methods to express their despair, helplessness, and unwillingness.

What is funny, and adorable as well, is the eastern heroine. She, in a self-assured and accusatory tone, castigated Ginsberg, who, in response, "gave a witty and helpless smile first, and then pitched a little forward like a Cheshire Cat, 'I'm,' he shrugged, 'headless in blisshood.' "

Sometimes, how I wish I could be forever free from being headless — not suspicious, not pondering, not illogical, not complicated, not even responsive or impulsive! A simple mind is lucid, and it is great because it turns any truth into falsehood and any decadence into magic.

Although I know it is ridiculous to wish for eternal truth, I cannot help doing so sometimes — wishing for the eternity of beauty, the eternity of life, the eternity of benevolence, the non-existence of a power that can destroy a life, and the non-existence of an evil life that can destroy power and determination.

What's more, very often, I cannot stand the cries of those on their knees, because human limitations and miseries are as irremovable and irreversible as mountains. Will God appear? Will our mythologies come true? Grievous cries are as useless as the morning haze.

What a hateful thing it is that one has to cope with this clamorous world! What a hateful thing it is that evil ridicules kindness! Therefore, I begin to educate myself to be insensible, wicked, dumb, and to talk nonsense. And the next day, I swear to clothe myself in rags, wear a shabby hat, and carry with me "the picture of the Cloth-bag Monk" to wander as a vagabond. And the day after the next, which happens to be brilliantly sunny, with the sky as clear as if it were newly washed, I order myself to put on a new jacket, dress in a long skirt, and hold a parasol to ramble in the wilds. But it is unavoidable that I end up throwing myself onto the ground, lost in a dismal wail...

Ideals are unreachable, purity unattainable, and beauty unachievable; benevolence sustains us but for a split second while ugliness lasts forever. And even love has been stripped down so that only a paradox is left: Fervent lovers have never felt so lonely.

So I start to think about "a small country with a small population," think about "picking asters beneath the eastern fence," think about the scenery of the picturesque, tranquil European countryside, and think about closing the door and drawing the curtains to isolate myself from the noisy world.

3. Tramp Alone without Saying a Word

It is winter again — a long winter pervaded by continuous and never-dispersing cloudy smoke. This northern winter, infused with drifting coal-smoke, annoys and frightens me. Every morning, when I want to take a deep breath of fresh air to drive the stale air from my lungs after opening my sleepy eyes, I am greatly disappointed and bitterly reminded of the fact that the place I live in is not the radiantly enchanting and limpidly beautiful homeland. What shrouds me here is always this nerve-wracking and breath-clogging dust, dust, and dust.

Dusty, sooty air is my deadly enemy. Once I inhale it, my sensitive body will be weakened and fatigued so much that I will be as though half-dead and half-alive. After I get up, it has become a routine to open the windows to circulate the air in the room, but what comes in is only coal-smoke and more coal-smoke.

With a headache bordering dizziness, and feeling half-asleep and half-awake for the entire night-like, tormenting long winter, I remain in an inactive state and sit there without a word; I do not even want to shed any more tears — the cold and dim winter is not worth my diamond-shiny, crystal-clear, and lingering tears.

Again and again I see my lonely shadow on the vastly sprawling desert. Thin and frail as this image may be, my back looks so firm and perseverant. Although the travel-pack is heavy and the chaos around is terrifying, what gradually emerges from a sense of helplessness, resoluteness, and grievous persistency and determination is beauty and radiance.

Although this beauty and radiance may not last long, the fate of the lone tramper is already rock-firm. As it is inevitable that artful feigning will overwhelm true feeling, night after night, you cry and pray, and sometimes you feel like you are dead and then reborn. But when the sun rises, you resume your dusty and weary trip and stride with your head held up high and proud. As tenacious as before, you continue your trip. You tramp alone under the scorching sun without saying a word.

When the hustle and bustle for survival rises like music and the echoing of desolation resounds everywhere, you are no longer lost or perplexed. Forever ringing in your heart is a sound, which is cold but firm, faint but beautiful, obtuse but persistent. You follow it to stride forward. No matter how vague and far the destination is, you quietly and firmly forge ahead. You tramp alone without saying a word.

The Howling Northwest Wind

◎ *Tang Datong*[1]

The First Night in the Northwest

The train comes to a halt on a pitch-dark night. Although it is still midsummer, ridden with a chilly northwest wind, the road ushers me into a quaint inn.

Exhausted, I sleep for the next few days and nights, my dreams jarred by the monotonous spinning of the wheels...

One midnight, woken by the noise of the inn owner opening the door, through a sleepy mist, I see a stalwart old man come in. His long, square face, wide forehead, thick eyebrows, high, straight, dignified nose, full, dry, and honest-looking lips, bold-looking wrinkles at the corners of his eyes like a woodblock painting, and his blue-green cotton gown covered with thick layers of dust, immediately remind me of the Loess Plateau...

A typical northwest man; a typical northwest wind!

When I get up in the morning, the old man is already gone.

But I can see on the vast desert the stalwartness, virility, and staunchness created by the back of a human body.

The early morning northwest wind whistles, like the sound of a Chinese *suona* trumpet.

The Road on the Plateau

A straight line, resistant to bending, leads directly to where the sun rises.

---

[1] Tang Datong (1932-), prose-poem writer.

In the distance, is it still a far stretching pasture, a pasture so broad, level, and far stretching? In people's eyes, the sky and the earth will eventually converge and end, but the road will not. The road extends on and on into infinity...

Oh, the wheel of aspiration that has once bumped along many rough and twisted routes, please awake to your ambition and spin forward!

A straight line, resistant to bending, leads directly to where the sun sets in the distance.

In the distance, is it still a horizontal scene of animals at pasture, a scene of harvesters reaping, and a scene that allows for magnanimous personalities? Will any road continue through the gap between the intimate convergence of Heaven and Earth? The life of a road is endless, but only the plateau can reveal that life.

Now, everything can be straightened up — even feeling and thinking... Oh, the wheel of innocence that has once been shrouded in darkness and twisted by complications, please awake to your true ambition and spin forward!

The road on the plateau is an imaginative comfort to a rough and tortuous life.

The Naked Sun

— Do you have the courage to visit the plateau?

The sun over the plateau is naked, without the slightest strip of cloud or any kind of mist to diffuse or shade its intimacy. Clinging to the vast, empty and radiantly azure sky is nothing but an enormous, dazzling, fiery orb.

The naked sun scorches the boundless, stripped land and desert as if the entire world and the entire universe were denuded to the point of an eye-piercing and skin-burning bareness.

Nothing here is hidden.

So I am no exception. The fervent, penetrating sunbeams have stripped me of my coat and of a sense of embarrassment. In this way, my internal organs, blood vessels, and collateral channels, my mind and soul, my integrity and sincerity, and the road I have taken and will continue to take are all exposed — exposed to the thorough sunning and searing, so thorough that everything is inside-out, and no privacy remains. What a sheer and transparent nakedness!

I am proud of being so transparently bright now. My transparently bright suffering and joy and my transparently bright life can stand the tight embrace and the thorough penetration of the naked sun.

Do you have the courage to come under the sun over the plateau? Be sure to bring your soul with you...

The Sun Rises Over the Plateau

In the serenity, who quietly draws up the curtains of a dark night?

The undulating mountain summits are quietly lit up first, and then the vast prairie, and then the herdsmen's kitchen smoke and the tips of their whips...

An enormous orb loaded with bubbling heat waves slowly and quietly rises from the serenity of the mountains in the distance. The incandescent, transparent blazes at the center of the orb billow out in all directions, casting a luminosity in light-yellow, golden-yellow, and golden-red. This vehement radiation progresses quietly, without calling out or singing.

Everything happens in the sacred quietness.

Quietly burning, quietly bursting;

Quietly moving, quietly sublimating.

The great desert, in deep and solemn quietness, greets the emergence of the great orb of life. Following the emergence of the great orb of life, everything grows up in quietness as well. Following the emergence of its brightness, vehemence, magnificence, and brilliance, everything rises.

This is the moment — the only moment — when I hear the rumbling of life, rumbling for the celebration of the unparalleled rising and sublimating. The rumbling is so intense and enormous that it preponderates any clamor in the terrestrial world and any roaring thunder in the celestial world...

Gold Rush

Are we still in the age of the gold rush?

The vast stretch of sand on the beach is scrawled with the scurrying footprints of gold diggers who, generation after generation, came here with their unquenched desire for fortune and used their ignorant blood and tears to have filled the upstream regions and even the sources of many rivers to the brim with barbarous stories.

I cannot help thinking of the painful history of a certain country's westward development.

Are we still in the age of the gold rush?

The heat waves of the contemporary gold rush swamp the headlines of west China. The frantic yelling and bustling of the equally frantic gold rushers cause the long undisturbed and peaceful horizon of the plateau to quiver sadly. What a release from the suppression of the long-accumulated poverty!

This wakens a nation and makes it long for the banishment of poverty.

Is the thick earth that has staged our history and reality deposited with the gold that will lead us to prosperity and strength or the gold that will give us the unshakable determination for prosperity and strength?

We always need the gold of such determination.

So who is the real gold-digger during this age of gold rush?

Tales Nurtured by Mountain and River

That hilltop is transformed from a fierce downhill tiger, ready to leap onto the evils that have snuck into the terrestrial world. That jutting crag is transformed from an eagle captured and tied there by a great immortal who chanced to see it trying to fly away after preying on the chickens, ducks, rabbits, and even toddlers in the village at the foot of the mountain. And there are that deep cave with spiritual rainbow clouds floating at its opening, that evergreen forest with the little singing creek meandering through it, and that dark-green gully with its unknown source and the thick-moss-covered, peculiar, craggy rocks on which the mountain god has sat. There are even the mystic calls, sometimes coarse and sometimes gentle, from an elf perched deep down in the dark gully...

Like trees in a forest, the tales here are ubiquitous. Is it the mountains and waters here that have nurtured these tales or, vice versa, the tales that have enlivened the mountains and waters?

And those humans who work in this story-laden place, separated from modern society — they have even become part of the tales.

Visitors envy the natives for their luck in having the mountains and waters, the stories and tales, and most importantly the serenity, while the natives themselves want to break through the bond of the antiquated stories and the miseries of mountainous poverty...

Mountains, Rivers, and Others

The landscape — the mountains and rivers with their jade-green and emerald-green colors, their unusual and graceful textures, and their winding and meandering lines — becomes the source of inspiration for the painter's brush and rendered in artistic scenes that intoxicate and appeal to viewers. (I want to distinguish between the landscape that has come out of the paintings and the landscape that has gone into the paintings, because a completely natural landscape free of the revelation and illusion of the soul possesses an eternal purity.)

The awesomeness of the unusually shaped crags and the haughtiness of the hovering eagles; the ethereality of the flying clouds and the boundlessness and height of the azure sky; the interlaced placement of dark green and emerald green of the lush forest; the tranquility in which even the breeze is careful not to startle with its nimble footsteps; the carefree and light-hearted twittering of the birds skipping on boughs and between leaves; the blur of the meandering mountains in the distance and the lingering imagination kindled by the undulating and continuing mountain ridges; and the mountain streams, the chain bridges, the hamlets, the quiet, rustic, and quaint kitchen smoke...

And the poetic lines that I have adventitiously plucked from or that are lost in the sacredness of the mountains and rivers — the poetic lines that have been green-tinged by the forests, washed bright by the streams, and tempered into steel by the depth of pain and the weight of worry...

In this way, finally, the modern life exquisitely constructed over the years has crumbled, while the new-born belief established over the ruins is pregnant with the sacredness of the mountains and rivers as well as their style and exquisite charm. A burgeoning, bright yellow message signifies to me that all the glories and humiliations are transient and will eventually turn into green leaves, to be assimilated into the eternity of the mountains and rivers.

The Rainy Season

◎ *Hei Hai*[1]

In Japan, when raindrops brush over my skin, they give me a feeling of pure chilliness. This often makes me feel that a Japanese summer is like moonshine at night — creating a sense of autumnal solitude.

One after another, the apartments nearby put out more "For Rent" signs, making them look very much like the calendar hanging on the wall of my room. Turning a few more pages of this calendar, I believe the rainy season should be over. But right at this moment, you told me that you would be taking a long journey, for a few days, to a place as far away as the other side of the ocean.

We had the biggest rain of the season on the day you told me this news. I can still clearly recall that you walked on sunshine into my room, but no sooner had you mentioned your trip than the rain abruptly started pouring down. My little wooden cottage, with you and me in it, was then submerged in grey. Because of the grey suit you wore, you simply blended into the color — or rather, you became a living soul manifested by the color. I had a feeling that the Japanese rainy season seeped out of the grayness and out of your grey suit as well. Pillowing my head on your grey suit, I now describe to you the grey scenery in my heart.

Probably affected by my grey mood and evoked by the solitude of a rainy day, you said that the rainy season in Japan this year was particularly long. It is usually quite warm at this time of the year.

What you said, I am afraid, is true.

But I was once again surprised by your calmness. Not everyone is

---

① Hei Hai (Geng Renqiu, 1963-), contemporary woman writer.

endowed by fate with an ability to capture a feeling inherent in the objective world, but, for the short period of time I have lived up to now, feelings well up in me as frequently as dreams do. Because they are feelings, they are not real. Quite a while ago, I discovered that I have a gloomy mentality caused by a sense of loss, because, apart from the cliché or platitude of the Anicca and Illusion of Life, I do not possess any supernatural power to understand nature and life. Quite a few times, whatever I have perceived of nature and life directly returns me to a sorrowful state — the type of feeling that has existed since ancient times. This is the very reason that my illness differs from those of most others. Mine is a depression, or an everlasting feeling of melancholy. I am always being haunted by a continuous, grey-colored, dreamlike feeling.

You, a placid person, are completely different from me. You are always so tranquil. A serious event, in my opinion, is nothing more than a natural happening in yours. Since the day I met you long ago, I have never seen you lost in emotion, but instead, I often hear you say these few words: "That's the way it is. It doesn't affect anything." Your pragmatic, calm personality always wakes me up when I am dreaming. I often wonder if your naturally peaceful demeanor and your urbane and resilient temperament are something transcendental that one can obtain only after going through mental and spiritual afflictions.

I have no idea if your peace of mind is indeed a natural reflection of the religious height that you have reached, just as I have no idea, either, if being in a state of uncertain wandering is a happiness to life or not. But what is certain is that, staying close to you, your placid disposition has gradually brought me closer to a transcendental tranquility and a state of nirvana, thereby curing my depression, because you always enlighten me with your feeling through actual events: consider the existence of nature and life a happiness to mankind, acknowledge temporal matters, and believe Anicca and Anitya as human destiny. If your peace of mind is indeed a natural reflection of the religious height you have reached, what you reveal to me, perhaps unwittingly, is that your peaceful temperament connotes the rich shine of nature.

This is how I had the luck to get close to you, the embodiment of peacefulness, and how my troubled heart was cured. It was just as if you suddenly caught my attention and instantly brought peace to my heart at a time when I was floundering through depression. By now, you have been away for quite a few days. If this had happened in the past, I would have felt lonely and dejected. But things are different now. This time, I feel that you are still in the city, right by me, and I can hear you if I pick up the phone or touch your body if I reach out my hand. Loneliness is no longer evoked by the lack of people around me, but by the lack of a person to miss in my heart. Temporal matters exist — and will forever exist — with life. For humans, to live is to live. Life is not driven by any will. Anicca is the sparkling of life.

Can we say that the most restless thing is the human soul? If we can say so, then the antithesis of a most restless soul is a state of complete peacefulness. Now I possess this antithesis, which is you. After you are gone, this world, to me, has narrowed down to just one person — and that is you.

Although it is still raining, the large spread of greyness in the dark has already snuck away. This is how I have discovered my heart, and thinking that it is your quiet personality that has actuated my discovery, I feel a consolation to relieve my depression and a sense of affectionate warmth.

You are the peace, quietly accompanying me, in the rainy season.

Summer and Autumn

◎ *Si Qing*[1]

From the sky come echoing serious and solemn voices that drown out the whistle of winds rolling through pinewoods and the lapping of waves sweeping the sandy beaches. Those voices come from a conversation between two members of nature — Summer and Autumn.

Summer: Oh, my friend, we have known each other for so long, but why do we always resent each other and not get along well? Don't you know me? I am Summer, who unveils his youthful appearance and exercises his robust body under the vast, bright universe; like the forever-swaying sea, chambered in my bosom is throbbing vitality; my feelings are so passionate that my heart is like the nucleons of the sun... Am I not beautiful? Don't you like me?

Autumn: Ha, my brother, you are beautiful and I do like you, but I also deeply pity those poor terrestrial dwellers, when your direct sunshine bakes the earth so that the air is filled with thermo-molecules, when those living in tight rooms without enough space cannot ease the suffering caused by your thermal radiation penetrating their thin roofs, when people can only use their willpower to protect themselves from your scorching torment, when...

Summer: Alas, my sentimental Autumn, you have a maudlin temperament. Aren't you talking about heat? That is exactly my merit — I am proud to be able to convey to the terrestrial world this first element of life.

Autumn: My dear brother, I admire your enthusiasm, but are you

---

[1] Si Qing, contemporary writer.

aware that you often go too far in the expression of your vehemence, which is only your one-sided wishful thinking...

Summer: My gloomy Autumn, you are full of recondite ideas and unknown thoughts. Your eyes flash chilly lights. You must be an abandoned child of warmth, or you must be jealous of me.

Autumn: No, my brother, I'm not jealous of you. Look, I have my beauty, too: During the daytime, I am balmily bright, clear, and high, naturally influencing people to be open-hearted and broad-minded; at night, I offer bright moonlight and breezy air, provoking people into profound thinking. I like to probe, seek, and search along the way of thinking. In autumn, I let everything ripen for humans to reap...

Summer: Hold up right there, my friend. Are you talking about ripeness? But without growth, where would ripeness come from? And I am the very season for growth! Winter freezes the surface of the earth; Spring just spreads seeds in the earth; and you, Autumn, enjoy the growing results at the time of ripening. But I am the only one that helps the growing to grow.

Autumn: Yes, my dear brother, but your vehemence, forthrightness, and single-mindedness are exactly where your misfortune lies. Have you ever thought that your "growth" symbolizes a primitive, brutal force that is apt to go wild? Have you ever noticed that your "growth" is just the wanton sprawling of life in nature, without any consideration of eugenics? Don't you know that in your chest, fresh flowers and sweet fruits have to flounder through the weeds and darnels for a bit of nutrition they need?

Summer: My respectable friend, are you in tears? Are you crying? What you have said shocks me. How can you blame me for this?

Autumn: Oh, yes, my brother, it looks like I am a little less enthusiastic, but my tempered warmth is hidden in my heart, like hot blood being cooled down and congealed.

Summer: Looking at you, I suddenly feel like I am looking at someone new. I now see something new in you and I am amazed by it... My respectable older brother, just a minute ago, I caught sight of your eyes glowing with enthusiasm. What a beautiful pair of eyes they were! What stately and lofty charm they convey, along with the facial expression that reveals your mature thinking! Oh, my supreme God, why don't you also bestow the same beauty on me?

Autumn: Thank you, brother, but you will have eyes like mine later, just as I had eyes like yours before. Although we were born with our respective merits and demerits, we cannot force ourselves to be one another. But in fact, we were also born a pair, related to each other, and inseparable from each other. Without growth, what would warrant ripeness? Without ripeness, what would secure the birth of new life?

From the sky, the serious and solemn voices are fading away. The winds are rolling in the pinewoods, whistling aloud; the waves are sweeping on and off the sandy beaches, lapping aloud. The dark mountain crags look up into the horizon, as if murmuring: Until next year, until next year!

Mother

◎ *Wei Hong*[1]

All for My Child

You are hospitalized the day I am released from the hospital. As is the case with me, fate has decided that something unexpected will always happen to you.

I look in the direction of the hospital — nobody knows how I feel. He doesn't know it, either. He is a man anyway, and no man can ever be a mother.

I now remember a tree that I like very much. Its fruits ripen only when winter is about to come. It is called Ginkgo and is also nicknamed Mother of All Trees because its fluffy sunlight-absorbing limbs and soft succulent trunk are good for grafting all trees.

Once, in winter, I looked up at the tree, crying, because I had learned what was called "giving" — to give always ends up in tragedy, although it always looks beautiful.

My grafting has worked for you, my child.

You have a good name: Summer Tree.

You are the biggest "giving" I have ever done in my life. My thirty-year-old life is already beginning to dry up. The summer rain is like a woman's tears, which, from today on, will nurture you. They contain the essence of life, the sacrifice of a woman, and my most passionate feeling. They will foster the spirit of your healthy body.

I look in the direction of the hospital — nothing can stop a mother's gaze. My dear three-day-old child, it is too early for you to go through

---

[1] Wei Hong (Li Weihong), contemporary woman writer.

pain. Besides, all you can do about the pain is to cry. But when the pain gets more intense, it will suppress your howling voice...

My child, what a profound beginning this is! Before you got sick, you had brought vigorous cries and charming smiles to me, your mother, and to this world as well.

Fatigue forces my eyelids to drop, but again I clench my teeth to hold myself up, for my child needs this gaze. For you, I can give up anything...

A Breeze Is Whispering

I put down my child on a paved path bathed in sunshine and covered in green ivy. Standing in the breeze, he looks like a small green tree sprouting with leaves. Sunbeams sway on the ground like gay snow flurries, while the breeze flutters his clothes. As he has lost one of his shoes, he stands in the sunshine and amid the green ivy with one foot in a shoe and the other bare. In a captivated tone, I call out his name. A breeze is whispering, sending from the recess of the nearby wood a natural and mysterious sound over and then far away. He tries to remain in a standing position, because he has felt the existence of his life. As he holds my two hands tightly, a sense of curiosity and thrill for life flashes in his eyes. The breeze ruffles his thin, never-trimmed lanugo hair. With his anxious eyes, he watches the world gradually unfolding in front of him and watches his dear mother. Firmly grasping my hands with his little ones, he uses every effort to remain standing.

Tightly holding his hands, my eyes are wet with tears as a sense of empathy for life runs through my heart. I look into his eyes with all the truth that has remained intact in me, after thirty years of mental and physical abrasion. In this way, I am telling him that this is the very life, the very power of life, and the very vitality of life; telling him that I am sending into his life the information of my life, which he can receive and understand even without the help of language; telling him that this sunlight is for the radiance of life, and starting today, he is also entitled to the radiance; telling him that he needn't be afraid, because his mother will never let go of him when he is in need of her, in need of dependence, or in need of strength...

The breeze is puffing.

He tries to remain standing. Cast onto the ground is a small, delicate, needy, but throbbing shadow.

There Is a Black Cloud over the Horizon

Whoosh — whoosh —

While imitating the sound of wind, you pattern your movements after the wind, with your small dimpled hands. Your babyish gesticulations look adorable and childish.

Whoosh — whoosh — Here comes the real wind.

Where there is wind, there will be clouds; where there are clouds, there will be rain. Pointing to a black cloud over the horizon, I explain the phenomenon to you.

Following your mother's pointing finger, you look into the far distance with your little eyes. High above the Customs House's bell tower on the other side of the sky, the wind is gathering, rolling, and driving over here massive clouds in yellow, grey, and dark colors. You now see those clouds and the changes in those clouds against the base color of the sky. You are fascinated by the mystery and by the scary phenomenon as well. Your baby boy's eyes are now completely riveted to that part of the sky.

Then, here comes the chiming of the bell of the Customs House, reverberating between the sky and the darkening clouds.

Suddenly seized by a sense of regret, I want to cover your eyes with my hands. Over there in the sky, the clouds are still gathering and rolling, and their yellow and grey colors are deepening.

These were the same weather conditions as when I left my hometown and my mother.

Back then, at the end of my childhood, I inadvertently glanced at the far side of the sky. Back then, the blue vault of heaven was arched, and the horizon was permeated with river-like ground-vapor of the spring. I tried to walk there and had gone quite a distance, but no matter how far I went and how exhausted I got, I couldn't reach that horizon, although it seemed within the reach of my extended hand. And that was the very moment when an urge to grow up sprang up in me. I thought once I grew up, I would be able to walk there.

Eventually, I left my mother and started to go toward the horizon. I outgrew my senile mother in shape, found for myself a more intimate life-long companion, made my own family, and now I have you — the continuation of my life. My mother nurtured me with her breast milk, but now that I am grown up, I rarely think of or take care of her. For so many years, I have found it hard to face this reality, because I am afraid that my sense of guilt in this will hurt the rest of the mothers in the world; I would rather that this guilty feeling of mine be a result of a sensitive response or an unnecessary worry of my long literary life. Countless times, I have blamed myself for negligence, denied it, and tried to rectify it, but each time, human expedience prevails and shocks me.

Now I have you, child. You have turned me into a real mother. I love you with more than what a mother can give. Although I know what type of mistake I have made by pointing out to you those clouds over the horizon, I am so sentimentally touched by the love that still sparkles in my nature. I know you will grow up, and when you do, you will know the relationship between this wind, the clouds, and the rain, and will know the relationship between karma and rebirth. But at the same time, I am afraid of your growing up — afraid that you will, on a windy or clear day, pack up and leave to go on with your own journey.

The moment when you no longer need your mother may be precisely the moment when she needs you most.

That side of the sky is now covered with dark clouds, my child.

The Best Song

You don't know how to sing yet. Everything is a first try for you. I have taught you a very simple but the most life-related song I made up myself.

Dad is good. Mom is good. The sun is good. The little tree is good.

In your babbling voice, you sing:

197

Da goo... Mo goo...

Although you do not know how to sing the rest of it yet, Father and Mother are already very happy with your singing. They think it the sweetest song they have ever heard. They sit around you. While Mother holds you on her lap, tapping out the beat for you, Father, without a word, fixes his eyes on this most heart-warming picture in the world until his cigarette burns his finger.

Again and again, you sing the song in a jumbled manner.

When you wake up in the morning, you have thoroughly wet the bed, and then you roll up to crawl to the window, babbling the song: "Da goo... Mo goo ..."

Again and again, you sing it complacently.

As I wring out the bed sheet, I suddenly notice that you can not only sing "Da goo... Mo goo...," but also two new lines in addition to the song, which your father and mother cannot figure out: "Ei goo..., Sis goo..."

Child, my less-than-a-year-old child, is this your own lyric substitution? Is this your first creation? Is this a choice you have made instinctively?

I look at you, surprised and perplexed.

Again and again, you babble.

Perhaps because of the closer genetic relationship, Father has cracked your lyric codes. He has found the link between the song and your eyes that look at the doll in a skirt, because Mother once told you that the doll is your sister, and when people ask you who Xiao Shu (Little Tree) is, you point at your own nose and say, "It's me."

Because you cannot make it out clearly, you have changed "Dad is good" and "Mother is good" to "Da goo" and "Mo goo", and "I am good" and "Sister is good" to "Ei goo" and "Sis goo."

"Da goo, Mo goo, Ei goo, Sis goo," you babble on and on freely, naturally, and happily. You may not be a genius in creativity or in the understanding of human nature, but you have made up the best song I have ever heard!

Da goo, Mo goo, Ei goo, Sis goo.

Protective Shell

I hold you in my arms, my child, letting your body that has just left mine come closer to me again. Let me give you all my heart, my little baby son. If all this world can give you is danger or pain, then I would rather still carry you in me than let you out.

It is already dark in this outside world. The trees and the earth are no longer pure and clean.

For a long time, I haven't heard you cry.

My little baby son, when you tried to climb with your feet, you didn't know you should hold onto something with your hands. So you fell out of the stroller heavily. What met you was not a mother's soft arm, but the hard concrete ground you didn't even know the name of yet.

Before you know what danger is or how to resort to the simple correlation principle, this world has already forced the unknown onto you. My son, my little baby son, your mother closes her eyes so that she doesn't see what has happened. She hates that her vision is limited so that she cannot protect you all the time. Child, you are shedding blood. The blood has got into my tears and is curdled with them as it flashes purple light.

My little baby son.

Please cry out and raise your finger to tell Mother where the light is, where the nursing bottle is, and where your mother is...

Mother does not want you to break any part of yourself. Anyone who has damaged his or her facial features or limbs is called handicapped; anyone who has damaged his or her brain is no longer considered a human... My son, my little baby son, please tell Mother where the light is that can light you, where the nursing bottle is that can feed you...

Mother — your mother is here.

Mother is your protective shell. If you fall, it should hurt your mother before it does you, my little baby son.

What's Behind Love

Here comes night again, when a boundless sea of darkness rushes into your view. Night shrouds whatever the lights fail to illuminate, shrouds your mother, who is now in a city residence very far away from you, and shrouds the asphalt road, the balcony, the stroller, and many other items unknown to you.

Night also shrouds your mother's love, preventing you from hearing her voice or seeing her face. But no matter how far apart we are, Mother can always hear you when you wake up and fail to find her.

For countless times, I go through your pictures, to see how a sprout of a life grows into different poses of a sapling, letting the pictures affect my mood and prompt me to act, letting my bitter smile bloom into a carefree smile.

Aged people always see their pasts through their children, and spring always brings hope and life to everything.

Although I always know you are another me and you are the most important and beloved part of my life, I always feel there is something more behind my ardent love.

Exhausted as I am, I continue watching you. You lie in my arms, one hand grabbing my corsage. Every night, how I wish you would fall asleep soon! Diapers, clothes, messy floor — all call for my attention, and that dust-covered unfinished women-writing also awaits me, and many grievances in life and unexpressed wishes also urge me to sit down for a moment and think about them. I lightly let your hand go and get off the bed, but even though I have been very careful, you wake up, and you then tighten your grip on my corsage. Then, I let your hand go and get off the bed again, and you tighten your grip again. This silent cycle has recently formed your habit of staying wide awake instead of falling asleep. You fall asleep only when I give up everything else, lie next to you, wipe the tears off your face, and stroke your lanugo hair; only then can you peacefully fall asleep.

Aren't love and feeling shown through nothing more than giving, protecting, providing warmth, and offering safety? Stroking your light-yellow lanugo hair, I begin to realize a cruel reality: You and I — a child and his mother — are fighting for something.

I am not willing to give myself up completely!

I am vying with you for something. Although I love you the most, behind this ultimate love hides my ego, and although this ego wears a mask of love and sheds tears of love, it is characterized by the unerasable darkness of deprival. And each deprival in the cycle ends up in your failure, for I am stronger than you are.

But every time that I am thus prompted to think that you will be deprived like this by more people and by this world to your last bit, I am in an agony of heartbreak. My child, the one who is not yet supposed to know all this, you will be forced to learn how to deprive others; you will, as I do, see with your own eyes a black hand of survival-driven selfishness behind every beautiful veil.

My child, I have deprived you of what you need because this world is born cruel, faulty, and incomplete. Someday, maybe, this world may force you to deprive me — your weeping mother...

The First Sigh

I do not have the courage to let my eyes linger on your picture any more. I flip it over and put it back in the photo album. Child, what has brought this blankness and grief into your nine-month-old eyes? Your extended hands halt in the air as if you know you cannot reach what you want. Your maternal grandma is holding you. Have you already felt that things there differ from those here? And the hands that hold you are not Mother's? Is it that the person more familiar and dearer to you has disappeared after waving her hand to you? Is it that you have woken to find yourself in a strange — hence colder and lonelier — place? What your extended hand has grabbed is but an aged woman's lapel.

My baby, your hand lingers there, and your eyes are filled with the blankness and grief that the change of environment and the puzzle about the change have brought about.

You have already felt the absence, the change, and the discomfort this change has brought about. Only I, the one who has given you life and who once shared the same physical body with you, can perceive what is revealed in your eyes.

Now I remember what you have gone through over the past nine months.

Your lanugo hair had been completely shaved off, and metal needles were inserted into your blood veins under your skin which had been exposed in the air for only three days. You kept crying until your voice ran out; you kept kicking until the skin on your little feet was abraded. Even this couldn't help release your pain. You were too weak to handle the pain. The disease, together with the summer climate, has racked you with bone-deep pain.

Rolling your little, red, swollen, tender body while cleaning it, I was at a loss as to what to do to assuage you and save you, wishing I was able to suffer for you. When we were back home from the hospital, you cried so much that you were too tired to burst into tears again. Lying down there, pain sank from your eyes down into your newborn soul.

You play by yourself. When you are tired, you go to sleep yourself. When you want to pee, you nudge your mother, once, twice, three times, until she is aware.

You no longer cry over many things that would cause other children your age to cry, or you just give a few light sobs over them. Once, while Mother was busy with something, she heard you sigh for the first time.

My child, my good child, many a mother has said that you are smart and mature, but, my child, your mother would rather you be like other children — naughty and immature.

The blankness and grief afloat in your eyes are your mother's tearful clouds that beckon me to come to get you! I am coming over to get you, my child.

Love, only love, is the sun that casts your mother's image into your view so that you will not extend your nine-month-old hand without reaching her.

I Am Your Mother

I look at you quietly and peacefully. Secluded, clean, and cozy — for those caring for each other — this is a place where rose branches have woven together to form a beautiful plant wall, old locust trees have spread out a large canopy, pedestrian footsteps can be heard but the pedestrians are not seen, and the wind blurs everything in sight.

I look at you quietly and peacefully — a mother's gaze fixes on you like golden sunshine streaming around the bower of a tree. A woman without such a gaze is not a complete woman. I lean against the rose wall, lost in a picture, a feeling, and a mood. I am so tranquil that I become stagnant. Time slips by, but I am still lost in my gaze, frozen in this wholehearted concentration that has disinterested me from anything but life.

Only you, my child, can put me in such a state.

Motherhood glorifies and sanctifies a woman, and becomes an inviolate image of the woman herself. In their true nature, mothers provide the origin of all humans' — including men's — lives, and they make concrete contributions to the maintenance of human dignity and the continuation of human life. Mothers are an asset to mankind. A woman who is a mother is dauntless enough to expose her breast to feed her child, while a woman who is not a mother is not so dauntless, proud, and confidant enough to do so.

I look at you, my child, devoting to you my gaze, my love, and the last minute available to me. I will nurture you with my love for your entire life. Now I have to tell you that I have to go. Having to leave you again for that distant city makes me feel that the sky is split in two, but I have no choice. This is life.

I like to watch you like this, hear you calling "mom" and seeing you again and again toddle into my arms and then toddle away.

I need you to need me.

The feeling of being needed is sometimes as uncontainable as the feeling of being loved. This is not a mere display of power, but rather the defense of a position — a way to signify love.

A young mother once told me in tears, "Because of my broken marriage, I have wanted to die quite a few times. If someday I do, I would first choke my child to death..." I didn't know at that time what she really meant and what a cruel method she was planning in defending her irreplaceable position as a mother. I thought she was a selfish mother.

But later, through what I have gone through, day and night as a mother, I have finally come to understand her mind — come to understand how desperately she loved her child and why "*mu-qin*", the two Chinese characters for "mother", must be written together.

To live is for love, and to die is also for love, if not more!

The Full Nighttime Is Yours

◎ *Mao Shi'an*[1]

The hustle and bustle of the day has gone away, as the last wisp of glowing cloud fades with the sunset; the din of social activities and the seemingly never-ending chores have also ebbed away as Venus starts to glitter. As the night gradually falls, you take off your "daytime mask" and slowly let out your true self.

Sitting in front of the desk, with your snow-white sheets of paper in the lamplight and your middle-aged face in the shade, you search in your mind for the ultimate meaning for living, life, and mankind — everything. Like a pilgrim trudging on a sea-like vast desert, you do not know how far away you are from that spiritual shrine, but you know where to head to find it. During this extensive night, you are using words to set up a conceptual and imaginary world upon all things existing. You sit there, with your assiduous and indomitable soul, trying to perceive the vitality of great nature, to merge your life into the vast star-strewn sky, to let the breeze caress your thoughtful mind. Like a northern wolf, you let your thoughts wander on a spiritual path and explore your soul again and again. Every word or every sentence, the result of brain-wracking effort, comes from the inner recesses of your soul.

The quiet night-world activates and enlivens your mind to its fullest capacity. This is just one of those countless creative nights, and you do not know how many more you will have in the future. You feel grateful to God for the nights he has created.

Lights studding the delineated dark buildings in the distance begin to

---

① Mao Shi'an (1948-　), famous literary critic, vice president of China Literary and Art Critics Association.

go off. One after another, they look like pairs upon pairs of eyes starting to close — a city also needs sleep. Gradually, the night falls quiet — very quiet, like a millennium-old water well on a remote, thickly forested mountain, sequestered, deep, dusky, and mysterious — unfathomably mysterious.

Now your mind turns to an ordinary woman, whose familiar face is remote yet gracious, blurred yet vivid. Beset by early senility, she had grey hair that fluttered in the wind coming through the north window, and her grievous and wishful eyes were fixed on the end of the residential area. It was like going through a purgatorial torture for her every time her child was late in returning home during those years of turmoil. You will miss her myriad times during your long, sleepless nights and remember her senile life. Like a prematurely extinct comet, all her life value lies in that moment of brilliant sparkles. Her simple life shows you that there is something in this world that money, lies, power, and fame cannot replace. One's value is not something attached, but is innate — the profound love carried in his or her heart. And such is the love your mother carried.

During the daytime, you live in the vanity of other people; only at night do you live your own solitary and sequestered life. From the deep end of the residential area comes a dog's gentle barking — keeping pets is now fashionable among the newly rich — which instead quiets and deepens the night even more, making it like a bottomless, dark tunnel. Standing at the window, you listen with your soul. You hear your heart still throbbing, like that of a young man.

To get away from the noisy tourists, you once quietly sat alone by the secluded, cold, limpid, and emerald-like lake in Jiuzhaigou, a natural scenic spot — for a spacious valley can contain all scenes, but only a tranquil heart can perceive the beauty of and feel the warmth of Mother Nature. The night before, the sky had been laden with glittering jade shards of snowflakes, but now, at this moment, the bright sun hung high up. From a corner, you took a view full of jade-green trees and graceful boughs. "Flop, flop!" Large, thick lumps of snow, as white as if they were transparent, thumped down from the branches of pine trees, producing a heavenly sound. That was the breath of the great earth, and therefore, only the sons of the earth could hear this divine manifestation of nature. Whether you encounter a blessing or a curse, an honor or a disgrace, a rise or a fall in your life, you will never forget that flopping sound of snow falling.

On such a sleepless night, which wraps around you as evergreen ivy does, you turn each of your tangled thoughts into fine words and sentences, through which you discover yourself: You are still ardent in feeling and young at heart. In my opinion, the Creator's initial purpose in making the night was for humans to enjoy their poetic tranquility and romantic mood, but on the contrary, modern people in this material-craving and profit-seeking age waste these nights in the indulgence of revelry, extravagance and racket — such an expensive waste!

But you treasure a full, sleepless nighttime, which is truly yours.

The Sluggish Wei River

◎ *Zhu Hong*[1]

Someday, the water in the Wei River will dry up. Every time I see the river, I cannot help thinking this way. This is not a curse, but a worry of my own.

The Wei River has never given me any sense of pleasure. Its hesitant flow, its murky, sandy color, and its tendency to butt up against and destroy its banks — all make me frown. Wherever it goes — whether to traverse the countryside, or to cross a city, or to weave through the farmlands laden with luxuriant crops and blinding sunlight — it always sneaks along. Its quiet, self-effacing demeanor creates an impression of somberness and horror.

The first time I saw the Wei River, I was taking a train from Xi'an to Baoji with my teacher and classmates for educational practice. We were laughing and singing all the way, until the river came into view. We abruptly stopped laughing and singing, and nearly all of us popped our heads out the windows to watch it. It was sometimes visible and sometimes not. We fell silent. It was so old and so all-encompassing that silence seemed the only adequate way to express our overwhelmed emotions.

The Wei River originates from the mountainous area in southern Gansu. After laboring through those barren wilds, it goes into the Central Shanxi Plain from Baoji, then merges into the Yellow River at Tongguan, and then recedes from the plain, its length totaling eight hundred and eighteen kilometers. When it approaches the Yellow River, it abruptly swamps the banks, spills over, expands to push further on both sides, and

---

[1] Zhu Hong (1960-), contemporary essayist.

floods a large stretch of land under its murky waves. One can see its true vastness only until it plunges into the Yellow River.

During its course, the Wei River absorbs the water from quite a number of tributaries. Otherwise, it wouldn't be able to form that final majestic force. When it pours into the Yellow River, it does indeed create a sense of imposing boldness and impact. That imposing boldness and impact come from its attitude of accepting all. On the south side, most of its tributaries come from the mountainous area of Qinling, and the famous ones are the Ba River, the Yu River, the Feng River, the Hei River, the Yuxian River, the Chishui River, the Luofu River, and the Qingjiang River; on the north side, most of its tributaries come from the Loess Plateau, and the most well-known are the Luo River, the Jing River, the Jinling River, and the Qishui River. Of these tributaries, the Jing River originates in Mount Liupan and joins the Wei River in the mountainous area of Gaoling, in Shanxi Province, after a long journey. Because in the history the Jing River contained less sand than the Wei River, after merging, each retained its own color for quite a long distance: one clear and the other turbid. Although they ran together, each kept its own color, hence the classical allusion "as distinct as the waters of Jing and Wei." But unfortunately, both the rivers now contain about the same amount of sand, and subsequently, those allusive scenes have disappeared. If we could clip out the Wei River and its tributaries from reality, we would have an image of a feather or a leaf system, as it flows and shimmers through the Central Shanxi Plain. In fact, it is the rush of the Wei River that has created and nurtured, with its numerous tributaries, the Central Shanxi Plain. A million years ago, our ancestors resided here, and back then the climate here was balmy and the land, beautiful and rich.

The earliest and oldest towns in China appeared by the banks of the Wei River, with Xianyang on its north side and Xi'an, its south. For quite a long time, the Wei area was a place of advanced civilization in China and even the world. The Tang Dynasty, the pride of the Chinese nation, for example, was established here. Its declining, however, led to a shift of the political center of the great country to the east. Such a shift is persistent, firm, and irreversible — there is no turning back, even if we stamp our feet on the ruins of old dynasty and cry for a comeback. Our ancestors left their large, tall tombs on both sides of the river. What they left with those tombs, however, was also a substantial culture, of which some are treasure and some, trash. The trash still stinks, even to this day, and I still bear the many wounds it has caused me. Xianyang and Xi'an are situated right by the sluggishly running Wei River. Despite the adornment of modern civilization, their ancient traces cannot be hidden in any means. Their antiquity was deeply rooted, and it oozes out from the cracks in the ground and the gaps between the clouds. The Feng River, skirting to the east of Xianyang, is where the ruins of the Western Zhou Dynasty were discovered — in its lower reaches. The sand in the Feng River, fine and white, is a good construction material, and when passing by, I often see farmers digging it up. The Ba River, frequently chanted about in classic poems, lies to the east of Xi'an and was originally named the Zi River. During the Spring and Autumn period, Duke Mu of Qin renamed it the Ba River and built a bridge over it to commemorate his admirable deed of establishing hegemony. Because the Ba River served as an important defensive line during those ancient warring periods, blood must have been spilt on it. The Tang was a prime dynasty in ancient China, when, in bidding farewell, relatives or friends would customarily walk to the Ba Bridge and snatch a willow twig to give it to the traveler, as a token of cherishing the memory. Our ancients had cultivated such a refined mental attitude, and I often longed for it. Soon after I picture in my mind the willows flanking both banks and a large spread of willow catkins flying, I feel that while humans absorb something new, they lose something old at the same time, and what they lose is often something beautiful.

One hundred eighty kilometers up the Wei River, after passing Xi'an and Xianyang, is another city — Baoji, called Chencang in ancient times, whose origin can be traced back to the Xia and Shang dynasties. In Baoji, however, the Wei River, I have always felt, takes a different posture as it enters the Central Shanxi Plain. Because the area west of Baoji is largely covered with hills, when the water of the Wei River goes through such a place, it, of course, meanders and weaves, hindered by something here and something there in its course. Upon entering Baoji, however, it meets an endless stretch of plain, which allows it more room to run on a more level and wider course. The State of Qin was once supposed to ship grain by vessel to the State of Jin, and Baoji was the starting port. Back then, the Wei River had a large flowing capacity. Riding its waves, boats could travel all the way to the Yellow River, across which was the State of Jin. In 656 B.C., Duke Mu of Qin married the daughter of Duke Xian of Jin, and this intimate relationship helped Jin obtain the support of Qin during its distressed years of drought and famine. At that time, Yong was the capital of Qin. Because it was situated to the south of today's Fengxiang, it was easy to access Baoji from there. After a few centuries' development, the State of Qin grew stronger and stronger before it began to expand to the east and moved its capital from Yong to Yueyang in Lintong. Here, it remained active for thirty-four years, before it moved again to Xianyang, where Qin fulfilled its wish to unite China. Qin's eastward movement all happened along the Wei River, for the land along this route was rich with resources and good for farming and herding.

The Wei River lacks a distinctive style, which does not pose any problem, because expecting it to have a style would be asking too much of it. The problem is, however, that it is so filthy. Its sandy color, in fact, covers up its filthiness. If it were born a limpid river, it could very well be one of the ugliest and filthiest rivers in the world. My soul shudders as if it had been struck by a thunderbolt for exposing the river like this, because I was born right on the plain which the river had formed and which still carries its water-washed texture. But the Wei River is indeed unclean and unsanitary. It is hypocritical to deny this. Many a human event is aggravated by hypocrisy. For this reason, I do not want to treat the river hypocritically. After all, it is an ancient river that has been soaked in history and reality. Treating it with sincerity is a way of respecting it.

Everywhere, in the cities of Baoji, Xianyang, and Xi'an, I have seen trucks carrying and dumping garbage into the Wei River. The garbage piled on its banks has a kaleidoscope of colors and shapes, with hordes upon hordes of unrestrained houseflies swarming up and down. In fact, apart from these cities, none of the many villages along the riverbanks make it easy for the Wei River. Every family dwelling near the river throws garbage into it. None of them has ever thought of this: We have only one Wei River for us, for our children, and for our grandchildren. Maybe someone has thought of this, but if the majority of the public does not share the same concern, the Wei River will still suffer. Those who do not love and protect their living environment, in my opinion, must have despicable and vile souls. In summer, under the scorching sun, the rising Wei water weaves along between the two banks, where wheat has just been reaped and corn and rice grow, and where the fields are so muggy and hot that even rabbits are reluctant to come out to look for food; in winter, the falling water is torn into rags by the protruding mud islets and lacerated into small streams, which are disconnected here and there, with the flow seeming to move very slowly, if not going completely stagnant. The suddenly widened river beaches look empty and cheerless. Shrouded under the dark grey sky, both the urban and rural areas remain silent. On a sunny day, the quiet beaches will see lovers, prostitutes, and loners sneaking around. The wind will suddenly sweep over these people, but they just ignore it. Where the beaches are torn apart, they are torn apart; where the beaches are level, they are level — there is no sense of integrity, but everywhere there are the bruises left by the waves of the Wei River.

I have long been thinking of visiting some of those families residing by the Wei River. As simple as it may look, I have never taken the journey. But many times, I have stood on the river beach, watching those villages: They are always silent. The towering poplars, locusts, and other trees huddle so densely together that they almost shroud the bungalows and buildings of various heights. There seems no human activity in those villages, but only the sporadic rooster crows or dog barks that drift over the river into the far distance. I do not know how they spend the dark nights. I do not know when they started to live there, if they originated there or migrated there — none of these things do I know. I do not, of course, know, either, what they think when they see the monotonous rising and falling of the sun and the moon. And if they like it there.

A Dusk of My Own

◎ *Xu Yunqian*[1]

In an aimless dusk, I wander alone on a street, merging into the vastness of nature and the anxiety of humans, and picturing myself as a detached, thin cloud transcending the clamor and crowds of the terrestrial world. Like an apparition, I silently and invisibly weave through the stream of pedestrians.

"So many people are blindly following the footsteps of others, seeking something." Those pedestrians rushing past me remind me of that song, and that illogical song, in turn, often reminds me of them, too. They seem to follow no order, yet there is an order; they look anxious, yet enriched; they have no time to think about what they are after, yet they have all broken through the confines of daytime to rush into this scene: one door, one lamp, and one person — the simple originality of life which is often acclaimed by poets, abstracted by philosophers, and sentimentalized by women.

The sun has pulled back its last beam in the west. Under the vaulted sky, we swarm like schools of fish in the darkness of the deep ocean, closely bound to each other; like fishing-boat lamps winking along the riverside, the lights in the stores flanking the streets give us a sense of warmth and closeness. Dusk is a touching moment: The beaming face of a baby nestling in his or her mother's arms, a family dining table placed at the roadside, a piece of saxophone music drifting from an amplifier — all soak a person's heart with gentleness and warmth and provoke a gratitude for life and an urge of returning something to life.

---

① Xu Yunqian, contemporary woman writer and editor.

Dusk is also a melancholic moment. When I was a child, I learned to read a children's revolutionary lyric from a Chinese language textbook. I can only remember the first two lines now: "Over the horizon a rosy cloud glows; the feedlot now has Fang and Hua as workers." These two idyllic lines somehow gave me an indescribable feeling of melancholy. Back then, I was unable to express such a feeling with words, but could only read this seemingly pretty idyll again and again, and the more I read it, the more depressed I felt. It is not that the teacher back then misdirected or damaged my aesthetic appreciation, but that the simple lyric lines inflamed my imagination of dusk. I see with my mind's eye a waning scene of melancholic beauty, which I was not aware of at that time, but from a pure subconscious level — feeling exists before it is filtered through language or images. Even to this day, I am not yet able to express the rich feeling I have when bathing in the dusk. Dusk, to me, is like a sad movie. I want to soak my heart and soul in it, but at the same time, I fear that I may be trapped in it too deeply to be able to climb out of it. This is still an inadequate way of expressing it, I am afraid, for many of my gushing sensations about dusk often sneak away like undercurrents.

Late autumn dusk enchants and perplexes me the most. The melancholic charms of the two — not just one — waning scenes agitate your heart as you stand amid the west wind and the falling leaves. All the feelings that you have suggest "rush and rush". In the late autumn dusk, pedestrians tend to quicken their pace, as if reaching home could ensure a peacefulness in their lives and an enjoyment of illumination forever. But I cannot help pushing my way to the front of the store counters with glowing lights, to buy a lot of food that I do not necessarily need, as if to fill my physical and psychological emptiness. When I was a child, at many a dusk, I stood alone on the balcony, waiting for my parents to return. Now I recall that that little girl, as she stood in the rustling autumn wind with a set of house keys hanging from her neck, for many times, was desperately scared by her own foreboding imagination. This indicates that memories sometimes deceive us, but those double melancholic charms, on the other hand, can serve most appropriately as an undeniably sentimental background.

Of course, not all dusks are that dolorous. I once wrote a very uplifting poem with railway tracks as its theme:

With smiles, three girls walk over,

Clad in three colors of spring —

White, blue, and pink,

And they stop where the sun sinks.

As I remember, that was the time when I was trying to release myself from the self-centeredness of mental imprisonment and throw myself into nature, into friends, into crowds, and even into dusk with a smile. My friends and I were walking back and forth on that hardly used railway track until we saw the sun slant to the other side of the sky. We wrote poems about the crazily bright-yellow rape-flowers around us — in fact, about ourselves: about women, their fates, and their sudden returns to happiness. That was almost like a fairytale at dusk — a fairytale that was like a scenic photo taken at the time of girlhood sealed in the deep recesses of her heart.

In this aimless dusk, I let myself go among the urban hustle and bustle, let my footsteps go, and let my thoughts go, reluctant to return home and unlock the darkness-filled room.

Enlightenment

◎ *Ai Yun*[1]

A perspicacious person resorts to his soul to sense the world and resorts to his body to feel the world. Once he reaches the pinnacle and the critical point in the course of the dual enlightenment of the spiritual and the physical, he will find everything instantaneously going crystal clear.

1. Spiritual Enlightenment

This type of enlightenment has more to do with the soul. It carries a sense of purity and sublimity and possesses a quality of religious piety and persistency.

To you, the spiritual enlighteners are saints, who position themselves on altars, who are solemn and unsmiling, who detach themselves from the terrestrial world and do not advocate life-related interests, who use their great willpower to pacify their passions even if those passions have once welled up inside their hearts, who contain their throbbing corporal lives to live by their beliefs which are their music, and who rack their brains and sacrifice their bodies every day in search of the final truth. These are the people who do not go beyond order for romantic escapism, but abide by classical principles in their behavior. Those who contain their desires to the minimum use the peripheral order as their final base, where they can settle into their metaphysical thinking. They do not let the fluttering of the flag of life distract them from the pure spiritual road into the terrestrial world.

---

[1] Ai Yun (Li Aiyun, 1957-), woman editor.

2. Physical Enlightenment

He who does not understand spiritual enlightenment possesses an uncultivated, ordinary or mortal body, which will not grow and blossom into a dreamy, brightly-colored orange bud.

But after his spirit is enlightened, his physical body longs for yet another awakening — that uncultivated land longs for a vernal rain to nurture it and for a pair of suntanned hands to plough it open with a hoe.

This is the enlightenment of the physical body.

You use your entire body to feel the world. This is the moment when your soul lingers in a half-asleep and half-awake state, although it is mostly slumbering. You always feel dazzled and mesmerized, and smell a thick fragrance.

And also, as if surrounded by various nether ghosts and demons, you feel their instigation, enticement, and guidance. But to your amazement, in the ghostly and demonic atmosphere, how come you also see scenes and images of exotic seasons? You see a large spread of brightly golden rape-flowers and a flock of wild rabbits dashing through a village in a vast open country at a time of vernal twilight; you also hear birds chirping before they leave the autumnal trees for migration... Your heart is filled with a primordial joy and the inspiration of being assimilated into nature. Invigorated and thrilled, you keep your dreamy eyes open while right at the moment, the luxuriant grass outside the window is ever more alive.

This is a day of discovery and boundary-breaking. Willing to be guided by the ghosts and demons, you follow them through the dark nether gate and then see May lilies, July lilacs, and October osmanthus coming up, all in brilliant, full bloom.

Now, you have forgotten all the missions, meanings, and historical appointments. You do not have a final goal, but only this wonderful feeling that permeates the air. You have forgotten all spiritual realities. You are carefree and indolent, reckless and unrestrained. And swimming in this free stream, you are often inundated with and suffocated by your quenchless desire.

The feeling of sublimating; the casting off of your old skin — you have talked about this feeling many times.

Thus, your physical body becomes sweet and fragrant.

This is physical enlightenment. Although such enlightenment is rough and faulty, you are fascinated by the thicker-than-blood wisdom pregnant in the primordial images. You believe that this time it is for real and irreversible, for it somehow has made you forget all those truths and meanings you have once heard of and experienced, and bathes you in the joy — the bodily joy that you can have for in life.

But you have indeed forgotten your genuine belief, because you are unable to abide by those eternal principles — you only live in the moment.

However, you are still fascinated by this physical enlightenment.

This world is characterized by an increasing level of freedom. You say: Let's build a heaven in the cottage — a heaven redolent of bean-pods and wheat, and thus that heaven comes into being in the terrestrial world.

But immediately following the emergence of the initial truth of physical enlightenment come many doubts and questions. Have you already reached the final stage of delivery? What does it matter if a life is lived for the purpose of living that life? Those questions you didn't have the time to brood about during those delirious days of life — they now set you to ponder aloud.

3. Questions Prompted by the Two Types of Enlightenment

After going through the dual parts of enlightenment, now come the days for questions.

Now that the eyesight of purity and bliss is cast far, far away from you, you are left alone again. This is the moment when time looks to you as clear as a precipitous cliff.

You begin to badger yourself. While you contemplate those old days, past events emerge. Anyone who has gone through such dual enlightenment will not waste time on common contemplation. Instead, he presses himself — for the innermost secret.

You now ask: Can anyone abide in eternity? Once you raise this question, you cannot contain your surging thoughts anymore. The question about eternity has at least two aspects. One: Your enjoyment of life, while it is available for such enjoyment, makes you forget the meaning of life and eternity. How do you explain this phenomenon? Two: While you enjoy every moment in your lifespan, have you betrayed your pledge to abide in eternity? And can you live for the purpose of living?

Now, by asking these questions you are trapped in the bitter torment of yourself.

Your thoughts tell you, in the meantime, that each type of enlightenment should complement the other. The spiritual enlightenment brews in your heart an awakening of life, because only this awakening, along with the kindling of the primordial images, can bring a timely spiritual rainfall which silently nurtures an exotic flower for the century. And in return, the physical enlightenment enriches and expands the spirit so that a significantly more intense longing and craving for the other side of the sea will well up in you. Thus, you turn yourself into a swimmer to reach the other side.

The Mighty Pass

◎ *Yang Guomin*[1]

Setting out from the city of Ge'ermu in Qinghai Province and then crossing the Lian-Bian Mountain Range, we have reached the city of Dunhuang in Gansu Province, from where we can head directly for Xinjiang Uyghur Autonomous Region, but we will sorely miss a meaningful experience if we do not visit the Jiayu Pass on our journey in west China.

Hailed as "the First Great Pass under Heaven", the Jiayu Pass boldly perches on the coordinate axis of Chinese history and culture, where it has developed a rich connotation. One cannot read Chinese history without studying the pass! But somehow, I am tenacious in my belief that this mighty pass is not necessarily the manifestation of a nation's sufficient confidence, but rather an indication of its diminishing mental strength. What lies shrouded and concealed in the spectral shadow of this towering, steep, and massive fortification is a helpless state of timidity and cowardice.

But still, we decide to go and take a look at the pass. Setting off from Dunhuang in the morning, we reach the city of Jiayu when it is already after three o'clock in the afternoon. We can very well continue our trip to the pass, but we would feel rushed in doing so, because we are not going there to tour a scenic spot, but to read an abstruse and recondite historical book, which requires composure and patience.

As if assisted by the god of climate, we come upon favorable weather. Shortly after noon, an abrupt, cooling gust of autumnal wind, with a few wisps of drizzle, has moderated the glaring sun that dominated the

---

[1] Yang Guomin (Gu Ming, 1957-), contemporary journalist and essayist.

morning. The temperature has immediately dropped four or five degrees, and a single day seems to span two seasons. We begin our trip to the Jiayu Pass the following morning, when the clouds clench together and sporadic raindrops fall, as if to create a sense of bleakness. As we arrive too early, the gate has not opened yet and we have to wander outside.

The Jiayu Pass is indeed extraordinary in its imposing appearance. Built on a small but widely stretching hill, with uplifting eaves, overlapping chambers and pavilions, and awesome battlements, it boasts an overbearing air that can tear apart winds and cut through clouds. The Great Wall, extending on both sides of the pass, snakes and ripples along into the distance, penetrating valleys and canyons and crawling along mountain ranges, like a pair of gigantic wings that rub and brush the clouds. Facing the Jiayu Pass is the Qilian Mountain Range, horizontally unfolding on the south with a long but narrow gorge in between. It indeed possesses an unusual formidableness against the perilous steepness so that "One guard can keep off ten thousand attackers".

The stationing of troops and establishment of military checkpoints at the Jiayu Pass can be traced back to the Han Dynasty. After the scourge of the large-scale wars that erupted toward the end of the Qin Dynasty, the Liu family took power and founded the Han Dynasty on the ruins of a war-ravaged China in the 3rd century BC. However, no matter how colossal and powerful the new dynasty looked, it was dwarfish and weak. By necessity, the Liu family was eager to retain its gains, shield itself from foreign military attacks and invasive raids, close its doors to recuperate and rehabilitate itself, and revitalize the spirit and dauntless will for its overdrawn and emaciated power. The earliest rudiments of the Jiayu Pass were the helpless expressions of an emperor's frailty. Shy as it may be, revealed against the rocky Gobi desert and wasteland, this frailty was explicitly exposed — so explicitly that it was as if a sharp bone poked out through ragged clothes. Of course, after the Liu family had fully developed its strength and spirit, this pass turned out to restrict the dynasty's swelling desire to seek hegemony. Like a hatched chicken pecking open its own protective shell, the heavily armed westward expeditionary force of the Han Dynasty, cloaked in rolling

221

smoke and dust, broke through this impeding pass, which had been built for the dynasty's protection, to carry forward the will of the dynasty's ruler into distant lands. Isn't the meaning of a pass clearly and fully illustrated here?

The historical progression later painted the Jiayu Pass with a more tragically stirring color! Soon after the great Ming Dynasty was established, Senior Crusader General Feng Sheng stationed his troops on the west side of the Yellow River. At first sight, he recognized the strategic importance of this bottleneck area — a militarily advantageous narrow junction. As the fort at the pass built during the Han Dynasty had long been buried under thick dust or simply had been so badly beaten by wind and sand that no single trace of it remained, they had to reconstruct the earthen fort on an even larger scale. Thus, a true heroic and majestic Jiayu Pass once again perched on the coordinate axis of the Chinese history. From the Imperial Inspector to the Minister of War, for as long as 130 years or more between the fifth year of Hongwu in the Ming Dynasty (1372) and the eighteenth year of Jiajing (1539), all had agreed to expand the pass in Jiayu and all had actually taken historically-attestable and important measures to facilitate the construction. They assembled civilian workers and forced labor from everywhere to construct the framework and to lay stones. An extravagant investment in time and expenses led to the creation of the wonder on this isolated hill in the great rocky desert — a great pass that amazed generations to come. They also strengthened the Great Wall on both sides of the pass to form a lock-like military position and thus created the sealed domain of a dynasty. But has this perilous terrain centered around a solid fort ever really kept away the raids of the fierce, iron-strong horses of the nomadic barbarians and the ravages of their bows and arrows? It is only a comfort to and a concealment of cowardice and timidity, I am afraid! Throughout the history, so many man-made heroic and perilous forts like this have collapsed under the iron heels and metal spears or became a ruin suitable for mourning only. What sadness it is that the sweat and blood of many a generation would result in but a few sighs and laments of men of letters!

The Jiayu Pass, at the starting point of the Great Wall, faces, across a great distance, the Shanhai Pass on the bank of the Bohai Sea. The land threading these two passes has witnessed the bright moon of the Qin and Han dynasties and the spring and autumn seasons of the Yuan and Ming periods, all of which unfolds against the northern wind a voluminous history book. And of this long history book, the Jiayu Pass forms the heavily and deeply meaningful preface. Some people compare the Great Wall to the ridgepole of our nation, but I have never concurred with that figurative image. Seen from the perspectives of time and space, if the construction of such a stupendous and complex project — able to weave together such a long historical time period — is the very manifestation of the creativity and cohesion of a nation, concealed in the extensive, bold, and sturdy structure of closed doors and locked forts are the cowardice and timidity of each and every monarch. The stronger and tougher a structure is, the weaker and more inane a mentality it reveals.

Amid the pitter-patter of the autumnal raindrops, the heavy iron gate of the Jiayu Pass slowly draws open. Climbing onto the roof of the battlements and wandering around on it, we see a plethora of ancient relics. Such well-preserved historical remains are obviously the result of the refurbishment by later generations for tourist purposes. Personally, I would rather see an unspoiled ruin with broken parapets or dilapidated walls, ramshackle buildings or tilted towers, and luxuriant wild grass with flapping pheasants or scurrying rabbits — ruins among which I can find concealed bitterness, stirring tragedy, dignified indignation, and grievous sorrow in history, for from the aesthetic perspective of history, vicissitudes and incompleteness are themselves a manifestation of depth and connotation while perfection is, on the contrary, an indication of shallowness and showiness.

Amid the pitter-patter of the autumnal raindrops, of the sparse tourists, a few couples of lovers, nestling together under their colorful umbrellas, are taking pictures before or in the corner of the attractive fort. Obviously, they are not here to read history, and therefore they have a carefree and detached attitude, as they do not have any mental pressure. Indeed, why should we weigh down our youths by putting the historical millstone on their hearts? Is it perfectly alright for them to come here just to enjoy a little touring flavor and, in the days to come, take the time to re-taste it? And by then, isn't the Jiayu Pass in those pictures going to be the witness of their visit to the west? We cannot be carefree, because we are sentimental, because we have knowingly or unknowingly tied the historical tow-rope to our hearts! Otherwise, why would a single visit to an ancient pass have provoked so much thought? What we need more is to construct our reality, wipe out the shadows of the mighty pass from our hearts without hesitation. I feel great release in thinking this way. By the time we board the train, bid farewell to the Jiayu Pass and continue our journey west, we are already engulfed in a longing for a bright future.

The Past Is a Boiled Silk Cocoon

◎ *Guo Cuihua*[1]

We have sunk deeper and deeper into reality.

In reality, no one would chase after the sun over immensely long distances like Kuafu, the sun chaser in Chinese mythology. Therefore, darkness always quietly swallows all the wonders of light.

Is it that the more something is unobtainable, the more we want it, or once we have obtained one thing, we want another?

Our childhood is gone forever. What remains is a broken dream.

What we cannot forget is that when spring arrives, we will still fly that ancient, beautiful kite, and when autumn comes, that broken-winged kite suddenly slams to pieces.

Why don't you come to the south? Why don't you start a new life? My friend has been enticing me over the phone in a sweet tone.

She is a well-off, single woman, comfortably living a life that she believes is the best for her. But things would be different if she were living in an inland town.

I often wake up in the dark night and then think about what I have just dreamt, but not about the following day, for all tomorrows are the same, and you cannot change much in them. A piece of news can travel in five minutes from the east of the town to the west — on a bus!

I cannot forget that the flying I once did has now turned into a deep-blue memory. Because I have once flown — flown with the transcendental feeling of crossing the blue sky and the clouds, I have carefully treasured

---

[1] Guo Cuihua (Hua Zi, 1954-) editor and woman essayist.

my pair of broken wings.

What I do not want to think about is the sorrow that we cannot go beyond ourselves — that deep, hidden sorrow.

When we are in pain or confusion, we are not moving forward, but back to the past, instead.

And the past is a boiled silk cocoon.

We have to learn to continuously temper ourselves in this age and learn to swim across the sea of cold reality. In this way, we will be able to enter tomorrow with a smile.

Time and again, I have visited Mount Hua, and time and again I have visited churches, in search of Buddhist and Christian sacred places with piety — not desire — to find a piece of pure land in which my heart can be at peace.

I told one of my friends: The true transcendental realm is not to avoid reality but to keep a peaceful heart in the turbulent terrestrial world.

Life is a flight of steps. We have to climb it step by step.

And this climbing may be time-consuming, exhausting, and filled with emotion, but it is all for the purpose of pacifying your heart.

It is like what happened the other day when a friend came over. He sat in front of me, taking his time to talk, while a scene rose from behind him: A blue sky projected white clouds; the white clouds rode the breeze; the breeze swung a tree full of golden-colored, withered leaves by the window. The quiet, light, and water-like flow unfolded my heart into a morning mist.

I knew my friend was standing on a mountaintop invisible to me, watching his past. He was not counting those trivialities, but instead, he counted how many steps he had scaled, measuring the height he had ascended. This took me into a realm where I saw a broader world.

I understand now that an ideal day's activity in my heart would be just to pick up a cup of light tea from an unclothed wooden table, sip at it bit by bit and taste it little by little. The nature of a true life is nothing more than that. What is plain is real.

An Age of Lost Childlike Innocence (Excerpts)

◎ *Liu Jianping*[1]

We are now getting old.

Like stooping, parentless children, we have abandoned our childlike innocence to the wilds of our dreams.

When we wake up and feel an intense itch for material things, we are deluded into believing that we have strong bodies, and as a result, we stuff the agendas of our already busy, full lives to the degree that we have no room to set up a crib or fly a kite for our childlike innocence.

Human's childlike innocence does not come from public donations or the celebration of Children's Holiday on June 1, nor is it affiliated with any prodigious welfare or "Hope Project". To save childlike innocence, one should not unduly resort to the rich for their mercy and ostentatious formality, or even worse, pin his hopes on money as a panacea.

Childlike innocence only sparkles on ordinary days and on small matters that grown-ups tend to neglect.

Many years ago, I read in an easily overlooked corner of a newspaper an even more easily overlooked little poem. Although I cannot remember it verbatim, I know the rough lines.

A mother asks her baby: Darling, what do you like best?
Pointing to the moon in the sky, the baby answers: That.
With a smile, the mother says: Want Mammy to get her for you?

---

[1] Liu Jianping (1956-), editor and writer.

Shaking his head, the baby answers: No, no, it will hurt!

Although I do not have the slightest memory of what the editorial had said in that day's issue — that newspaper's editorials were once the cynosure of all eyes in China and the world — I am moved even to this day by the childlike innocence expressed in that little poem.

I still firmly believe that although mankind has already walked on the moon and will have the power and ability to capture it (It is reported that the "Moon Development Plan" and the "Mars Development Plan", generally referred to as the "Outer Space Development Plan", are already budgeted and being implemented in many countries.), this does not necessarily mean that the prevailing industrialized civilizations can replace a humanistic spirit that has the childlike innocence as its intrinsic core. What gigantic enterprises or international consortia — scary, monstrous machines that appear right now in the guise of saviors to a panicked crowd with forced smiles — can finally annex are at most just a few research institutes and public relations departments in humanities, which lack more in spirit than in finance. This menacing pecuniary and technological influx will never be able to smear, in the hearts of our children, the pure moon with the dirty footprints of their leather boots with furry cuffs and large toe caps. Maybe this poetic line is the only shield children — what bliss it would be if we could all turn into children — have to protect themselves from being invaded:

"No, no, it will hurt!"

One of my friends is a surgeon, whose medical contributions over the past decade have been to remove countless appendixes from his patients. Every day after he gets off work, he will cast aside his dignity and play rubber band-skipping or shuttlecock-kicking games with his daughter in public — in our lives, we have little privacy in our gardens and on our lawns — while laughing like a child. In the eyes of the people around him, he lacks the seriousness of a father, and as a result, when his neighbors have problems with their appendixes, they are afraid to seek his help because they are worried about whether he is mature or professional enough to perform his duties. Bewildered, he asked me with a frown one day as we were chatting:

"Is childlike innocence less useful than an appendix?"

I was tongue-tied at this question.

Once, when visiting me at my home, an elementary school teacher complained that her students always tried to get to the bottom of issues such as "Does the sky have an edge?" "Can anything be endlessly divided?"

I asked how she answered the questions.

With a baffled look, she replied, "There is no clear clue in the textbooks."

So I gave her my opinion and some materials I had about the questions, but she cried out, "No, no, that won't do. Your opinion is not from the viewpoint of dialectic materialism. It does not comply with our teaching guidelines. I cannot let your opinion poison our children."

I gave a helpless smile and felt a dull pain, just like appendicitis.

Grown-ups often say: Don't argue with children. But I'd rather not see the forced, rhetorical, feigned, or muddled seriousness of grown-ups.

Besides, we grown-ups do not necessarily live as serious a life as our children may think we do.

Of course, we can use "textualism" or "structuralism" as an excuse to shift the responsibility to this world.

But nowadays, in the structures or texts of this world (What a grotesque expression!), there is no room for gentleness or childlike innocence. What is left in this world is only either the market or the battlefield, which does not refer to the analogical concept of the term "a market is a battlefield" but to actual issues being reported on the regular TV news every day, such as corruption, bribery, unemployment, bankruptcy, terror, blood, war, refugees... The trend of materialism (used in a different sense from the one that elementary school teacher was defending) is sweeping the traditional idols from the human spiritual antique-and-curio shelf, while metaphysical meditation is now an extravagance or a bad habit to be gotten rid of. Everything has to be provable and operable. And history has since put on a new uniform called "Neo-historicism," which is receiving its pre-work training. Like Jacks-of-all-trades, philosophers tactically decipher charts, data, formulas, established laws, and ideologies and, to show their employment qualifications and their courageous commitment to the current age, they once in a while answer the above-mentioned types of questions asked by the elementary school students, introducing something about the "wave-particle duality" that appears when matter is divided into the smallest unit in quantum mechanical tests. Attention: It is the unit, not the ultimate end (although the conclusion is yet to be proved). However, in explaining the mysterious, elusive and slippery phenomena of the state of matter in microcosm, the inventor of this patent, the Copenhagen School, hemmed and hawed like the elementary school teacher. On an emotional level, many people refuse to accept the fact that the world of matter cannot be proven or operated when it is merely approaching the ultimate state (which pays no heed to the teaching guidelines that must be followed without equivocation), as it insolently disappears from the vision of current human knowledge. It is as mysterious and abstruse as Buddhism or Taoism that Chinese sages often like to mystify. If that is the case, then we can be fully at ease — give up if you cannot figure it out, for thinking itself is unnecessary. "Materialism" can still help us reify the "abstract" to the "concrete" and "nothing" to "something". The creator of Chinese characters seemed to have long given consideration to this: Isn't the character *wu* (nothing) homophonic with *wu* (something)? That is why we have easily turned Qigong (Breathing Kungfu — the Taoist method of cultivating the heart) to Qigong (Apparatus Kungfu — the method of cultivating health.) There are countless achievements to enlist in other aspects. No matter what, we continue to feel reassured, continue to feel at home, and continue to value "worldly possessions" — which are solid and tangible in a practical life. So we continue to hold fast to our lifelines — to be qualified, fitting and accurate bolts on an assembly line. We are so used to covering the cruelty and despicability of industrial times with our well-mannered professional smiles. We spend days upon days managing our official affairs and household chores; we look busy and fulfilled outwardly but feel empty at heart. We are no longer in a leisurely and carefree mood; we no longer cherish our old dreams and no longer gaze up at the star-strewn sky. We give up our kindness to grab wealth and suffocate our childish chastity to save profits.

We have debased our souls for advanced technology, and smart technology has dulled our minds. For these reasons, we can hardly live without science and technology attending on and caring for us completely; we begin to suffer symptoms of bone loss; the comfort of "civilization" has diluted our life essence so much that our complexions turn pale and our blood is clogged with black deposits. (No wonder cerebral thrombosis and myocardial infarction are two frequent modern diseases.) We lack sunlight, greenness, and direct contact with nature... What fills our blurred vision are only dense forests of high buildings, detached pedestrians, cold family relationships, stock market clamors, and corporations that emerge and disappear suddenly, like that "wave-particle duality" and such, which, grotesque in shape and gaudy in color, together with the noises and fumes of the industrial civilization, impose on us a feeling of overwhelming drowsiness and endless, dreadful monotonousness.

The decline of humanities and the dominance of industrial technology have turned the world into a picture with two sides: an ostentatious display of infinite merchandize on one and a scene of destruction and ruin on the other. Like a model in a pair of red dance shoes who has lost self-control, modern life puts on a never-ending, wild fashion show, frantically swaying and spinning. It makes our jaws drop, our heads whirl, and our eyes glaze.

During these clamorous festivities of singing and dancing and of displaying and selling patented products everywhere, I suddenly hear a Dane, engaged in a marginalized job (as an author of children's literature), crying out:

— "He is naked!"

This is a fairy tale by Hans Christian Andersen. This is the true nature of the world that the fairy tale has exposed.

This childlike innocence has turned into a sharp bullet, which whistles along, tearing apart a modern lie — a lie that nobody wants to point out and nobody wants to disprove.

Counterfeits

◎ *Lei Da*[1]

With the abrupt boom in antique collecting, from the south to the north, a myriad of shopping malls specializing in cultural relics, antique markets, folk art and craft streets, and the like are popping up everywhere before we even notice it. The scale of the business and the number of the people involved are marvelous. Unknown to those who haven't seen it, the Panjiayuan Sunday Market in the southeast corner of Beijing is a stunning place for newcomers. At its peak, the antique corner alone is crowded with nearly a thousand stalls, around which swarm tens of thousands of visitors, cheek by jowl, speaking different kinds of patois, and displaying on the stalls are all kinds of items ranging from chinaware to bronze-ware, jade articles to ancient coins, agate and crystal stones to emerald stones, rare tiles to unusual ink plates, stone carvings to wood carvings, oil lamps to ancient Buddha statues — so numerous and so diverse that in a moment of aberration, you suspect that this is actually happening in a modern China after the Cultural Revolution and on the margin of a modern capital, Beijing. What has made such a large number of antiques appear overnight?

In fact, not very far from those Panjiayuan stalls, there are other antique markets, like Beijing Antique City, Handicraft Promenade, Chaowai Cultural Relic Market, etc., each of which boasts an impressive scale and sells approximately the same types of items; moreover, there are those flea markets in Crown Park and the Shichahai tourist attractions. This may lead to some worry as to whether there is really such a high

---

[1] Lei Da (Lei Daxue, 1943-), editor and writer, vice president of Chinese association of contemporary literature.

demand for antiques or whether such businesses are profitable for those vendors who stand like magpies in the chilly air from morning till night in the hopes of coming into a windfall. That worry is unfounded, though. Generally speaking, the supply of the market equals the demand or, vice versa, the demand creates the supply. The antiques boom today, I am afraid, is a commercial and cultural phenomenon worthy of attention. As the old saying goes, an indulgence in hobbies saps the will, but without the proper environment, what can cultivate indulgence? Generally speaking, antique collecting will thrive when the country is in peace continuously and all is well; antique collecting can also thrive when life improves and people have a little extra money. As China is an ancient civilization, we have a historical penchant for the old. A person actually appreciates a culture as he strokes a carved piece of jade, plays with a bronze mirror, or turns a porcelain vase in his hands; the attraction lies not only in the object's outward beauty, but also in its meaning and artistic value. Besides, apart from real collectors, there are also people engaged in storing, possessing, and scalping; how can such a market not flourish? From the perspective of antique sellers, the biggest possible impetus for traveling long distances in extreme weathers for a special item or sitting glued to the stall for a prospective customer is that there is no fixed price for an antique, which can be sold for a couple of dollars if the seller is unlucky or for tens of thousands if he is lucky — the business can be a shortcut to getting rich. Besides, because it is hard to determine if an antique is real or fake, the business gives the people involved a lot of opportunities to put their own knowledge into practice.

What amazes me is that I have been gradually enticed into the great mass of antique collectors. This enticement is indeed trend-driven and irresistible. My friends suspect it is a sign of my early aging, but I don't think so, for I was fond of stone or wood carvings even when I was a child. I believe that seeking our roots is human nature and so, likely, is antique collecting. When the weather is right, the markets flourish. So over the past few years, I have bought, for very little money, some small articles such as jade carvings, Buddha statues, bronze items, and the like. At the beginning, I was in high spirits, showing off my trophies to my friends, believing that I had a unique eye in appraising antiques. But, to my dismay, through my repeated flaunting, I realized that I had bought not only fake stuff mostly but also at unnecessarily high prices. Take the mass-produced bronze tripods or the bronze Buddha statues, for example; they cost only 40 RMB apiece in the south corner of Panjiayuan, but I got each for 100 in Shichahai. Take the so-called Ming Dynasty imitation of the Ge Kiln chinaware of the Song Dynasty, as another example; the vendor boldly shot out a price of 5,000 RMB, but if you bothered to shop around, you would constantly come across similar "treasures," and if you really wanted to lay your hands on them, after some bargaining, the price could slide to 50 RMB, which is hilarious. The current curios are mostly imitations and exist mostly to satisfy people's casual interest in collecting old things. Otherwise, why would a Xuande incense burner be called a Xuande incense burner if it is available everywhere? My antique fever cooled down by the time I understood the true nature of all those counterfeits.

Nevertheless, my interest turned to fossils. Compared with the overwhelming number of fake curios, fossils are straightforward. If you doubt me, let me ask you: Is there anything more down-to-earth or more solid than a fossil? So I made up my mind to be a fossil collector. I really love fossils, which can take me to the remote, boundless and ancient past, when a trilobite, a swimming fish, or a piece of fir was suddenly buried in a stream of lava during a natural cataclysm and eventually turned into a fossil after having been sealed in the dark for millions of years — yet still remains a real bug, a real fish, a real tree, displaying an inexorable will of life through its eternal appearance. Stroking such a stone wing, such a stone fin, or such a piece of stone tree bark or leaf, how can one not marvel at the oneness of time and life? Of all the carvings, fossils are the greatest! Think of it this way: A bird circling over a river or a fish swimming in the water was abruptly frozen in place in a lightning-fast mutation — a tragedy from an apparent perspective, but, in nature, the most solemn realization of nirvana in the world, a retreat into an eternal nest. This reminds me of the famous sculpture *Apollo and Daphne*, which tells the story of Apollo, the god of the sun, who pursued the nymph Daphne, daughter of the river god; seeing that Apollo was about to catch her, his hand almost reaching her long hair, Daphne, a sworn virgin, panicked and called upon her father Peneus to help her by changing her beautiful form. No sooner had she made her plea than her hair transformed into leaves, her lovely bosom turned into bark, and her feet became rooted to the ground. Fossils have a similar artistic effect. The lack of human fossils due to the short human evolutionary history, so to speak, well illustrates the difficulty of creating a fossil.

I started my collection with two pieces of petrified wood I managed to acquire. Standing on the windowsill like two wood stumps, each with a distinct bark and growth rings, they are great fun to look at. Soon, I got hold of a few small stone slices resembling larch fir leaves, which looked like a miniature forest — quite a spirit booster. Following that, I started to collect animal fossils, because I believed that they were more dynamic and rich with the fun of life. I bought what was called a Jinzhou wolf-fin-fish fossil and a lizard fossil, which were available on the market. My friends thought they were fake, because the animals looked like they had been carved into the stone, but I was firm in my belief that they were real. Before long, I saw a knoll-like pile of them in Panjiayuan and became suspicious of the origin. So I asked a vendor, an honest-looking guy in a military overcoat, if any of this type of fossil was counterfeit. He answered with an honesty that surprised me: "Some are and some are not." He casually pointed at a little piece and told me it was a fake, but he then pointed to a large pile of fossils and said that those were real. Impressed by his honesty, I posed another question, "Do you have fossils that bulge from the embedding rocks, those fish fossils that have completely turned into stones?" "Oh, yeah," he said. "I do, I do." Then, he mysteriously dug out two large stone slabs from a strawboard box, and they did have traces of fossilized fish. Pointing at the slabs, he told me that the two pieces came from one complete fossil, cut open in cross section, and that was why one bulged and the other was caved in. "Look," he said. "They match. How can this be man-made?" Without any hesitation, I bought it for 180 RMB. Back at home, I found a little dirt on the bulging piece and so proceeded to wash it. No sooner had I started to brush dirt off than an ochre-colored "fossil skin" began to scale off, exposing a different color inside, which was white just like an ordinary slab. Taking a closer look at it, I found that to make the fish stand out, the surface layer of the slab had been peeled off. That helped me to know what it really was. I sat there, angry, picturing how the disgusting counterfeiter was doing his job. The next morning, I rushed to Panjiayuan, and found, to my surprise, that the honest-looking guy was still there. Looking each other in the eye for some time, he began to dodge my stare somewhat. I shouted out, "Your fossils — oh no, your slabs — I don't want them anymore!" I waited there for a stormy quarrel to break out. But to my surprise, he remained quiet. He began to blush a little in the morning sunlight. Without saying anything, he fumbled out the exact amount of money I had given him the day before. I turned to leave, not wanting to see him in his embarrassment. I wondered what kind of look he gave me behind my back.

At the same time afraid of and angry at the frauds, all at once, I made a firm decision that if I bought anything again, I would buy a real fossil — a highly authenticated, bona fide fossil. As I knew that a luxurious Antique City nearby had a tortoise fossil, I put all my money together for the purchase. If that was not enough, I would be willing to throw in any additional amount I had with me at the time till I was able to get my hands on the fossil.

What a spacious and well-illuminated hall! What a large variety of unusual attractions! As soon as I entered the luxurious and grand mall, I felt much more secure. People said that all the counters here had been leased to individual private businesses, but what was wrong with that? Such a highly elegant mall would have no place for low-grade items! At one of the counters there, Little Jia, the saleslady, full of high spirits, brought out the rare treasure for me with much ceremony — the tortoise fossil. As I had expected, it looked mysterious and extraordinary and was permeated with an air of antiquity, as if it had survived for eons and happened to be left in a rock cleft. The fossilized tortoise didn't have a head or legs, but only the complete, rigid shell. Although it was only palm-sized, it revealed the vivid crawling movement of the tortoise. The shell, embedded in a large stone, was completely fossilized, but the texture was distinct and as transparently bright as mature jade. The most fascinating thing was that the fossil had a fragment of the carapace. Tiny as it was, it was oily and shiny black. Oh, I was completely lost in rapture at the miracle of nature. Caressing it, I was bedazzled by happiness. And through our conversation, I learned that Little Jia was something of a fellow-townsman. She told me that her boss had once served on the Qinghai Geological Exploration Team. He wanted to keep the fossil for himself, but since I wanted it, and I was half a fellow-townsman, he could give up the treasured fossil. The asking price was 1,800 RMB. We could negotiate the price, but because their cost was already 700, they would go no lower than 800. Yes, what else could I say? OK, 800 it was. When I was paying, I had a spectacular, gigantic feeling, thinking that I could make the money back by sitting up late and writing a few more articles. I told her that once I got home, I would wash the tortoise fossil, because it looked a bit dirty. Little Jia casually warned me not to use water to fool with such a valuable object; she said I could use a brush in order to maintain its integrity.

That night, under the lamplight, I abandoned myself to the pleasure of repeatedly fondling the precious tortoise. I couldn't help marveling at it: It was indeed the pinnacle of Mother Nature's creation. Its only imperfection was an unnecessary lump sticking out at the back of the stone and that lump kept the fossil from resting properly in the glass box I had prepared in particular for it. Why shouldn't I flatten that lump? So I pried it with a knife, and "flop," it went off. I twisted it between my fingers, but why had it turned into powder? So with the knife, I scratched at a concealed spot at the back of the tortoise, and again, some powder sprinkled down! As if empowered by some spiritual being, my train of thought, like lightning, flashed to the mud on the plateau of the Great Northwest — wasn't the rain-washed and then dried-up mud there in exactly the same texture? And wouldn't it make all those shapes and textures if you pressed a tortoise shell into it while it was wet? But, then what about that small piece of carapace? That could not be fake! It must be fossilized. Let me scrape it with the knife. What? Why did it contain fiber? That is to say that the piece of carapace must have been glued to the stone. What an exquisite composition! What a scheme!

Suddenly, I felt horrified — horrified by my discovery, by the hideousness of human nature; I also felt foolish and ludicrous. Looking at the darkness outside the window, I felt as though I was suffocating. I was too stunned to think about anything else, but I felt in horror that lurking in a distant corner was a schemer, who designed that mud tortoise particularly for me and who knew that I would come and buy his stuff, as he used to be a fossil enthusiast like me. I seemed to have already seen his dark and guileful back. I was kind of scared. I would rather not have discovered anything. I would rather the fossil was real. And I suddenly had an "Ah Q Complex" — a complex of self-consolation about a ridiculous situation: If it is a fake, then let it be; it doesn't make any difference if it is displayed at home or in a museum. Besides, "Where there is a being, there is a non-being; where there is unification, there is separation." But my heart ached, after all. I felt something collapsing bit by bit, like that mud tortoise. What had collapsed — my trust in people?

The following day, my friend Dawei and I showed up at the Antique City. I quickly caught sight of my half-townsman Little Jia at the counter. She was still wearing a smile on her face, which now suddenly reminded me of a facial mask made of mud instead. I told her I didn't want the fossil anymore. With a smile, she asked me what the reason was for my decision, because I had taken such a close look at it before buying it. I told her that even though I had looked at it for a while, I still hadn't figured it out at that time and that only indicated how skillfully it was made. "Are you implying," with a domineering expression on her powdered face, she suddenly turned into a high-pitched voice, "that this is counterfeit?" I smiled and replied, "Yes, it is. Let's leave it to your boss on the Geological Exploration Team." By then, quite a crowd had gathered, and one curious guy even picked up a little chip, put it in his mouth and then spit it out, saying it was indeed mud. Finally, Xiao Jia gave me my money back. An honest-looking middle-aged man working at the mall approached me surreptitiously and told me that it was complicated there so it was in my best interest to leave quickly with my money. The subtext seemed to be that if I didn't leave quickly, something bad might happen.

By the time I walked out of the Antique City, it was noon sharp, when the dazzling sun beams looked like unreal incandescent lights, and the surrounding buildings floated like mirages or rootless duckweed. All at once, I started to wonder if I myself existed. Involuntarily, I touched the stone pillar in the hallway, which felt hard and cold, indicating that real things did exist. Taking a deep breath of the fresh air, I felt as if I had just crossed a big threshold of life or skirted a steep-banked inlet. From that day on, I settled down to do many of the things I was supposed to do.

The Revelation of a Soul

◎　*Geng Zhanchun*[1]

He is sitting by a radio, listening to Gustav Mahler's *The Song of the Earth*. He does not understand its lyrics, but, in his opinion, that is even better, for in this way, he has to focus on listening. He is familiar with the titles of the movements, which are inspired by poetic imagery of the Tang Dynasty: reminiscence, high-spirited youths drinking alone in the chilly autumn, beauties, and farewells. While he listens, the terrestrial world gradually fades away from his consciousness. He begins to breathe a different air — a musical air as fresh as that over an earthly valley; a new sunlight begins to shine on him — the one being sent from Mahler's heart. Floating in the melody are the sorrows of the terrestrial world and the fantasies of the Supreme Ultimate. From within the broad and deeply thematic melody and its ample variations, a melancholic bass — he does not know what instrument it is — faintly resonates in a way that is soothingly sad. It is as determined, recurring and hesitant as a belief, but keeps a thin attachment to the heart.

Songs or music always cause him to think about human sorrows and man's sanctity and angelic nature. The melancholic music can resurrect the singer and guide the dead to heaven. In the name of a song, we can be forgiven, for the song is our repentance, our lamentation, and our prayer to heaven. With this music, this earth will sustain us forever. Even if destruction is imminent, something as miraculous as music will come to our rescue.

Can we humans express anything better or fuller in speech than we

---

[1] Geng Zhanchun (1957-), professor and literary critic.

can in songs or music? He believes that our speech is not even half as good as songs or musical phrases. Our speech is vague. It is vague because it is too distinct — definitive concepts in our speeches prove ambiguous in terms of truthfulness.

Music is conclusive argumentation. Whether you are hung on the seesaw of conflicting viewpoints or trapped in the whirlpool of a duel of skepticism and nihilism, the moment the music rises, all will be reconciled. Music is the absolute thought above all other thoughts. Violin music or vocal music do not need grounds for argument, because they themselves are arguments that we must accept.

He is pondering: I am listening for the moment when I will reshape myself into a new being; I am listening for the moment when a new spirit and a new way of thinking are reborn in my internal music. He is hoping for the appearance of a musical viewpoint that will rise after the death of metaphysical thinking, historical standpoints, economic viewpoints, etc. — that is to say, the Orpheus outlook. Of course, music does not have any viewpoint.

But music is impregnated with the seed of belief — "the seed of a holy song." Music must bode a different arrangement for and a different insight of our world. He is trying to understand what they are. He is also trying to understand the intrinsic nature of music: to sing a hymn. He is pondering: We should place our lives in it, but instead, all our miseries lead us in the opposite direction. To move in the direction of singing a hymn is the ultimate affirmation.

Odysseus asked his crew to tie him to the mast, because he was afraid that he might not be strong enough to resist the lure of the singing sirens and that he might fail to complete his voyage. So he bore the dual afflictions of being lured and of resisting. But he couldn't budge in his bond. All he could do was to chase that singing in his heart and stop the lure where it arose — his heart. He ordered his crew to seal their ears with wax. Because they never heard the sirens' seductive singing, which they knew was will-consuming, they kept rowing their oars hard.

Some people know that the passion of a tender song can also weaken their resolve to act in the practical world, making them especially sensitive to matters and to injuries, compassionate and sympathetic to others, and liable to have pity for people's losses. But at the same time, they want to act, to control, and to dominate. They consider the voice of God as the lure of sirens, and a well-intended call for good-heartedness as an evil temptation towards disaster. They act at the cost of muffling the inner sound. They suffocate their souls in exchange of social status and material wealth of the outside world. They lose the spiritual power of the inner heart, but like the crew with wax-sealed ears, they gain the power of action.

He is pondering: All human miseries are caused by the detachment of the internal voice from the external actions; like me right at this moment, an Odysseus chained to a chair, I am listening to a song — the compassionate greeting from the eternity of the music — but cannot respond to it, or apply it in the world of actions. That world does not tolerate the way of music, the concept of singing hymns sincerely, or any friendly actions. He is pondering: So my activity in listening to music is, in nature, the feeble, cowardly action of my innermost being. As soon as it makes contact with that world, it collapses and shatters. How fragile a musicalized heart is! But he always has a guilty conscience. In the innermost recesses of his soul, he blames himself and has a sense of sin, guilty, uneasiness and compromise, of screaming and praying for help, and of pleading to be forgiven. His internal music weakens him.

While accepting the tapping of the music on his heart, he is pondering: As long as humans hand down the music or folk songs they have composed with their myriad grieved souls, mankind will not perish, and the value of the heart will still take root in a song and will germinate and sprout.

A Trace Remains When a Bird Is Gone

◎ *Xu Fang*[1]

I have a strong yearning for a moment of peace in the city's hustle and bustle — to do nothing but think, such as to thoroughly think about my old, late maternal grandpa. But this seems so difficult: I have always been busy — so busy that I do not even know what I have been busy doing; so busy that I do not even remember who I am. But, no matter what, I have already begun to think — to think that perhaps because he lived for so long, we have forgotten the phrase "time flies," to think that perhaps his quiet, even silent lifestyle has made us hallucinate that he is still with us, sitting or lying in the reclining chair, watching us without saying a word. He was always watching — watching us rush around.

He was not always that quiet, though. He was once active. But now — I mean, long before he died — he, of course, had become inactive. Although he had long been "aging," in the eyes of a child (me), he was already an old man some thirty years ago. It was indeed so: The wrinkles on his forehead, his hunched back, and his hoarse voice — all attested to what the child believed thirty years ago.

About twenty years ago, he had already started talking about the arrangements after his death. Mother stopped him in a firm tone: "Don't talk nonsense! It is not auspicious to talk about this!" A moment later, after she seemed to have thought for a little bit, she murmured, as if to herself: "Far too early..." Even so, I was still shocked. Back then, I was a child who had only learnt what birth was but knew nothing about death — and I didn't want to know what death was. Therefore, I didn't want to hear such

---

① Xu Fang (Xiao Chu, Fang Xu, 1962-), contemporary poetess.

a conversation between them. And if I chanced to hear it, I would rush to cover my ears or shake my hands, for this was indeed something that would leave me at a loss: How would a human life have such a frightful end? I had never thought about this. Later on, Mother no longer tried to stop him from talking about "death," because she got used to it, but I became the one to come up and stop him, because I grew up and had the courage to do so. This was what they didn't expect, although they were supposed to. I am not sure if this perennial topic is a good thing or a bad thing in the growth of a child. Anyway, this is how I grew up.

Despite the afflictions of worldly matters, my sisters and I had finally grown up, become independent, had our own families and raised our own children, and thus established a new generation. After going through an unexpected adverse event, Mother aged a great deal, while Grandpa aged more and more. And after quite a few relocations, he finally settled down with Mother in our old apartment, in a "new residential district" built during the 1950s in the northwest corner of the city. The neighborhood of the old apartment was not as boisterous as before, and this was the same situation with many families like ours: getting quiet with only the aged or the pre-kindergarten toddlers at home. In just the blink of an eye, gone were the days when children romped everywhere on the streets, rolling iron wheels, kicking shuttlecocks, doing knee wrestling, skipping ropes, etc. — just as we were gone, too.

And unlike in the past, too, the door of our old apartment was kept closed most of the time. In the past, when our home was teeming with family members, it was hard to keep that door shut even if we wanted to. Parents, kids, and our friends kept bustling in and out. What a jolly period of time! But nowadays, of course, our friends wouldn't come over to the old apartment to visit us, and apart from holidays, we didn't come over often, either.

Neither did Grandpa's friends come over. They stayed in the place where Grandpa had lived nearly all his life before his last relocation. It was called some kind of a lane in the old district of the city. He lived there until he could no longer take care of himself. Grandpa was a widower. He hadn't remarried since Grandma died of disease at the time when Mother was about ten years old. His life was quite lonesome, but he enjoyed all the freedom that an aged widower could have. He had many old buddies to drink and chat with. But they could not come over anymore. Even if they wanted to, they were not physically able to. In fact, they couldn't physically make it at all, for, according to Mother, Grandpa had outlived all of them. They all went ahead to the other world before him.

Grandpa had two old birds. One was green-colored, and the other, green-colored, too. No one knew how long Grandpa had had them. All I could vaguely remember was that he began with the parents of those two birds — or, maybe, even the grandparents, two generations back in their family line. But before he moved, Grandpa was almost firmly determined to give them away, together with the birdcage and all other necessities. He didn't care about his other belongings, which we could dispose of at will, but about the birds, he had never been so tenacious. He was obstinate sometimes, but never like that time. Mother, of course, tried to change his mind, but to no avail.

That day, Grandpa looked quite different: Something crystal was glittering over his cloudy eyes. Exerting himself to keep his back straight, he clapped his hands — that was how he communicated with the two birds, a language only he and his birds knew; at that moment, the birds were circling in the narrow garret. They were familiar with that sloping ceiling, dormer window, squeaking bed and chairs, water-marked gable walls with the corresponding part of the sky over it, and the smell of the wind there — they adored that place, for that was their "home" where they were born and where they had grown up. Following the established clapping language, they flew into the birdcage, but they didn't expect that to be a farewell forever — their owner was going to move out of the house while they had to stay in the garret, a place that had a particular odor they were so used to...

He said that those two old birds were accustomed to their old home, and he didn't say anything else — besides, he was only talking about the birds. So, we had to honor his wishes. By now, those two birds should be truly "old." Although we haven't seen how they are now, Grandpa was prudent about this, I think — he didn't want to be sad. So he prepared for all the partings he had to go through. I don't know how Grandpa looked at life and death, but his nonchalance (or, at least, what seemed to be nonchalance) has left me endless sorrow.

I was familiar with Grandpa's senility — so familiar that I became numb to it, but out of this numbness came, unexpectedly, a moment of surprise. Recalling this incident now, I feel quite dumb myself.

For the first time in my life, I was denied entrance to our old apartment. I did have a key to it, but because I had never needed to use it before, I believed subconsciously that the door would always be open to me... That was the stupidity of a person who was not aware of what aging was like. I kept knocking on the door for about ten minutes — or maybe fifteen minutes. I was anxious and tenacious, because I thought that even if Mother went out for something, Grandpa must be at home. Therefore, I hastened in my knocking. For fear that Grandpa might not know it was me, I even yelled out his name, but it was not Grandpa who responded to my knocking. It was a neighbor woman, who told me that my grandpa was at home. So I started to knock again... Finally Grandpa came to open the door, and that was when I saw how he had struggled step by step on a walking stick to get to the door. Damned me! It was I who bought that walking stick for him, but I had never expected that it would be such an effort for him to walk, for every time I saw him, he was either sitting or lying there.

So in the end, the old apartment often had its door closed. For some time after Grandpa died, Mother kept saying that she heard the door squeaking. I told her it must be because the door was so old and the hinge may need to be oiled — but in my heart, I wondered if Mother was delusional. Grandpa was gone, and that old apartment looked older and quieter, and everything there seemed to be followed by a shadow. Sometimes I wondered if I was delusional too.

About this time last year, during the National Day or the Mid-Autumn Festival, he was sitting in that reclining chair I mentioned before with a little square table in front of him, loudly "smacking" (not drinking) his wine from his cup and following it with a bit of food. It took him an hour to drink that small cup of wine — he had plenty of time. His enjoyment delighted all of us. One of his granddaughter's husbands said, in great admiration, "Isn't Grandpa doing better than we are? He has so much leisure time, while we are born in a competitive age, always up to our eyes in work. Most likely, we won't have as peaceful an old age as Grandpa."

My son was at an age of inquisitiveness and curiosity, and always insisted on getting to the bottom of everything. It was no surprise that he shot out a question: "Who told you so?"

All of us "busy adults" burst into laughter. Loud as it was, the laughter was quite panicked in nature. We grown-ups have too many "practical" problems to tackle. As a matter of fact, we are not able to figure out what our future will be like, and neither are we able to understand what "senility" really means and what life and death really suggest. We lack time — I mean, the transcendental approach to time. We all live in a very concrete world. This concreteness creates not only profusion and complication, but also tiresome trivialities. But is this our choice? No, not at all. It seems they are the consequences of our own choices, but can we ignore the influx of the choices imposed upon us and pretend that we don't see them? The environment shapes a man. Tension and competition are too great a social power, and are a manifestation of social progress. Who is able to resist? Therefore, that is why we are "pragmatic".

Laurel blooms fall for leisurely persons;
Spring hills vacate under a serene moon.

That poetic line describes a life only like Grandpa's. It is like a blank scene in a movie, or the "empty space" in a Chinese painting — blank, but not necessarily blank; empty, but not necessarily empty — like those traces Grandpa's birds had left in the air: They seem to have existed and seem to have not existed. Grandpa already lived a marginalized life. He didn't know about stocks, mortgages, futures, etc., didn't quite understand the daily TV news about international and domestic events, stories big or small, that seemed to concern us... But using his intuition, instead of knowledge (he used to be a chef), he figured out how to fix an electric kettle in a week. That was after his ninety-third birthday celebration, when it would take him a few minutes to slowly bend over towards the bowl to take a bite out of the food, as he was not able to hold the bowl up to his mouth. What an amusing and touching movement — I was moved by his projecting, old, and quivering lips that were pallid but vigorous, slow in response but rash in action... It seemed that from a weather-beaten, almost rotten statue I had seen the power of real life, a life that was revealing itself.

Yes, indeed, even in such a senile body, an actively lived life is fighting or competing to survive. It never considers losing or giving up. External serenity or peacefulness is extrinsic, but the internal warfare is intrinsic. Although his body already looked like a mummy, it was alive; although many years ago, from the perspective of natural law, the owner of that body had already calmly prepared to accept "death" and had narrowly slid over it a few times, one day last year Mother abruptly exclaimed with a thrill that Grandpa had new hair growing out on his head.

So we saw, with our own eyes, miracles on your bald head where the earlier white hair was all gone — it was a lock of thin hair, extremely soft and similar to lanugo hair, and it was black in color! It came from the "blankness" and the "nothingness". Grandpa, you didn't seem to have done anything, but just peacefully waited, waited to the last minute. You were a calm and patient person. To be honest, there was no way for me to know what your eyes had absorbed from the void you were looking at, but it looked as if they were saying something like: Why fight it?

But you fought. Except for the last period of your life, you had been "independent": You fed yourself without any support, you walked outside with your walking stick to enjoy the sunlight, you went to the bathroom by yourself and took a shower by yourself. (The shower was something like a messy but determined fight.) That is how I knew you were fighting. In the hospital emergency room, you told me "directly" through your grip on my hand that you were fighting — that was when I cried. And that was the time when a young woman doctor, expressionless but nimble enough, wrote and issued to us a note of Critical Illness about you, at which I wept — wept so hard that I ignored the reserved manner I had adopted for urban life. I cried to the doctor, saying, "Doctor, I beg you. All our family hopes our grandpa can start the new millennium with us..." Grandpa, you must have heard me and therefore, once again, you started to fight. Once again, you didn't surrender. Once again, you let us see a miracle. I could hardly bring myself to tell you while you were fighting: Your life is bidding farewell to you, although it is an irrefutable fact. It was indeed an odd feeling to see you completely leave yourself at the disposal of pain without making the slightest moans and to see you completely leave your intractable body to Mother or me to "handle".

Grandpa left us, in the end. He was tired. Mother was tired, too, attending him. He was asleep — forever. Mother was asleep, too, but when she woke up, she could no longer wake him up. He was in an extremely peaceful sleep, but I always believe that he died of exhaustion, like an oil lamp that has burned out its last drop of oil, yet the flame continues for another quarter of an hour, another minute, or another second... I want to set that picture of the last minute in a beautiful frame and hang it in my heart.

Normally, I do not have to mention the dates of Grandpa's birth or death to anyone outside of our family. He was not a prominent or great figure, but as it is said, every ordinary person has a "world history" in his or her heart. If that is the case, Grandpa's "world history" was longer than the time since the Revolution of 1911. Speaking of history, he could be considered a subject of the Qing Dynasty; he had gone through many wars, suffered from starvation, traveled up north and down south, and trod on many roads, big or small. All this — even the mere thought of it — would startle me as I come to realize how fast time has flown by and how much time has changed us. Thinking this way, our road ahead seems endless. — Am I too impatient?

Life requires patience. That is what I have deduced from the life journey Grandpa has gone through: Although our long journey is pitch-dark here and there — so dark that we cannot see anything — and although this fairly long journey and the fairly long time it will take to cover the long journey always seem daunting to our patience, it does not at all justify our pessimism or impetuousness, for life itself holds the overwhelming power. Although I am still busy and muddle along, I am now filled with confidence. No matter where I come from or where I go, no matter if it is daytime or nighttime, no matter if it is a windy or a windless day, no matter if there is a bird to accompany me or no bird at all, I have a peaceful heart now.

Night at the Summer Palace

◎ *Wu Cen*[1]

Perhaps not many people know how to appreciate the nighttime scenery of the Summer Palace. Each night at dusk, after a hasty visit and some feeble impressions, streams upon streams of tourists rush out of the palace and return to where they sojourn during their "golden vacation week." Will they reflect on or talk about their daytime visit, or will they just go ahead and let their exhausted bodies and senses relax as quickly as possible? Will such a short-term "eye-opening" visit have any impact on them, provoke any thoughts in them, or affect their lives? I have absolutely no answer to these speculations — perhaps they have never had any such thoughts! They may very well come here just for sightseeing. Modern people's travels differ greatly from those of the ancients, who traveled to broaden their personalities and preserve their integrity, as described in the poetic couplet, "Read thousands of books and travel thousands of miles." Modern people's travels also differ greatly from those of the religious pilgrims, who travel to experience hardships and to communicate with God during their lonely "Pilgrim's Progress". Modern people's travels, to the utmost, are pure consumerist behavior. We should not expect any spiritual improvement to come of them.

After every tourist has gone, and so have most of the night joggers, I wander the east bank and then sit on a bench to wallow in my leisure, lingering my gaze at the vicissitudes of the twilight over the West Hills. From behind those hills, the setting sun sends out a residual, dazzling glow, silhouetting more distinctly the continuous chain of the hills. Soon,

---

[1] Wu Cen, contemporary writer.

the sky begins to turn red. While the clouds around the setting sun look refulgent, the evening orange-red twilight keeps spreading — I used to believe that a twilight glow appeared before a sunset, but in fact, it is the other way around. In just a short while, the last renewed glow will fade away, just as the Russian poet Pushkin once described in his poem, "The evening glow is waning", and the lingering glow looks languid. Under the gradually dimming grey sky, the rolling West Hills appear even more solemn and dark, permeated by a steadfast and stately tranquility. But as the night thickens, the darkness of the hilly area, on the contrary, becomes fainter and fainter and finally dissolves into the dark night, leaving only a blurred outline. On this moonless night — moonless despite the gleaming of the Hesperus toward the edge of the sky and the glittering of a few stars between the thin clouds — the night sky and the Kunming River, their boundaries vague, also shimmer with grey light.

At night, the famous palace is dark, with only a few lights in the houses where the palace staff live. The daytime clamor has died out, and the hustling and bustling of the past have gone. Where is Empress Dowager Cixi? Does her soul occasionally come back to visit the Happiness and Longevity Hall, where she restlessly spent her "peaceful senile life"? Where is Emperor Guangxu? Are the days in that pretty prisoner's cell, the rooms in the wing of the Jade Ripple Hall with the exit bricked over, "too harsh to recall"? Perhaps, many years from now, when science has enabled humans to travel faster than light, past events that perplex current historians will reappear in a man-activated replay of time, before the surprised but unbiased eyes of future generations.

One is justified in saying that the night at the imperial palace naturally has different connotations for people to ponder. Shrouded in the darkness of a moonless night (back then, only millennium-old illuminating devices, like paper lanterns and candles, were available), the entire Summer Palace was but a great pitch-black sprawl, with only the lake faintly shimmering. The ostentatious resplendence and magnificence of daytime became meaningless when the Creator shifted time to the night. This is the will of Heaven. However supreme and magnificent a power can be, it has to abate for a moment, otherwise the people involved will all be exhausted. But does this diurnal shift affect the feelings or mentalities of us humans? What were the "monarchs" doing in the Happiness and Longevity Hall and the Jade Ripple Hall when they returned to their imperial sleeping chambers, after holding court and meeting their ministers in the Benevolence and Longevity Hall? This question is not raised out of naïveté or curiosity, as a country girl would imagine how an Empress consumes her roast sweet potato. This question is raised because, during the nights when there was no ostentatious grandeur or stately show-off of power and prestige, what the "monarchs" thought or did would, all the same, affect our history.

From what I feel about this place at this moment, the Summer Palace is more of a tourist mecca after nightfall than it is during the daytime, when one can see its red walls and yellow roof tiles. It is now quiet, sprawling, and massively mighty — quiet hills and woods, a sprawling lake, and massively mighty night wind. Try to picture yourself standing by the lake with the waves gently lapping the bank, with one of your hands resting on the white-marble balustrade under the night's thick mantle beyond the reach of the dim glow of the lamps — isn't this a place where you can converse with Heaven and Earth, and isn't this a moment when you can communicate with your heart? Thinking, in fact, requires space (although some ancient sages could do it in dungeons or dark cells), and the famous landscaped garden of this Summer Palace could be an excellent space for thinking, especially on a voiceless, tranquil night, because this palace possesses the quietness and peacefulness of the mountainous wilds and forested areas, without their desolation; this palace boasts the sublimity and solemnity of the Forbidden City, without its overbearing weight; this place was the residence of a small group of people, but it does not feature the homeliness and trivialities of most residences... — Isn't this the best place for pondering such serious topics as history and political situations, life and sentient beings, or God's will and man's fortune? That is exactly the way a tiny room tends to suggest daily necessities, a dark cell tends to provoke thinking in theories and social reformation, and the Suzhou garden landscaping tends to conjure up lyrics and poetry... If, from this perspective, we examine all the people who owned or visited this palace to find out what they have left for themselves and for us and what they have done in history, I dare say that they have failed to use this place as the best thinking space. As a researcher of history, I am not so naïve as to believe that rulers must attend to myriad affairs every day, read and comment on memorials at midnight, peruse classics by candlelight, and endlessly (or secretly) discuss national affairs with their courtiers. I know that what filled the living space of an imperial monarch's palace more than anything else was his bedrooms and eunuchs, hordes of concubines and favorite officials of the court, palace banquets and exquisite delicacies, and all kinds of antiques and Western wares. The monarchs were also humans, and those were the objects that they used to satisfy their greatly inflated and abnormal feelings, senses, and desires; those were the objects that formed the living circumstances of the monarchs as biological beings; and besides, those needs kept pace with time. The monarchs also needed contact and exchange with the outside world, hence the necessity of all kinds of secret reports and memorials, envoys for minorities and officials handling tributes, Secretaries of State and Privy Councilors, Princes and Princesses, reincarnate Buddhas and monk heads, and even the Peking and Kunqu Operas in the Harmonious Virtue Garden and the famous actors Yang Xiaolou and Tan Xinpei. Besides all those necessities, however, the monarchs needed time to relax and meditate in solitude, time to face themselves, and time to think over the rise and fall, the survival or destruction of the empire they ruled — even if it was a "legacy" inherited from their ancestors. No matter what, they needed time to face themselves somewhat as human beings, at least — to take off the masks required by their social status as monarchs, and to really ponder their lives and responsibilities, their fates and raison d'étre. Did they have such moments when they temporarily detached themselves from their political roles and biological selves to return to their true nature as themselves and as human beings? If they did, I believe, those moments must have taken place after nightfall, when they were alone, and when they stood by the lake — does that high mast by the bank in front of the Happiness and Longevity

Hall indicate the antecedents of Cixi sailing on the lake at night? As a late Qing ruler who was extremely artful and astute at politics and who had controlled the supreme power for almost half a century without ever having ascended the throne, would she just board the boat for fun with her men? It cannot be that she never stood there, in the shadow of the dark pine by the stone balustrade along the bank, gazing and pondering.

If we do not limit the scope of our historical scan to the late Qing Dynasty, we will then find that this palace has also witnessed the sojourning of some other personages who have shaped the Chinese history: Mao Zedong, the first Chairman of the People's Republic of China, arrived at the Longevity Enhancing Hall on the very first night after he arrived in Beijing in 1949; and then, Liu Yazi, a South Society poet, lived in it; Hu Qiaomu, the literary gallant, lived at the Harmonious Fun Garden; Lin Biao, the "Deputy Commander-in-Chief", lived in the Clouds which Fostering House; and Jiang Qing, the "Flag-bearer of the Cultural Revolution", lived in the Lucidly Splendid House. Did they do any thinking in these abodes which provided good venues for letting out thoughts? Did they leave anything behind? We have no way of knowing the answers to these questions. Mao had the mind of a poet-politician, a mind that never ceased thinking — thinking about "the future of our motherland and the fate of mankind", thinking about philosophy, politics, and power, and also thinking about poems and the fate of poets. But, unfortunately, he didn't stay here long, and therefore, we shouldn't expect too much from his relations with the place. Poet Liu must have been thinking as he walked along the edge of the lake, reciting his poems; that is why he was "too much a complainer", and his complaints always involved political figures, extraordinary opportunities, and strategic plans for the stabilization and prosperity of the nation — only that his complaints carried the flavor of the Warring State Strategy cliques. That is why Mao Zedong classified him as one of "the old literati with democratic thoughts", that is, "a scholar-bureaucrat" left from the old time. Hu Qiaomu must have done more thinking, but his thinking then was intended at making him deviate from his true self and become the voice of the Party and part of the leader's will. We, perhaps, have to agree, however, that that type of self-effacing thinking was pious, to a considerable extent. Perhaps Lin Biao didn't think a lot when he stayed here to recuperate in the early 1950s, although he was widely known for his substantive thought. Firstly, he was in poor health after going through such a long civil war. Secondly, the thinking on military strategies and tactics, Lin Biao's strong suit, was no longer useful for the time being, as the gun-smoke over the battlefields in the mainland had completely dispersed. And thirdly, his thinking on political power-juggling trickery perhaps had not yet reached an intensified peak at that time; instead, based on the political structure, "scrawling" a few "notes" or setting up a few principles was good enough for him to pass muster — we have seen, for nearly a decade, that was how he managed to conceal his abilities, keep a low profile and bide his time. As for Jiang Qing, I dare say, her sojourn here brought to the palace more drama than peace. Although no more opera was played in the Harmonious Virtue Garden, this woman with a background in acting surely didn't come to the Lucidly Splendid House to study philosophy or engage in meditation. Even if she did read philosophy, she would have produced a gong-and-drum din. I believe that, apart from enjoying the palace and garden, leading a leisurely and extravagant life, and creating assemblies and clamor, she must have been thinking about something — as Cixi, when staying here, did. Women share similar characters, as do women entitled to ultimate power and old women entitled to ultimate power. Therefore, I believe that Jiang Qing and Cixi, when staying here, were more likely to use their women's instincts to play political power games rather than thinking. From what I believe, only when such "play" was made possible could they thoroughly express their destructive nature — let loose their bigotry and prejudice, arbitrariness and dictatorial natures — which look like reckless, headstrong behavior but, in fact, are nothing short of shrewdness and tactics, all aimed at exerting their destructive nature to the fullest extent. When these women reach such a state or height, the country, the nation, and the progress-makers were all likely to suffer. Is this not so? To Cixi and the like, this relatively (I wouldn't say "mostly") suitable thinking space may not have anything to do with thinking. Looking at it from a different perspective — the perspective of an individual or of a pure human being — I believe this thinking place does have a potential effect on them, though. Let's assume — there is no harm in assuming — that the nights at the Summer Palace could only have affected Cixi — and hence, the entire late Qing political situation — in two extreme ways: Either during a peaceful, mild, and tranquil night, a proper measure of gentle feelings and sentiments was woken in her which led to kind, undramatic, and rational decisions or, at the other extreme, under the cover of night, a narrow-minded, evil, and vicious human nature was unscrupulously released, which caused despicable palace conspiracies or schemes. Take the Political Reform of 1898, for example. Cixi's dramatic change, from allowing Emperor Guangxu to "do as he wishes" to abruptly entering the Forbidden City and again attending state affairs from behind the curtain, happened right here. I believe that a detailed textual research on certain related documents and files will easily prove this so.

Excluding the sojourners, of those who have resided here long enough to be the palace owners, Cixi and Guangxu should top the list, and we have already elaborated a lot on the former. Although I can easily speculate about the political power-juggling trickery of this imperious, dissipated and voluptuous old woman ruler (There is no lack of women with similar personalities throughout the Chinese history.), I can hardly figure out her way of "thinking", for "thinking" was too much to expect of her. Therefore, Emperor Guangxu must be the only one left on the list to have done some "thinking" here in this most suitable thinking place. One is justified in saying that he more or less made use of this space, and due to his thinking he summoned and interviewed Kang Youwei, Yuan Shikai, etc. during the Political Reform of 1898, when this young man, frail in body but strong in desire to strengthen the nation, must have been thinking about various issues. But since he was again turned into a prisoner of the deep palace as two end-to-end walls were erected in the lobby to confine him after the failure of his short effort to revitalize and strengthen the nation, he was badly beaten — so badly beaten that he was like a political puppet: He was unable to save his beloved concubine, he diverted his interest to the fun of music boxes, and he became frail in both body and spirit. There is a possibility that he lost his mind after many years of imprisonment. As the records indicate, he "saw that foreign aggression was advancing and that the nation was in danger after he returned from Xi'an to the palace... he then started to suffer mental disorders." Once, in a fit of derangement, the Emperor "thrust two bamboo poles through a chair, and ordered two young eunuchs to carry him in it. He held a little copper vessel in one hand and struck it with something he held in the other to produce sound, and he murmured, 'What happened, what happened now that foreigners are making such shambles!' He kept talking as he was carried on the chair, but the bamboo poles unexpectedly broke and he fell... He jumped up and raced into the inner room." Was this the last trace left in him of his ambitious political reform? In the end, he was completely "done for" a day ahead of the death of the person who had doomed him. But, in fact, there is something quite suspicious in it. Reformation could fail, power could be lost, a career could be wrecked, but thought should never be curtailed — if one does really "think". Thought never gets curtailed by an outer force, but by inner factors. Therefore, I always believe that if there were no deep, unrevealed secret plan behind the interruption of his political reformation and of all his changes — from a young ambitious emperor determined to strive for the prosperity of his country to a puppet who indulged in the entertainment of a music box, the only explanation of his sudden change would be that he was not a qualified "thinking" person — not to say the executor of the historical mission that had been entrusted to him. But the complete failure of his one-time effort has greatly affected the fate of our entire country. What a grand and mighty thing that the Manchu people, a tribal nation rising from the northeast grassland, with a few hundred thousand metal spears and gallant warriors on armored horses, could sweep, conquer, and reign over a territory of over ten million square kilometers and as many as a few hundred million people! But was it because the spell of good fortune for this small Tungus tribe had run out that two hundred years later, a few frail young men — so frail that they couldn't even have sons as heirs — ended its history? But what tremendous and unbearable consequences it has brought to the huge empire of a few hundred million people — so tremendous and unbearable that the country still lingers in a mentality of restlessness and uncertainty a hundred years after the end of that dynasty...

But was that fate really determined during those peaceful, tranquil, and remote nights at the Summer Palace?

Looking for the Lady with the Dog

◎ *Wang Meng*[1]

"It was said that a new person had appeared on the sea-front: a lady with a little dog."

There might be a period of time in your life when you think that Anton Chekhov's novels should be and are extremely easy to memorize. Filled with gentleness, sentimentality, and a sense of holier-than-thou, you lament with your eyes half-closed — memorizing his novels is enjoyable. Although he died at only forty-four, through mere translation, he won much literary acclaim and appeal, smiles and tears. You seem to have seen him; you seem to have heard his melancholic and urbane voice. You can hardly imagine that the world, especially pre-revolutionary Russia, would have produced such a gentle, kind-hearted, shy, talented, and exquisite man, playwright — and novelist. I got the order of this list — playwright and novelist — from the Encyclopedia Americana (not the Encyclopedia Britannica).

"She was a tall, erect woman with dark eyebrows, staid and dignified, and, as she said of herself, intellectual. She read a great deal, used phonetic spelling, called her husband, not Dmitri, but Dimitri, and he... was afraid of her, and did not like to be at home. He had begun being unfaithful to her long ago — had been unfaithful to her often, and, probably on that account, almost always spoke ill of women..."

Chekhov was somewhat weak in character. He was afraid of tall, erect women who claimed to be "intellectuals", and maybe also of men

---

[1] Wang Meng (1934-), influential writer, scholar, essayist, and once Minister of Culture of China. He was awarded the Mao Dun Literature Prize for *Scenery on this Side* in 2015.

of the same type. Anyone who sells himself or herself as an "intellectual", or labels his or her social circle as "intellectual", is either pretentious or arbitrary. I wonder which of the two is better. When he was alive, the late author Liu Shaotang abhorred those who posed as intellectuals when they wrote. Although biased, this opinion of his was justified, to a certain extent.

Many persons have written about Chekhov's home in Yalta. I visited it on November 3, 2006, after seeing the Massandra Winery. My feelings were somewhat different, though.

Massandra's wine smelled really good, and some of the wine tasted sweet. Because it is primarily for the magic flavor that one drinks French wine, the tongue plays an important role. However, in tasting the wine made in Massandra, now belonging to Ukraine, both one's nostrils and tip of tongue are crucial. I had been fascinated by the Massandra Winery since 1952, when I read *Happiness* by Pyotr Pavlenko. What an attractive writing! In the story, even as they drank, they would sing of the Soviet Union, praise Russia, and ridicule Americans. But what a pity it is that Pavlenko was said to be an extremely bad character — a mischief-maker, and an informer! Tipsy from wine-tasting, and tired from traveling under a gloomy sky with alternating rain and drizzle, I noticed that my footsteps became heavy. After all, I was already seventy-two years old then, but I had outlived Chekhov by twenty-eight years; I was 1.63 times as old as he was. Then, my mind drifted to Chekhov, the lady with the dog, youth, Pavlenko, Ukraine, the Orange Revolution, Russia, and the Union of Soviet Socialist Republics. I got off the bus, went down the stairs, and then I was there: Everything around me was seen for the first time, yet everything seemed familiar; everything seemed to have gone back to the time of my youth as in a dream, yet everything seemed so long ago; the memories were fading, but were more cherished.

"Then they spent a long while taking counsel together, talked of how to avoid the necessity for secrecy, for deception, for living in different towns and not seeing each other for long at a time. How could they be free from this intolerable bondage?

"'How? How?' he asked, clutching his head. 'How?'"

In fact, I had no deep feeling about life when I read these lines in my youth, because at that time I had no experience for it in my life. The dilemma of choices, all kinds of plights, a sense of guilt and helplessness, especially when it comes to a life involving a tall, erect, and intelligent woman, quite a number of frivolous women, and the true love of a strange woman — how could Wang Meng have comprehended any of these back then? But I was deeply touched, "How? How?" I could still remember those laments.

Having felt the afflictions of so many "hows" by now, somehow, that lady with the dog is, on the contrary, fading away.

No matter what, Chekhov was too delicate and sensitive. Born in 1860, he died in 1904, a year before the 1905 Russian Revolution; he certainly had not experienced the February Revolution of 1917 and the Menshevik Provisional Government, had not experienced Lenin's Red October Revolution, had not experienced the Stalin Era, the Great Patriotic War against Nazi Germany, the Cold War between the two super powers, and the collapse of the Soviet Union. Nor was his home in Yalta affected by the Yalta Conference, the wartime meeting of the three magnates of the United States, the United Kingdom, and the Soviet Union, which laid the basis of the post-war world order.

What a cruel experience the Russians had gone through! It should have left no room for Chekhov. It may have suited Nikolai Gogol, Fyodor Dostoevsky, Ivan Turgenev, and Alexander Pushkin, those passionate, optimistic, and romantic writers, but not the plain Chekhov. This, therefore, rarefied him, rarefied the cherry orchard and the three sisters, and rarefied even more the lady with the dog on the Yalta bank. Didn't tall and erect intellectuals also need the gentleness and melancholy of someone like Chekhov from time to time?

Chekhov's cottage in Yalta was described in some writings as white, but it impressed me that day more as green. It was a rustic two-story cottage, relatively simple, but with an undulating orchid in the yard. All the numerous trees, plants, and flowers, and the outdoor chairs were green.

Weaving amid the green clusters on a slope was a limpid stream, gurgling mellifluously day and night. The tour pamphlet and literature about the cottage seemed to me like dreams or reminiscences, early epistles or old friends, time-worn pictures or photos. Maksim Gorky, Isaak Levitan, and Tchaikovsky — their images all seemed to have bubbled out of the stream. Leo Tolstoy was in the photos on the wall. Some said that in his early years, Chekhov had been a great admirer of Leo Tolstoy, but after visiting Sakhalin Island, Chekhov developed a strong antipathy to Tolstoy's advocacy of non-violence against evil. But a different story said that Chekhov disliked the arrogant and pretentious attitude of Tolstoy's wife. I wonder if she was of the same type as the wife of Dmitri Dmitritch Gurov, the protagonist in *The Lady with the Dog*.

Chekhov's cottage wouldn't be considered large, but it had multiple rooms. It was said that he already knew he was suffering from tuberculosis when he bought the property in 1897. He planned the construction himself and set aside rooms for family members, including his mother, wife and sisters. Such a spirit of caring about family easily won the understanding and support of the Chinese.

The Massandra Winery had also been built in 1897 — a beautiful coincidence. Overlapping or synchronicity was also something that could touch our hearts.

More important about the cottage was perhaps its location. It was in Yalta. Not far from the yard was the Black Sea beyond the dam — a great stretch of the dark, surging water. And Verney's pavilion, which Chekhov mentioned in his *The Lady with the Dog*, was still there, in as good a shape as it had been in the story.

"And there sprang up between them the light jesting conversation of people who are free and satisfied, to whom it does not matter where they go or what they talk about. They walked and talked of the strange light on the sea: the water was of a soft warm lilac hue, and there was a golden streak from the moon upon it. They talked of how sultry it was after a hot day... And from her he learnt that she had grown up in Petersburg... that she was staying another month in Yalta, and that her husband, who needed a holiday too, might perhaps come and fetch her. She was not sure whether her husband had a post in a Crown Department or under the Provincial Council — and was amused by her own ignorance. And Gurov learnt, too, that she was called Anna Sergeyevna."

The sea water had remained the same. The sunlight and the moonbeam, the climate and the temperature had remained the same. Yalta had remained the same. Crimea had remained the same. Just as the lady with the dog had not been sure where her husband had a post, I was not quite sure if I had remembered it right. It was possible that the cottage was in Yalta, Yalta was in the Autonomous Republic of Crimea, and this republic was in Ukraine. But one thing was certain: Chekhov's cottage was still Chekhov's cottage, and it remained undamaged even during the German occupation in the Second World War.

I was told that there was a bronze statue on the bank. It was of Anna, the lady with the dog, and Gurov, her boyfriend. Due to inconvenient circumstances, I had missed many a chance to visit the statue. Finally, encouraged by Zheng Wantong, Secretary-General of the CPPCC National Committee, I went out into a rain to visit the statue, carrying an umbrella but still exposing myself to splashes of raindrops. I found Anna, Gurov, and the dog, but unfortunately, no Chekhov flavors could be found in the photos I took, because the surroundings of the statue had not been well-preserved.

Once, I looked out the hotel window for a long time, ardently hoping to see a lady with a dog. They did appear, much to my expectation, yet the dog was not a puppy, but a huge, fierce borzoi, and the lady had lost her youthful charm. During the years when I had been obsessed with Chekhov, my life had turned upside-down, which had left no room for him anymore. I was not sure if that was a good thing or a bad thing.

Finally, I was back to where the lady with the dog had been, and at last I had recalled the past, reread *The Lady with the Dog*, and for the time being, was as carried away as I had once been in my youth. Then, I bid farewell to the statue, got on a bus for the Simferopol Airport in the capital of Crimea, and returned to China.

The Walking Stick of the Founding Father of the Multicolored Mosque

◎ *Zhang Chengzhi*[①]

Unintentionally, all my prose involves geographical areas, whether big or small.

So does this piece of prose. It involves a piece of land through which the Yellow River weaves, with Qinghai Province on one bank and Gansu Province on the other. This piece of land is surrounded by big mountains, corroded in rain storms, and honeycombed with deep ravines and perilous gullies. Although widely known as a drought area, it is ridden with damp pockets everywhere. With the main transport roads winding far beyond the mountain encirclement, the natives simply take different routes — ferries on the Yellow River or paths wedged in the throats of the mountains.

Let me describe this area in a different way: The Yellow River cleaves through this piece of land in Xunhua. If you disembark in Xunhua and head into the deep, barren area to the left, you will reach the mountains of Kaligang; if you continue your trip down the river in the eastward direction, after exiting the Jishi Pass and reaching the bank at Dahejia, you can disembark and the town of Guanting is within a few paces. This is where the land and the water finally break up: The Yellow River turns to head north, leaving behind it a row of villages in Ximaying.

I saw the date-wood walking stick twice: once in Ximaying and the other in Kaligang.

[①] Zhang Chengzhi (1948-), famous contemporary essayist and novelist.

1. Ximaying

This happened during those days when I was in an unsettled state of mind. Wandering around, I somehow roamed into the Ximaying area.

Ximaying refers to the mountainous area where Minhe County of Qinghai Province and Yongjing County of Gansu Province share the same border. Like a calf that has just galloped out of the Qinghai-Tibet Plateau, Ximaying crouches in a corner, perspiring in the dankness of the pastureland. It does not look like a truly rural area, what with its tough folkways from the northwest, and most of its villages are in the damp and chilly mountain area, where it drizzles all day in the summer and the quilts on the brick kang-beds are damp. A look from the mountaintop reveals, at the foot of the distant mountains capped with dark rolling clouds, a vast stretch of golden rape-flowers. Alas, no matter how you look at it, this place does not look like a part of China's Loess Plateau.

The villages situated unpretentiously along the borderline of the Tibetan pastoral area are called Ximaying (West Horse Camp) by Ningxia farmers, who like to give nicknames. Geographers are not aware of this name, nor do they know why the area is called "West". It is said that the name is used to distinguish the place from the East Horse Camp, whose whereabouts remain ambiguous.

Ximaying has a very prestigious senior resident, called Grandpa Mansur. He was the one who regaled me during my few days' visit there.

When you reside in Ximaying, you will get used to considering the neighboring villages part of your family. One day, as I had nothing serious to do, I followed Grandpa Mansur around. Because all the scholars in the neighboring villages, far or near, were his disciples, I looked like a colleague of his as I accompanied him. Wherever we went, I was treated well.

While chatting in a village mosque, a junior imam abruptly said:

"We have a Khutbah (Islamic public prayer) walking stick, used by the Founding Father of the Multicolored Mosque, here in this Naqshbandi Mosque. It is made from a Chinese date tree. You want to take a look?"

This Founding Father of the Multicolored Mosque, mentioned by the junior imam, is no ordinary man. He was Ma Laichi, a historically renowned Sufi master — but his Islamic sect was not under the same roof as this small Naqshbandi Mosque, the result of some squabble, a "family split" between two brothers.

So I asked with interest, "How did this stick find its way into your hands?"

He replied, "Legend has it that the Founding Father left word that only by leaving the stick to us could it be retained. That is how, and that's all there is to it."

"So can you keep it safe? Are you guarding it carefully?"

"Of course. We usually hide it and only take it out for Khutbah on Friday Prayers."

"Do you really have to hide it?"

"If not, it will be stolen!"

So I urged him to take it out for a look, and he turned to fetch it. Before long, I was holding a quaint-looking stick. When I laid my hands on the stick, it felt like bronze — very heavy.

It was a solid date-wood stick. The entire black-red rod was glistening from the repeated application of varnish and oil and from the sweat that had soaked into it. Starting below the first curved joint, along the sinuous tendency of the stick, ran an inscription, in relief, of the opening chapter of the Koran, with the strokes exquisitely rendered and the words proportionally composed. Paragraphs were separated by carved patterns of flowers in circles and looked neither cramped nor crowded. Groups of related paragraphs of the chapter were arranged around the natural date-wood joints. Rhythmically, the inscription progressed along to the middle of the stick.

What a treasure! I marveled silently.

Holding it in my hand, I gave free play to my imagination. How fantastic! It was far more than just a work of art! Two brothers studying abroad under the same teacher in Yemen later had a disagreement and thus separated, leaving to later generations endless conflicts. However, a sense of comfort and happiness welled up in my heart, as if I had come across some kind of revelation. Since the Naqshbandi Mosque was guarding the walking stick of the Founding Father of the Multicolored Mosque, it meant that the "family split" that had taken place two hundred years before was about to be resolved.

A strong emotion choked my voice. Embarrassed, I rushed to change the subject: Look at the texture of the dragon's beard and the phoenix feathers! Look at the vigorous marks of the gold chisel and iron brush!... In this way, while caressing the stick in admiration, I ran my eyes along the inscription on the stick and read the entire *Al-Fatihah* with the disciples.

Only after I satisfied my desire to fully appreciate the stick did I think of asking the necessary questions.

The Founding Father of the Multicolored Mosque achieved his major success in Hezhou and Xunhua. But why hadn't his stick stayed in Xunhua, where he had risen to prominence, or been brought to Hezhou? Why had such an important item taken the trouble to travel all the way to this place, Ximaying, instead of being displayed as a relic for sale in Jiezigong or Huasijie?

Neither the disciples nor the junior imam could answer these questions.

Grandpa Mansur, who had just been listening, took over the questions.

"Our Ximaying was the very preaching place of the Founding Father of the Multicolored Mosque. Would you like to go there tomorrow or next day and wander around? Go and take a look at the places where he once lived."

It suddenly struck me that ordinary people always preferred a happy ending. To them, all family disputes were a source of sorrow. Ximaying always considered the Founding Father of the Multicolored Mosque their family member, so it guarded his relics and remembered the places that had been important to him.

"Have you heard of Kaligang?"

"Wasn't it the place where the Founding Father achieved his greatest success by persuading the Tibetans there to become Muslims?"

In Qinghai patois, they agreed in chorus, "Aye! —"

Grandpa Mansur was enchanted: "Our Ximaying is the very east gate of Kaligang, which is not very far from here — just a straight route along the diagonal."

2. Kaligang

Some years later.

Purely on a whim one day, I decided to make for Kaligang!

The only reason for my decision was that everything concurred for the trip: The enthusiasm of my friends, a new cross-country vehicle, a first-rate driver, and a reliable co-driver — all seemed to favor a big plan. Instantly, I decided to fulfill my wish to visit the mysterious Kaligang.

If it had been during the 1970s or if it had been in Xinjiang Uyghur Autonomous Region at the time when I was in my twenties or thirties, I wouldn't mention the perils of these few twists of the winding mountain paths. But it was already 2002, when asphalt roads had been paved from one end to another in those scarily steep and precipitous mountains in Dongxiang, and when "tar paths" had been laid, crisscrossed like a net, among the sheepfolds in the Uzhumuchin prairie. You would be astonished by the types of roads you see here, if you happen to reach the top of a mountain in Kaligang. That outwardly tilting earthen path hanging on that thousand-meter-high cliff! That lifetime of regret if you slip! Sudden awareness can also surprise you: This is a tiny, isolated world encircled by high mountain walls on all sides, and locked in the center is a piece of level land with a dozen hamlets on it. My imagination soared as I jolted along, unable to believe that this slippery path as oblique as a human shoulder would throw me off it.

I was told that in just the past few days, three vehicles had ended up bungee-jumping from one of the two roads, and a moment before, I saw, from the road we were on, a big truck lying belly-up with its wheels spinning in the whistling wind at the bottom of the valley.

Holding my breath, I was both excited and tense. Like an animal probing its way, the cross-country vehicle labored along with great effort, bumping up and down as it hummed aloud. It crawled up first and then edged down, exerting itself in Kaligang.

Finally, we descended into the relatively smooth, hilly area inside Kaligang. We drove our vehicle into the big Mosque of Yelichun. And then, with the help of a newly made friend in Yelichun, we finally reached the center of Kaligang.

I would never have categorized the natives of Kaligang as Tibetans: Squatting on the steps in front of the main hall of the mosque whose frescoes had chipped, the natives — in white skullcaps, black waistcoats, thick Hezhou-style beards, and padded cotton jackets draping over their backs, with their faces tanned a bronze color, their hands crossed in their sleeves and their caps pushed far back on their heads — all looked very much like a group of Hui people attending a village fair.

But my friend from Yelichun kept saying, "Listen, listen, they are talking in Tibetan."

They were authentic Tibetans and authentic Muslims. Back then, Kaligang was isolated from the outside world, and life here was incomparably abject. Once in a long while, a peddler would cross the mountains to bring in tea-bricks, salt, hoes, plows, and plowshares. Ma Laichi, in his old age, came here and taught the natives many new things, including wearing pants and hats. "But we still speak Tibetan," an old man said with a smile, though I was not sure whether he was proud of that statement or something.

The Tibetans in Kaligang believed in the Founding Father's miraculous power and told me that some old folks had seen, with their eyes, the Founding Father clap his hands and then walk across the Yellow River without getting his pants or shoes wet.

"From which part of the river?" I asked them.

"..." They cried out a name of a place in chorus.

Their reply struck me. This was not something ordinary. It was a sign of acceptance and respect from an ancient ethnic group. I was so moved that I was unable to speak. I felt an impulse to find that part of the beach, but then, I thought, what was so important about the location of that place? The important thing was that the Tibetans on this piece of land had accepted the Founding Father, and thus, the isolated, mountainous area began to open to the outside world, and the Yellow River thus began to turn into a smooth course.

My friend from Yelichun was an impetuous person:

"What's are we waiting for? Just take out the Founding Father's walking stick!"

Walking stick? Then, I understood: There wasn't only one walking stick of the Founding Father of the Multicolored Mosque. That was to say, the Ximaying story had a Kaligang version here.

I was just smiling, eyeing these hesitant Tibetan Muslims. I told them that it was okay if they couldn't show the treasure, because even if they showed it to me, as an "unenlightened" man, I wouldn't be able to see anything special about it... But my friend from Yelichun was the opposite kind. He was determined. He was born charismatic. When we were leaving Yelichun in the afternoon, he sank into the car seat and demanded of the driver: "Straight! Straight to the mosque!"

Now, he started a tirade to educate the few heads of the mosque.

This made them take out the walking stick. We were not allowed to take pictures of it at the beginning, but later they relented, so I took some close shots of the inscriptions while the native Tibetans held the stick for me.

This stick was the same as the other one: a solid date-wood stick with the same black-red-varnished sheen, glistening from the repeated strokes of the farmers with their big, rough hands. The difference was that it didn't have the opening chapter of the Koran inscribed on it, but deeply inscribed on it were the two lines of eulogy: "Shahe Aibufutuha."

As with the other one, the calligraphy of the inscription on this walking stick was vigorous, graceful, and flowing. I cradled it in my hands, lovingly and admiringly. The tactile sensation it gave me was beyond description; it felt smooth and warm, transmitting pleasant information to my palm. I was magnetically attracted to it, as I was aware of the brevity and importance of the moment. Everyone in the yard, Muslim or not, crowded around me, but none of them understood the whispers between the stick and me. Alas, although I understand now what the stick was saying, the past time has already gone!

Postscript

I didn't tell Kaligang that the distant Ximaying had kept another stick, and neither did I have the intention of introducing to Ximaying the idea that Kaligang had one, too; in my belief, the most distasteful thing to do was to haggle over which stick was authentic and which was not, and the most unwise thing to do was to ignore the fact that the two sticks tell the two sides of the same story.

We can assume that the old master Ma Laichi must have entered Kaligang from the west entrance — most likely the area of Qunke — by crossing the Yellow River; it also seems natural that he, too, took the east opening to travel to and from Ximaying. We can trace his life this way: With a walking stick in his hand and a travel pack on his shoulder, he had been trudging on his journey month after month and year after year, and spent his old age in the rocky mountains and at the Yellow River berth.

Now, the era of the Founding Father is over.

Only the date-wood walking sticks remain like a message or an enigma to us.

Both sticks are made of date wood — with one heavy and the other solid, one bright and the other shining, one slick and the other smooth, one returned as a gift and the other hidden as a treasure — in a way, they are simply like twin brothers.

The Reed Marshes at the Estuary of the Yangtze River

◎ *Zhang Shouren*[1]

The bank I stand on is where the river ends and the sea starts. As I gaze into the distance from here, a boundless stretch of reed marsh lies ahead of me. When the balmy wind of the early summer sweeps over the tips of the dense reeds, it heaves up layers upon layers of green waves and pushes them to the very edge of the sky. Pulling at a reed and caressing its jade-green leaves, I feel its soft and smooth silk. These aquatic plants of the Poaceae family grow together by the thousands, millions, or hundreds of millions, sprawling out onto hundreds of miles, forming a magnificently overwhelming scene and making up the Dongtan (East Beach) Wetland of Chongming Island as well — an important nature reserve designated as the Wetland Site No. 1144 of the Ramsar Convention in 2002.

The Dongtan Wetland of Chongming Island lies at the midpoint of China's coastline — a point that the intercontinental migratory birds from New Zealand and Australia in the south and Alaska and the Arctic Circle in the north all must pass. Each year, millions of birds, including Northeast Asian cranes, East Asian geese and ducks, and Australian shorebirds, extend their powerful wings and hover in the sky above the Yangtze estuary, perch on the tideland, or retreat into the reeds to look for and feed on small fish, shrimp and other creatures to replenish the energy they have exhausted during the long journey. So this point serves as a resting place for the migratory birds from the western Pacific Ocean and the eastern coastline

---

[1] Zhang Shouren (Qing Jiang, 1933-), modern writer and editor.

of Asia.

A furrow, created through the lashing of tides, breaks open the walls of dense reeds and winds its way to the place where I stand. Along the furrow, against the shallow water, a sleigh, drawn by a galloping Chinese buffalo, slides up, sending out flying splashes. When it reaches the bank, I see on it a fisherman, in a raincoat and long boots, carrying a bag of amphibious crabs, which may very well be delicacies for the flocks of migratory guests temporarily perching here.

Chongming Island, my hometown, is an alluvial island that emerged in the Yangtze estuary during the reign of Wude in the Tang Dynasty, as a result of the deposition of silt carried here in the Yangtze River over a long period of time. The island now has a history of one thousand three hundred years. It began as a small sandbank, to which fishermen from both the south and the north of the river sailed to fetch reeds or catch fish and shrimp at different times. They were the ones who built the first reed huts, trod the first paths, and became the first generation of inhabitants working on the island. The population of Chongming Island gradually increased in time. Therefore, in the first year of Shenlong (705) in the Tang Dynasty, the year when Empress Wu Zetian died, the island was established as a town, and in the twenty-ninth year of Hongwu (1396) in the Ming Dynasty it was upgraded into a county. By February 1950, when I left for the East China University of Military Affairs and Politics in Nanjing, at a time when Chen Yi was its president, the population of Chongming Island had surpassed three hundred thousand, but the island then was much smaller than it is now. Today's East Beach is a new land of three hundred square kilometers that has emerged through the deposition of silt in the sea since I left. It keeps expanding to the east at a pace of more than ten thousand *mu* per year. In shape, Chongming Island closely resembles a silkworm wriggling on jade-green water. As it keeps growing every year, it looks as if this enormous silkworm longs to break away from the mouth of the Yangtze River and swim into the boundless Eastern China Sea...

Gazing at the reed marshes ahead, I cannot help recalling my childhood, when the reed marshes were my old haunt. In spring, when those purple-red reed sprouts emerged in the bare beach by the greenish-blue water, my joy began to grow with them. By the time the rape-flowers began to bloom, the reeds were already exuberantly graceful and green, beautifying our waterfront land. This was when I would snap off a tenderly-green stem to make a reed flute. I would then climb a tree and sit in a fork of its branches to toot on the reed flute in musical accompaniment to the butterflies fluttering amid clusters of the broad bean flowers. Although my song was tuneless, I felt as if those butterflies would hear my flute music and dance more gracefully and merrily. Sometimes, I would climb a willow tree and stand on a thick bough to gaze into the distance, where, behind the great marsh of reeds, a few bellying white sails trailed from one of the branching streams onto the river, looking like white clouds gliding close to the earth. And they took my dim imagination to the world beyond the island, where the sails were heading... In summer, I would sneak away from my parents and swim naked in a small river, or wade into the dense and lush reed marsh to catch frogs, fumble for crucian carps, or hold my breath to nip dragonflies perching on the water as the slender reeds brushed my back. The green shade was my personal paradise. The water then was so clean that I could just cup it in my hands and drink it to quench my thirst. Sometimes I pulled out a reed to appease my appetite. The roots of the reeds, shining with a smooth white luster and perspiring with thin sweetness, tasted better than sugarcanes. On summer nights, when we burned mugwort to drive away insects, my playmates and I would hold a hurricane lamp in our hands and walk along the riverbank to chase the small amphibious crabs that hurried away in all directions and caused an endless rustle in the reeds. When the reeds opened their white flowers in autumn, I would climb onto a Chinese tallow tree surrounded by reeds on the riverbank, snap off some twigs, and stroke off from them the seeds like white pearls. I would sell the seeds to a Chinese herbal medicine store in town to earn some money for the exercise books, pencils, and erasers that I needed very much at the time. And then, I would go to Miaozhen Elementary School, where our lady teacher taught us to sing *Reed Flowers Are White, Reed Flowers Are Bright* while she played the accompaniment with an organ.

Reed flowers are white;

Reed flowers are bright.

When reed flowers bloom, autumn wind is to broom.

When autumn wind is to broom, geese are southward flown.

When geese are southward flown, winter will loom.

...

Listening to this beautiful lady teacher's charming voice was my greatest joy in elementary school. When an early winter came, my playmates and I would gather dried catkins and cut them from their reed stems, and we would ask our neighbor, an old man, to make us reed catkin shoes. Shaped like hedgehogs, the warm and downy shoes helped us endure the long, cold winter, keeping our toes and heels from getting frostbite. Recalling all those now, I realize what enjoyment the reeds brought to my childhood!

The reed is a goldmine of treasure. In my hometown, every bit of people's lives is related to the reed. Its tender leaves, rich in protein and sugar, can be used as animal food. When the leaves grow longer, they can be used to wrap rice dumplings. Reed stems can be used to weave mats, fish baskets, door or window curtains, and vegetable-field fences to keep out chickens or ducks. Reed stems are also flammable and can be used as firewood for the earthen kitchen stoves in farmers' homes. Cold in nature and sweet in taste, reed roots can be used in Chinese herbal medicine for heat clearing and detoxifying. Because of its high density of fiber, the reed is a high-quality raw material for paper-making.

Of all the plants, I like the reed best. It is ordinary and simple, lowly and upright; it emerges from sludge but is not stained, dwells in the marshes but guards the bank; it is content and humble, feeling at home no matter where it is, and always gives without grudging. In my study of foreign literary history, I learnt to my surprise that Tokutomi Kenjiro (1868-1927), a Japanese writer, liked the reed — especially the reed catkin — even more than I do. He liked it so much that he named himself after the plant: Tokutomi Roka, which means Tokutomi the Reed Catkin. It became the only pseudonym he used throughout his life, by which he was widely known in the world. This probably shows that anything that is plain in nature may be adored both at home and abroad.

The Chinese buffalo, with its yoke removed after reaching the bank, is now standing on a slope, leisurely grazing, while a long-billed white bird is standing on its back, leisurely gazing into the distance, where a few girls, under red parasols, stand on the pier behind the emerald-green reed clusters, leisurely watching the birds and the various wetland scenes with lively gesticulations; a few red flowers here and there adorn the vast sprawl of green clusters, forming a mesmerizing painting that could be called "The Rustic Fun of the Estuary".

Diagonally across the island is Liuhe River in Taicang, Jiangsu Province, which was the port of departure for Zheng He's westward voyages. In 1405, ordered by Emperor Chengzu of the Ming Dynasty, also known as Emperor Yongle, Zheng He the famous Eunuch Sanbao commanded the world's greatest fleet, which was composed of over 240 ships and 27,800 well-trained mariners and fully loaded with China's special products such as porcelain, silk, tea, and gold, silver, bronze and metal ware, in several legendary voyages from the port of the reed-flanked Liuhe, out of the Yangtze estuary, and southward along the Chinese coastline into an international journey of peace past South Asia and East Africa to the Red Sea. That was over half a century earlier than the so-called feat in the history of world navigation — the travel of Columbus from the late 15th century to the early 16th century, who navigated through the Atlantic Ocean and discovered America, the "new continent." It was also from the port of Liuhe in Taicang that my ancestors crossed the Yangtze River to move to the island. My great-grandparents, my grandparents, and my parents were all born there, farmed there, and were buried there — they are resting there. My hometown is the root of my life. How can I not love with all my heart the land where I was born and raised? How can I not feel a lasting nostalgia for it? In English, a globally popular language, there is a word "motherland," meaning a land of parents; in Russian, a powerful language for literary writing, the translation of "motherland" refers to the place where oneself and one's ancestors were born. People anywhere in the world all address their birthplace as "motherland" with intimate affection. This is the most accurately depicted, deeply impassioned, and precisely chosen name for it.

Blaise Pascal (1623-1662), a French thinker, held that man lives to think. He once employed a classical and wonderful metaphor: "Man is but a reed, the most feeble thing in nature, but he is a thinking reed." As I gazed silently at the vast stretch and distant sprawl of the marsh, an enlightened thought flashes in my mind: Smallness can make greatness! Having a fine stem and thin leaves, a lone reed is delicate, feeble, and shaky in the wind, but wantonly and tenaciously growing together in luxuriant and dense clusters, many reeds can form an impenetrable Great Wall with their thick foliage. How tiny was that first transparent drip that melted down from the glacier in the Tanggula Mountains on the Qinghai-Tibet Plateau! Yet it is such countless small drips that rally to form a thin flow, and such countless thin flows, streams, tributaries, and rivers — after running 6,300 kilometers over our land through Qinghai Province, Tibet Autonomous Region, Yunnan Province, Sichuan Province, Hubei Province, Hunan Province, Jiangxi Province, Anhui Province, Jiangsu Province, Chongqing City, Ningxia Hui Autonomous Region, Shanghai City, etc. — converge to form in front of us this great eastward-running Yangtze River, the third longest river in the world, after the Amazon River and the Nile River. By the same token, how tiny a grain of sand is! Yet billions upon billions of such grains of sand, deposited together through time, have formed the world's largest estuarine alluvial island — Chongming Island, the third largest island in China, after Taiwan and Hainan Island! Something small can become big! Therefore, in life, we shouldn't ignore anything small.

About a decade has gone by since I left my hometown. Such great changes have taken place that I hardly recognize the people, roads, rivers, bridges, and towns here. Townhouses have been built to replace the thatched cottages and reed huts popular during the 1940s and 1950s. Roads wide enough for international bicycle races have been paved to replace the narrow, muddy, and rugged paths of the past. A tunnel-bridge has been built across the water from Pudong to Chenjiazhen in Chongming, so the native people no longer need to take small sailboats or steamships to downtown Shanghai. In the middle of the island, Dongping National Park, the largest man-made plain forest in east China, has been planted; in the northern part of the island, the North Lake is now open, and it is double the size of the West Lake in Hangzhou. With verdant forests, abundant flowers, crisscrossing rivers and roads, blue sky and clean roads, my hometown today is the largest ecological island in East Asia. Tourists who have been here during these years all praise my hometown for its beauty. I believe that as Long Island is to New York, Chongming Island is now a backyard garden to Shanghai, as well as a vacation resort of the Shanghai people.

Those Shanghai girls in fashionable dresses, standing on the pier and watching the birds, are here to tour and relax. On their way back to the bank, they pass by me and get on the bus to leave; I overhear their excited conversation about what they have seen and heard among the reeds — the gracious flying and the mellifluous twittering of shrikes, wagtails, turtledoves, kingfishers, swifts, herons, corncrakes, white cranes, and gulls; I also hear their conversation about a frog leaping up and opening its mouth to lick in a grasshopper hopping under the reeds, about mitten crabs crawling on the mud between the reeds with their pincers raised high, about big tortoises in the shallow water popping out their heads and swinging their limbs... The conversations among these girls have prompted me to think: Now that the whole world shows great concern for the effects of global warming and pays more attention to the protection of the environment, in my hometown, this newly grown wetland and reed marsh that can purify water and conserve biodiversity can provide inestimable geographical and ecological value to the densely populated and crowded city of Shanghai.

Now back in Beijing, with great passion, I am writing this piece of prose as a farewell song for the Yangtze River, my mother; for Chongming Island, my hometown at the estuary of the Yangtze River; and for the reed marsh like a virgin forest on the East Beach of the island that exemplifies the importance of conserving the world biosphere...

Aerial Roots

◎ *Xiong Yuqun*[1]

Over twenty years ago, I happened to see a painting that inscribed in my memory the name of Kaii Higashiyama. It was an emotional picture! An enormous system of tree roots filled the entire frame — no trunks, no branches, and no leaves. The exposed roots were curved, twisted, and tangled, looking as if they were snapping and gnawing at each other; they were robust, tough, and vigorous, looking as if some tremendous vitality was blazing out of them. It stirred my imagination: What a haughty and vigorous tree those roots must support! What violent storms, intolerable cold, and intense heat it must be able to sustain! It is a source of power, the mother of life, and the blood veins for the birth of everything! It is a symphony of life and beauty! I did not know what tree it was, because at that time, I had not yet seen the southern banyan — a tree charged with great vitality and steeped in rich legends that have originated from the southern land itself. When such a root finds itself in a tight space, it can even lift a megalith or a house.

Later, I saw this kind of trees growing on the red earth in the Leizhou Peninsula in the southern Guangdong Province — a tree that had its root system completely exposed above the earth. Those roots randomly huddled up like a batch of snakes in a way it was hard to tell if the roots were eager to creep into earth or out of it. The tree's flattened and exposed roots spread wide, in all directions, like a huge web. Its root system was so large that it eclipsed its huge crown in size! A group of children crawled

---

① Xiong Yuqun (1962-), engineer, poet, essayist and senior editor, who had won the 5th Lu Xun Literary Prize.

on the roots. Although they wore shabby clothes and had the dark tan from the southern sun, they smiled as happily as singing streams, revealing their snow-white teeth. The tree's roots were a playground filled with childhood happiness. When I looked up at the crown of the tree and the sky, the clouds flying past the azure depths reminded me of the sea and the fierce storms from the ocean. From where the banyan tree stood, I walked into the village and then over a few miles of gently sloping plains. Then, my ears were filled with the sound of the sea waves. This was where the continent leveled off into the ocean, the sky drooped, and the waves and the clouds stretched so far away that the peninsula looked like a sampan. Without such gripping strength, how could the tree confront the ocean?

In the south, this was the first time I felt the impact of a tree!

A banyan tree growing on a huge rock created a different scene, which caused me to get lost in deep, long thoughts. Like vines wrapping a bare rock, the banyan tree rooted on a cliff on Mount Yuexiu in Guangzhou was an artwork of complicated craftsmanship. Standing by the roadside, it formed an abstract painting of vitality that completely revealed the secret of life.

In Lingnan, south of the Five Ridges that cover Guangdong and Guangxi, all banyan trees have profuse roots and buttresses. What is it in the nature of the south that produces this magic? What has charged the banyan trees here with such stunning, enormous vitality? Our ancestors asserted that the south was a place permeated with miasma and inhabited by barbarians. They must have been awed by the wanton growth of the trees here when they made such assertions!

In the south, where the flora flourishes, banana trees, as widely-crowned as plump skirts and as thickly green as mellow wine, blanket the earth in emerald. Kapok trees, as haughty and high as pines, toss their flaming red flowers high and wide in the air. Before their leaves burst out, the kapok trees are already laden with flamboyant flowers, and when their large and clumsy flowers shed in the spring, they fall like hammers beating the ground, loud enough to wake people from their vernal dreams. Like tasseled arrows, the coconut palm trees shoot high into the sky. Densely drooping in the thick shade of various trees all over the hills and dales, lushly abundant fruits — exotically shaped in the eyes of northerners — such as jackfruit, litchi, pineapple, papaya, star fruit, wax apple and mango indulge themselves in wanton growth all year round...

This constant greenness overshadows individuality, though, because here in the south, among a myriad of luxuriant trees, an entire forest could well be formed from just a single banyan tree. The paradox that "one tree forms a wood" seems to make sense with the banyan. For the visitors to the south, reproduction of this plant remains a mystery, because only time reveals it.

The rainy season comes as early as March in Lingnan. This is the time when the swelling waters all around find nowhere to go, and everything, up and down, is soggy. It was during such a misty drizzle that I arrived in Tianma Village, Xinhui Town, Guangdong Province. The earthen part of the islet in the middle of the river was already submerged. When water rushed over its top, all one could see was a large stretch of bright greenness, which looked like spring water gushing out of a riverbed in waves upon waves and tides upon tides. It was a flow and rush of greenness. In lapping flashes, the water heaped up thousands upon thousands of waves, as high as those in the Qiantang River, towering above the low surface of the river, making it look like a jade plate shining with beautiful light. Upon this plate, myriad green living things, sparkling with beads of water, hopped, leaped, and danced on each leaf... This is one of the scenes on the rivers that crisscross Xinhui — the famous Bird Heaven. For over the last three hundred years, a little banyan tree has grown into a small forest, large enough to cover one hectare of the islet.

Looking out at the river from my hotel balcony, I saw light-green water accentuating the dark-green trees and gently rippling to where the banyan tree branches and leaves drooped. The small forest looked like a green mass of cloud and mist afloat over the river, with tens of thousands of egrets flitting up and down, twittering. But they were completely hidden from sight in the deep recesses of the jungle.

I couldn't help wondering: Is the banyan tree the paradigm of southern trees? Of all the countless, large and tall trees, although each has its own unique shape, the banyan tree is, at least, the spiritual mirror of all the verdant lives in the south.

I rowed a wooden dinghy into a creek in the Bird Heaven. Beneath the crown-shaped foliage was a mysterious world. It was shadowy. Rain-and-fog-diffused white lights slanted into the forest in strips, like the uncanny illumination of heaven; tree branches were crisscrossed and entangled like randomly piled wood logs; hanging densely from the trunks, like clusters upon clusters of thatch, were the miraculous aerial roots of a banyan tree. New-born aerial roots are as thin as fine threads, swinging and drifting like floating dust. They are sepia in color, and their tips are beige; the beige tips are new sprouts that burst out in the spring. With the moisture and nutrition they absorb from the air, these newly bursting sprouts race to the ground, as quietly as flowing water. At first, you think they are withered and that they grow as slowly as human beards do, showing no intention or purpose at all, but as soon as they touch the ground, a miracle happens: As if abruptly awakened or energized, they clutch at the earth, quickly squeeze into its depth, and turn suddenly into roots. They abruptly stand erect and then gradually thicken, from something as thin as hair gauze into something as thick as a tree trunk. They quickly become thicker than their mother trunks. Then, they will produce their own branches, from which the second generation of aerial roots will drop like cascades, in a place farther away from the main trunk...

In this way, one generation after another, the banyan tree keeps extending outward into new spaces. And in the course of this extension, the difference in generations has been lost, for the various "generations" of trunks have grown into one tree, and even the age of the tree becomes difficult to determine. The vitality of a new life belongs to the entire banyan forest. The different trunks cluster together and share the thriving glory together! This is just what the saying suggests: "One banyan tree can grow into a heaven."

This miraculous quality of the banyan tree manifests itself only in

Lingnan, an area saturated with moist air. When the moisture clashes with warmth, however, it produces what our ancestors blanched at — "humid heat," which is a typical condition in the south. In ancient times, this hot and humid area served as a place of exile for the banished, but it is a blessing to natural life.

The Chinese of the Central Plain were leery of the south, but they finally arrived in this place. For the past thousand years, their footsteps into the south have continued unabated, despite the "humid heat", the "miasma", and the fierce prejudice against the south as well. This sparsely populated Baiyue region has gradually developed to reach today's population of a hundred million. This exuberant vitality naturally reminds one of the banyan tree. These migrants have dwelled along the dense tributaries of the Pearl River Delta. And the dense tributaries are to the Delta what the trunks are to the banyan tree. Wars, banishment, or ostracization drove these people — prominent officials, eminent personages, and commoners — here from their homes afar. Harboring a fear of nature and traveling with their families, they crossed the Nanling Mountain ridges and finally settled in this land. In Guangdong, over a long period of time, they have formed the three demographic lineages today: Guangfu, Hakka, and Chaozhou.

These migrations occurred as the underprivileged groups in the north fled their hometowns and came all the way to Lingnan to live a peaceful life under the towering southern trees, secluded from the outside world. Along the crisscrossing, branching streams and in the foliage-shaded woods, they have tenaciously survived and continuously increased their population until the banyan trees, previously growing on the wilds and now standing guard in their villages indistinguishably entwined with the curling kitchen smoke, turn into a symbol of their homesteads. Thus a new type of life, completely different from that in the Central Plain of China, has begun in Lingnan. As these migrants grow vague about the customs and habits, language and culture of the Central Plain of China, they grown familiar with the trees, plants, and flowers of the southern land, which gradually become a part of the landscape of their yards.

The defiant spirit revealed in the persistent growth of the banyan trees has enlightened these people and has now become a part of their own spirit — a spirit that is never tired, never daunted, and never deterred from developing and expanding itself, like a banyan tree extending its aerial roots into new spaces — keeping the lineage growing on and on! After they have opened up their land, groups upon groups of local people have gone abroad to all corners of the world. And wherever they go, they carry with them their clan pedigree books to record the courses of the lives of their ongoing generations, like torches being carried on from one hand to another. This is the root system of a life unfolded in time.

Banyan trees are famous for their deep roots, thick leaves, and the returning of the leaves to the roots. It is because of these metaphorical implications that the Lingnan people love banyan trees and are fond of growing them next to the shrines of the Gods of Land and Grains in their villages. When the Lingnan people are far away from their homes, they often miss a big banyan tree. In the dreams of their childhoods, those aerial roots, ruffled by the wind, are the most cherished memories of their homeland.

The banyan tree, which has shaped and fostered the culture of the Lingnan people, is in harmony with the primitiveness, ruggedness, and simplicity of this borderland. The ancient Ancestral Temple of the Lei Family in the Leizhou Peninsula, for example, boasts a stunning beauty in its thick gable walls, wide beams and large tiles, and even the absence of the typical overlapping eaves at the corners and the use of double brick seams as the vertical ridges of the roof — these rough features don't resemble any aspect of southern architecture but are rather closely related to northern architecture. The poetic grace and blitheness of the south find no place in Lingnan, for the so-called "south" only refers to the refined and graceful, natural and exquisite aesthetic characteristics seen in the downstream and midstream parts of the Yangtze River. The Chen Family's Ancestral Temple in Guangzhou features carved beams and painted pillars as well as animal statues adorning the roof ridges and overlapping eaves in extremely exaggerated and overly elaborate designs and bright colors — none of these styles has anything to do with the southern elegance, either. And even the Chaoshan culture, closest to the southern culture, also has far too much detail in its ornament. All of these stylistic choices bear the same kind of tribal traits in remote lands. All of these stylistic choices show the primitive roughness and wildness of Lingnan as a borderland that almost seems to defy the rules and normalities. And these stylistic choices resemble the banyan tree in spirit. This is the ruggedness and unruliness of Lingnan, the gushing of the banyan's vitality, and the sincere and naked temperament and aesthetics of the south. Subtlety, indirectness, symbolism... the typical features of the downstream and midstream parts of the Yangtze River are absent as if they had been swept away by a Lingnan typhoon.